The Works

The Works

A Consolidation

Danny L Shanks

iUniverse, Inc.
New York Bloomington

The Works
A Consolidation

iUniverse books may be ordered through booksellers or by contacting:

iUniverse
1663 Liberty Drive
Bloomington, IN 47403
www.iuniverse.com
1-800-Authors (1-800-288-4677)

ISBN: 978-0-595-53072-4 **(pbk)**
ISBN: 978-0-595-63126-1 **(ebk)**

Printed in the United States of America

Table of Contents

1 Eclectics 1

2 Eclectics II 85

3 Eclectics III 149

4 Conversations 240

5 Conversations in the Spring 290

6 Final Conversations 334

7 Eclectics Revisited 376

8 The Poet's Curse 440

9 Questions Matthew 7.1 495

10 Short Stories 530

11 New Poems 589

12 Poeantasy II 615

13 Poeantasy III 640

Eclectics

Within these poems lies 35 years of a family.
A man seeking answers,
a devoted husband to his wife,
and a grateful father to his child.

No.	Title	Date
1	The First Baby	12/11/1975
2	Remembrance of Rain	9/20/1983
3	Kaleidoscope	9/26/1983
4	Could I Make a List	10/4/1983
5	Katie's Sandcastle	10/4/1983
6	What was Stolen	10/11/1985
7	The Answer	1/22/1986
8	Short and Sweet	12/2/1986
9	Fast Reading	12/2/1986
10	Yes, I went to Viet Nam	6/3/1987
11	Christmas Spirit	11/29/1988
12	Alien Breakfast	5/15/1989
13	The Universe	9/16/1992
14	Our Walk through Life	9/9/1995
15	Strength For The Future	8/25/1995
16	Valentine Day Gift	2/14/1996
17	Eulogy from a Father	6/25/1996
18	Chivalry	12/8/1996
19	To Dell on Katie's Wedding Day	3/14/1997
20	To Katie on Your Wedding Day	3/14/1997
21	A Hippocratic Band	10/1/1997
22	Immanuel Kant Can Kiss My Ass	10/21/1997
23	The Veteran	10/21/1997
24	Getting a College Degree	11/19/1997
25	Song of Earth	11/20/1997
26	Dandelion	1/15/1998
27	The Oceans of Time	2/7/1998
28	Another Valentine's Day Poem	2/14/1998
29	Immortalization	4/7/1998
30	A Farewell Poem	5/15/1998
31	Victory Poem	7/8/1998

No	Title	Date
32	Thoughts from an Afternoon Walk	10/10/1998
33	Ecologist Unite	11/2/1998
34	The Philosopher's Stone	11/4/1998
35	An Alien Question	6/22/1999
36	Civilization?	7/11/1999
37	The Conceit of Advice	8/21/1999
38	Nomads of the Wind	11/22/1999
39	The Uselessness of Deep Thoughts	1/31/2000
40	The Ballad of Danny and Dell	2/5/2000
41	The Understanding of Life	3/7/2000
42	To Dell Happy 48th Birthday	6/1/2000
43	My Life so Far	7/26/2000
44	The American Dream	7/26/2000
45	A Good Night's Sleep	6/26/2001
46	You Make Each Day My Life	8/28/2001
47	Veteran's Day	10/20/2001
48	The Beginning	11/4/2001
49	30th Anniversary	12/11/2001
50	Prose for Fifty	6/1/2002
51	Thoughts on a Cold Afternoon	12/11/2002
52	Two Halves	12/11/2002
53	Happy 51st Birthday	6/9/2003
54	Happy Birthday Mom	8/15/2003
55	An Old Shirt	12/11/2003
56	To My Daughter	1/12/2005

The First Baby

When talking about a baby,
    If you listen to the man.
It sounds as if he's done it all,
    Never needing a helping hand.

He's got ideas, and got a plan,
    To make everything go right.
Even the colors for the baby room,
    He states, "They must be bright."

The baby bed, the diaper pail,
    The carpet, and the rest.
A newborn authority, he takes charge,
    To determine what is best.

While with loving eyes the watchful wife,
    Lets him have his fun.
And with a gentle hint or two,
    She accomplishes what need be done.

She listens to him brag and boast,
    Knowing it's fear that makes him lie.
And chuckles to picture such a brave strong man,
    The first time he hears the baby cry.

She loves him and he loves her,
    They're happy in their life.
This strong protective husband,
    And his loving patient wife.

December 11, 1975

Danny L Shanks

Remembrance of Rain

The rain is falling gently,
    Down from a cloud-filled sky.
Creatures of the wood take shelter,
    And birds refuse to fly.

Sitting in my office,
    Warm and protected from wet and cold.
I ponder the effects of age,
    Wondering why I feel so old.

The rain sparks my depression,
    Yet why I cannot understand.
For in memories of my youth,
    It was always so glorious and grand.

Boats were sticks of wood,
    Dams of fist-sized rocks.
There were no thoughts of time,
    No need of watches or clocks.

Every puddle an ocean all my own,
    Each ditch a "River of no Return."
It passed ever so quickly,
    With so much to see and learn.

Maybe my depression comes from yearning,
    To return to such a carefree day.
When all I could see of rain,
    Was an exciting new way to play.

Perhaps I should not be remiss,
    Nor let such a day pass in vain.
I shall, when I get home today,
    Take my daughter for a walk in the rain.

September 20, 1983

Kaleidoscope

I am a kaleidoscope,
　　Turn the wheel and see.
The changing color of emotion,
　　That make up the essential me.

Nostalgia on the radio,
　　"Living in the Past."
It feels so good to remember,
　　But the feelings never last.

See my daughter playing,
　　And behold the present day.
Blissful joy of being alive,
　　Wishing it could stay.

Television on, volume low,
　　Talking to my wife.
Such promises the future holds,
　　Of a better and carefree life.

Idealistic talk and philosophy,
　　Give thoughts, like peace from a dove.
Yet, holding a knife, I relish in,
　　The weapons of war I love.

Healthy and sound the atheist talks loud,
　　Then the heart flutters late at night.
Logic and reason turns to piety,
　　I fight it with all my might.

Simple, poor, intellectual,
　　Rich, powerful, self-destruction.
Hate and joy, peace and war,
　　Each with consuming passion.

Round and round I go in my life,
　　Each emotion dominating what is real.
But as the kaleidoscope, what I really ask,
　　Is who is turning the wheel?

September 26, 1983

Could I Make A List

How do I love you?
I wish I could list the way.
When or where I met you,
I can't remember enough to say.

What were you wearing?
What was the time of the year?
The fact that I can't remember,
Doesn't mean I'm not sincere.

When were we married,
What vows did we exchange?
Was it a thousand years ago,
How many ways did we change?

So many things forgotten,
Memories people say I should retain.
They say, "Remember the happy times".
I guess love forgets the pain.

Romantics curse me,
What a beast I must be.
Unfeeling and uncaring,
But what I feel, they cannot see.

I refuse to say how I love you,
Nor compose a list of the ways.
My memories and love for you,
Come from simple common days.

Yes, where we met eludes me,
The day, the time, the place.
Yet vivid does my memory recall,
Dirty jeans and an oil-stained face.

The intense concentration,
To bait a hook just right.
The heat of you body next to me,
Watching the stars on a summer's night.

Bending over the kitchen sink,
    Raking the leaves in fall.
What Romantics say is important I forget,
    It's only the common days I recall.

So let the world curse me,
    Call me an insensitive cad.
The common days they cannot remember,
    Remind me of the love I've always had.

Katie's Sandcastle

Rising from the ground proudly,
It declares its strength and might.
A truly aesthetic work of art,
An Architect's delight.

It was not there yesterday,
Yet, how could it be sculptured so fast.
Perhaps permanence wasn't the objective,
And only in my memories can it last.

I did not see it made,
But can picture how it went.
The dedicated work of tiny hands,
The face determined and intent.

The Seven Wonders of the World,
Though they be majestic and grand.
Pale to insignificance beside,
My Katie's Castle, made of sand.

October 4, 1983

What was Stolen

What has happened to our poetry?
The whimsical carefree style.
Enjoyable to read with a simple verse,
Understandable and devoid of guile.

A joy to the common man,
It eased the burdens of life.
A chuckle, a tear, a thoughtful pause,
And strength for worldly strife.

Yet it was taken from us,
Stolen, not so long ago.
The thief was the intellectual,
Stolen to feed his ego.

He proclaims that " simple" poetry,
Has no redeeming worth.
Poetry should aspire to a higher plane,
Solemn, morbid, and devoid of mirth.

This thief ponders the meaning of life,
Inspirational confusion in his head.
He converts these ramblings to paper,
Using the thesaurus beside his bed.

The words must be majestic,
The thoughts subtle, yet sublime.
He cannot be distracted,
By trivialities, such as rhyme.

No one understands this trash,
Fellow intellectuals proclaim it magnificent.
The common man cannot denounce it,
His credentials are insignificant.

Thesaurus groupies now run the schools,
    Teaching trash the children can't understand.
Forgetting poetry was made for the joy,
    And happiness of the common man.

Someday we will steal it back,
    The common man will win somehow.
And then, the world won't be embarrassed,
    When I recite, "The Purple Cow."

October 11, 1985

The Answer

Theology, numerology, physics,
Stoicism, logic, and math.
Searching for the answer to life,
I've strode the intellectual path.

One answer to explain it all,
That fits every case in life.
The whys of anger or lust,
Of happiness or strife.

A thousand theories have come to me,
Each indisputable and true.
Yet when put to the final test,
They, one by one, fell through.

Then one day I saw a dog,
Lying in a field of clover.
Enjoying the sun and gentle breeze,
Onto his back rolled over.

He did not strive to better his lot,
No guilt to spoil his fun.
He took the day for what it was,
And reveled in the sun.

And as I looked, I realized,
With joy and yet remorse.
I would never find the answer I sought,
And the reason was, of course.

If I seek,
I cannot find.
Yet as a man, I'm driven to,
By the ego of my mind.

December 2, 1986

Short and Sweet

I ask you noble poet,
Of the intellectual sway.
That if you write a poem,
For me to read today.

Please use a rhyme scheme,
And do so be a sport.
Make it sing, but make it clear,
And do please make it short.

December 2, 1986

Fast Reading

Poetry's like eating,
    Nourishment for young and old.
If you gulp it down too quickly,
    It misses the taste buds of your soul.

December 2, 1986

Danny L Shanks

Yes, I Went to Vietnam

Ah yes, I went to Vietnam,
    In the early days of my youth.
That I was proud and unafraid,
    I felt I needed proof.

War and blood and shells galore,
    It was a living hell.
But the worst thing I remember,
    Was the burning body smell.

But I made it, my family relieved,
    That some god had spared my life.
Then they promptly forgot it all,
    The only hell endured, was by my wife.

We're happy now we have a kid,
    Damn near twenty years gone by.
She stuck by me, but I regret,
    That alone, she had to cry.

And now they decided to have parades,
    To tell us we did great.
Memorials, speeches, and tremendous praise,
    But damnit, it's a little late.

So I'll keep my wife, and quiet life,
    With jokes and laughs, at the moon we'll yell.
So keep your parades and thoughtless praise,
    And damn you all to hell!

June 3, 1987

Christmas Spirit

You had better watch out,
    You had better not cry.
Believe in Christmas,
    And I'll tell you why.

Remember the tears,
    That wet your face.
When told your parents,
    Were in Santa's place.

Told Christmas was a gimmick,
    The ad man did create.
Spend money, buy gifts,
    Mail packages by a certain date.

Bah! Humbug!
    Don't be naive, you were told.
It's simple to see,
    It's been packaged and sold.

I tell you don't believe them,
    Christmas is alive and well.
Cynics can't damper,
    The Christmas tree smell.

Relish the feeling,
    Of gaudy decorative lights.
While driving around,
    On cold winter nights.

Let your stomach rumble,
    Let your taste buds swell.
Remember warmly,
    Each Christmas dinner smell.

Don't be afraid to be silly,
    Or laugh loud and long.
Relish the spirit,
    Join in the song.

Enjoy the season,
    Do not reason it out.
For belief and feelings,
    Is what it's about.

See the excitement,
    In the children's eye.
Then catch yourself looking,
For reindeer in the sky

The spirit is there,
    It cannot die.
Catch yourself smiling,
    To strangers passing by.

Don't sell me logic,
    Forget morbid dark thought.
From the heart comes the spirit,
    Not to be sold or bought.

It's tinsel it's lights,
    It's the ringing of bells,
It's opening of cards,
Received in the mail.

I wish you a merry Christmas,
    And a Happy new year.
Confusing facts and feelings,
    Is our only fear.

Danny Shanks

Alien Breakfast

An alien from outer space,
Came to visit me last night.
We sat in my living room talking,
Till dawn brought the early light.

He declared, "We need nourishment,
To start this new Earth day."
Having studied he knew of breakfast,
And being a good host, I agreed to pay.

The restaurant was empty,
As we casually took a seat.
The waitress came to wait on us,
A stoic face no easy feat.

"Please take one dead pig," he said,
"And grind up the meaty part.
Then stuff it in its intestines,
And tie up each end so smart."

"Then incinerate the pieces,
Till the fat cells ooze out hot."
The waitress looked uneasy,
Getting weirdoes seemed her lot.

"Next take unborn seeds,"
Continued my farout guest.
"From grain growing in dirt,
I believe your wheat is best."

"Pulverize the seeds.
Then bake them till they're white.
Slice the mass in sections,
I believe I'm getting this right."

"Burn each single section,
    Till the carbon turns it brown.
Then cover each with bee vomit,"
    The waitress's smile turned down.

Next abort two chicken fetuses,
    And put them in a pan.
Cook them on one side,
    Then flip them and do it again."

The waitress looked slightly green,
    But asked what he cared to drink.
"Extract from the mammary gland,
    A cow it's called, I think."

The waitress turned to me,
    Her look could bore cold steel.
"I think I'll just have coffee," I said,
    "I'm feeling a little ill."

We finished our fateful breakfast,
    Wished the waitress, "A happy day."
And for the first time, I realized,
    It's not what, but how the what you say.

May 15, 1989

The Universe

If you have ever lain outside at night,
And pondered a star-filled sky.
Philosophies will flow rampart through your mind,
To be followed by the inevitable, "Why?"

"The Universe" is such a quaint little term,
Yet its creation we cannot understan.
Such energy, mass and light,
All for the benefit of man.

So why would a superior being,
Or a God make such a fuss?
Perhaps we missed the intention,
And it was not created for us.

September 16, 1992

Our Walk Through Life

Of all the songs that we have heard,
And the songs that we have sung.
I still recall one, when we wed,
Saying, "We have only just begun."

And as we've traveled down the road,
With many a stumble and slip.
I'd never take back a single step,
And I've never regretted the trip.

The hills and valleys of our life,
The twists and sharp edged turns.
Have been illuminated by my love,
That torch forever burns.

We've walked so long together,
Seeing the wonders of the road.
And though at times we got tired,
We always shared the load.

Walk on holding my hand tightly my love,
For we've never lacked the will.
To see what adventures await us,
Lying just over the very next hill.

I wish you a Happy Birthday and
I love you.

June 1995

Strength For the Future

Poetry is passion,
Of that there is no doubt.
Each of us has such feelings,
All screaming to get out.

So take up pen and paper,
And let pour forth what you dream.
Let it flow from deep inside you,
Like a fresh clear mountain stream.

Don't listen to the critics,
They hold no exclusive rights.
To thwart your heart's expressions,
Of life's doubts and loves and fights.

Write it down on paper,
To cleanse your very soul.
Be not shy or timid,
Let your passion make you bold.

And when you've finished writing,
Fold it neatly and put it away.
For it will give you the strength you may need,
On some far off future day.

August 25, 1995

Valentine Day Gift

Here I sit, February 13th,
And once again I find,
I have not gotten a Valentine gift,
And I'm really in a bind.

I thought of buying you a card,
But, they're really such a bore.
Plus, if memory serves me correct,
I've done it about 27 times before.

Perhaps I could sing you a love song,
Naw that idea just won't float.
After all these years, we both know,
I can't begin to carry a note.

So I inquired about some roses,
Which caused me to severely wince.
I mean, $45 for a few dead plants,
Just didn't make much sense.

Well, I know I could always get candy,
But on my way to buy it.
I remembered how hard you've worked,
Staying on that damndable diet.

So I thought and thought,
Despairing alack and alas.
What could I get, my Lady Fair,
That could possibly save my ass.

What would I give you,
If not a song, candy, card or rose.
But of course! I would tell you of my love,
By using simple rhythmic prose.

I need a new way to express the feelings,
I so desperately want you to know.
With hopes the poetry will be cherished,
And the rhythm will gently flow.

For hours and hours I toiled,
    Many a page was cast away.
But finally, I had it right,
    And knew exactly what to say.

I can't just say "I Love You",
    You've heard it so many times before.
Like the kiss, before going to work each day,
    As I'm walking out the door.

But like Bathsheba, who walked the Persian Land,
    And Cleopatra, who floated on the Nile.
You are the Goddess of my life,
    The only reason I ever smile.

So if the world should fall apart,
    Or the heavens be suddenly gone.
Together shall we be forever,
    Together in Babylon.

Happy Valentine's Day

February 14, 1996

Eulogy from a Father

The breeze passes gently,
    It causes the lilies to sway.
Clouds float, on a deep blue sky,
    As I ponder, what to say.

I have had such a wonderful wife,
    Upon whose strength I've drawn.
And a child, who was a joy to behold,
    So do not mourn me when I'm gone.

I danced my way through this world,
    I've sung my own life's song,
I've had more happiness than sorrow,
    So do not mourn me when I'm gone.

Remember me for compassion,
    There is no greater right or wrong.
It is the self-worth of a lifetime,
    So do not mourn me when I'm gone.

I feel your tears and sorrow,
    But do not let it last for long.
Yet keep my memory as a joy in your heart,
    And do not mourn me when I'm gone.

July 25, 1996

Chivalry

The darkness was upon us,
Barbarism ruled the land.
The Middle Ages held no hope,
To continue the existence of man.

As society fell apart,
And civilization on the brink.
There had to be an answer,
If only we could think.

Then there arose a thought,
That stemmed straight from the human heart.
We could reverse the madness,
And Chivalry was the start.

A code for a man to live by,
That aspired to his better half.
A code of honor and goodness,
When facing adversity, allowed him to laugh.

A code to protect the women,
To protect the poor and infirmed.
The warriors had to set the example,
By the common man, it could be learned.

There must be honor in your life,
Fairness is not bought or sold.
For if you have not self respect,
What good is all your gold.

The gold will not buy you,
The peace of mind at night.
The feeling of well being,
And joy of doing what's right.

For right and wrong is intrinsic,
Known by every human soul.
We may lie to others, how we feel,
But the lying leaves us cold.

And so the centuries passed us by,
To bring us to this day.
In America the code of Chivalry,
Seems to have lost its way.

It's no longer how you played the game,
But who has won or lost.
And as the importance of winning rises,
I feel the moral frost.

Do unto others first,
And greed now seems the best.
Take care of yourself only,
And to hell with all the rest.

To sacrifice for others,
It is a sucker's game.
And forbid if something does go wrong,
Make sure you're clear of blame.

Alas my friends, I fear the dark,
Again descending on man.
Who gives a dollar to appease his guilt,
But gives not a helping hand.

I beg you to forestall this fate,
No longer declare you're number one.
But declare, you are part of the human race,
On the third planet from our sun.

Forsake superiority of winning,
That gives us vanity's hold.
Forsake competition without honor,
For nothing but the sake of gold.

For if we forsake our honor,
And Chivalry dies, on history's pages.
I fear we are doomed again,
To a time called "The Dark Ages".

Dec 8,1996

To Dell On Katie's Wedding Day

Roses are red,
    Violets are blue.
Katie's gone,
    And there's just me and you.

It's the way that we began,
    And the way that we will end.
You've always been the woman I loved.
    And always my best friend.

So on we go with our life,
    All the ups and downs of the road.
But together we'll overcome it all,
    For we've always shared the load.

It's almost kind of scary,
    Yet being scared is sometimes a treat.
But reassuring that we're still walking,
    Down our own "Baker Street".

March 14, 1997

To Katie on Your Wedding Day

And so my treasured Princess,
Today you are to wed.
I do not know what I feel,
Unbounded joy or dread.

The emotions pull so strongly,
My chest feels as if it's torn.
For wasn't it only yesterday?
I remember you being born.

I held you in my arms,
Announced you Katherine Ellen Shanks.
Then offered up a silent prayer,
An offering of thanks.

My life was changed that day,
Though I could not see.
The road of ups and downs,
Awaiting there for me.

And so I watched you grow,
Learning to roller skate and ride your bike.
Which music you listened to,
Which foods you did or did not like.

I watched you learn to swim,
Tell jokes that all began "Knock Knock".
The thrill that was in your eyes,
When you skipped your very first rock

Walking through the forest,
Body surfing at the beach.
Watching your confidence grow,
Realizing nothing was beyond your reach.

And my pain of realization,
That you needed me less and less.
But pride as you grew so strong,
The conflicting emotions I confess.

So today I retire,
Another has taken my place.
But that is the way life is,
Or should be in any case.

I've never been at a loss for words,
Yet today it's hard for me to say.
Out loud of how much you mean to my life,
In every facet and every way.

You begin a new adventure today,
But really you cannot go.
For in my heart you shall always be,
With the memories of watching you grow.

And on some future day at work,
Wading through file after countless file.
I'll remember you fishing at dawn on Lake Hartwell,
And my face will start to smile.

The past is always with me,
The future belongs to you.
I can only wish a life of happiness,
And joy in all you do.

I wanted to tell you so much this day,
Of memories, joy and pride.
But all I can say is "I Love You",
And hang on for a helleva ride.

March 14,1997

Danny L Shanks

A Hippocratic Band

I was admitted to the Columbia St. David's South Hospital,
    In October, on the 13th day.
With little knowledge or forewarning,
    That my life was slipping away.

A group of people took me in,
    I knew them not at all.
But soon realized they worked with a diligence,
    As if it were "their" backs that were against the wall.

I did not understand their care,
    I mean, wasn't it just a job?
They go to work, they draw their checks,
    How could they become involved?

For I'd heard the Congress speak before,
    And the press decry their price and style.
But a soft hand on my brow at night,
    I could not reconcile.

You cannot buy the compassion,
    I felt displayed for me.
Though God knows I didn't deserve it,
    They gave it to me for free.

I've never met a band of people,
    Such as I met there.
A band with such unselfishness,
    And compassion to show such care.

To work in such a stressful job,
    Must take its wear and tear.
To endure the strain and endless hours,
    Is more than I could bear.

I would like to thank these people,
    From a middle-aged old fat guy.
And though I know the words will fail me,
    All I can do is try.

You will always be in our hearts,
    Wife, daughter, son-in-law, and me.
For we shall never forget,
    The looks in your eyes, that we could clearly see.

Immanuel Kant Can Kiss My Ass

Immanuel Kant can kiss my ass,
B.F. Skinner take a hike.
Your philosophies professed as sublime,
To me are merely contrite.

You profess the understanding of life,
Yet your arguments are so weak.
The only souls converted to you,
Are the self righteous and the meek.

Never has such vanity held,
An unfettering of bounds.
And never has so much time,
Been devoted to such clowns.

Perhaps your vision has been obscured,
But I offer hope unto the masses.
Just grab yourselves by both ears,
And pull your heads out of your asses.

October 21,1997

The Veteran

The sun is setting gently,
    On the African plain.
There lies a tired old veteran,
    Scarred with too much pain.

I watch the jackals' circle,
    What cowards are the pack.
But they cannot change their nature,
    For it's character they lack.

And so I rise on tattered legs,
    And give them one good scare.
A toss of head, a twitch of tail,
    A shaken mane of hair.

I move off toward the jungle,
    Knowing it all too soon but true.
Before long I'll be one step too slow,
    But what else can I do

For I remember dimly,
    In a time so long ago.
Reading a book on an airplane ride,
    When I was far from slow.

The plane was taking me to a war,
    In a far off distant land.
What it was for and why it took place,
    I still don't understand.

Don't remember the title, the author,
    Or much of what it said.
Only a character named Daniel,
    With a voice inside his head.

The voice kept saying the same thing,
Like the lyrics of a song.
Get up and do "something", Daniel,
Even if it's wrong.

October 21,1997

Getting a College Degree

The days they come, the days they go,
    The classes never end.
It seems you finish with one test,
    Only to have another begin.

Another late night of studying,
    More homework to complete.
Make a "A" in classes,
    When passing seems a feat.

What's the point, you sometimes ask,
    As frustration claims your soul.
Is it really worth the effort,
    To attain such a lofty goal.

The knowledge is worthwhile,
    But what application for higher gain.
It comes after you get the college degree,
    Life calls it , "The Food Chain".

Nov 19,1997

The Song of Earth

Do not let this day pass,
Without looking to the sky.
To hear the song of the Earth,
To see the clouds float by.

Enjoy the heat of summer,
Relish in the cleansing rain.
The touch of winter's briskness,
Will help to keep you sane.

Just see the colors of the Earth,
Such joy in the array.
The birds, the ants, and the animals,
Ignore them not, a single day.

For you have to make a living,
But no requirement to make it grave.
Be careful viewing money,
Be its master, not its slave.

For in every city that we build,
All concrete walls and steel.
The dandelion breaks the pavement,
To show us what is real.

Mother Earth she sings a song,
To teach us joy and trust.
A way to live our lives,
Our buildings, she turns to rust.

So try to meet your deadlines,
To make your schedules tight.
The Earth scorns your depression,
And makes her flowers bright.

I tell you fellow mortals,
    Be yea enemy or friend.
Relish in the song of Earth, because,
    You shall not pass this way again.

Nov 20,1997

The Dandelion

Behold the lowly Dandelion,
    Truly every gardener's bane.
They dig them up, time after time,
    Only to have them grow again.

But, I must ask you, my good fellow,
    Does it deserve such universal scorn?
I mean it does have such a pretty little flower,
    And not one single solidarity thorn.

Its leaves can make you salads,
    The heart gives us a soft sweet wine.
And how many childhood memories are built,
    Blowing its seeds in the summertime.

Its yellow flower is vibrant,
    When highlighted in a morning's dew.
It gives its all, without self reward,
    It gives it all for you.

So do not scorn my little friend,
    It should not be the object of scorn and rants.
For it's king among the growing things,
    A true hero of the plants.

January 15,1998

The Oceans of Time

A drop of human life,
Lost in the ocean of time.
We strive to understand it's meaning,
Be it malignant, or benign.

Analysis, sacrifice and reason,
Seeking achievement of the perfect state.
While our lives slip by unnoticed,
What an ironic twist of fate.

Our senses tell us all we need,
Yet, we ignore them and try to detect.
Some complex meaning of life,
Such simplicity we reject.

Meditation will not give you life,
Perfect health nor perfect mind.
All the moments spent in striving,
Are but a simple waste of time.

Yes, greatness is a myth,
But, the human egos are so sublime.
Lost, as the tides come and go,
Lost in the oceans of time.

February 7,1998

Another Valentine's Day Poem

It's Valentine's Day again,
    No gift, flowers nor card.
To be original as the years go by,
    Is really getting hard.

I could play on being sick,
    Say the medicine's to blame.
That you are the light of my life,
    And my love burns, like an eternal flame.

You've heard all that before,
    Romantically, the first few times.
You say you love my poems,
    All those original rhythms and rhymes.

But we been together so long,
    I'm beginning to suspect.
That you would love anything I wrote,
    So I figured what the heck.

Therefore, here I sit composing,
    Something short, sweet and sappy.
Because if you lie, or really like it,
    It seems to make you happy.

And despite all the crap in the world,
    To make you happy is my life.
Don't really give a damn about anyone else,
    Except for you my wife

So take this poem for what it's worth,
    I'll believe any lies whispered in my ear.
Fact is you're the only reason I get up each day,
    And losing you is my only fear.

So you keep on telling me,
    You like what I have to say,
And I'll keep on writing them,
    Till we're both just old and gray.

Truth is, I do love you,
    And I'll do whatever makes you smile.
All I ask is that you put up with me,
    And stick around awhile.

Feb 14,1998

Immortalization

Ah, to be remembered,
When you are dead and gone.
To be forever immortalized,
In written word or song.

What is this kind of reasoning,
That such thoughts comprise.
For surly, it cannot be considered,
As logical, or wise.

And yet we find, initials in concrete,
Names painted on a bridges' side.
Buildings, schools, and statues,
All named for someone who died.

I hate to cast dispersions,
Upon your intellectual sway.
But when you're dead, you're dead,
And only the worms have the final say.

So you want to be remembered,
Why is beyond my grasp.
But something in man, seems to believe,
If you're remembered, you will last.

Well, if it makes you happy,
Then try with all your might.
Just recall they also remember,
Black plague, syphilis and blight.

April 7,1998

A Farewell Poem

Katie and Chris are gone,
    They're heading out today.
Gone to storm the castle,
    Gone to find their way.

We are so proud of them,
    So young and full of life.
This strong protective husband,
    And his worrying, but loving wife.

It doesn't seem the same two,
    We've watched the last few years.
Seeing them roll with laughter,
    Seeing them challenge all their fears.

And so we stand and wave goodbye,
    Our breast feeling such an ache.
We will miss them so terribly,
    It seems too much to take.

But mingled with the pain is joy,
    No, better described as pride.
As we watch them take the world head on,
    They feel no need to hide.

Those crazy kids belong to us,
    We claim possession of the two.
No matter where they go,
    No matter what they do.

So to Katie and Chris, we say goodbye,
    Adventure and happiness, we hope you find.
And until we see you again,
    Stay one, in heart and mind.

May 15,1998

Victory Poem

Well, they went and stormed the castle,
Their victory is now at hand.
They conquered all the dragons,
They rule a brand new land.

All the fears, are now banished,
Washed away in just one day.
They said it, and, then they did it,
What more can anyone say?

Nothing can stop them now,
It's all within their reach.
This strong determined Texan,
And his lovely Georgia peach.

They've accomplished something glorious,
Something money can never buy.
They've earned the right to walk the world,
Erect, with heads held high.

So relish this day of victory,
Let your faces split with a grin.
Laugh until it hurts your side,
Cause damn, it feels good to win.

Congratulations to you both,

July 8,1998

Thoughts from an Afternoon Walk

Our species is not proactive,
We're reactionaries all the way.
Dealing with problems without planning,
Seems the order of the day.

Knowing a storm is coming,
That event we cannot change.
Yet people stay in its path without moving,
Such behavior is extraordinarily strange.

"It sounded like a freight train",
As if they had ever heard such a sound.
I guess they have heard it said before,
By such traditions we are bound.

So in life there are many storms,
Only planning will get the desired results.
Avoiding the mental rigor mortis,
Propagated by politics, religions, and cults.

Dare to ask those questions,
Whose answers no one seems to know.
Exercising your mind in this fashion,
Is the only way to grow.

It keeps you out of trouble,
Gives you philosophies you can trust.
So live each day yet plan ahead,
And by the way, what the hell is rust?

October 10, 1998

Ecologist Unite

Save the rain forest,
    Save the Whales.
Save all of life,
    All living cells.

Well, at least save the cute ones,
    That goes without being said.
I mean who really cares,
    If spiders or snakes are dead.

And don't forget bacteria,
    Tuberculosis don't count.
Cancer, Flu and Pneumonia virus,
    Deserve the best defense we can mount.

And for the love of God, save the porpoises
    For they are soooo smart.
Screw the rest of the fish,
    They're just too slimy, to have a real heart.

Save the rain forest,
    All the creatures living there.
The Sahara desert used to be one,
    But now it's just bare.

Obviously Mother Nature,
    She doesn't know what's best.
So we must save the smart and cute,
    And kill off all of the rest.

Dam the rivers,
    To flow where we wish.
Save the trees and flowers,
    Damn the dandelion and fish.

It is truly amazing,
    Where we draw the line.
Of what is life and worth saving,
    On this planet we call "mine".

Humans are so damn arrogant,
    We can justify anything we please.
Yet, we kill so indiscriminately,
    Can you call us, an intelligent species??

November 2,1998

The Philosopher's Stone

Tales told over and over,
    By a camp's firelight.
Until they became mythical legend,
    Man's fancy taken flight.

I speak of "The "Philosopher's Stone",
    Speak with reverence it's very name.
For it has enough magic,
    To bring the owner, riches and fame.

Alchemist hid it's source,
    Only a few could understand.
So, over thousands of years, it was kept hidden,
    Safe from the eyes, of the common man.

But I have discovered the secret,
    And, I give the Stone to you.
It's a simple chemist equation,
    $Ag + SiO_2$.

November 4, 1998

An Alien Question

Does a computer know it's a computer?
    Does an ant know it's an ant?
If I say either is intelligent life,
    Does that make me a miscreant?

We search the skies for UFOs,
    Seeking an outer space connection.
But if we ran across such a different life form,
    Would it escape our detection?

I hear people declare we can't be the only intelligence,
    The galaxy is much too large.
Yet lurking close, intelligent life could be,
    As close as their back suburban yard.

Arrogance is our species' only enduring trait,
    It seems to never leave us.
And it seems to have been around longer,
    Than Confucius, Mohammed, or Jesus.

But say on one momentous night,
    An "alien" lands on the Whitehouse lawn.
Everything then could change, but wouldn't you still,
    Have to go to work with the dawn???

June 22,1999

Civilization?

When is a society civilized?
    Philosophers question and brood.
Could it be when competition is for,
    Self esteem instead of food.

July 11,1999

The Conceit of Advice

I'm starting to push 50 years old,
And, as I lay in bed at the end of the day.
I feel compelled to write out my thoughts,
For I have so much to say.

Well it dawned on me, as it sometimes does,
Illumination for the millionth time.
That I should express myself in prose,
With all that wittiness of rhyme.

Yes, I can tell you all, how to live your life,
For I've been writing for nearly 30 years.
Addressing thoughts, philosophy, and hopes,
Giving answers to all your fears.

What a bunch of conceit, I have collected,
Such vanity so totally unbound.
To think I understand anything so much better,
That such answers only I have found.

I have read all the greatest thinkers,
Discarded some and kept the rest.
Collated it all into a philosophy of life,
Which I have determined, is the best.

The drive to write such drivel,
Is an amazing twist of fate.
But once again I find myself writing,
After taking vanity's bait.

Well after a lifetime of such wasted effort,
I find such conceit, life's ironic trap.
Yet great thinkers and I have a common ground,
We're all pretty much full of crap.

July 18,1999

Nomads of the Wind

Nomads of the wind are my wife and I,
    We blow wherever feels right.
Judge us not if you fail to understand,
    If you cannot view life, with our sight.

For we are creatures of this earth,
    Like leaves upon a tree, our lives play out.
Each season different and changing answers,
    To what this life is all about.

In the Spring, we are born,
    Feeling the breeze and growing strong.
Seeking answers and meaning,
    Each day redefining, right from wrong.

By summer we've grown,
    And our concerns are for the seeds.
Nurturing and feeding them,
    Supplying all their needs.

Fall comes and the seeds are gone,
    Our beliefs change with the loss.
So we leave the security of the branch,
    On the winds are we tossed.

Winter finds us pressed to Mother Earth,
    Perhaps to rest awhile,
To reminisce on a full and happy life,
    Content to be together, and sharing a simple smile.

November 22,1999

The Uselessness of Deep Thoughts

I've always thought the meaning of life,
Would come in a dream some night.
Well it came, but was so strange,
I wasn't sure, if it was right.

I have been told for years,
Of the power of the brain.
Of how mankind must meditate,
Of how hard, we must train.

To spend our lives just thinking,
Contemplation of life, a worthy goal.
Dedication to a higher awareness,
To provide sustenance for our soul.

The brain is an amazing thing,
It's analytical power, something to see.
Yet that's all its purpose is in our lives,
And all, it ever will be.

The brain is in fact the analyzer,
But of our senses, and that is all.
It gives us awareness of life,
Tells us summer from the fall.

It does not explain the universe,
Those who have tried it for that use.
Have found after a certain point,
The explanations become vague and obtuse.

Let your brain do its job,
Stop trying to reason why.
It interprets our senses to give awareness,
And we hardly have to try.

Do not waste time trying to understand,
    It's your life and the experience is nice.
Get out and enjoy it while you can,
    Cause you won't, get this chance twice.

January 31, 2000

The Ballad of Danny and Dell

She was a Tarheel from North Carolina,
He an Arkansas Razorback.
They hooked up down in Georgia,
And they never have looked back.

Running from here to there,
Never settling for long.
They seem to dance to another tune,
A self composed sort of song.

Never playing by all the rules,
Just enough to get by.
Never managed to win the game,
But seemed to really try.

They would get so very close,
Then off again, to run around.
Folks and family just shake their heads,
Will those two ever, settle down?

They are just searching for paradise,
A pipe dream if you may.
They flit from here to there,
Hoping to find it, one fine day.

Well that isn't quite the whole story,
Finding paradise, ain't what's cookin.
Cause after thirty years it ought to be obvious,
The fun is in the lookin.

February 5, 2000

The Understanding of Life

Oh I have spent my lifetime,
    On such a grand endeavor.
To understand this life,
    And the universe it uses as cover.

I have wrestled hard with logic,
    Held physics hostage with fear.
I have conquered time's spatial dimensions,
    Unraveled man's need for smile or tear.

I have discovered forces as yet unnamed,
    Understood how the humans thought.
No matter how long it took,
    I won every battle that I fought.

But in the end my own ego beat me,
    For I was so sure that once I understood.
Mankind would be eager to hear and learn,
    What makes us evil, or makes us good.

That everyone would want to know,
    How atoms and energy related.
Even the inner workings of the brain,
    And for what destiny we were fated.

Alas, I realized that I had failed,
    Truly, I had been such a fool.
No one wanted to hear the truth,
    When fantasy is such a useful tool.

So now I must use what time,
    I have left in this present life.
To try and salvage some joy,
    To be a good husband to my wife.

Yet I burn with painful desire,
    To share the knowledge I have won.
But no one wants to hear it,
    Neither wife, nor daughter, nor son.

And so I must resign myself,
    To suffer silence until my death.
To the grave goes my hard won facts,
    Expiring all with my last breath.

But if you perchance read this,
    Please embrace this fact yourself.
A better mouse trap sells very well in this world,
    The "Meaning of Life", gathers dust on the shelf.

To Dell....Happy 48th Birthday

Another Birthday,
Another year.
And living without you still,
My only fear.

Sometimes up,
Sometimes down.
We shared our lives,
From town to town.

Washington State is now our home,
We chose this place to live.
Give what we must to the bad,
And take what good it will give.

For almost thirty years this is the way,
We chose to live our life.
I do not regret a single day,
Since I took you as my wife.

We will survive the daily woes,
If you'll just hold onto my hand.
Still dancing to the music we can make,
With our own two person band.

So hang with me, my dearest one,
And remember all the fun.
Cause you gotta ride in the rain,
To be able to enjoy the sun.

And on this day we celebrate,
Your birth that made me whole.
For all that has gone, and all that will come,
I love you Mind, Body and Soul.

June 1, 2000

My Life So Far

I was the youngest of six children,
    My father never finished the eighth grade.
And so I learned very early in life,
    To dance, the piper must be paid.

I decided to go to college,
    I worked hard to pay the bill.
At times it seemed the road I'd chosen,
    Was constantly uphill.

And then there was the Army,
    My abilities they could not see.
For Viet Nam awaited,
    As they classified me infantry.

I did my time for country,
    Graduated college and was set.
Then society told me to wait awhile,
    Hiring minorities was the best bet.

My father died at fifty two,
    I turned to alcohol as a crutch.
And after ten years I fought it off,
    Aware of it's lure and clutch.

I fought injustice where I could,
    Faced prison just to take a stand.
Only to realize no one wanted the truth,
    I was branded un-Americian.

I faced the challenges with head unbowed,
    Getting up whenever knocked down.
I kept my beliefs untarnished,
    I felt my reasoning sound.

For I had studied the masters,
    Read philosophy and theology for years.
I felt if I understood the world.
    The knowledge would alleviate all my fears.

Took care of my family,
    Provided for child and wife.
Devoted time and energy,
    None wasted for a vanities life.

So the years slid by the pain intrudes,
    And suddenly I feel old.
Only now realizing,
    How such efforts took their toll.

I never took the time,
    To make my body a temple place.
Between school plays, graduations, vacations,
    And generally the whole rat race.

I do not do drugs or alcohol,
    Chase other women or any such vice.
Mine is only the cigarette curse,
    Which makes me sociologically, not so nice.

And while the world lies quiet at night,
    The nightmares haunt my sleep.
With the things I've seen in my life,
    And the secrets I must keep.

At fifty people tell me,
    "You're not all that old."
Yet if they had walked in my shoes,
    Perhaps they would not be so bold.

The daily pain grows old,
    I wish to play no more.
Only to find each day,
    They still are keeping score.

My eyes are old, my knees are gone,
    Each day seems harder than before.
I sometimes wonder if I fall again,
    Can I get up off the floor.

And so once more I struggle,
    To get up and pass their test.
Yet it seems such a small thing to ask.
    If I could just, take a rest.

July 26, 2000

The American Dream

Laugh and the world laughs with you,
    Cry and you cry alone.
Stop your whining and complaining.
    And answer that god dam phone.

The American Dream, that's the ticket,
    That's what life's about.
Work hard, pay bills and hopefully you'll die,
    Before you figure it out.

Buy a house, a car and a boat,
    It all just makes such sense.
Then put it on a piece of land,
    And surround it with a fence.

Nothing matters, and what if it did?
    Is not a suicides song.
It's for people who have begun to think,
    And no longer play along.

So be the best that you can be,
    And please don't think me crass.
But you can take your American Dream,
    And stick it up your ass.

July 26, 2000

A Good Night's Sleep

A good night's sleep, those four words,
Leave me shaken to the core.
A sad and tortured soul,
Exhausted, tired and sore.

For beyond the edge of darkness,
And the shadows whispering of sleep.
Behind the lids of my eyes,
Lies the realm of the demon's keep.

With evil eyes and hideous grins,
They lie in wait for me.
From these screams and fear and sweats,
Will I ever again be free?

Where is the wonderful innocence?
That youth once fondly held.
What door of consciousness did I open?
That spelled a peaceful sleep's death knell.

I do not fear the demons so much,
As I dread the games they play.
For how can you fight such tortures?
When unmoving and defenseless you lay.

So they play their games,
And with darkness I fight their fight.
For I know as surly as the daylight fades,
Soon comes another night.

How I envy those of you,
To whom sleep is a restful interlude,
Who dream of simple things,
With no demons to intrude.

Yet would I then change places?
Given the chance for dreamless night.
I think the answer is no,
For I keep searching for the light.

The light that is itself a dream,
Of a universal understanding of man.
For the answer lies somewhere in the demon's keep,
And I must find it, if I can.

June 26,2001

You Make each Day My Life

My knee is aching,
    My back is tight.
My eyes are burning,
    And I didn't sleep last night.

So here I sit,
    Another endless day.
In pain and boredom,
    Just to earn my pay.

But I have a secret,
    That makes it worthwhile.
It's just twenty feet away,
    Plus it comes with a smile.

Because when things get so tough,
    I feel I must scream.
I just get up, walk to next row,
    And there sits my dream.

That smiling face,
    Those sparking eyes.
Honesty that's almost painful,
    And never once tells lies.

Yes, you are the reason I live,
    You make me able to face each day.
To endure such endless crap,
    So I feel I must say.

Thank you again,
    For giving me my life.
And I will love you forever.
My life and my wife.

August 28, 2001

Veteran's Day

It's Veteran's Day. It's Veteran's Day.
A day off from work to share.
To tell Veterans they're appreciated,
To show how much you care.

And as the speeches continue,
And the parades go mile after mile.
Has it ever crossed your mind?
Why you almost never see them smile.

How could they be so callous?
All you want is to show you care.
But look into they eyes, as the eyes film over,
With the famous, "thousand yard stare".

I do not mean to spoil your fun.
I'm sure you're concerned with their plight.
But if you wish to really help,
Be there when they wake up sweating, in the middle of the night

I'm sure the intentions are honorable,
All of societies' obligations will be met.
But maybe they don't want to remember,
And all they want, is to just forget.

Yet year after year, the pattern repeats,
It invariably never seems to fail.
Old wounds torn open again
Exposing memories of a season in hell.

So please don't think me an insensitive cad,
Deserving scorn, like a thoughtless child.
If I don't participate in the festivities,
And want to be alone for a while.

The past is done, so let it lie,
    Let the memories become a blur and a haze.
Look forward, not back, to better times,
    To a future, with brighter days.

Oct 20,2001

The Beginning

Once upon a time,
    Long, long, ago.
Or maybe it was just a second,
    Who's to really know?

There was just energy,
    But not out in space.
Not in the void, nor in chaos,
    Or any such imaginable place.

Suffice it to say,
    If you dare.
It was its own Existence,
    That it was in fact, just there.

Then came a spark, origins unknown,
    Perhaps an evolutionary combination.
And it created an independent thought,
    Thus beginning a conflagration.

And with the fires, the energies roared,
    As if the thought recognized or even cared.
Time slowed, matter was created, and
    Validation of the equation, E=mc2.

An Existence was created,
    Call it a universe if you need a name.
And unto this place of new beginning,
    Swiftly the Fire Lords came.

The Fire Lords are creatures,
    Of what we would call light.
They protect us from the darkness,
    And depressions of night.

They helped develop this universe,
So the Existence can understand.
They created the states of matter and time,
And a creature we call man.

Yet the Existence is very limited,
It's comprehension beset with strife.
Three dimensions, only one universe,
And what is the definition of life.

Yet how, can any creature hope to understand,
And here I come to its defenses.
For it is limited by a spoken language,
And the restrictions of only five senses.

So the Fire Lords created,
More than the Existence deserved.
A time frame to develop it's thinking,
A modified learning curve.

And at the end of this curve,
A change, in its state of being.
A new perspective of existence,
Or, if I may, a new way of seeing.

Eventually the creature called man,
Began to believe it was the Existence.
Fabricating beliefs, sciences, and legends,
Destroying any and all resistance.

Yet even limited by understanding and fear,
And denying what is plainly in sight.
Defer if you must, and ask a physicist,
What is the nature of light.

Is it a particle? Is it a wave?
Call it a photon if you must have a label.
For the Fire Lords appear to be,
The only beings that are stable.

So do not worry, if confusion reins supreme,
And at the end of your learning curve, you will be.
Changed to a different being, existing as pure light.
An energy, with the capacity to "see".

A uniformity of existence,
A totality of it all.
With time, dimensions, and states of nature,
All at your beck and call.

Becoming a Fire Lord,
To instinctively know wrong from right.
To exist without such definitions,
At one within the Light.

November 4, 2001

30th Anniversary

Thirty years now, where'd they go,
Thirty years now, I don't know.
I sit and I wonder,
Where they've gone.

But sometimes when it's late at night,
When I'm bathed by the firelight.
The moon comes callin, a ghostly white,
And I recall, I recall.

I recall, Fire on the Mountain,
Lightning in the air.
Gold in them hills,
With you waiting for me there.

I remember giving myself to you,
All my Mind, Body and Soul.
A love I gave to you freely,
Never for Silver Threads, or Needles of Gold.

Yea, we've seen paradise, by the Dashboard Lights,
We've even had our Afternoon Delights.
We've had more laughs than I can count.
And even at first we had some fights.

And I recall, Grovin to La Freak,
Back in a time when it was, so Chic.
And Dancing in the Dark,
Just us two, Cheek to Cheek.

There was a time, all we did was Celebrate,
And Dance to the Music, with our own special beat.
Living in a Fifth Dimension,
Down on Baker Street.

God, the times and music.
    That have defined our life.
Never could a guy ask for more.
    Than to have you for his wife.

So if I go crazy, would you still
    Call me Superman?
In a Gadda-da-vida,
    Or on a beach just, Walkin in the Sand.

Caused Lord it's Hard to be Humble,
    When your Wife is perfect in every way.
Yet when we look in the mirror,
    We keep getting older by every day.

So what I guess I'm asking, after 30 years,
    With your daily quick kiss, before walk out the door.
Is will you still need me? Will you still feed me?
    When I'm Sixty-Four.

And I will Always Love You,
Happy Anniversary to you Dell
My wife and My life.

Dec11,2001

Prose for Fifty

Fifty years have passed,
Since you came into this world.
Thirty two years have passed,
Since I first called you, "my girl".

You've been called by many names,
By one person or another.
And about twenty-four years ago,
A young girl first called you "Mother".

Good years and bad years,
They blend into a fog.
Once we had Tropical fish,
Twice we had a dog.

Always taking care of each other,
We walked the path we chose.
We listened to our kind of music,
Dressed in our style of clothes.

So now there's gray in your hair,
But I love when it looks that way.
Your smile, your eyes, I must confess,
I love more and more each day.

So "Happy Birthday" to you I wish,
May true joy come your way.
But my gift to you, is my heart and soul,
Forever and a day.

June 1, 2002

Danny L Shanks

Thoughts on a Cold Afternoon

It's cold today,
    And it's raining too.
I sit her alone,
    And miss my Boo.

I'm at home, and she is gone to work,
    It's all quiet, but I have no fear.
Cause everywhere I look,
    Are bunches of friendly Reindeer.

UPS, they brought a package,
    It was from my mom, today.
Then she also called too,
    Just to say "Hey".

So I washed the dishes,
    Took out the trash.
Used some hand lotion,
    To prevent getting a rash.

Anyway, I still miss my Boo,
    Maybe cause she's such a fox.
Decorating a Christmas tree,
    Or just playing, Word-Ox.

So I'll play on the compute,
    And I'll bide my time.
Till she's home again,
    No more sharing, she'll be all mine.

Then tonight I will be thankful,
    In my heart and in my head.
That after 31 years, we can still,
    Snuggle together in a warm, soft bed.

Dec 11,2002

Two Halves

One half am I, and she the other,
Put us together, and you will see.
These two halves make a complete whole,
The way it was meant to be.

For in our youth, I was the knight,
Who rode a two-wheeled steed.
She my maiden fair,
Who fulfilled my every need.

We rode from adventure to adventure,
Across this enchanted land.
We saw castles of beauty and dragons of fire,
We faced each, hand in hand.

And now the years slip by,
My armor is not so bright.
Her hair is streaked with silver,
But she is still, my guiding light.

And when we leave these Earthly bonds,
Her light becoming blue to my green.
The adventures will begin anew,
With new places to be seen.

For the universe will be our playground,
We'll ride the currents of space.
Constellations, planets and moons,
Each a new and wondrous place.

We are one, and we are whole,
She is my maiden fair, and she is my life.
Me just a knight of old,
And she? She is my wife.

Never could a man ask for more.
With all my love,

12/11/02

Happy 51st Birthday

I lay here out of shape, overweight , and depressed,
    I await the dawn's opening light.
And as the room's darkness fades,
    I adjust my pillow and turn to my right.

There lying next to me,
    The reason for my life.
Her face in sweet sleeps repose,
    My lovely magnificent wife.

For when the world is too much for me,
    And I feel I can no longer get along.
She's always there to pick me up,
    When did she become so strong?

I remember a cute little thing,
    Short skirts, boots and long long hair.
Laughing smile and sparking eyes,
    She seems to say, "Hey the world is fair."

No cynicism, sarcasm, no brooding thoughts,
    Everything reliable as a tide.
So I signed up for the whole nine yard,
    And I thank her for the ride.

Oh I have read God's noblest poets,
    Philosophy and theology by the ton.
Yet as instructive as it seemed at the time,
    She and only she, taught me to enjoy the sun.

She taught me about life,
    Gave me strength when I was down.
Never complaining about bad luck,
    When I was sad, she acted the clown

What forces led me here,
    What did I do to deserve such a life?
How do you place a value?
    On such a magnificent wife.

So on your birthday, I would say,
    Thank you for picking me.
Letting me come along for the ride,
    For teaching me to see.

I would do anything for you,
    No cost would be too much.
But, I could not bear to lose you,
    Your smile, your love, or your touch.

So let the world be warned,
    This old man will truly tell.
Take her from me and you'll free the Dogs of War,
    And loose the Hounds of Hell.

I will rip the stars down from the sky,
    Lay waste to all the land.
Defy both Gods and Demons,
    If you try taking her from my hand.

Anyway, "Happy Birthday to you my love."
    Again I thank you for my life.
You will always be, forever and a day,
    My lovely magnificent wife.

Happy 51st Birthday,

June 9,2004

Happy Birthday Mom

There is a place called Arkansas,
    It's about half way across this land.
And there, was born , a wisp of a girl,
    Next to the Mississippi sand.

She married early in her life,
    Brought six children into this world.
Three were in the form of a boy,
    Three were as a girl.

She taught them well, she brought them up,
    She taught them wrong from right.
She taught them to appreciate the good in life,
    And to never run from a fight.

And as they grew, their opinions firmed,
    They wanted to argue their point of view.
Never realizing their strength of character,
    Nor the source from which it grew.

They disagree with her,
    Disagreed with all their might.
But if forced to admit to it honestly,
    In the long run she was usually right.

They may not have agreed with her logic,
    But when it came to push and shove.
None of them could ever doubt,
    Her devotion or her love.

Her ups and downs in this life,
    A roller coaster ride
She faced all of life's challenges,
    She was never one to hide.

And on this day, you look at me,
    And measure my worth as a man.
Remember all I am was taught to me,
    At her loving gentle hand.

Yeah she is my Mom, and I love her so,
    But after the toil of years taken by this world.
If you look real hard as I often do,
    You will see the wisp of a girl.

August 15,2003

An Old Shirt

We've been married a long, long, time,
    You are like an old shirt to me.
How unromantic others may say.
    But what I feel, they just simply cannot see.

I do not wish a new shirt,
    One that says spruce up and go out on the town.
My old one does not feel the need,
    To "Boogie" or "Get Down".

It accepts me for what I am,
    It does not make accusation or render judgment.
It just let's me live my way,
    And just gives my life contentment.

It wraps itself around me,
    It keeps out all the cold.
It does not seem to care,
    That I am getting old.

No it does not shine with newness,
    It's kind of wrinkled and gray.
But it's the kind of shirt,
    That I could wear each day.

It's reliable as the rising sun,
    Never complains about being worn.
You could never ask for more in life,
    It makes you glad that you were born.

And on this day, I'm thankful,
    For this old shirt I call my own.
For the comfort, protection, and strength,
    And especially for the support that it has shown.

Well it may not be romantic,
    A dozen roses should be for a wife.
But to me it's the comfort that it gives,
    And this old shirt gives meaning to my life.

Happy Anniversary,

December 11, 2003

To My Daughter

I sent my daughter a message about a comet,
And I got back her reply.
That she was working very hard,
But look into she would try.

I hope she does not lose the wonder of life,
And her excitement of when she was young.
Trapped by a world gone mad,
With deadlines, politics, work, forgetting earth's simple tongue .

I tried to teach her everything and she listens politely every time,
To each bad joke, each stupid pun, and badly worded rhyme.
She is so much more considerate than I was at her age,
When I was so consumed by my arrogance I thought myself a sage.

That I knew so much and could give it to her all,
Was a dream every parent had.
But there is no blueprint or project notes in being a parent,
To tell you if you've done good or bad.

I also realized how dumb I'd been
Yes, dumb in every way.
For how can I teach her anything.
When I find myself still learning things every day.

I tell her to always listen,
That is the way to true knowledge.
Perhaps I should listen to her,
After all she did better than I when going to college.

I once wrote a poem called "The Answer",
Which explained the simplicity of being.
I realize now that I saw the answer,
But did not understand it's meaning.

Maybe some things you can learn,
    And some things only, with age can you understand.
I can only do my best,
    And try to be the leader of the band.

Eclectics II

Eclectics took me 34 years to write. Eclectics II is going faster. I am retired with nothing to occupy my time except trying to put down in rhyme some of my thoughts and fears of today's life in America. From fireworks, to selling pet rocks, to the politically correct. I tried to cover it all.

June 1, 2005

1	Introduction	6/1/2005
2	What Happened	6/3/2005
3	Stop Smoking	6/7/2005
4	My Lady Fair	6/8/2005
5	Pets	6/8/2005
6	Professional Sports	6/8/2005
7	Retirement	6/8/2005
8	Early Morning	6/9/2005
9	Gambling	6/9/2005
10	The Ballad of Tom and Leslie	6/9/2005
11	The Secrets of Aging	6/9/2005
12	Early Morning at the Beach	6/11/2005
13	Early Morning Touch	6/11/2005
14	Oxymoron	6/11/2005
15	Competition	6/13/2005
16	Minimum Wage	6/13/2005
17	Growing Older and Wiser	6/13/2005
18	Proud to be an American	6/15/2005
19	Panic in the Streets	6/16/2005
20	A Failed Lesson	6/19/2005
21	Middle of the Night	7/2/2005
22	Fireworks	7/4/2005
23	I Miss God	7/5/2005
24	Small Wooden Spoons	7/5/2005
25	Light Brown Hair	7/8/2005
26	Politically Correct	7/9/2005
27	Marketing	7/9/2005
28	Sex	7/11/2005
29	We've Only Just Begun	7/12/2005
30	A True American Hero	7/14/2005
31	Wants versus Needs	7/14/2005
32	The 60's	7/15/2005
33	Emergency Broadcast System	7/15/2005
34	Air Conditioning	7/15/2005

35	Reading	7/15/2005
36	Breaking Even at the Casino	7/16/2005
37	Grocery Shopping	7/17/2005
38	Language	7/18/2005
39	Country Summer Night	7/19/2005
40	Operation Iraq Freedom	7/20/2005
41	My Poetry	7/20/2005
42	Bacon and Tomato Sandwichs	7/22/2005
43	Invasive Questioning	7/23/2005
44	My Sister Diane	7/23/2005
45	The Present	7/25/2005

What Happened?????

I lost my son in law,
 A man whom I respected.
I lost the love of my daughter,
 Both slipped away undetected.

They both now think,
 That I am just a fool.
When did that change,
 From me being a dad that was ever so cool.

My health is gone now,
 No matter what I do.
As my health declined,
 I lost my paying job too.

I'm in debt,
 Mostly from trying to help the ones I cared about..
So now my wife has to work.
 And I can't seem to help her out.

I don't even have the courage,
 To try and end my life.
A full bottle of percocet would do it,
 But I worry about my wife.

Because I checked and the insurance won't pay suicide.
 A solution that would finally ease my pain.
So how much would my selfishness
 Result in her financial gain.

If there is a God, it must be laughing,
 What a joke has been my life.
Imagine, all I ever wanted, was to just have a job,
 With nothing more than a home, a child and a wife.

Stop Smoking

The government officials tell us, Stop Smoking,
They sound so righteous and sincere.
Yet they continually subsidize the tobacco farmers,
Their tax and intentions, to me are far from clear

Just stop smoking, it's easy,
Try and do what's right.
If they believe it so much, just ban it,
And dig in for the fight.

They say you should try to quit,
What moral character do smokers lack?
But who would want to give up the loss of taste buds,
And the bad smell, for just $5 a pack.

Well I admit it does give one pleasure,
But I'm jealous of those who quit, or try.
Cause it's obvious from what they say, if you quit,
You'll never get sick, feel pain, or die.

My Lady Fair

Well its Birthday time again,
    This will be number 53.
No present could I buy, that would equal my love,
    And that, you have for free.

You are indeed My Lady Fair,
    The cool breeze on a hot summer day.
The showers of April.
    And the flowers of May.

You make each day a joy,
    Give meaning to the world.
A world that had nothing for me,
    Till you agreed to be my girl.

So what can I say on this day,
    To stress how much you are worth to me.
All the gold and silver in the world,
    Mean nothing when you are all I can see.

Your smile, your touch, your love,
    All comprise the you I cherish so dear.
So on this day I celebrate your birth,
    And losing you still my only fear.

But my armor is tarnished,
    It's embarrassing in the light of day.
A lady fair deserves so much more,
    And so for the world to hear, I say.

I Love You . My Lady Fair.
Your tarnished knight and grateful husband,

Pets

Our pets are special,
What a wonderful breed.
For they are unique,
For their looks, intelligence, and speed.

Sorry folks, but I don't see it,
They're animals, and us they really don't need.
They could survive fine without humans,
They don't have to count on us for feed.

But we give them human characteristics,
Names that we think are cute.
Buy them presents, have parties,
And have birthdays for them to boot.

So why do we spend the money,
To fulfill their every need.
When people are starving around the world..
It's them, that we should feed.

Professional Sports

We revere professional athletes in America,
    Adopt them as our own.
But what devotion to the fans,
    Have these people ever shown?

I hear people brag,
    About the winning of our team.
What position did these people play?
    Or was it only in a dream.

So your team won,
    And it's really a big deal.
But have any to these players,
    Ever asked you to share a meal.

Ever invited you to their house,
    Ever invited you over for a drink,
Do they even know you exist?
    I don't know, what do you think?

Fact is they are only a group,
    Of grown men playing a game.
Does that really qualify them?
    For all such riches and fame.

Well I guess they're the reassurance,
    And for this, all athletes together I can clump.
For if the world has a pandemic,
    We can at least count on them to jump.

Retirement

Retirement, Retirement, Retirement,
It has to be the universal dream.
So you stop working to watch the sunsets,
And after about an hour you are ready to scream.

It starts in kindergarten,
You go to school for seemly for endless days.
Grammar school, high school then college,
All accomplished to get a job that pays.

Days in, and days out,
With vacation once a year.
Building up a retirement plan,
Surviving it all, your only true fear.

And so you retire,
Ready to kick back and relax from daily strife.
But what in the hell did you ever learn,
To prepare you for such a life.

So many people get another job,
Maybe a hobby you can call mine.
All done for the express purpose,
To occupy your time.

Our brains took us out of the caves,
Raised us up to a civilization where we are now.
You can't just turn it off,
And turn into a contented cow.

You can't just turn off your brain,
Nothing has prepared you for a life that lazy.
So find something to occupy your time left,
Or you will eventually just go crazy.

Early Morning

I sat out on my patio,
    Waiting for the beginning of a new day.
It came on soft creeping feet,
    Slowly the light felt its way.

I listened to the sounds,
    The earth sang in that morn.
Of a world waking from its slumber,
    And thought why we were born?

Maybe mother earth could give me,
    The answer that I sought.
And so I sat there listening,
    In my mind I held the thought.

It's amazing that in all my years,
    I had never listened and just sat outside.
The animals would have their say,
    The secrets they would confide.

And so I sat and listened,
    An hour came and passed.
I realized that if nothing else,
    I had learned one important truth at last.

The birds of our world,
    Spoke to me as I drank my coffee by the cup.
They may in fact have the meaning of life,
    But the damn things never shut up.

Gambling

I go to the casinos a lot these days,
    To test out Lady Luck.
To try and win a fortune,
    But the odds there really suck.

The lights, the smells, the staff,
    All waiting there it's true.
Well it's simply not paid for,
    By giving money to you.

But it is refreshing,
    To see so many people all full of hope.
And it could happen at any time,
    So you don't feel like such a dope.

Yeah you know the odds are against you,
    It's that simple and it's a fact.
But what joy to see such unbounded hope in the people's eyes
    Of winning their money back.

You play 35 hands and lose them all,
    So what sort of reason, or simple mind set.
Would compel a person in that case,
    To double their very next bet.

I go to the casinos,
    I relish in the place.
For unlike the rest of the world, they always welcome me,
    And always remember my face.

The Ballad of Tom and Leslie

He was a Tar heel from North Carolina,
She a South Carolina Southern Bell,
They married on October 1, 1950,
And since then, things have gone pretty well.

They first lived in North Carolina,
Then for a while, made Augusta, Georgia home.
Then moved to live in Houston, Texas,
Must have been the lure, of the famous Astro Dome.

They brought three children into this world.
By the time that they were done.
Two were as daughters,
One was as a son.

The oldest daughter is my favorite,
Sorry if I'm a little prejudice there,
But I married her 34 years ago,
So I feel my choice is fair.

For she was a child of the Wild Blue Yonder,
That trait they gave her in style.
By their example and by their love,
Cause you could never call them wild

Their lives are a living example,
Of what is sought after by most.
Yet they were not the self-righteous type,
Never given to brag or boast.

They live their lives with honor,
An example of goodness for all of us.
They just live that way all the time,
Never feeling the need to make a fuss.

So Happy Anniversary on this day,
That began a full and happy life.
And by the way, I must say to you both,
Thank you for my wife.

The Secrets of Aging

As I grow older in this life,
I find I'm learning more and more.
About what this life is about,
And what it has in store.

I remember in my youth,
Seeing older people in the park.
Smiling at all the children,
Out playing until it was dark.

I now realize they weren't just smiling,
At the children from emotions that were soft.
Cause they knew what was coming,
But telling no one, and laughing their asses off.

It takes longer to get to the bathroom
So why warn the children of what lies ahead,
When you sit on the side and think about it,
Before you get up from the bed.

I now take long showers,
With the water turned on really hot.
It's not to feel better physically,
But to steam up the mirror a lot.

I don't want to see my body naked,
In that mirror on the bathroom sink.
It could give me a heart attack,
To see that stranger looking back, all soft, wrinkled and pink.

For I heard all my life,
That the body a temple should be.
Well an amusement park was mine,
And the price I paid was not free.

But hey, it's not all bad,
It's not all pain and hurt.
When simply your only concern or worry,
Is on which side you are of dirt.

Early Morning at the Beach

I went to the beach this morning,
    It was a little after nine.
June the tenth it was,
    The beginning of summertime.

White cotton ball clouds filled the sky,
    A deep rich texture of blue.
Salt air on my face,
    Seemly promises of a perfect day were true.

I saw two children playing,
    Building castles in the sand.
A beautiful woman, probably their mother,
    And I guess their father, a young strong healthy man.

He was trying to fly a kite,
    A seagull watched, with a smirk on its face.
It seemed to say, "Just spread your wings and take off",
    Then executed the maneuver with perfect grace.

Sitting on a bench,
    I watched the waves roll in.
Wow such noise,
    But it was a constant, and relaxing din.

What a way to start a day,
    Fresh air, sights, and sounds.
I felt all my worries drifting away,
    As the beauty of the earth abounds.

No schedules to keep,
    No stress to intrude.
No rush hour with drivers,
    All seemly trying to be rude.

So if you feel depressed one day,
    And it carries into the night.
Get up and begin a new day,
    Enjoying such a day, in a beach's morning light.

Early Morning Touch

I can't sleep this evening,
    I toss and look over to my right.
The clock says three fifteen,
    So I turn to the left and behold a beautiful sight.

There lies my wife,
    Sleeping sweetly in the bed.
A small smile on her face.
    Her long hair cascading round her head

So I move to my left gently,
    Snuggle my leg up next to her.
She feels so soft and cuddly,
    Like a puppy's new grown fur.

Then electricity flows,
    Powerfully from her to me.
It's calming energy I feel,
    She unknowingly gives it to me for free.

I dare not wake her,
    I just relish in delight.
That feeling she has shared with me,
    In the middle of the night.

She will never know,
    And this secret I will keep.
Of the love and calming energy,
    She shares even while asleep.

Oxymoron

Oxymoron by the dictionary
    And the definition that it refers,
Means the juxtaposition,
    Of the two normally contradictory words.

Examples are "big baby", and "common sense".
    A "sad clown" or the "front end".
But my concern is societies oxymoron of thinking
    And the message it does send.

At the ATM in the banks drive thru,
    Why does it have a Braille keypad?
And why on school buses,
    Are there no seatbelts to be had?

What is "government efficiency?"
    What are these references for?
What is a "jumbo shrimp?"
    And please tell me, what is a "Holy War".

No wonder kids don't understand the language,
    And for "higher education" expressing the plead.
I guess lower education, just doesn't work,
    Doesn't fulfill their every need.

Well it's an "obvious secret,"
    With a "rush hour" to fill the void.
To give us the satisfaction.
    Of being "pleasantly annoyed".

Competition

It's 3 AM and I'm playing poker on the computer,
    Playing the game, just for fun.
It will not change the world,
    If I've either lost or won.

But I find myself getting angry,
    Every time that I lost.
The realization chilled me,
    Like a winter's morning frost.

Why are we so competitive?
    As a species on the whole?
Why is winning so important?
    What is the ultimate goal?

It's not the competition for food,
    Or even shelter do we strive.
It's not a simple matter,
    Of trying to survive.

Yet I see kids yell that they are number one,
    Of what. If I may ask.
Is it so important, the winning?
    Is it that much of a task.

It's not how you play the game,
    It only counts if you win.
To come in second or third,
    Now seems a mortal sin.

What the hell are we teaching the kids,
    That everything counts as a score.
Have we really sold ourselves so cheaply?
    As a late Saturday night whore?

It's ingrained in our minds so,
    That everything counts so much.
That every thing matters,
    That you must come thru in the clutch.

I'm sorry, not everything is so important,
    Like the late evening drive.
Yelling at someone who cut you off,
    Like that matters somehow to make you survive.

So relax the competition,
    Stop making it live or die.
Just chill out a bit,
    And if you can't, then a least just give it a try.

Minimum Wage

I am now retired,
I worked most of my life.
Putting up with deadlines, production schedules,
And all the office's political strife.

Well I stopped in a restaurant the other day,
Just to grab a bite to eat.
I noticed the people working there,
Spending all day on their feet.

I spent some time reflecting on the jobs,
I had known, or done over the years.
Some stressing me out
Almost to the point of tears.

But upon reflecting on those jobs,
I remembered thinking how some people worked so hard,
Just to keep a job,
And kept punching a stupid time card.

Yes, I'm now retired,
Writing poetry and thinking myself a sage.
But why do the people who work the hardest,
Always seem to make minimum wage?

Growing Older and Wiser

I heard a woman talking one day,
    And she stated to me.
That her children would never love her till she died
    And that her reasoning was clear to see.

How horrible I thought,
    Those children would not love the parent till they die.
But determined I was to listen,
    Giving her a chance to explain or at least to try.

She said its human nature,
    Not morbid so be not distraught.
For time wins every battle for wisdom,
    That it has ever fought.

Do not confuse she said,
    Youth's intelligence with the mature's wisdom.
For only life's experiences give it,
    And only time can give them some.

Example she says of thinking for humans,
    When young and maybe still in school.
They believe everything a coach says,
    Thinking the coach has every tool.

Talk to them later in life,
    Once they leave the confines of school,
Their opinion of the coach changes,
    They now think, "What a Fool".

The coach didn't change,
    Only their perspective did.
They see things more clearly now,
    Things their youth just hid.

But beware, she went on,
    And using the word ignorant I can't .
They'll never hear another word,
    They just think I'm on a rant.

But ask them if they feel bad
    About being ignorant of surgery for the brain.
Then it doesn't carry, the insults,
    Slurs, innuendos, or pain.

Ignorant is just a word,
    Meaning the person lacks certain knowledge.
It doesn't mean their stupid,
    Or didn't to well in college.

And so I realized she was right,
    It didn't mean there was no love.
Just that they hadn't reached the heights,
    And that understanding was still high above.

But it is common enough,
    Every child seems to believe and use.
Thinking their parents are putting them down,
    Giving their egos a short lived fuse.

So if I feel bad,
    That my child loves me no more.
I just need to be patient,
    And wait for the final score.

Although I may not see it,
    While my body still has life.
But I feel better knowing it will happen,
    And will probably be seen by my wife.

Proud to be an American

Yes I'm proud to be an American,
That feeling is ever so true.
The swelling emotion felt in your breast,
When seeing our colors of red, white, and blue.

Our turf protected by the military,
They defend us with pride and zeal.
Not just anyone can come in,
Only those who believe and feel what we feel.

Serving in the military,
Is something done with pride.
Out front for the world to see,
No need to sneak or hide.

For they will fight,
And readily take any life.
Of anyone perceived,
As a threat to children or wife.

A country defended by everyone,
And to have pride in it we must.
Convinced our belief is so right,
Our motto is "In God We Trust."

Old glory is our flag,
Never dipped to another state.
To show such weakness,
Would indeed predict a dismal fate.

Then one day I was thinking,
And a thought came to me like a bell it rang.
Aren't these the same descriptions?
And accusations we use when talking about a gang?

Panic in the Streets

Americans thrive on panic,
The media feeds this fear.
For how can we survive without?
The local news broadcast to hear.

They recently tested the tsunami warning system,
And it failed to warn the people in time.
How could the people survive the wave?
If the warning bell didn't chime.

As far as I know, no tsunami has ever hit the west coast,
But if it did how many people would have died.
Maybe none if they moved inland,
About 5 miles and put up with a little drive.

When I lived on the east coast,
We had shark warnings without end.
I checked and guess what? No man-eating shark
Has ever been seen on third floor of the Holiday Inn.

Tornados in Kansas,
Stay tuned to channel 5.
How in the world could we make it?
How could we ever survive?

Buy a barometer and learn to read it.
The only time to lose your smiles.
Is if it reads less than 29 inches of pressure,
The tornado is less than 5 miles.

And look at the people,
In Kansas for their thinking is sound.
There seems to be no threat to life,
If you dig a hole and hide under ground.

But how did the people live,
    Without TV updates to warn them what to do.
They seemed to survive for centuries,
    Just reading the Mother Nature weather clue.

In Seattle we had an earthquake,
    My supervisors railed at those who took no cover under their desk.
But if the 80 foot ceiling beam fell,
    Would I have been protected by my Formica topped desk?

Mother Nature loves us,
    Like the cherub Cupid.
But she can't protect us,
    If we all just act stupid.

Just think of the time we waste in Congress,
    Debating a flag-burning bill.
Just pass a law making all American flags flame retardant,
    Or would that be to simple a law to will?

How about a nuclear attack,
    Fearing fallout we should.
But no advanced country with any sense,
    Would explode a bomb on the ground, for it would do no good.

Exploding it about 50 miles up,
    Would disable a society like a well-placed fist.
But a small hill would protect us from the blast,
    And the fallout would not exist.

Yet the media rants and raves of the dangers that we face,
    A daily threat to our being resistant.
For without the threat to hold our attention.
    Their ratings would be non-existent

As far as I know,
    Only one person died in the Seattle quake.
They had a heart attack,
    The media's fear they could not shake.

As far as for me,
    If the ceiling beam fell.
I may have at least been able to dodge it,
    If not hidden under my desk's fragile shell.

So listen if you must,
    And stop giving in to the fear.
Some things just happen,
    Life goes on with a smile and a tear.

A Failed Lesson

The woman I married is unique,
    A better woman has not been born.
So to keep her from harm I must do,
    Things that leave me emotionally torn.

A better woman there has never been,
    Since man began with Able and Kane.
Yet as much as I love her,
    She sometimes drives me insane.

For she knows not how to hide her emotions,
    She wears them all out there on her sleeve.
It is an enduring trait.
    But perhaps a little naive.

She listens to our son in law and daughter talk,
    Interested in their jobs, fears, joys, and life.
Always interested and paying attention to it all,
    Not knowing how to fake it, that is my wife.

But she asked me one day,
    Why no one wanted to hear, about her.
Her job, her day, or even her thoughts and
    Views on the use of animal fur.

Sometimes they would ask,
    Then interested they would pretend.
But it was obvious to all concerned,
    They only half listened till the end.

So I decided to teach them a lesson,
    With two parts if you may.
So about two years ago I began to talk about myself,
    In an overbearing and obnoxious sort of way.

It took a full two years.
    But part one finally came to light.
They couldn't take it anymore, and said essentially "Shut Up",
    And of course they were right.

However part two of the lesson,
    Fell on hallowed ground.
They did not recognize their actions and mine.
    No relationship to be found.

They just didn't get it,
    That their actions were unjust.
That they had treated their mother so badly,
    That emotion they could not trust.

Well I tried and I failed,
    To teach them how humans felt.
Just the caring about another person,
    A worse failure I had never been dealt.

Just to be interested in someone else's life,
    Other, than one's own self.
Was an emotion they could not handle,
    So it was pushed to their emotional back shelf

So how do you teach a child ,
    To be honest and sincere.
To care for others without faking,
    Their joy or their tear.

For she had always been there for them.
    Through the laughter and the pain.
Never had one parent given so much,
    Than she did, apparently given in vain.

Middle of the Night

It's three A.M,
It's the middle of the night and once again I find.
That I simply can not sleep,
As rhythms run rampant through my mind.

So I rise quietly,
Don't want to awake my lady fair.
I sit by the sliding glass door,
In my reclining lazy boy chair.

I gaze out at the world,
Bathed in the soft moon's light.
I watch the silent clouds slip by,
In their never ending flight.

How peaceful seems the world,
How the quiet controls the sound.
Such conditions I crave,
This life that I have found.

I wish I could give it to all,
Share my joy with everyone I know.
I wish it could be there during the day,
And that I could make it so.

But it passes ever so swiftly,
And comes the rising sun.
The light intrudes and traffic builds,
Another day has begun.

But I treasure my time,
My peace in the middle of the night.
When all the cares just disappear,
And the world it just seems right.

So some night if the world seems too much,
    And thoughts keep you awake.
The problems, the worries, and life itself,
    Appears too much to take.

Just get up from your bed,
    Make your way to gaze upon the night.
See the world, as it should be,
    When everything just seems right.

Fireworks

I went to the Emerald Downs Raceway,
It was July on the third day.
It was an Independence celebration,
To see the fireworks display.

Ten thousand people were there,
I was lost in a maddening crowd.
Pushing and shoving each other,
Most drunk and really loud.

The show started around ten P.M,
Everyone watched the sky.
But I could not be impressed,
No matter how hard I did try.

For myself it was not so impressive,
It did not make me want to cry.
For in my past I had seen much bigger,
A 105 howitzer round, with white phosphorus in the sky.

The booms were loud,
People shrieked, it was too much to take.
Sorry, I again was unimpressed,
For the howitzer had caused the ground to shake.

I looked around at all the people,
Hypnotized at the sight.
I was reminded of a bunch of monkeys,
Fascinated by a loud noise and a bright pretty light.

Every time I think,
Human beings I understand.
I again find myself shocked,
At what impresses this being we call man.

I do not mean to spoil your fun.
    Or tell you something you don't know.
But it can not compare to Mother Nature,
    And her summer lightning show.

So rave about the rocket's red glare,
    Rant about bombs bursting in air.
People's imaginations deceive the reality of history,
    And what it meant to actually be there.

They say it's patriotic,
    That we must support our boys.
If you really want to support them,
    Tell your congressman to find new toys.

How many of our young men,
    Do we lose in a fruitless war?
Only to have the losses covered up,
    With some patriotic lore.

What did the killings accomplish?
    That would end some young man's life.
Nothing enduring or long lasting,
    Except he would never hold his child or wife.

For what did all the wars accomplish?
    Blood shed and drying in the sand.
For all the rhetoric and promises,
    It's still about some insignificant piece of land.

So I'll shut up for now,
    Go celebrate and play.
Enjoy the fourth of July,
    And the fireworks display.

I Miss God

I miss my youthful innocence,
When God was dominant in my life.
When I could count on the belief.
That he could relieve all my misery and strife.

Catholic high mass, and Latin,
I served my time as an alter boy.
Such belief and simplicity,
I never knew such joy.

But the church changed their beliefs,
Ecumenical council changed most of the law.
No longer would I go to hell,
For eating meat on Friday as did my Pa.

So I denounced the church,
Angry with the hypocrisy they did display.
For without the church, I could still believe in God,
So I continued to pray.

Then I went to Viet Nam,
With what I saw my faith they did kill.
They brought my body home,
But left my faith on some south Asian hill.

There is a saying that states,
"There is no atheist in a foxhole."
For me the opposite was true,
And it left me morally cold.

I lost my faith in that war,
Of what I saw and did over there.
To steal the faith of one so young,
Hardly seemed really fair.

I did not see it coming,
    They did not ask permission.
I just woke up one morning,
    To find my faith was missing.

I came home and went to college,
    Learned history of man and what he created.
Opening Pandora's box of knowledge,
    And how it all related.

I cannot close that box now,
    Cannot forget what I have learned.
For the lies and deceit of mankind,
    Stay in my mind forever burned.

But I miss the joy of youth,
    Innocence in believing what I now know is false.
For it was the same as putting Santa Claus,
    Up there on a cross.

I am angry no more,
    Just sorry that it is forever lost.
The same as parents replacing Santa Claus,
    And the knowledge came at such a cost.

Yes I miss my God and the religion,
    That gave me reasons to try.
But I would rather die knowing nothing,
    Than put faith in such a lie.

Small Wooden Spoons

There was a gathering at the Fair Haven Methodist Church,
To celebrate the Fourth of July,
The congregation all coming together at the gathering,
And the main discussion was "Why".

Not the why of the universe,
No discussion of planets stars or moons.
But the question of why when served a cup of ice cream,
Had they done away with the small wooden spoons?

Even as a child I remember,
The joy of a small cup of ice cream.
And to eat it with a wooden spoon,
Was every person's dream.

Well things change,
Is the reason that they gave.
But they should consider tradition,
And some changes should not be so grave.

Light Brown Hair

Have you ever heard the song?
About Jeannie with the light brown hair?
That describes my wife,
The long beautiful tresses of my lady Fair.

I coveted those long locks in my youth,
Her hair a beauty to behold.
But that was in our youth,
Before we began to get old.

Rapunzel Rapunzel , let down your hair,
The fairy prince he called.
Now she let down so much of it,
I can not believe she is not bald.

I can trace where in the house she's been,
As she goes about her day.
Making the bed, doing the wash,
Watching the TV, or bringing my supper on a tray.

She leaves it to mark her presence,
Strands of that long lovely hair.
On the bed, bathroom floor,
And just about everywhere.

I pick it up daily,
At first that she would lose it all I did fear.
Picking it up each day,
Only to have it magically reappear.

So I realized she would never lose it all,
Those locks I so coveted in my youth.
It just reappears on the bathroom floor,
Each day, and that is the truth.

The shower drain, the bathroom floor,
Under the refrigerator and everywhere.
But today the last straw was broken.
When I found it in my underwear.

Politically Correct

If you hear me talking about America,
    And a slight cynicism you detect.
It could be I am discussing,
    The language of the politically correct.

It seems that we are unable,
    To describe simple things for fear we may offend.
I myself was amazed to find,
    Such changes in the language trend.

It seems I misjudged myself in my youth,
    I did not acknowledge my condition really.
I was not fat but horizontally challenged,
    And my beer gut was just a liquid grain storage facility.

The poor were economically marginalized,
    The crooks ethically misguided.
Vomiting a reexamination of recent food choices,
    No stupid people, just not intellectually provided.

It seems the homeless were into mortgage free living,
    There are no losers just people in second place.
Heaven forbid we call anyone ugly,
    They are just cosmetically different in the face.

No one is considered lazy,
    Just motivationally deficient.
We dare not offend anyone,
    That's not the message we want sent.

So someone is not balding,
    He's into follicle regression.
And people are not looking at the dark side,
    They just suffer from depression.

Could it be the reason people,
Can not find the help they need.
Is because we call their problems something else,
Afraid of planting a bad seed.

Just renounce the politically correct.
Call a spade a spade.
Give people more credit than you do,
And their needed changes can be made.

Marketing

America is the land of the free,
    And is the home of the brave.
But selling things seems to dominate,
    Everything from a car to the grave.

We can sell anything here,
    A land of watches and clocks.
Where else could you find a place?
    That actually sold its people "Pet Rocks".

The fourth of July is an example,
    For when did you ever see?
A fireworks stand that sold you what you bought,
    Without the pledge to buy one get one free.

Buy a mattress or box springs,
    Apparently people didn't buy the set.
So they match the different pieces,
    And look at the saving that you get.

It's almost insulting,
    How stupid do they think we are?
Telling us they will sell it for less,
    Than they actually paid for the car.

Buy a diamond for 10 cents,
    And you soon will find.
It's not worth two nickels,
    Where did they get such a thing mined.

Just ask a fair price,
    If it's reasonable we will buy it.
And stop selling me fattening food,
    Then sell me plans for a diet.

Sex

I have spent my lifetime,
    Trying to get answers to the human mind.
But the answer to, "what is sex?"
    Has eluded me ever time.

It is a powerful force,
    Truly a constant affliction.
For cocaine, alcohol, or marijuana,
    Never have given a greater addiction.

To satisfy this craving,
    We create reasons and some laws.
For how can we justify?
    Defining spousal rights as a cause.

What turns us on?
    From one day to the next?
Looking at a picture, pornography,
    Or reading some erotic text?

Forget all the silliness,
    And use your brain, to foot the bill.
For if it's nothing but procreation,
    Why did we produce a birth control pill?

Perversions, bondage, and fetishes,
    The variety is daunting.
Yet after centuries, we can not discuss it openly,
    Then our sexuality we are flaunting.

It seems we fear,
    If someone knows our mood.
We will lose it all,
    And their knowledge will intrude.

But think about it,
    What leads us to such fate?
The combinations of such thoughts,
    That gives us a climatic state.

It is not logical,
    This orgasmic state.
So we label things as right or wrong.
    To fill our arousal plate.

For as we grow older,
    What physical characteristics do we most miss?
And why do people still remember,
    That exciting very first kiss?

I don't know the answer,
    Tried to figure it out all my life,
I don't have any intention of more kids,
    So why do I love to watch the undressing of my wife?

For the naked human body,
    Is such pleasure to behold?
But it's really unattractive,
    Yet such pictures are constantly sold.

The angles, the joints,
    The acres of hairless skin.
Yet it holds our fascination,
    And has so since time began.

No matter who you are,
    You can not escape its lure.
And if you can not function that way,
    We have found a pharmaceutical cure.

The subject is taboo,
    Polite society will not talk.
Try to discuss it openly,
    And the people will just balk.

To say making love,
    Sounds ever so romantic.
Procreation is biological,
    Yet using these terms do not cause panic.

But we have cuss words for it,
    That simply are not allowed.
They all three are the same act,
    But no cussing in a crowd.

So no more discussion,
    Understanding it our greatest fear.
And try to accept it as a fact,
    Then come and blow softly in my ear.

We've Only Just Begun

There was a marriage ceremony,
    On December 11, 1971.
The final statement made was a song,
    Saying "We've only just begun."

Marriage of two so perfectly matched,
    As there ever was under the sun.
That they became everyone's dream,
    The fabled two into one.

Anyone who encountered them,
    Tried to figure out the connection.
He really loves her, she really loves him,
    This simplicity escaped their detection.

This lovely gift of joy,
    And a grumpy old grizzly bear.
You don't get one without the other,
    You can only get them as a pair.

People try to figure it out,
    It must be done with mirrors and smoke.
Others attempt to copy their love,
    And it comes off as a pathetic joke.

It must be her sacrifice,
    She gave up all she had.
Yet they have never seen this timid princess,
    When she really does get mad.

She has a spine of steel,
    He grumpy enough to topple nations.
Never have two been so perfectly matched,
    Dealing with life's joys, sorrows, and frustrations.

So if you by chance encounter,
    This unlikely and unbelievable pair.
Just accept them for what they are,
    A grumpy old man and his lady fair.

A True American Hero

Buzz Aldrin was born in Montclair, New Jersey,
    In January 1930 on the 20th day.
With parents of military legacy,
    Heritage seemed to pave his way.

For the West Point graduate,
    Finished third in his class and great things were in store.
Trained as a fighter pilot,
    He flew 66 combat missions in the Korean War.

Then on to NASA,
    To become an astronaut,
The future looked brighter,
    Than he had ever thought.

Every thing turning up roses,
    Yes everything was going just fine,
Then he landed on the moon,
    It was July 20, 1969.

People around the world listened,
    To the frequency of the NASA crews.
To the few people who heard it,
    It was forbidding news.

"Oh My God", yelled his teammate Armstrong,
    "I'm telling you there are other spacecraft out there,"
"You wouldn't believe it."
    "They're on the moon watching us." He did declare.

They warned us off,
    But no details could he disclose.
National security had to be maintained,
    And secrecy did the CIA propose.

But after coming home, our hero,
    Locked himself in his room.
Disconnected the phone and drank a lot,
    What scared such a man that his home became a tomb?

He got divorced,
    An alcoholic he became.
What had scared such a man?
    That he rejected all riches and fame.

But NASA had to keep up appearances,
    Continued the Apollo Missions, for they had to appear bold.
For the next three years,
    Then put the project on indefinite hold.

What did he see?
    That almost ruined his life,
This proven man,
    That he would turn to drink and then divorce his wife.

But what troubles me, in the middle of the night,
    Is I cannot discern fiction from fact.
But even more disturbing is that after 1972,
    We never have gone back.

Wants versus Needs

When did Americans change?
From having wants to having needs.
Where did the transition take place?
When did we plant those seeds?

I, myself, personally think
It started with Sesame Street.
Learning could be fun,
Not hard work but really just a treat.

Use a calculator,
No need to memorize higher math.
Was this the thinking?
That led us down this path.

And if by chance,
You believe my thinking strange.
Then next time in a store,
Ask a young clerk to count back your change.

We must be entertained at all cost,
Not to think about the message coming from the great beyond.
As Bruce Springsteen put it so clearly,
There are 57 channels and nothing on.

When young parent plan on a child,
The concern is what day care they will attend.
Both parents must work,
To earn enough money to spend.

Surviving now seems to mean,
Having things that were wants in the past.
Our society has changed so much,
But will the changes last.

The one that drives me crazy,
And waiting at the bank sets the tone.
Watching people cash a welfare check,
While talking on a cell phone.

The 60's

The decade of the 1960's,
    If you wish to judge it and be fair.
Consisted of a nation of young people,
    Who really seemed to care.

Never in the history of man,
    For we had Camelot, the Great Society and Civil Rights.
Had a population banded together,
    So ready to fight for rights.

Never had there been such unity,
    Displayed by a single nation.
Even the advertisers jumped in,
    And named us the Pepsi Generation.

Physical fitness, education, and
    Even the Peace Corps.
We came together as a people,
    To right history's wrongs and settle any old score.

The politicians were trusted,
    And they never ever gave pause.
To correct wrongs of the past,
    And stuck to passing such laws.

The music was a variety,
    The world had never seen.
Songs of joy and happiness,
    And what it meant to be green.

The young people of today,
    Have no unifying plan.
Of working on anything together,
    For the betterment of man.

Then the money of the world,
    Became really scared.
For they had not encountered,
    An entire population that cared.

So first they killed john,
    Martin was close behind.
Then they killed Bobby,
    That broke the camels back and to them, that was fine.

It was a time of change,
    A naive dream from which we could not shirk.
But dammit overall it was a great idea,
    Even if it would never work.

Emergency Broadcast System

Are you old enough to remember?
Driving around on a Saturday night.
Listening to the radio,
Feeling everything in the world was right.

Then an interruption,
Of your favorite radio show.
Of the Emergency Broadcast System,
Designed to let us know.

A warning if we were under attack,
Time to get to a shelter and protect.
All of our loved ones,
And anyone else we did select.

For we were proud and Americans,
It was a constant in my youth.
The government would always,
Share with us the truth.

Irritating it was,
But a necessary pain in the ass.
For whatever country cared enough,
To tell it's people of disaster so fast.

Well I grew older,
Didn't hear the tests any more.
But upon inquiring I was advised it still existed,
To tell us what was in store.

Then came 9 11,
Reports we were under assault.
The chance to broadcast and legitimately use it,
But it never came, so who was at fault.

Air Conditioning

In the history of mankind,
Many inventions have made life worse.
But overall air-conditioning,
May end up as the greatest human curse.

You may ask,
What let me to deduce this fate?
Well it's really very simple,
It cost us the ability to communicate.

To cool down in the summertime,
People would go outside with the coming of the night.
Everyone was exposed to each other,
And shared their beliefs, fears and insight.

Settling down after a summer day,
So hot that it could scorch,
Everyone eventually gravitated,
To sit out on the porch.

So you learned to talk,
Learned your neighbor's name.
What differences you had,
And what beliefs you had that were the same.

We now live in caves of steel,
Giving rise to all my fears.
For you can live next to a family,
Never knowing their name for years.

People now live in apartments,
Without communication resources.
Even the houses we now build,
Are void of any front porches.

Churning homemade ice cream,
    Watching the kids play kick the can.
Seems a long lost activity,
    Gone forever from the 21st century man.

We ride in air-conditioned cars,
    Shop in an air-conditioned mall.
Work in air-conditioned offices,
    Such luxury mandates the communication skills would forestall.

Our muscles protest,
    Cramps come not feeling like tickles.
As we have slowly become,
    A generation of living room Popsicles.

For everyone has said,
    At one time and it's true.
How about the heat?
    Is it hot enough for you?

I see no solution,
    We are doomed to such a life.
To reside in our cool cocoons,
    And deal privately with our strife.

For not only did we learn,
    And the loss is clear to see.
The lost art of communication,
    But also of courtesy.

So if the summer finds you,
    Locked in your cave of steel.
Try to share with another human,
    By going outside and talking about how you feel.

The air-conditioning may cool you down,
    With the fading of the light.
And as uncomfortable as the heat is,
    You may find your sleeping thru the night.

Reading

Oh I have trod the wind swept heights,
    Drank from the eternal spring.
Dined with wizards and dragons,
    Drank mead with an ancient king.

Rescued a fairy princess,
    From atop the dragon's keep.
With a soft kiss I awoke her,
    From the witch's enchanted sleep.

Rode a comet to the stars,
    Searched for life's answers to truth.
Sought out all the questions,
    And then brought them home with proof.

These memories run rampant,
    Through the confines of my head.
As I review them all,
    As I lay reading in my bed.

The worlds that reading opened,
    Belong forever to me.
It is so much more,
    Than I ever thought I'd see.

So if your world is depressing,
    And you can't deal with your life.
Escape to my world of fantasy,
    Where good always triumphs over strife.

Just pick up a book,
    Lose yourself in its pages.
All the dragons, kings and queens,
    And all the courtly sages.

There are no clocks here,
    No time to thwart your stay.
Enjoy it till you come home again,
    To start another day.

Breaking Even at the Casino

I went to the casino,
Broke even for the day.
It is said if you leave with what you brought in,
It's considered a very good stay.

Well I didn't get rich,
But also didn't lose my shirt.
Generally you lose more than you win,
And those loses can make your wallet hurt.

But it's really irritating,
Sensitive like a newly popped blister.
And breaking even is as exciting,
As the thought of kissing your sister.

Grocery Shopping

I have become a vegetarian,
    And to reconcile it now.
I eat only vegetables,
    Reprocessed by the cow.

Retired but my wife still works,
    And with free time, I thought I would help out.
I cut meat in my youth,
    So to buy it, my knowledge I did not doubt.

But in the store,
    There was such a display.
Of various meats,
    Spread in the array.

From what part of the chicken,
    Do the tenders come?
I suspected one or two,
    And I believe they made up some.

And what part of the cow,
    Is ever consider petite?
Who would ever consider eating?
    Such a piece of meat?

What have the done to the labeling?
    Of the different pieces of meat.
Are they trying to be nice?
    Not to offend the cow by being discreet?

Completely baffled I was,
    By the variety of all these things.
But I finally lost hope,
    When they tried to sell me Buffalo wings.

Language

Foreigners have trouble with English,
    Just listen and it is heard.
Our use of words that contradict,
    From the ridiculous to the absurd.

An example is boxing ring,
    But their confusion seems only fair.
Ring they understand,
    But why is the match always held in a square?

Another is ice tea,
    Their confusion do they voice.
Is it ice? Is it tea?
    Is there a hidden third choice?

We drive to work each day,
    The parkway takes us there.
Then we park in the house's driveway,
    Is it just to make it fair?

We mail a note to someone,
    We call such thing letters.
But it has many such characters,
    By people claiming to be their betters.

They see an inventory sale,
    Are they just being dense?
But to them what else would a business offer?
    But their inventory, that makes any kind of sense?

Another is Good Friday,
    We crucified our Lord's son.
Could we not find a better word?
    Or is it intended as a pun?

Our food labeling,
    Tells us what's in the can.
Then what the hell is Baby Food?
    Their confusion I can understand.

It seems the only thing,
    That we named correctly, and I don't want to fuss.
Is an animal that is a contradiction in itself,
    We called it a platypus.

Country Summer Night

If you have ever been,
    In the country on a summer night.
The experience is pleasant,
    Something about it just feels right.

It is softly lighted,
    The moon's light caresses the land.
As if it was designed,
    By a greater being's hand.

The crickets chirping to each other,
    Their evening to be determined by fate.
That diligence and persistence,
    Will tonight find them a mate.

An owl glides by slowly,
    On feathered silenced wings.
On it's endless quest to find,
    Mice, chipmunks and other such things.

No noise from the city,
    No cars or buses to intrude.
No blaring of horns,
    To break the quiet's mood.

Time slows down,
    Peace fills the land.
It seems the world remains untouched,
    By the hand of man.

You can not find this peace,
    If you live within a city.
Such a loss is sad,
    And their loss is such a pity.

For they are the ones who need it,
    In a world infested by thieves and thugs.
So they lock their doors,
    Then go to sleep, using pills and drugs.

Yes, I miss the summer country night,
    When I was young and didn't have a care.
I miss the silence, the heat,
    And the smell of honeysuckle on the air.

The still and the peace,
    Only found on a summer night.
With the land softly lit,
    By a caressing moon's light.

The sounds of children laughing,
    Their play lit, by a firefly torch.
The sounds of people talking,
    In rocking chairs on the front porch.

Young lovers staring at stars,
    That completely fill the sky.
Poets dream, old men doze,
    No one wastes time questioning why?

The clouds they pass,
    Their endless flight unarrested.
In their houses city folk miss the sight,
    And so their flight passes undetected.

It is a world so different,
    From the one we see during the day.
It's as if the world has had enough of man,
    And wants to have its say.

To scoff at man's persistence,
    He that creates labels of wrong and right.
So if you want to experience peace,
    Just go outside on a country summer night.

Operation Iraq Freedom

On September 11th the world,
Was shaken to the core.
Americans had been attacked,
The attackers called it a holy war.

The president called them cowards,
The ones who took over the flight.
But for someone who knowingly dies,
For what they believe, I'm not sure the term is right.

Our intelligence soon found,
Osami bin Laden had orchestrated the attack.
So we immediately went for Suddam Hussain,
The leader of the country of Iraq.

Is it to finish the job his daddy started
Whatever the reason for.
By starting the first attack on Iraq
In the famous 1991 Gulf War.

Yes, the war for Iraq freedom,
Leaves me shaken all the more.
For I remember Viet Nam,
When we sent our boys to die on some distant shore.

Three thousand died in the attack on us,
Almost two thousand soldiers have died since then.
To try and impose democracy on the Middle East,
And make a new and global friend.

They use suicide bombers,
To accomplish their religious ends.
One or two I understand,
But almost five hundred sets dangerous trends.

Then yesterday I heard the president speak,
    And his thoughts became clear as light.
For no matter what I believe,
    The man believes he's right.

Yes, I support America,
    Our troops and our way of living.
But how much can we ask of our soldiers,
    How much more can they be giving.

Iraqi's don't think like us,
    That much is clear to see.
They don't relish the idea,
    Of dieing to be free.

The horror of what is happening,
    Awoke in me, like taking an ice cold shower.
And who in the world should impose their beliefs,
    And who have we given such power.

And so we impose our beliefs,
    On another country and try.
To explain freedom and its advantages,
    That it's an idea for which to die.

I don't feel much smarter,
    Having lived all my years.
Just dismayed to find my life,
    Dominated by such fears.

I wish the Iraqi people,
    Joy and a long long life.
I harbor no hate for them,
    Their children or their wife.

So I may be naive,
    But stupid or not, my feelings are still strong.
Why can't we respect each other's beliefs?
    And try and get along.

My Poetry

My poetry is simple,
Yes simple, and that is good.
Designed to rhyme the words,
So they are easily understood.

I don't need to expound philosophies,
Discuss the universe or the existence of man,
I feel that such discussions should be left,
To philosophers and not in a poets hand.

For what can a poet offer?
But joy from daily strife.
Not the answers to the universe,
Much less the meaning of life.

For what could I say?
That has not been said before.
Nothing that would prepare you,
For what this life has in store.

So read my poems happily,
Look only for a chuckle or a smile.
To ease the burdens of life,
If only for a while.

Bacon and Tomato Sandwiches
(With credit to Ted Shanks)

When writing poetry,
You call upon any thoughts in your head.
Well I remember one from forty years ago,
Given to me by my brother Ted.

He once told me early in the morning,
When his stomach seems to say.
Four bacon and tomato sandwiches,
He could put away.

He rushed down to the table,
For breakfast he was never late.
And there he spyed awaiting him,
Four sandwiches on his plate.

He rushed up to the table,
And turned upon his dish.
And o fright, he lost delight,
The sandwiches were tuna fish.

First he coughed,
And then he sneezed.
For how could he enjoy a day?
When his stomach wasn't pleased.

Questioning

I worry about our society today,
And the questions they ask of you.
I feel as if they doubt my answers,
And wonder if they are true.

It seems when I've speaking to someone,
They need to see, and they feel it only fair.
To see if I've stolen something,
So they inquire, "Take Care?"

No I didn't take any thing,
And I'm sorry for the belief.
That I would take something they own,
And that they believe I'm such a thief.

Another question often asked,
When seeing a person for the first time of the day,
They always ask, "High?"
So if its games they want, I'll play.

I always answer "No",
Then they look a me and I feel,
They really believe I have been drinking,
But in denial to what's real.

The one that bothers me most,
Is "Have a good one?"
Well that is between my wife and I,
The last thing to discuss under the sun.

Whether I have a good one or not,
Is not information they could buy.
But they feel no embarrassment,
And feel they need to pry.

Maybe I'm just getting old,
And I really don't want to fuss.
But the questions seem personal,
And more than I want to discuss.

My Sister Diane

I had a sister growing up,
    Diane was her name.
However being a great sister,
    Does not seem to qualify for riches or fame.

By the time I got to high school,
    Had no car and that was a pain.
Yet she had finished high school,
    Got a job and bought a new Ford Mustang.

On the weekends,
    She would come up to me.
Say "Have Fun" then give me the keys,
    These were always given where no one else could see.

After high school,
    I was sent to Viet Nam.
She never once forgot me,
    My other siblings didn't seem to give a damn.

She wrote me constantly,
    Sent cookies always wishing me well.
It helped to ease my pain,
    Making tolerable my season in hell.

She moved away from the family,
    But I never told her how much she eased my pain.
That regret I carry with me,
    Forever burned in my brain.

So if by some chance she sees this,
    By whatever means, being published or some other.
I would like to tell the world and her,
    "Thanks for everything", from your young stupid kid brother.

The Present

I worked for the IRS in Austin Texas,
    About 12 years before moving to Washington State.
And ask anyone and they will tell,
    How I railed about the country's future fate.

The injustices done,
    And the ones who were to blame.
Lunch and breaks included,
    My soapbox was my fame.

Bill Boyd, an old friend there,
    Upon my departure gave me a gift.
He said that it should help me,
    If I ever needed a lift.

As I opened to package he gave me,
    And confusion filled my head.
This will give you your answer he stated,
    Better than anything he could have said.

"You are the voice against injustice",
    "Truly a leader of the band".
"But look at the only one having a heart attack",
    As I looked in the mirror, that I held in my hand.

Eclectics III

Eclectics III is the third and final book in the series of poems called Eclectics. Eclectics is the story of my life of 34 years with my wife and daughter. Eclectics II is best labeled as my soapbox. Eclectics III is simply poetry. It is a continuation of the rhythmic analysis of life in America and on this planet we call Earth. It is old-fashioned simple poetry. Easy to read and understand. Hopefully something for everyone, and something to spark a thought or a smile.

Eclectics III

1 My Little Friend
2 Why
3 Having Babies
4 Hope
5 Taxation Without Representation
6 My Dad Has Passed
7 Suicide
8 Youthful Knowledge
9 Let It Ride
10 Writer's Block
11 Best That You Can Be
12 High Blood Pressure
13 Founding Fathers
14 Nature's Songs
15 No Fault
16 Dropping Soap
17 Time Warp
18 Time
19 Hunting and Fishing
20 Language Stupidity In America
21 Pink Inner tube
22 Great Smoky Mountains Vacation
23 Going Bald
24 Katie and Chris are Dead
25 Understanding Sucide
26 Six O'clock
27 What Excites Me
28 Labor Day
59 The Zippo Lighter
30 Daytime Noise
31 Hurricane Katrina
32 Hurricane Relief

33	War
34	The Purple Cow Revisited
35	The Philosopher's Stone Explained
36	Judgment of a Smoker
37	Religion
38	Stan Rogers Songs
39	Getting Old Emotions
40	To Dad Macon
41	Exercise Bicycle
42	Collision
43	Congressional Spending
44	Going to College
45	Wasted Time
46	Hearing the Song
47	Boo
48	Rain
49	Lighthouses
50	Intelligent Life
51	Heisenberg vs Kirshoff
52	Dr Patti Robbins
53	I've Gone Insane
54	Taking MY Blood
55	Waiting in Line
56	Global Warming
57	Super Tork
58	A Wife's Reasoning
59	The Zippo Lighter
60	Last Poem

My Little Friend

The sun creeps over the mountains,
    Daylight comes slowly in.
And there on my back patio,
    Sits the reliable one, my little friend.

He's a furry little creature,
    With a long and bushy tail.
He comes to visit each morning,
    A task in which he does not fail.

If we slide open the door,
    He will scurry off, but not far.
If we don't show up, then he comes to look in,
    Wondering where we are?

We only set out three or four nuts,
    But keeping that schedule we must.
For we dare not spoil him,
    But we dare not violate that trust.

Just the other morning,
    Sitting out he came and sniffed my big toe.
As if wondering who the big guy was,
    An answer that he just had to know.

It will not change the world,
    It's a tradition that is not far reaching.
Just a communion with Mother Nature,
    And one that I will be keeping.

Why

Why is the question?
And what, who and when.
Man is the most inquisitive creature,
That there has ever been.

We have to know it all,
We torment ourselves to see.
An answer to every question,
And we expect it to all be free.

But something's have no answer,
At such ignorance we all rail.
For we feel if we don't know it all,
That lack means we did fail.

But keep in mind, your opinion was not asked,
For you are a creature just called man.
And on your understanding,
Was not how the universe began.

So enjoy each day,
A blessing the creator did bestow.
He did not deem it feasible,
All the answers you should know.

Having Babies

Today I was pondering,
    The miracle of giving birth.
I realized I didn't have a clue,
    Of women's real place on earth.

I heard a man explain why he had six kids,
    And that having many kids wasn't bold.
Hopefully one of them would like him,
    And take care of him, when he got old.

But no one explains to the parents,
    Cause they don't want to give them a scare.
That soon the kid turns 13,
    And Nikes are $85 a pair.

So to the expectant mother,
    For your new child I wish you joy.
And a healthy new baby,
    If its a girl or its a boy.

For children are the reason,
    In that we must place our trust.
Our inventions, machines and buildings,
    Mother Nature turns to rust.

Relish the child, to which you give birth,
    Do not listen to the critics long.
They simply do not understand,
    They cannot hear Mother Nature's song.

The giving of life,
    Is what its all about.
It is a good reason,
    To celebrate and shout.

Take care of yourself,
    I'm jealous of you and your mate.
But realize you have contributed,
    To a world's future and brighter fate.

Hope

What is this thing we call hope?
We revere the trait above all the rest.
And why must we continually,
Put it to a test.

Have you ever gone into a casino,
And the people just have to know.
The odds are all against them,
Yet their confidence does show.

See people skydiving,
It's really such a feat.
And their parachutes will always open,
It will be such a treat.

Bad things always happen,
To the other guy you know.
It never happens to you,
So to the wind, caution you do throw.

Do overs are in the movies,
Some things don't allow a second chance.
But people do things,
That seems stupid at a glance.

But hope is universal,
And so we all tempt fate.
Because while it may be dumb,
It's man's only enduring trait.

Taxation Without Representation

Taxation Without Representation,
Was an ideal our forefathers did sell.
Well folks taxation, with representation,
Isn't doing all that well.

They have less than us so we help out the world,
Such a noble thought I would not decry.
But our fathers worked their butts off all their lives,
Is the only reason why.

Give millions of dollars,
It all must be sent.
Couldn't they first just fix?
The cracks in the town's pavement.

I may not be altruistic,
But I didn't work all my life.
To have no choice of spending the taxes,
Paid for by me and my wife.

They're starving children in Africa,
Send aid to help them out.
Well they're starving children in Tennessee,
So what's that all about?

I didn't put my kid through college,
To give her a better life.
So she could work to pay for others,
Deal with their daily strife.

So you think I'm crass,
You think that I don't care.
Well whatever happened,
To a system we used to call fair.

I don't wish them harm,
    But in the long run they must.
Provide for themselves,
    Or the whole thing is a bust.

If you give a man a fish,
    You will feed him and maybe his wife.
Teach them how to fish,
    And they will feed themselves for life.

My Dad Has Passed

It's been 30 years,
April 1st was the day.
They called to tell me,
That my father had passed away.

I remember the agony,
When they said that he was dead.
All I could think of was,
The many things I had left unsaid.

Why was I so hardheaded?
Are all children that way?
Do they believe any parent ever woke up thinking?
"How can I screw up my child's life today?"

Is every child so blind?
That to such a future fate.
That when they all decide to say those things,
That it all comes a little late.

I didn't get to tell my Dad,
How much I appreciated what he did.
The sacrifices he made for me,
I felt like such an ungrateful kid.

But he comes to visit me,
Slipping into my dreams in the middle of the night.
Reminding me of how to look at the world,
And not to be blinded by the sight.

Only then can I tell him,
In that somewhat mystical way.
But he always gives me his smile,
As if to say its O.K.

So if you've not told your parent,
Do not be subjected to my fate.
Tell them now how much you appreciate,
Their sacrifices, and their life, before you are too late.

Suicide

I wanted to know the meaning of pain,
 So I went to Webster's Dictionary.
I wanted to see what definition,
 These enlightened people would carry.

The first word they used was punishment,
 That was followed by ache and torment.
So I began to think to myself,
 Do these people really know what it meant?

Physical or mental, the pain.
 Brings only one response giving us a reason to pretend.
The person afflicted,
 Only wants it to end.

Reason and logic go out the window,
 All one can do is think of making it stop.
So we will try almost anything,
 And we now have a variety of pills to pop.

They generally only treat the symptoms,
 But never touch the cause.
And we don't give a damn,
 We only want a pause.

Suicide is studied
 And is the most misunderstood.
Most people who do it,
 Don't understand it will do no good.

They don't care for reason,
 Talking does nothing but demonstrate a doctor's guile.
They don't care if it makes any sense,
 They just want it to quit for a while.

When I had my heart attack,
    I reached the point of taking the shotgun off the shelf,
Only looking at my wife,
    Gave me time to realize it didn't just affect myself.

The need was physical,
    Much like when you feel the need to eat.
All you can think of is food,
    Be it vegetable or meat.

You will do whatever eases the hunger,
    Anything to end the strife.
Even if it means something so final,
    As putting an end to your life.

The church preaches suicide is a moral sin,
    That can result only in a trip to hell.
Is that a myth or knowledge?
    And more importantly how can they tell.

There is a story about Jobe,
    Who asked God why his persecution was far from soft.
And God replied,
    "Cause you just piss me off".

Life is generally good,
    Or was God just in a bad mood.
And made pain a part of life,
    Just as he did the need for food.

So if you feel the need,
    To stop the suffering and do something to end your life.
Just remember it will end the pain for a moment,
    But you don't get a chance to live twice.

Youthful Knowledge

The knowledge I had when I was young,
    That I knew all the answers, of that I was sure.
The meaning of life and the universe,
    For any problem I had the cure.

Any questions that you had,
    Any question under the sun.
I could answer them all,
    I reveled in the fun.

But with age came wisdom,
    The realization left me cold.
The fact that I didn't know it all,
    Hit me hard when I got old.

I had such arrogance,
    In the early years of my youth.
I could argue with anyone,
    For I felt I had the proof.

I don't know if the realization,
    Or if the truth be told.
Had I knew then what I know now,
    I would not have been so bold.

So now I try to listen more,
    And not be such an ass.
For the knowledge I thought I knew,
    Had left me arrogant and crass.

So I beg your forgiveness,
    For being an overbearing youth.
For my intentions were honorable,
    And I thought I knew the truth.

But old age has set in,
    And now I'm not so sure.
That even for the common cold,
    I could come up with a cure.

Let It Ride

I went to the casino,
 It was a lovely summer's day.
My favorite game is Let It Ride,
 And I decided to play.

It takes three chips to start the game,
 But on five cards is your final bid.
The dealer deals three cards face up,
 The next two face down are hid.

In the long run it only takes one chip,
 This is the actual fact.
Cause if you feel unlucky,
 You can always pull two of them back.

Suddenly I felt Lady Luck sit next to me,
 As if against me she had brushed.
I felt so good that I knew,
 Her good luck I could trust.

The dealer gave me three hearts,
 My hope did suddenly swell.
If I got two only two more,
 You could say I did very well.

So I said, "Let it Ride".
 Determined to do my part.
The dealer also seemed committed,
 And turned over another heart.

Five hearts would be a flush,
 Each chip left on the table pays eight to one.
Plus a flush pays a fifty-dollar bonus,
 So the total could be a tidy sum.

The total on this hand,
    Was one hundred seventy dollars I could make.
With Lady Luck with me,
    I felt it was a risk I should take.

"Let it ride" I said,
    With Lady Luck sitting next to me.
Visions of a nifty payout,
    Was all that I could see.

For I had all three chips,
    Still bet out on the table.
I would trust the lady,
    As long as I was able.

Four hearts already,
    One more and the flush is made.
Then the dealer then turned over the fifth card,
    And the dam thing was a spade.

The dealer raked in my chips,
    It was a depressing sight.
When I thought of what could have happened,
    If my feelings had been right.

I thought Lady Luck had set down,
    But all she did was pass.
And I realized all the good feelings,
    I now believe was just gas.

Writer's Block

I'm tossing and turning,
    I turn on the light and it says 2 o'clock.
I believe I am experiencing,
    What people call writer's block.

I never expected it to happen to me,
    For when I cannot sleep at night.
I simply get out of bed,
    Go to the kitchen and write.

I use my writing as a tool,
    To purge and cleanse my soul.
The thought of losing it,
    Has left me feeling cold.

I have examined life, family,
    And the universe.
I put down all my thoughts and fears,
    Then converted them to verse.

So if you are having trouble,
    Of going to bed and falling asleep.
Get up and write down your thoughts,
    It's easier than counting sheep.

Put down your fears,
    Express it in any way.
Your thoughts and plans,
    That you had during the day.

Be not timid or shy,
    Write anything down that comes to mind.
And after you have put it on paper,
    I think that you will find.

You've cleaned your thoughts and worries,
    That kept you awake as you tossed and turned.
Then put them away to read later,
    Or if it bothers you, get them burned.

Best That You Can Be

The last few years I've often heard,
  "Be the best that you can be".
The phrase seems vague and obtuse,
  And kind of a stupid statement to me.

Children blame their parents,
  But if they look closely they will see it's true.
The high expectations came from only one place,
  And that one place is you.

You don't need to validate your existence,
  No need to prove you worthy of life.
You don't need to explain any of it,
  To Father, Mother, Husband or Wife.

What is perfect?
  The best in what area of living?
What expectations do you hold?
  What explanations are you giving?

So the days of life they come,
  And the days of life they go.
What expectations do people have?
  What line must they toe?

They set the standards,
  Judge themselves by some test.
Of what is worthy of living,
  And what is perfect and best.

You are alive and that is all,
  No need to prove anything to anyone.
So stop all this madness,
  And go out and have some fun.

The meaning of life,
  "To be or not to be".
Everyone asks the same questions,
  So why, oh why, ask me?

High Blood Pressure

Today I read that over 300,
Is the blood pressure for a giraffe?
To suggest that for a human,
Would cause most people to laugh.

But where do they get human measurements,
Where do they get such samples?
Cause the last time that I checked,
We both are considered mammals.

So they studied the Eskimos,
And the Pacific islanders, who lived so long.
They looked at what they ate,
To figure out what made them strong.

Well folks guess what?
Some day you will die.
No matter how hard you fight,
No matter what you try.

Twenty, forty, or eighty years,
Learn to take what this life will give.
And stop worrying so much,
Of how long that you will live.

For the fact of the Eskimos,
The fact that they did not find.
Was that maybe they did not worry so much?
And they had found peace of mind.

Hypertension they say,
Is our greatest fear?
Ironically we live our lives fast paced.
Afraid of losing something so dear.

For our one true fear is death,
    We fight it with all our might.
But the fact is, we will die,
    On this you know that I am right.

So on this day in august,
    The year of 2006.
I have decided no more pills,
    If I live longer, it will be on a Mother Nature fix.

I worried all my life,
    That the time when I retired.
I would still have enough of my health,
    And not in a hospital would I be mired.

For one thing is certain,
    And is true for mostly all.
When most people die these days,
    It is in a hospital.

Death is a part of our life,
    I never accepted that as true.
So I took vitamins and prescriptions,
    And ate health food till I was blue.

I probably would have done as well,
    If I had been really clever.
To accept the fact of my death,
    And that I would not live forever.

So wish me luck
    On this glorious day.
When finally realizing the truth,
    I decided not to play.

For I found out a fact,
    That had eluded me for so long.
That I was so caught up in living,
    I had missed most of Mother Nature's song.

So I'll just try and relax,
    Accept whatever time I have left.
And not worry about my life,
    For it was not stolen by some theft.

My only regret will be my wife,
    And my child when they hear the news.
Of my plans to just live,
    And to stop paying the doctors dues.

For the doctors are overworked,
    Seeing so many people is a real trick.
But maybe they wouldn't be so busy,
    If they only saw the people, who were really sick.

Do not worry too much,
    Be not beset with so much strife.
Just try to relax,
    And enjoy the rest of your life

Founding Fathers

The Founding Fathers of America,
    What a motley crew.
Upon studying history,
    I'm not sure all their praise is due.

Most were well off,
    Had farms or a plantation.
What a questionable group of men,
    To found a budding new nation.

Most had slaves,
    That worked when they were told.
A good investment it was,
    Cause if they caused problems, they were sold.

It troubles me a lot,
    And for answers, I crave some.
Because weren't these the men who fled England,
    Searching for an ideal called freedom.

But freedom did come,
    At the cost of a civil war.
It was eighty-seven years later,
    When they decided to settle the score.

So the wrong was righted,
    What more about it can be said?
Well one thing that sticks out to me,
    Is it didn't happen till they were all dead.

Nature's Songs

It's four o'clock in the morning,
Daybreak did not yet begin.
I'm sitting on my back patio,
Enjoying the night like a long lost friend.

Suddenly I noticed the wind,
Weaving gently through the trees.
They're swaying rhythmically seductive.
Saying come dance with us please.

For I know the wind scientifically,
Fronts, gradients, and pressure.
But I had never listened to its song,
And thought of it by that measure.

It is a form of music,
I had never realized before.
The trees heard it and danced,
Emboldened by the score.

Slowly I heard a new sound,
It was starting to rain.
Relishing my new awareness,
Hoping a new song I could gain.

Sure enough it was there,
Different but beautiful in its right.
So I sat and listened to the medley,
In the middle of the night.

So I pondered what other songs of nature,
I had heard but not recognized.
That it was singing a song to me,
One that should be prized.

I thought of ocean waves,
    Of a cascading waterfall.
The gentle tumbling of leaves,
    Heard softly in the fall.

As I listened for the first time,
    I came to realize that it was so.
That I was changed that morning,
    And may never again listen to a radio.

The gentleness of it,
    Seemingly calling to me.
It played on and on,
    All of it for free.

I wonder how much,
    Of nature's songs I had heard.
Never realizing the beauty of it,
    As put out by a bird.

It's complex in its simplicity,
    Subtle, yet seductively strong.
The variety was overwhelming,
    This nature's propensity for song.

So if you see me swaying,
    And wonder what I'm listening too.
It's nature's song I'm hearing,
    Just listen and you will find it's true.

What a prize I have found,
    In the middle of the night.
Nature singing to me,
    Making the world seem rhythmically right.

No Fault

The year was 1969,
    A law signed by the California governor's hand.
A trend that swept the nation,
    And changed the traditions of this land.

What you may ask?
    Did he sign that set us on this course.
A law simply labeled,
    No Fault Divorce.

The law changed marriage,
    An arrangement for all to see.
Not a lasting commitment,
    Just sign a paper and you are free.

Free to go out on dates,
    Free of the children you created.
No more restrictions,
    Your choice is not how your future is fated.

Marriage is no longer
    The commitment it had been?
All done in a second,
    With the simple stroke of a pen.

Two people got married,
    Not many now last so long.
Most will not concede,
    The no fault experiment has gone horribly wrong.

But if one is committed,
    To make it all work out.
Folks it takes two not one,
    To last the fight and to finish the bout.

Convenience now seems the trend,
    And being available most will try.
Why should they suffer?
    And spend the time to cry.

Yet I feel sadness for the people,
    Victimized by the trend.
I'm not so sure that is the message,
    The Governor wanted to send.

My wife and I went out,
    Our thirtieth anniversary to celebrate.
We ran into a man,
    His story he did relate.

"I've been married forty two years,"
    He told us with a grin.
Then explained the reason was,
    It was to five different women.

He was not embarrassed,
    And his attitude set the tone.
I didn't have the heart to tell him,
    He will wind up old and alone.

I myself got lucky,
    Been married thirty four years,
We've had our fair share,
    Of happiness and tears.

But to trade it all for passion,
    Which got lost in time I find.
The comfort I have instead,
    Gives me peace of mind.

So to young people of today,
    I give you this advice for free.
Get married and stay that way,
    And over time I think you will see.

It's not like in the movies,
    Where singles have all the fun.
For comfort and peace of mind,
    A long race must be run.

Dropping Soap

Why does every time it seems,
    I take a shower to wash away my grime.
I drop the soap on the floor,
    And it seems to happen every time.

You would think I should be more careful,
    And that I should not be irritated.
But why does it happen so much?
    Is that the life to which I am fated?

Nothing to hold onto,
    But it's not that far to bend.
But to happen almost every time,
    Seems like it's setting a trend.

I've dropped things in my life,
    I've had many a stumble and slip.
But why the soap every time,
    On a floor that is so slick.

I guess it's just one of those things,
    That I will never figure out.
No need to lose sleep over it,
    Or something to feel persecuted about.

Time Warp

I went out to get the mail,
To see if it had been delivered so soon.
It was around 3 P.M.
Just a summer's early afternoon.

The next-door neighbor was outside,
With her child of about age 2.
So we stopped to talk awhile,
Not to discuss anything important or universally true.

I said that yesterday
My daughter was the same age as hers.
Yet today she was 29,
As the child ruffled the cats soft fur.

Yes, she was just a baby yesterday,
Today she is grown with a family of her own.
Yet I have pictures to remind me of her being young,
And those pictures I have repeatedly shown.

I must have watched too much science fiction,
And was thrust into some sort of time warp zone.
I don't remember so much time passing,
Just her being there when I got home.

But if I want reality,
I go no further than the bathroom sink.
The mirror shows me the truth,
No matter what I think.

And I find myself in that room often,
More and more as I get old.
And the reflection I see, haunts me.
Cause I don't want reality to be so clearly shown.

Where did the time go?
    With my daughter and my wife.
It has slipped by so quickly,
    This thing I call my life.

But I've had a ball,
    From being on the bottom or the top.
And the only thing I ponder these days,
    Is that I don't want any of it to stop.

Time

Have you ever watched a movie?
    Time passes before you know it.
But waiting for someone for half that time,
    And you are really in a fit.

Sixty seconds to a minute,
    Sixty minutes to an hour.
Time is kept meticulously for us,
    By London's Big Ben Tower.

But I wonder sometimes,
    If we understand time at all.
It seems perception is what counts,
    And it may not be at our beck and call.

We keep track of time,
    It's how we measure speed.
But how important is its keeping,
    And why do we feel the need.

It passes slowly in traffic,
    It passes fast when playing a game.
How should we feel its passing?
    If the time measured is the same.

I've ponder the question long,
    Have no answers to give to you.
For the perception of it changes,
    That much I know is true.

Our science is based on it,
    Frequencies used to tell.
When to get up for the day,
When to ring the bell.

We accept it all so blindly,
    This measurement we call time.
We base so much of our life on it,
    That it sometimes leaves us in a bind.

But do not fret so much,
    There is really no need to worry.
Just spend your time wisely,
    For in life there should never be a need to hurry.

Hunting and Fishing

I only went hunting when I was very young,
Past age 18, I never went again.
I fished until I was 30,
Then stopped, wishing I had never began.

What are you people asked?
Some kind of whimp or some such.
No I am not, but I am aware,
And that awareness has taught me much.

As far as for hunting,
Did you ever wonder why?
The animal will run away from you,
Escaping or giving it a try.

The fear they feel is tangible,
Their sweat reeks with fear.
The thought of doing that to any creature,
To my eyes will bring a tear.

For in my youth, I had been hunted.
In the jungle of a far off distant land.
Outnumbered and for the first time,
You learned to fear man.

If my survival depended on it,
I would hunt without a doubt.
But the grocery store provides everything,
And I don't have to do without.

I had never thought of fishing,
In the same light as a hunt.
That was the naiveté of my youth,
Because the similarities are very blunt.

As I got older I became more aware,
    I started seeing Mother Nature's true self.
So except for when it's absolutely necessary,
    I put the fishing rods and guns back on the shelf.

Hopefully I will never have to kill again,
    Of that I am happy to report.
But if forced to do it, I will,
    But I'll never call it a sport.

Language Stupidity In America

I would like to get a steak the customer said,
    I would like to have it lean if I may.
The waiter looked puzzled and asked,
    "No problem sir. Which way?"

A man told me "I've been seeing spots,"
    "They are before both of my eyes".
So I asked "Have you seen a doctor?"
    "No, Just the spots," He replies.

If a convenience store is open,
    Twenty-four hours, three hundred sixty five days a year.
Then why do they have locks on the doors?
    What do they know or fear?

Why did the jelly roll?
    Because it saw the apple turnover.
And how do you keep a bagel from getting away,
    Put lox on it for cover.

The man stated,
    "I have changed my mind."
The woman replied,
    "Well I hope this one you can find."

And why shouldn't you say two hundred and eighty eight,
    When using polite conversation the most.
It is simply because,
    The total is just two gross.

Hear about the silkworm's race,
    Each wanted to win and so they did try.
But in the end it didn't matter,
    Cause they ended up in a tie.

I heard about two antennas getting married,
    Hopefully it did not determine their fate.
For the ceremony was a disaster,
    But the reception for it was great.

Pink Inner tube

What can you imagine?
As a more refreshing interlude.
Than floating on lake Sinclair,
In a pink inter tube.

The hot sun of August above,
Cool water down below.
I can't think of a better place
To be in that I know.

Hours pass slowly,
As you relax and enjoy the sun.
What better way can you think of?
To enjoy the summer's fun.

Yes it is a joy,
Best described as a treat.
Best be careful though,
Or you will get sunburned feet.

The Great Smoky Mountains Vacation

The Great Smoky Mountains,
What a treasure to behold.
With all the mountain streams,
Running crystal clear and cold.

I remember playing there,
Playing and splashing, it was fun.
And what better way,
To beat the summer's sun.

What a better way to vacation,
To spend all the day through.
Than watching the children playing,
Till the cold just turned them blue.

The sky was always clear,
But even rain could not spoil the fun.
Just watching the children playing,
Watching them swim and run.

So enjoy your vacation,
Enjoy it all the day.
For the joy of watching someone's,
Unbridled fun in every way.

For soon it will come,
As it did to me.
The pressures of the world,
When you can no longer feel so free.

Soak up the sun,
Splash and play in the stream.
For it should be cherished,
Like remembering a long lost dream.

And on some day at work,
Working on file after countless file.
Just remember the children playing,
And you will start to smile.

Going Bald

I was listening the other day to Jeff Foxworthy,
Speak of going bald.
Well is appears to be our perception,
And not really a problem at all.

Ever day we get older
Yet continue to shave the beards from our faces.
And we are not losing it from our heads,
It's just coming out in other places.

It now grows out my nose,
Eyebrows and my ears.
Losing such growth from these places,
Is not one of my fears.

He told a story about a man,
Who needed a new hearing aid.
Well what he needed, was a hair cut,
His ears had long since felt a blade.

So do not despair,
Of going bald before your time.
Mother Nature just redistributes it,
She is not concerned because to her, it all seems fine.

Katie and Chris are Dead

Katie and Chris are dead,
  We will truly miss the two.
But as I told my wife we must survive,
  For what else can we do?

They faded from our lives
  My daughter Katie and her husband Chris.
Like the sun burning off,
  The early morning mist.
‘

The pain of the loss,
  Will last a long long while.
For no parent should have to endure,
  The losing of a child.

So destroy all the pictures,
  Burn the memorabilia fast.
Have nothing to remind us daily,
  For in our memories they will last.

And so we go on with our lives,
  Just a memory of the pair.
And hope when they passed,
  They will have remembered that we cared.

Understanding Suicide

My mother called me up the other day,
I had used the word suicide in one line.
She called to find out,
If I had lost my mind.

The word causes panic,
When ever it is heard.
There is a really pejorative feeling,
When anyone uses that word.

It seems to call up mystery,
Speak it in hushed quiet tones.
It seems to strike fear,
Deep within your bones.

Well I have considered suicide,
And come to understand.
Where the thoughts come from,
Unbidden into the head of man.

The first time it happened,
It caught me unaware.
My ability to think,
Is the only reason why I'm still here.

For it is a physical thing,
Like being hungry or being cold.
All one can think of.
Are any solutions that can be quickly sold?

The craving for it is strong,
When it comes creeping into your head.
And you have to really think hard,
Of what it means to be dead.

I was amazed to find I considered it,
 Because all I felt at first was fear.
The horror of what it meant,
 That would result in my wife's tear.

I beat the demon it was,
 Then thought about from whence it came.
Who was responsible?
 And who was there to blame.

I realized it was the drugs I was taking,
 Not anything illegal you understand.
Just pills given to improve my health
 Given by a doctor's hand.

 I'm sure he meant well,
Such a side effect had never been said.
They never considered that such a drug,
 Could put such things in your head.

Like when he gave me Prozac,
 That it eases anxiety, is a fact.
But taking it the first time in my life,
 I experienced a panic attack

The doctors will not discuss it,
 Cause no drug effect it the same.
And they don't want to hear,
 That it was them who were to blame.

Every human is different,
 You must look closely to see a clue.
Of how we respond to them,
 To see what final payment is due.

My death was not what he wanted,
 Such a response was not anticipated.
The drug companies never foresaw,
 The final result of something they created.

Only my years of introspection,
    Carried me through it all.
The love for my wife, was so overpowering
    That it's final answer I could forestall.

For I needed to understand,
    What had brought on such a thought?
And after analysis of many months,
    I realized it was the drugs that I had bought.

Drugs to lower blood pressure,
    Drugs to lower high cholesterol.
Just pop a pill to control it,
    No need to correct your lifestyle at all.

To be fair the doctors said,
    I needed to stop smoking and exercise.
But I knew that already,
    So popping the pills just seemed wise.

The human mind is complex,
    Mother Nature's mystery to behold.
And why do we think we can control it,
    In each bottle of pills that are sold.

So if you feel depressed,
    That the world has treated you so bad.
Think and you will realize that after awhile,
    You are not the first human these feeling to have had.

Take the time to think,
    About the drugs that you take.
Use reason and logic,
    Before any such a decision you make.

But our egos override our feeling,
    And prevent finding any such cure.
That we are somehow superior,
    To those who have fallen to its lure.

For we always ask, why?
    When hearing about suicide.
They had never done anything like that before.
    So what caused them to decide?

A course of action,
    They would have passed on before.
Because once that door is opened,
    The physical cravings they could not ignore.

So if some one speaks of it,
    And they confide such in a confession.
Just try to help them understand,
    What has sparked their overriding depression?

Everyone has had it bad,
    Life is no easy trick.
But it does not mean,
    They are wrong and unchallengably sick.

Mother Nature gave us the mind,
    But drugs change the thoughts we have.
So don't discount the physical cravings,
    By saying they are just bad.

Six O'clock

It's six o'clock in the morning,
I go out of my back door.
I'm looking for my little friend,
Hopefully my presence he will not ignore.

I take some nuts to feed him,
To start his day off right.
To stave off the depression,
I had felt during the night.

And there he is,
Greeting the coming day.
He sits and waits for me,
And if he could talk he'd say.

Hey old man,
I've been waiting here with a smile.
So get with the program,
Feed me now and then, you can sit for a while

The sun is coming up,
I don't have all day to wait.
For I have this sweet little thing,
And I don't want to be late.

So I toss him the nuts,
He comes up quickly to feed.
As if to say it's appreciated,
But not a real necessary need.

I sit and watch him,
Snack with the nuts that I have fed.
Then off to run around awhile,
The image stamped into my head.

How I enjoy him,
As we greet the beginning of each new day.
He reminds me of the joy of living in this world,
And why I want to stay.

What Excites Me

My wife asked me,
It was just the other day.
What in this world still excites me?
And makes me want to play.

What gets me going?
And puts that sparkle in my eye.
Something that revs up my engines,
So that I don't even have to try.

Well I have raced motorcycles,
Fought a war on the other side of the world.
Rebuilt engines, rewired a house,
Got married and had a girl.

Had women throw themselves at me,
For vanities sake I kept score.
Well such things no longer work,
Or excite me anymore.

Flew across the oceans,
Saw a cascading waterfall.
Man's philosophers don't excite me,
For I have read them all.

About the only thing that works,
Is seeing my wife's love in the end.
Well that and one other thing,
And that is feeding my little friend.

My little friend is a squirrel,
I feed him nuts with each morning's light.
He and my wife are the reasons,
I make it through the night.

People say how boring,
    With nothing to light my fire.
Well seeing my little friend and my wife's love,
    Are things of which I never tire.

So go to a concert,
    A ball game or go across the country driving.
Take part of the countries activities,
    For each day they are thriving.

But as for me, I complain no more,
    And here let me set the tone.
Just let me feed my squirrel and see my wife,
    And leave me the hell alone.

Labor Day

The first Monday in September,
It's called Labor Day.
But even if you don't to go to work,
They will send you pay.

It's set aside to celebrate labor,
The unions made it a day.
To celebrate working,
To celebrate how you earn your pay.

Yet some people blame the unions,
Say they are too greedy by far.
To pay their salaries they had to jack up,
The cost of buying a car.

Well it's not all their fault,
They try to support their families and compete.
With countries who pay employees fifty cents an hour,
To win such competition, really is a feat.

The forty-hour week,
The eight-hour day.
Were given to us by the unions,
Who fought for it in their way.

For the employers fought them,
They wanted their products sold.
They even saw nothing wrong
With working a twelve year old.

Every new idea,
That the unions did suggest.
Had to be paid for in blood,
As the employers put them to a test.

Nowadays people take for granted,
    Each idea for which they did fight.
Assuming the employers,
    Saw it and just thought it was right.

So study the history of labor,
    And you will find it true.
They were fought at every turn,
    Of any idea that was considered new.

Eating Broccoli

I am growing older,
    More clearly do I see.
The need to protect my health,
    So I am eating broccoli.

My wife had always eaten it,
    But her I could never please.
By eating something,
    I referred to as little trees.

So I finally tried it,
    Forced to eat it made me sad.
But shock and wonder awaited me,
    For it was not all that bad.

That it was good for me,
    Was not debated.
But the taste of it not being so bad,
    Was something she had never related.

So now I eat Broccoli,
    Introduced to me by my wife.
And to stay healthy,
    I will do so the rest of my life.

Daytime Noise

I went outside my backdoor,
    To enjoy the nighttime solitude.
But I had waited too long,
    And the daylight did intrude.

Gone was the silence,
    Cars sped by at a frantic pace.
And with no pun intended,
    I realized why, it's called the human race.

The sounds of a city awakening,
    With the coming of the light.
Declared sure the noise was loud,
    But it is within our right.

The sound a city makes,
    Is as part of the world as food.
That I at first could not hear it,
    Had caused my petulant mood.

But it has its beauty,
    Different, than the middle of the night.
For it announces it's coming,
    As life, seen in the light.

Hurricane Katrina

Hurricane Katrina while it was still out in the ocean,
The forecasters had a ball.
For it appeared the hurricane would hit maybe two states,
When it finally made landfall.

Category 1 or Category 4,
Please vote for your selection.
Well Florida got the 1,
So it appears, Jeb won another election.

Hurricane Relief

Hurricane Katrina hit New Orleans,
It was a devastating blow.
And in a time of crisis,
The true character of a person will show.

Everyone was asked to sacrifice,
Give to relieve the victim's pain.
And they would prosecute anyone,
Who used the disaster for gain.

Well maybe I'm confused,
Or maybe I'm just dense.
Because the guilty feeling they are imposing,
Just doesn't make any sense.

The aid needed was there,
No more money should be sent.
The money comes from the taxes we pay,
It's just how the government sees it's spent.

Spent not to help the world abroad,
Or to finance some such war.
We have paid enough over the years,
To pay for relief here at our front door.

There is enough military,
To relieve the stress they feel.
And who over sees the spending,
And who is turning the wheel.

Speaking of sacrifice,
How about the cost of gasoline,
Why don't the oil companies?
Do their share, and not profit from such a scheme.

Aren't they profiting from our misery,
    Where is their sacrifice?
Wouldn't freezing the prices,
    Be a move that was considered nice.

Or why doesn't the president,
    Prosecute them for gouging, and take an active hand.
President Nixon froze them,
    And imposed the freeze across the land.

They try and make us feel guilty,
    That we don't give more.
Well I just don't see how, and the vision,
    Of what's happening, leaves me shaken to the core.

The government pleads inability
    To help the people in need,
To get them in some shelter,
    And food for them to feed.

Yet we spend billions,
    To fund the war in Iraq.
While the oil companies profit,
    And those two things are a fact.

So sorry if I use logic,
    To come to my defense.
Cause overall the government's actions,
    Just doesn't make any sense.

So I don't toe the line,
    And give more when they ask.
Yet it's not that I don't care,
    But I've given too much already to pay for such a task.

Why don't we hold the government accountable?
    Of how our money's spent.
To regulate everyone's expenses,
    From gasoline, food and rent.

President Nixon did it,
    And he paid the price in pain.
And no politician,
    Wants to see that reaction again.

For we heard all the rhetoric,
    Didn't think for ourselves and act.
We let them get away with it all,
    And the trend is now a fact.

Well we don't seen to give a damn,
    We don't throw a fit.
So I guess it's true,
    We then deserve, what we get.

War

Mankind's greatest insanity,
    Would have to be what we call war.
To understand it, we must examine,
    What is the fighting for?

It stems from our leader's insecurity,
    And their overriding thrill.
To dominate other humans,
    And to simply impose their will.

Yet time after time,
    And year after year.
Old men send young boys off,
    To overcome their insecurity fear.

They inspire the boys with rhetoric,
    Of ideals and promise of a better land.
But it's simply to conquer another rule,
    A rule held by another man.

Fact is we should never elect someone,
    To rule over the tower.
The fact that they run,
    Should disqualify them from such power.

For over the years the wars,
    Never have resolved for long any strife.
The only thing ensured, is that a young man dies,
    And never again holds his child or wife.

But if the answers were written,
    And universal under the sun.
Then there would be only one book,
    And everybody would have one.

And what ideal is so important,
    That they would go and forsake their child and wife.
And what belief so correct,
    That it would end a young man's life.

For any soldier who has fought,
    Asks the question at one point in time.
What the hell they were fighting for,
    And for what purpose did they spend their life's dime.

But they wave a flag,
    Tell you your country is the best.
Never analyzing the results,
    When put to the final test.

Most people live their lives,
    Not caring how others live.
Just going day by day,
    Till the leaders tell them to give.

To sacrifice their lives,
    To an ideal they are told.
That their belief is the best,
    And that thought they should hold.

So why do we never question them,
    On their ideas of what's right.
And to prove it to the world,
    And that it's worthy of any fight.

With any war it's true,
    For no matter whoever finally won?
The leaders soon change,
    And so do the ideals, like the setting sun.

So stop the madness of war,
    Our leaders should have no say.
Of how another people live their lives?
    And what beliefs they hold and how they live their way.

The Purple Cow Revisited

A poem was written long ago,
It was called the Purple Cow.
Intellectuals derided it then,
Much as they do now.

It was a whimsical quatrain,
But they ask, "What is it worth?"
Well if it caused a chuckle or a smile,
It is the most valuable thing on earth.

For in a world so morbid,
Where everything is bought and sold.
An unforced smile or laugh,
Is worth more than all of mankind's gold.

So do not deride Gelett Burgess,
For writing such a simple rhyme.
For it's value stands today,
And has survived the test of time.

The Philosopher's Stone Explained

I wrote a poem called The Philosopher's Stone,
    Gave it the chemist's equation at hand.
I exposed it all,
    For the benefit of the common man.

But it needed more than an equation,
    For most people did not see.
They did not major in the sciences,
    Nor understand the chemistry.

I gave it as Ag + Si O2.
    Well Ag is the symbol for silver that much is true.
And earth's most abundant material,
    Is Si O2.

Silicon dioxide is quartz,
    We use it to make glass.
Just put silver on it's back,
    And you make a mirror fast.

So how can a mirror bring,
    The answers for you to begin.
Happiness and wealth only comes from one place,
    And that place comes from within.

So get a mirror and look into it,
    Examine your beliefs and you must.
For introspection will give to you,
    The only meaning of life, which you can trust.

Judgment of a Smoker

Today I was chastised,
For my smoking is a fact,
All previous achievements would not make up,
For my obvious character lack.

I do not drink,
Or take any illegal drug.
Been married 34 years,
But because I smoke, I'm still considered a slug.

The youngest child of six,
I put myself through school.
The college degree I earned.
Seemed to give me a useful tool.

Then I worked all my life,
Put child and wife through college, the two.
Don't chase other women,
Or anything else forbidden, that you might construe.

But all these accomplishments mean nothing,
If my character is lax,
If I smoke a cigarette,
They don't seem concerned with the facts.

For it has been shown that people who smoke,
Don't develop Parkinson's disease.
As far as for Alzheimer's,
The studies are unclear and still out there in the breeze.

The ones at highest risks,
To develop childhood allergies.
According to the CDC study, are the people not exposed to cigarette smoke,
To report such finding surely did not please.

As a child I saw commercials,
Of how good it was to smoke.
Then the Army supplied them in C rations,
If I couldn't afford them or if I was broke.

So now everyone condemns it,
And in doing so, also condemns me.
None of my sacrifices made,
Mean much for them to see.

For why should they complain?
Or be concerned with the facts.
When everything they now enjoy,
Are paid for by my cigarette tax.

They only think its fair,
That I pay for my character lack.
For surely I can afford, the loss of taste buds,
And bad smell for just $5 a pack.

What will they think up next to tax?
Maybe fast food if they dare.
For the injustice shown in the taxing,
Seems more than the government is given to care.

Just so it meets no opposition,
And can be taxed with an open mind.
They seem no longer concerned,
If it puts the common people in a bind.

So before you judge someone,
See how they lived their life.
If they drink or work hard,
Of if they cheated on their wife.

To be considered a good person,
Means more than having one or two flaws.
And what they have done with their lives,
Should give one a judgmental pause.

Religion

I once wrote a poem called The Answer,
But discussing it I find.
I was not so clear,
To express what was in my mind.

Life exists on it's own sake,
No final goal for which to strive.
Just relish in the fact of being here,
Just happy to be alive.

Yet we seek higher answers,
But research if you dare.
The history of mankind before,
Nirvana, Shangri-La and Heaven were there.

The people that preach these thoughts,
Say faith will get you by.
Have faith in the beliefs,
You need no proof to try.

These people ask you for money,
Offering nothing but a dream of hope.
For not having any belief system,
Is more, than most people can cope.

Yet every culture has a story,
Of how it all began.
Offering hope unto the masses,
Of an over all-existing plan.

The only thing I find in these people,
There are no longshoremen, or even an accounting clerk.
The only common factor displayed,
Is that none of them have to work.

I am told that if I don't believe,
    Kill myself, if so filled with doubt.
How stupid of an argument is that,
    For the joys of being alive is what it's all about.

There was a hurricane in Florida,
    The news channel showed a sign written on a wall.
"God will protect us," it said,
    Then who created the hurricane at all?

They say Jesus came to earth,
    To die for the sins of man.
Yet if this is the Supreme Being,
    Could he not come up with a better plan?

Communion we now have,
    To eat the body and blood of Jesus.
How barbaric is that idea,
    An act designed to please us.

The belief that we just don't end,
    Seems too attractive an idea to pass.
So we create stories and myths,
    To ensure our being will forever last.

But keep in mind,
    That existence is ased on joy.
So if such belief gives comfort,
    Use them, for me they're just a ploy.

To help some people,
    From dealing with daily strife.
To give them a means of surviving,
    This short-lived thing we call life.

Stan Rogers Songs

Stan Rogers sang two songs,
Two songs that relate to my life.
Mary Ellen Carter for everyone whom I have helped.
Witch of the West Moreland reminds me of my wife.

Like the Mary Ellen Carter,
I went down last October in a pouring driving rain.
The kids they had been drinking,
And they did not feel my pain.

But they left me there,
To crumble into scale.
Even though I had saved their lives so many times,
Living through the gale.

So the laughing rats,
Left me to a sorry grave.
And they kept laughing,
For another day.

For adversity has dealt me,
The final blow.
With smiling bastards lying to me,
Everywhere I go.

And so I put out all my heart and strength and grain,
But my only hope is by my wife's hand.
For without her I will not rise again.
For she is like the Witch of the Westmoreland.

She said braze thee thy silvery sword,
Lay down thy Roland's shield,
For I see by the briny blood that flows
You've been wounded in the field.

She stood in her gown of the velvet moon,
  Bound round with the silver chain.
She kissed my pale lips once and twice,
  And three times round again.

Then she bound my wound with the golden rod,
  Fast in her arms I lay.
And I have risen hale and soon,
  With the sun high in the day.

She said, ride with your grand old hounds at heel
  And good gray hawk in hand.
For none can harm the knight whose lain,
  With the Witch of the Westmoreland.

Getting Old Emotions

Throughout my lifetime,
I have reflected on what makes me tick.
What makes me laugh?
And what makes me sick.

But as I get older,
A new one has arrived.
Mother Nature's rule over my emotions,
Its purpose cannot be derived.

Emotional outburst has come,
Uncontrollable as my fears.
Because at the drop of a hat,
My eyes unbidden fill with tears.

I used to be a stoic,
Nothing ever got to me.
But I cry now,
At almost everything I see.

A movie, a song, a card,
Saying goodbye to a loved one.
It seems I have no control,
Over anything under the sun.

But my wife says not to sweat it.
And once again she is right.
For it comes at weird times,
So I should accept it and not put up such a fight.

I shouldn't feel it makes me,
Weak, or even much of a wimp.
Just accept it as I do,
My walking with a limp.

Still it is disconcerting,
This emotion I now call mine.
But I have no control over it,
It just comes as does the passing of time.

To Dad Macon

I heard the wife talking the other day,
    About you having a dream.
Thought it was Christmas,
    And should be getting a tree and not go down to the stream.

Everyone thought it amusing,
    When told about the news.
I don't think they would have thought it funny,
    If they had ever walked in your shoes.

Myself I've had disorientation,
    Last month while shopping at the grocery store.
I got lost in the place,
    That we had shopped in for five years or more.

It is upsetting,
    And yourself you begin to doubt.
No one seems to understand,
    Or to let you talk it out.

Don't be upset if it feels like you're in a prison,
    For they always have a trustee.
For through it all remember, no one could ask for more,
    Than the woman you call Dusty.

You have earned the right,
    Not to water ski for fun.
You worked your ass off all your life,
    So relax and just sit in the sun.

No need to explain,
    To anyone how you feel.
To try to make it through each day,
    To experience fears that are real.

You are not alone,
    To fight the body's battles and it's true.
For you are surrounded,
    By people who only want to love you.

Exercise Bicycle

My wife bought me an exercise bicycle,
    It's to help me keep my health.
She seems more concerned with it,
    Than worrying about any wealth.

So I reluctantly agreed,
    That we should buy it.
And I would put aside some of each day,
    And spend my time to ride it.

So I sat there pedaling,
    Going nowhere fast.
When I happen to look out the back door.
    Out the sliding glass.

There sat my little friend the squirrel,
    Watching me pedaling quickly to nowhere.
Not seeming to worry about it,
    And didn't seem to care.

Then his face split with a grin,
    And quickly hit the trees and went aloft.
To tell his friend the gerbil about it,
    And laugh their asses off.

Collision

I once wrote a poem called The Beginning,
    And rereading it years later I find.
I was not very clear to express,
    How such thoughts came into my mind.

Let me start by stating,
    We live in a galaxy called the Milky Way.
Our closest neighboring galaxy is Andromeda,
    And will eventually come into play.

It seems both galaxies are heading,
    For the Virgo Super Cluster.
And the collision of the two will happen,
    Before they reach its luster.

For they are heading together,
    At 300,000 miles an hour.
And will collide with each other in about 7 million years,
    Which makes many forecasts sour.

Each has a black hole at its center,
    And the gravity encountered when they collide.
Is not something we will live to see,
    But from it's happening we cannot hide.

The results of the combination,
    Of silicon and carbon given off.
May create a new life form,
    And that's a fact so do not scoff.

The black holes will merge,
    And the only emission will be light.
As the the black holes evaporate,
    The results of a universe's fight.

For the stars are burning out,
    They were not meant to last.
It will occur when they collide.
    For the stars are running out of gas.

And so the stars run out of gas,
    And the black holes will evaporate.
The only thing left is light,
    And this may be our fate.

For it's not a question, of it happening,
    But of when, because it will.
The ending of our knowledge of the laws of physics,
    Will have to be a thrill.

Congressional Spending

I heard on the news of the hurricane Katrina costs,
    The congressman said it would be a bitter pill.
They said it would exceed,
    A one hundred fifty billion dollar bill.

The loss of lives and property,
    The appropriations are well meant.
But I cannot help but wonder,
    If the money couldn't have been better spent.

I do not mean to deride the congress,
    And don't want to be a heavy.
But couldn't they have spent it before,
    And built a bigger levy.

Going to College

When thinking about going to college,
Once you have left high school.
How to set up a schedule and to matriculate,
Could be a useful tool.

Just jump right in,
Don't sweat it if you don't know.
For they will tell you all the rules,
And the line that you must toe.

Do not be judgmental,
Keep and open mind.
And after a bit,
I think that you will find.

It's not so bad,
As you previously thought.
You have everything with you already,
With the high school tools you brought.

Just put up with it all,
Four or five years of strife.
But the degree will then be with you,
For all the rest of your life.

Wasted Time

The days they come, the days they go.
What schedules must I keep?
How much of my life have I wasted?
Unconscious and asleep.

My eyes are gone, my back is bad,
Out went both my knees.
Mother Nature does not seem to care,
She calls, "Come dance with the trees".

So I go outside, it's 3 AM.
Dawn is still far away.
And there is Mother Nature,
Waiting for me to play.

The warm wind caresses me.
So gentle is the breeze.
And there they are awaiting me,
The dancing rhythmic trees.

How many nights did I miss it?
While trying to get some rest.
It seems I missed Mother Nature,
When she was at her best.

So now I go outside,
In the middle of the night.
I no longer ponder the meanings,
Of what we call wrong or right.

My eyes, my back,
Even my worn out knees.
They don't seem to care,
If I'll only dance with the trees.

So do not worry so much,
Or struggle with the fight.
Just go outside and dance with them,
In the middle of the night.

Hearing the Song

Many people have heard me speak,
    Of Mother Nature's song.
Yet trying to hear it and failing,
    They assumed that I was wrong.

Material possessions are best,
    In those they put their trust.
Well observe those possessions,
    As Mother Nature turns them to rust.

Just go out into the night,
    Let it softly caress your skin.
Think not of the darkness as foreboding,
    Think of it as a friend.

Let the breeze blow over you,
    Close your eyes if you must.
And you will hear her song,
    A song that you can trust.

She makes no demands,
    No schedules for you to keep.
Yet sit there long enough,
    And she will lull you gently into sleep.

The song is not complex,
    A simple rhythmic flow.
Just relax your muscles,
    And make your breathing slow.

So I tell you believe me,
    The song is really there.
But to hear it, the only requirement,
    Is that you become aware.

Boo

I have a nickname for my wife,
　　It may seem silly but its true.
For years the name for her,
　　I simply call her Boo.

We've been married 34 years,
　　More than most people our age.
It is because, we read Earth's songbook,
　　From another page.

Yes I call her Boo,
　　She gives meaning to my life.
And I am thankful every day,
　　For such a lovely magnificent wife.

And she has a name for me,
　　A nickname she calls me too.
Not very original,
　　She simply calls me, Boo 2.

Rain

The rain is coming down,
    Down from a cloud filled sky.
I sit on my back patio,
    No longer wondering why?

The rain it is so soothing,
    It fills my heart with joy.
It takes me back to a time,
    When I was just a boy.

I do not watch the clock,
    Just sit enjoying the rain.
I do not consider the world,
    And it's daily dose of pain.

Just sitting there,
    Listening to the song.
That Mother Nature sings to me,
    Inviting me to sing along.

I do not know the words,
    So I just hum along with the tune.
Morning passes quickly,
    And soon it is noon.

But what a way to spend the morning,
    Just listening to the rain,
It was not time I wasted,
    Or a morning spent in vain.

Lighthouses

My wife loves lighthouses,
When I asked her why, she said.
It's the way they face the ocean,
Usually at a peninsula's head.

They give the light,
To warn the sailors away.
To offer hope,
That they will see another day.

They stand so tall and proud,
From midnight until noon.
Offering hope to the sailors,
That they will be home soon.

To guide them on their way,
It's light is very strong.
It warns them but does not lure them,
Like the sirens song.

They cover the earth,
Each ocean has its share.
To give a chance to the sailors,
To make the playing field fair.

They are simple,
Their purpose clear to see.
It all sounded so simple,
When she explained it all to me.

So cherish the lighthouses,
They allow sailors to cope.
And more importantly they stand,
For an ideal that we call hope.

Intelligent Life

If you consider yourself intelligent,
    Do not read beyond this line.
For you may not like the questions,
    It raises in your mind.

It seems to me intelligent life,
    Is the worst oxymoron ever said.
That is if you believe,
    Everything that I have read.

Life in the dictionary terms,
    Means the ability to animate.
And intelligence is merely.
    The ability to solve problems and communicate.

Well a plant creates a flower,
    Its color vibrant and pure.
It attracts other creatures to pollinate,
    It's survival to ensure.

That is solving a problem,
    Communicating its need.
To continue its existence,
    By other creatures spreading its seed.

And what of mankind,
    The competition for our fate.
So myths of an afterlife,
    And gods and legends we create.

One of the legends says,
    Thou Shall Not Kill.
Well its not to be taken literally,
    For that would be too bitter a pill.

But kill we do ever day,
    Another human or a plant.
For each has life,
    By the definitions that we grant.

Ever watch a spider,
    The webs architecture is a problem resolved.
Yet we wipe it out with the swing of a hand,
    No thoughts of a life being involved.

For we kill to survive,
    To live if you may.
A plant or an animal,
    Even the horses, eat the hay.

But we don't call a carrot intelligent,
    Man's ego won't go that far.
For our need to feel superior,
    We try and raise the bar.

But what is life,
    Carbon based and all.
Yet even the leaves they die,
    And from the tree they fall.

We seek answers,
    Of life and what is it for.
For we feel the need,
    Not only to survive but to keep a score.

Well what in the universe is counting?
    To determine what is our fate.
And why do the answers we seek,
    Always come too late.

An ant has the intelligence,
    And further more the right.
For it can communicate and solve problems,
    To grant it this thing called life.

Every creature I know communicates,
It solves the problems at hand.
Even if we don't relate its messages,
And cannot understand.

For communication is not just verbal,
Our voices do not fill every need.
To continue our existence,
Much less to spread our seed.

So what is it all about,
Well this much I know as true.
For the questions of life and the universe,
I haven't got a clue.

Maybe its just to live,
Day by day until we die.
And not try so hard, to solve the answers of life
Or spend so much energy to try.

Heisenberg vs Kirshoff

The Kirshoff voltage law states,
That if we have the flow.
Each position of an electron,
In a current we do know.

Yet the Heisenberg Uncertainty Principle says,
We cannot determine any such position.
If both are taught as true,
The consistency I am missing.

For if one is correct,
The other must be false.
But to teach both as true,
Has left me somewhat lost.

Yet physicists say just trust us,
The details you just don't know.
Well in that they are correct,
So maybe I'm just slow.

But on the surface it appears,
That they each contradict any such law.
So I cannot accept it as fact,
And am baffled by such a flaw.

So I'll sit outside,
And I'll feed my little squirrel.
For the logic of the physicists,
Has left my mind in quite a whirl.

Dr Patti Robbins

November 1st it was,
Till 3 AM I sat outside.
Depression had taken hold,
As I considered suicide.

I had been to my doctors,
They ran blood tests and X rays.
They could find no problems,
For my fatigue and depression days.

I had almost given up hope,
Told my wife it was not if, but when.
That the depression would finally take over.
And my life I would simply end.

In a last ditch effort.
To try and to save me.
She made an appointment,
To a doctor of Naturopathy.

Dr. Patti Robbins was her name,
She then took control.
Ran tests to see the heavy metals,
In my body that had taken hold.

She was aggressive in her care,
Told me it was not too late.
She would correct the fatigue and depression,
And suicide would not be my fate.

Yet the insurance companies would not recognize her,
No payments to her would they offer.
As if it would cost too much,
To touch their billion dollar coffer.

But the doctors they did approve,
  Could offer no hope to end my plight.
For all the tests they ran,
  No solutions came to light.

She tested and found no Lithium,
  One neurotransmitter in my brain.
My normal doctors sent me to see a psychiatrist,
  I think they did not believe that I was not insane.

For they did not use the blood work,
  But for Dr Patti it was clear to see.
My problems were simply,
  My body's chemistry.

Adrenal fatigue had set in,
  Liver enzymes were one problem at fault.
Simple foods and herbs were a remedy,
  From Mother Nature that she sought.

But for my normal doctors,
  I do not put the blame.
They had been taught differently,
  And played the pharmaceutical companies game.

How many people could she help?
  And my disgust I could not disguise.
If only her skills and knowledge,
  The medical community would recognize.

My nickname for her is Gia,
  The goddess that gives the planet its life.
For she saved me and I will always give thanks to her,
  From me and from my wife.

I've Gone Insane

Greetings friends,
    Please don't be shy or balk.
Once more I find myself writing,
    For I feel the need to talk.

I'm trying to reason, a new development,
    That has just come to light.
I seem to be in a battle,
    In which I will lose the fight.

I rose from poverty,
    The stigma of being poor.
And I was challenged when,
    I tried to advance thru each and every door.

I worked to take care of,
    My child and my wife.
To deal with every problem,
    To conquer every bit of strife.

To balance every problem,
    And to make my world tick.
Just recently I was told,
    That I am really sick.

I never shirked my duty,
    You could never say will, I did lack.
Till in the last year,
    My daughter and son in law turned their back.

No longer could I answer their questions,
    Or fulfill any need.
My advice wasn't asked for, any advice given,
    Wasn't for them to heed.

My wife stuck by me,
    And that was a trick.
Till she told me the other day,
    That I was just sick.

The sickness that I had,
    And this is what she said.
Was not anything physical,
    But was all in my head.

The children I needed to talk to,
    Didn't want to bring me to my knees.
But they were too busy to listen,
    So now I just talk to the trees.

I take medicine to help me,
    Get thru every day.
But keeping away the darkness,
    It's not a high price to pay.

So I will have to accept,
    No one wants to hear my voice.
But deal with it, I must,
    For I haven't any other choice.

Danny L Shanks

Taking My Blood

I'm going to the doctor's office,
　　To give a sample of blood today.
The nurse who will take it,
　　Is a kind woman named Renee.

In the past the nurses just stuck the needle in,
　　They would not shed a tear.
They appeared unconcerned and unbelieving,
　　That a grown man could have such fear.

Renee instead, gives me comfort,
　　She says," It will not hurt".
Then she lays me down,
　　And tells me to roll up the sleeve of my shirt.

True to her word it does not hurt,
　　Quickly its over and done.
If they ever held such a competition,
　　Hands down she would have won.

The procedure is expensive,
　　The office will send the bill to me.
Her caring and compassion,
　　That she gives to me for free.

So on this day I thank her,
　　For the caring and if truth be told.
Her compassion is like a gift from God,
　　It can never be bought or sold.

Waiting in Line

Have you ever noticed?
    That no matter where you go.
The other lines move much faster,
    While the one your in is slow.

Whenever I'm in traffic,
    And I move to the fast lane.
Sometimes I feel as if I could move faster,
    If I got out and walked with my cane.

And if I sound paranoid,
    Believe me cause it's true.
No one is going slower,
    And stuck in a line like you.

So why is everyone afflicted,
    Is it some kind of time warp or such?
And why does it happen,
    To me so awfully much.

Is it a cosmic conspiracy?
    To make me have such a fate..
Is it the world's lesson?
    That I should be content to wait.

That life goes on,
    In a fast line or a slow.
It is an important question,
    And that answer I should like to know.

For it will not change the world,
    If I arrive a few minutes late.
It only goes to show me,
    That I have no control over my fate.

Global Warming

The earth is warming up,
Global warming is the term.
The reasons given to us,
By the scientist all seem firm.

Yet common sense tells me,
That it is not so complicated.
Our life style gives us the problem,
Determines how our future will be fated.

The oceans not the rain forest,
Gave us life upon this planet.
Absorbing carbon dioxide,
The plankton survival was frantic.

Then the plankton died,
Settled to the ocean floor.
Over the years it turned into bedrock,
The carbon dioxide it did store.

We released the gas with every batch,
Of concrete we did grind.
To build our homes and parking lots,
To the consequences we were blind.

Well releasing that much gas,
Has finally taken its toll.
The buildup goes on unprecedented,
As mankind builds on in a roll.

So we build,
But realize that it's a fact.
We will be protected from the rain.
But breathable air we will lack.

Super Tork

My sister Carol who was closest to my age,
And her nickname was the Super Tork.
When playing cowboys, she always got to be Stony,
I was Lullaby, who was pretty much a dork.

I remember frying bread,
On an iron cast skillet, and if truth be told.
It tasted awful on the morning,
When we explored the famed blue hole.

We climbed up the sides,
And when I slipped in the sand.
There was Super Tork,
To save me with her helping hand.

We both got older,
Moved away and pretty much lost touch.
She lost her husband to alcohol,
He couldn't escape it's clutch.

As for me I drank also,
But was only ever drunk twice.
The first lasted about ten years,
Before I could conquer the vice.

We played all the summers of our youth.
Tanned and under the sun.
I had visions of being a priest,
She had visions of being a nun.

Then college called,
We both of us went.
Discussed the world and the universe,
With beer and pizza the nights were spent.

Divorce and children she survived it all,
    As I kept track through my mother.
Yet I feel remorse for the support I didn't give,
    Even if I was only a half assed brother.

Twenty years gone by,
    She raised her girls to care.
How to deal with life,
    How to deal with people and be fair.

Yet sometimes I feel remorse,
    Which hits me like a well-placed fist.
For I remember our youth and innocence,
    When we danced the Peppermint Twist.

A Wife's Reasoning

My wife told me to retire,
I was shocked by the news.
She said I had worked enough,
That I had paid my dues.

She told me this as we went out,
To get an ice cream cone.
She said many women have a house on the hill,
But many of them are alone.

She said she wanted me with her,
Till we were old and gray.
And eating green beans instead of asparagus,
Was a price she was willing to pay.

So I retired to regain my health,
To rebuild what was left of my life.
To try and just be there,
A living husband to my wife.

She took the job head-on,
Her responsibilities she did not shirk.
As for me I now tell people,
I've got a watch, a TV and a wife and they all three work.

The Zippo Lighter

Of all the inventions,
    Americans have put to the test.
The Zippo lighter,
    Has always proven to be the best.

Ask any veteran from the Viet Nam,
    Korean or Second World War.
They all will tell you,
    Never had a piece of equipment shown a better score.

It never let you down,
    A little maintenance was all you would need.
To supply you with a light,
    If fluid to it you would feed.

A better piece of equipment
    Has never been made.
It kept you company,
    Gave light when in the shade.

It lit the cigarettes,
    That came in every C ration.
A more reliable piece of equipment,
    That never went out of fashion.

So if you see a veteran,
    With a Zippo lighter you can tell.
It carried him from hometown and back again,
    Through his season in hell.

Never a better object,
    Will you see.
And if by chance it breaks,
    They will replace it for free.

It is an icon,
    Of the American way of life.
Probably as revered,
    As Mom, Apple Pie, and wife.

So use it as a signal,
    To tell you of a veteran's plight.
For in the darkness of war, the Zippo lighter,
    Was by far the only reliable light.

Last Poem

Today I write my last poem,
I have written for 35 years.
I have explored mankind's emotions,
All his thoughts and fears.

Explored suicide,
And what it meant to be alive or dead.
I have put it all down in prose,
And there is nothing left to be said.

Told of love and marriage,
What it meant to have a child.
Expounded on the universe,
And I think it's time to rest for a while.

Three books on it I have written,
From my soapbox I have given life's clue.
Of what I have learned,
And what part was false or true.

So no more 3 AM poems,
Written to clear my head.
I hope you have enjoyed them,
I now await the end in which I am dead.

But do not morn me,
For I have had a wonderful life,
A child who was a trial at times,
And a lovely magnificent wife.

So if perchance you read some,
Of my thoughts put down in rhyme.
Just rest easy as I go my way,
Lost in the Oceans of Time.

Conversations

Introduction

Below follows conversations between four friends. Daniel the retired civil servant. Bartholomew the tall stately Elm. Patricia, the young voluptuous pine, and Little, the sarcastic almond loving squirrel.

Conversations Index

	Introduction
	Nature's Songs
	My Little Friend
1	Contact
2	Black Hole Trouble
3	Exercise Bike
4	Baseball
5	The Most Important Thing
6	A Day of Rest
7	Hurricanes
8	World Series
9	Houston
10	Coming Home
11	Halloween
12	Daylight Savings Time
13	Smoking
14	Thanksgiving
15	Smart and Dumb
16	Retired
17	Writing
18	The Day After Thanksgiving
19	Winter Solstice
20	Depression
21	Disagreements
22	Winter Rest

This book is dedicated to Leslie Macon, my mother-in-law. Without her knowledge and inspiration I would never have known about, or ever achieved the alpha state. With thanks and love.

Danny

Nature's Songs

It's four o'clock in the morning,
Daybreak did not yet begin.
I'm sitting on my back patio,
Enjoying the night like a long lost friend.

Suddenly I noticed the wind,
Weaving gently through the trees.
They're swaying rhythmically seductive.
Saying come dance with us please.

For I know the wind scientifically,
Fronts, gradients, and pressure.
But I had never listened to its song,
And thought of it by that measure.

It is a form of music,
I had never realized before.
The trees heard it and danced,
Emboldened by the score.

Slowly I heard a new sound,
It was starting to rain.
Relishing my new awareness,
Hoping a new song I could gain.

Sure enough it was there,
Different but beautiful in its right.
So I sat and listened to the medley,
In the middle of the night.

So I pondered what other songs of nature,
I had heard but not recognized.
That it was singing a song to me,
One that should be prized.

I thought of ocean waves,
    Of a cascading waterfall.
The gentle tumbling of leaves,
    Heard softly in the fall.

As I listened for the first time,
    I came to realize that it was so.
That I was changed that morning,
    And may never again listen to a radio.

The gentleness of it,
    Seemingly calling to me.
It played on and on,
    All of it for free.

I wonder how much,
    Of nature's songs I had heard.
Never realizing the beauty of it,
    As put out by a bird.

It's complex in its simplicity,
    Subtle, yet seductively strong.
The variety was overwhelming,
    This nature's propensity for song.

So if you see me swaying,
    And wonder what I'm listening too.
It's nature's song I'm hearing,
    Just listen and you will find it's true.

What a prize I have found,
    In the middle of the night.
Nature singing to me,
    Making the world seem rhythmically right.

My Little Friend

The sun creeps over the mountains,
    Daylight comes slowly in.
And there on my back patio,
    Sits the reliable one, my little friend.

He's a furry little creature,
    With a long and bushy tail.
He comes to visit each morning,
    A task in which he does not fail.

If we slide open the door,
    He will scurry off, but not far.
If we don't show up, then he comes to look in,
    Wondering where we are?

We only set out three or four nuts,
    But keeping that schedule we must.
For we dare not spoil him,
    But we dare not violate that trust.

Just the other morning,
    Sitting out he came and sniffed my big toe.
As if wondering who the big guy was,
    An answer that he just had to know.

It will not change the world,
    It's a tradition that is not far reaching.
Just a communion with Mother Nature,
    And one that I will be keeping.

Contact

Morning had come and Daniel upon completing his daily workout retired to his back patio. There Bartholomew and Patricia greeted him with Good Mornings. Responding to them each he then heard "Almonds!"

"Little," he projected. "Almonds, is not a greeting."

"Sorry Daniel." Came the reply from his friend the little squirrel. "It's just the first thing that popped into my mind."

Daniel stated,"That, I can believe, and yes I brought your Almonds."

"Daniel," Bart projected in a somewhat somber tone. "Patricia and I have had some of our brothers and sisters questioning us about you. Why are you the only human, anyone of us has ever made contact with?"

"Almonds," interrupted Little.

"What the dead bark are you talking about Little?" inquired Patricia.

"Well," explained Little. "Everyone knows eating almonds results in a higher form of intelligence. Daniel had them in his cave, so he must have been eating them and hence his higher level of intelligence and the resulting contact."

"Irrefutable logic Little," said a bemused Daniel. "However, there's a bit more to it than that."

"If you don't mind." Bartholomew went on. "Patricia and I would like to know. Then we could answer some of the questions from our brothers and sisters and they would give us some peace."

"It's kind of a long story." Replied Daniel.

"Long is a relative term," expounded Bart. "We have time."

"Please," pleaded Patricia.

"No problem," he acknowledged. "Just try and keep fuzzy butt quiet and I will explain."

"Hey," cried Little. Feeling unappreciated, "I'm just trying to help."

"Well," Daniel began, "It all started with my mate's mother. She gave me a book on getting the human mind to the alpha state."

"What's a book?" Quipped Little.

"I see now, what you mean by a long time," Patricia said. "Little shut up and let Daniel explain."

"A book is how humans communicate ideas," Daniel went on. "You see the signs on the road out there. Each has a set of symbols on it. The symbols each mean something and humans use those symbols in a book to communicate ideas."

"How primitive, no thought projection." Bart stated. "Sorry, Daniel go on."

"The book explained how for a human to get into the alpha state, which results in astral projection." Daniel patiently explained. "You have to hold a thought in your mind and repeat it over and over. You may become distracted by random thoughts but you must continue repeating the original thought and soon you will transfer into the alpha state. I myself use the number one. Usually you slip into the alpha state and fall asleep because there is no other being to communicate with."

"What is sleep?" asked a confused Bartholomew.

"It is a state of unconsciousness where the human mind shuts down and is controlled by random thoughts."

"What a horrible state to be in." Patricia said and actually shivered. Her pine needles quivering.

"It's not so bad, Patricia." Daniel defended. "It's how humans recharge their minds."

"I guess that's what was happening when we would see you motionless for a period of time."

"Right," explained Daniel.

"Well what changed," Bart asked.

"One morning I was sitting there relaxed when a thought exploded into my consciousness." Daniel went on. "Almonds."

"Told you," quipped Little.

"I then started to question where such a powerful thought had come from, that it woke me up." Explained a perplexed Daniel. "Obviously Little. So I started to try and listen closer. I was truly amazed when I heard you and Patricia talking. I then tried to talk to you two and was even more amazed when you answered. I was delighted when you answered and even more so when you invited me to dance."

"Dancing with the wind is truly a joy in this world," explained Patricia.

"I couldn't agree more," said Daniel. "I had just never heard the music before."

"Mother Nature puts it there for everybody," Bart expounded.

"I realize that now, I had just never heard it before." Daniel said sadly.

"Well we are glad you heard it, enjoyed it, and made contact." Patricia intoned. "Talking with you has been a real joy."

"For me too." Daniel responded. "Even getting to know Little has its rewards."

"You bet your no tailed butt," Little chirped in.

"Thanks for the explanation Daniel." Bartholomew declared. "Maybe now we can get some rest."

"Maybe so but if you please," asked Daniel. "Dance with me first. And Little you just eat your almonds and maybe someday you can learn to dance."

Black Hole Trouble

Daniel woke to the early morning light coming through the window into his bedroom. He slowly got out of bed and went to wash his face. He then proceeded to the sliding glass door and went out onto his back patio.

"Good Morning Daniel" projected his friend Bartholomew.

"Hello Bart," replied Daniel. As he observed the tall elm tree he had come to know as Bartholomew.

"And top of the morning to you Patricia".

"Hey good looking," replied Patricia. The pine tree he thought of as a female because of her curved trunk.

Daniel had only recently begun to understand he could communicate with the trees by allowing his mind to go into the alpha state. His mother in law had given him a book on how to do it so he had been practicing it one morning when he got the shock of an unexpected reply from the trees. Since then he talked to them each day and really enjoyed their company.

"Hey no tail, you gonna feed me or stand there all day talking." He looked down to see he other new friend the small squirrel who he had taken to calling Little One.

"Sorry Little, I didn't know you were starving to death out here."

"You bet your bushy tail I am." Replied Little, "Well that is if you had one", came the sarcastic reply.

He really loved the little squirrel even if he could be a trial at times.

"We seem to have a bit of a crisis this morning" Bart intoned. "That is other than Little's starvation obsession."

"Hey kiss my fuzzy butt" came back Little's rapid rejoinder.

"This is serious," Patricia went on. "Andy has stopped collecting light."

"Are you kidding me?" Suddenly Little lost his humorous attitude.

"What?" asked a puzzled Daniel.

Andy is the black hole at the center of the galaxy Andromeda answered Bart.

"Well what does that mean?" asked Daniel.

"I will try to explain it to the human", answered Little. "And I will use small thoughts so maybe he can understand."

"Just stop being a smart ass and explain it to him", Patricia replied barely able to contain her irritation.

"Okay,"said Little. "I'll try".

"Daniel" he started. "You do realize that light is energy? And all life comes from energy." Little explained.

"Yeah so what?"

"Well in about 7 million years the Milky Way galaxy and the Andromeda galaxy will collide and the black holes of each will merge and give off light. That means the continued existence of the cosmos and all of us including my great grandchildren as you think of them. If Andy stops collecting light there will be no continuation of life, as we know it.

"Ok" Daniel replied, "How will that affect us?"

"Stop thinking like a human for a second and think of the overall picture," and exasperated Little explained.

"There is more at stake here than your existence."

"You need to have a talk with Andy" Bart explained.

"How do we do that", Daniel asked.

"O great" said Little, "I suppose all of this will all fall to me".

"Now think closely Daniel and I'll try to explain, plus I'll use small concepts so you can understand."

"Life is energy. It is created by the interaction of the cosmos. It is stored in black holes, till it is needed to start a new universe. Then the black holes come together and evaporate releasing the stored light and creating a new universe. It is really very simple."

"Well how do we talk to this Andy?" asked Daniel.

"We have to go see him," was Little's reply.

"If he's 7 million light years away that sounds impossible".

"Ever hear of astral projection?" asked Little.

"Yes but how does that relate to us?"

"How do you think we are communicating now?" an exasperated Little asked.

"But the time difference is massive," Daniel went on.

"Only because you think small. Wasn't it only recently that human's thought there were only 4 dimensions instead of the 11 that exist. Well, we will go to him by astral projection."

"I don't mean to rain on your parade Little, but that will be a little late by the time we get there. I mean 7 million light years takes a long time.

Little's exasperation was becoming obvious. "You still think the fastest thing in the universe is the speed of light."

"Well isn't it?" asked a confused Daniel.

"Look Dan. Thought makes the speed of light in your understanding, a turtle. We can go talk to him and be back by suppertime."

"Okay,"chirpped in Patricia, "Before we let you two take off. We need to talk to Sam."

"Who's Sam?" asked Daniel.

"Sam is the old oak out here." replied Bart. "He was old when I was just a sapling, and if anyone knows what to do it's him."

"Great," said Little.

"I don't know him," commented Daniel.

"That's because, he's a pain in the tail and never responds to conversations."

"Never the less," Patricia continued. "He has forgotten more than most of us will ever learn."

"Good point Pat," replied Bart. "Let me call him."

"Hey Sam."

"What!" came a loud cranky voice.

"Hi. This is Bart and we need your help."

"Did you forget how to drop your leaves in the fall? Is that Patricia with you? She doesn't need to drop anything she's an evergreen."

"No Sam. We need help to explain something to a human."

"Explain something to a human, that is the dumbest thing I've ever heard."

"Yeah, well maybe you just can't explain anything to anybody, human or otherwise," chirped in Little.

"Is that Little I hear". Boomed Sam "I can't communicate with him because I don't speak stupid."

"O Yeah,"cried Little. "Then just get someone else to bury your nuts next year."

"Okay. Everybody calm down. Sam the problem is with Andy. He's stopped collecting light and the human has agreed to try and talk to him and Little is going to help any way he can."

"Well shut little bushy butt up and I will try. I assume he can hear me in the alpha state.

So here's the situation. This has happened before. Last time was with Virgo. It was just a bad case of depression. Jim and I talked him out of it but it took about 50 years. I was much younger then but Jim was older with a lot of experience and wisdom. Experience and wisdom results in a higher level of intelligence. Something fuzzy butt wouldn't know about."

"O yeah!" yelled Little. "Well just kiss my bushy tail you old relic."

"That's enough Little," chided Bart.

"Same goes for you Sam. Both of you are being immature and we need to focus on the problem at hand."

"Sorry," said Sam.

"Me too," Little chirped in. "But nobody can get me going like he can."

"I apologize Little. It's sometimes too hard to pass up at my age. Maybe I'm just jealous of your youth."

"Apology accepted", Little said chastised. "Guess I can be a little irritating at times. It's just my inferiority complex from being so small, compared to you.

Well" said Sam, "Let's get started. Daniel, is it. Sit down in your chair. Little jump up into his lap and I will transport us all to Andy. Time will fold space, so it may seem like a long trip, but you will be back here in what passes for about an hour's time in this dimension, but longer when traveling. We will need to stop by the Orion Nebula to talk with the fire lords, so keep a stiff upper lip as you humans say and Little don't start complaining about the smell. The problem is simple to understand but harder to resolve. Andy probably feels unappreciated. He works for centuries and centuries, and most creatures that owe their existence to him don't even know he exists. How do you think that would make you feel?"

"Okay, I'm ready", Little declared.

"Me too" Daniel said unsure of what to expect but felt compelled to ask. "Sam, can you explain some of this to me".

"Sure" replied Sam, "Humans usually only think in 3 dimensions, but think if 3 blind men grab a lion. One grabs the tail and declares string theory explains it all. One grabs the lion's ear and says no, it is all flatland and two dimensions will answer any questions. The third grabs the lion's leg and says you are both wrong. The universe has 3 dimensions. Well they all are right, and wrong. Their observations are correct for what they experience, but they miss the total picture of the lion. Humans have recently come up with an M Theory to explain it. In my opinion the M stands for Magic. They try to explain everything in terms of the physical but ignore the essence of life. Ask a physicist what is light and they will argue for an hour about whether it is a particle or a wave. The only thing they agree on is that it is energy. Therein lies the complete answer. Life is what it's all about, and light is the source of life's energy. Understand?"

"I understand", said Little," but where do almonds fit in?"

"Look," stated an exasperated Sam. "The only one who even came close was Einstein. E=mc2, is the correct equation but most physicists miss the main point. Time is a perception. And once it is noticed, it slows down. and at that point, the energy becomes mass. Hence the universe is created." The discussion of dimensions is irrelevant. Just as is our travel across the galaxy, so here we go."

Daniel felt a slight disorientation and was soon looking at the Orion Nebula.

"Nebulas are the greatest source of light in the universe," explained Sam, "and therefore life. For this part of the galaxy the Orion Nebula, is where the fire lords live and our first stop."

Daniel marveled at the colors in the Nebula and was dumbstruck when it spoke to them. "Hello Sam. Long time no see. Who are your friends?"

"Just a couple of dreamers on a fools mission." Replied Sam.

"Anything we need to worry about?" questioned the fire lord.

"No just Andy's stop collecting light and the known universe will end".

"Okay" came the slow reply "Let us know if we can help."

"Well we would like some advice on how to change his mind.," replied Sam. "After all you did create him for the purpose of continuing the existence of life.

"Sure no sweat. Just offer him something to show he's appreciated."

"Great", said Little, " A neurotic black hole with an inferiority complex."

"Be quiet Little and listen," scolded Daniel.

"Okay,"said Sam. "Thanks for the tip we will think of something."

"You call that a tip?" Screeched Little. "I could have gotten that from a fortune nut."

"Hey, it's a starting point," offered Daniel.

"Well I think that it was a total waste of time," Little complained.

Daniel grinned and replied," As Donald Sutherland said in the movie Kelly's Heroes. Just stop with the negative waves."

"That's the answer!" shouted Little. "He's just lost a couple of protons and is feeling a little negative."

Sam groaned. "That has got to be the oldest joke in the cosmos.

Suddenly they were facing the Black Hole but did not feel the gravity pulling them in.

"Hello" Sam called. "Andy you home."

"Who wants to know?" came the sullen reply.

"It's just Sam with a couple of earth creatures," he explained.

"Go away," mumbled Andy.

"Come on Andy. We've come a long way to talk to you."

"Yeah, and I skipped breakfast," complained Little

"Well forbid I caused any such creature, so small and fat, to miss a meal. What do you want?"

"We heard the you had stopped collecting light." Daniel explained. "And we wanted to know why?"

"No one cares anymore so why bother."

"I care and so do my friends. We need you." Daniel pleaded.

"Why," Andy's question boomed.

"Without you life and the universe would cease to exist."

"And why should I care?" came the sullen question.

"Because it is the reason you exist, for one thing" Daniel reasoned.

Andy asked "Why should you care if I exist or not,"

"Because that is what life is about for us. And only you can make that happen. No one else can do it."

"And why should I believe you. Mr. Carbon Based Biped."

"Because I will forgo waiting. To kick start your gravity fields again, and to save this universe I will come into the light right now," Declared Daniel.

"You're joking." Said Andy incredulously.

"I will forgo the fire lords learning curve, and go right now." Daniel stated.

"That is some sacrifice you are proposing," said Andy, his respect growing.

"Not really," explained Daniel. "If it will start you up again I will just go now. I won't have that chance later if you stop forever."

"Good logic my friend. Hadn't really thought of it that way," reasoned Andy.

"Okay," I'll restart. But only because of your willingness to make such a sacrifice, and start now instead of several million years later if at all.

"Glad we got that settled." Daniel replied relieved.

Soon he felt the gravity pull start up again as he, Sam and Little retreated.

He soon found himself back in his chair sitting in the sun with Little on his lap.

"Well that was refreshing" Daniel quipped.

"I'm glad you enjoyed saving the universe," Little stated. "Myself, I was scared to death. Plus I missed my breakfast."

"Don't worry," Daniel said seriously. "Long as I'm around you won't go hungry. And Sam, it was nice to meet you and I hope we can talk more sometime."

"Be more than happy to accommodate you human," replied the Oak.

"And Little, if you will get the hell off my lap I will get the almonds."

"It's about time," complained the little squirrel. "Saving the universe has left me starving."

Exercise Bike

Daniel woke with the rising sun. He made his way to the living room and began his workout for the day. As he sat on the exercise bike he noticed his little friend at the sliding glass door looking in. When finished he went out the glass door onto the back patio.

"Good morning Little," he said to his friend the squirrel.

"And a fine morning it is",replied Little.

"Hello Daniel," Boomed Bartholomew, the tall elm tree. "You look chipper this morning."

"Hello Bart," mumbled Daniel. "And hello to you too Patricia. A fine good morning it is and you are looking good in the morning mist."

"It is really great to get a full day's drink and let the mist dress you up to look pretty," Patricia replied.

"Well what's happening today to get you all up so early and for Little to be peering into my living room."

Little shook his head. "You know Daniel we've all been watching you and are kinda worried. We see you working out every day, pedaling to nowhere and don't understand why. We all have seen the bicycle invention with people pedaling to go somewhere, but you don't go anywhere."

"I believe it's man's inferiority complex kicking in," Daniel explained. "We are slow, clumsy, with no fur and no claws, so we invent things to make us feel better."

Little thought for a minute, then expounded. "You invent the wheel, put it on a frame so you can travel faster, then remove the wheels so you can put it in your cave and pedal madly going nowhere. Is that about it?"

"You got it Little" Daniel answered.

"Well cut off my tail and call me a gerbil," Little said sarcastically. "If that isn't the dumbest thing I've ever heard, then it's solidly the second dumbest thing."

"Well," said Daniel patiently. "It's just a way to improve my health and keep my blood pressure in check."

"Bart . Patricia," asked Little. "Do you guys worry about high sap pressure?"

"No Little," replied Bart. "We don't. If we get bigger our sap pressure increases to compensate. Humans think one measurement applies to everyone regardless of their age or size, and judge themselves accordingly. Ironic thing is, that worrying about high blood pressure is what gives most humans high blood pressure."

"Great." Moaned Little. "Another thing I have to worry about. Daniel's blood pressure goes up, he explodes and I starve."

"Relax Little." Daniel explained. " I won't explode. Worst thing that could happen is that I have a heart attack, and I have already had one of those before. So, as Sam called you, fuzzy butt, don't get in a jerk. I'm not going anywhere."

"Well that's a relief off my mind," said a relieved Little. "Like I don't have enough to worry about just getting my daily almonds. So come on out here, sit in your chair and take a nap. Napping is one of the most underrated activities in the world today."

"Little," Daniel said sadly. "I don't know how to tell you this, but napping is not an activity."

"Well kiss my furry tail," exclaimed Little. "You learn something new every day."

"Little," said Patricia. With her irritation showing. "Just climb up here, eat your almonds, shut up and let Daniel take a nap."

Soon the sun came over the horizon and found Daniel sleeping sweetly in his chair surrounded by his three friends.

Baseball

As Daniel made his way out to the patio Wednesday he was greeted by his three friends. Bart the large old elm tree, Patricia the young voluptuous pine, and Little One his friendly but sometimes maddening squirrel.

"Well folks," he greeted them. "What's on your minds today."

"Well," intoned Little. "We were watching you and your mate last night. You were watching that box with pictures of other humans on it."

"It's called a television," explained Daniel.

"We don't understand it," Bart asked puzzled. "They seemed to be angry at something because they kept throwing rocks at each other and swinging limbs at the rocks. Help us out here and explain what that was all about."

"It's called baseball," Daniel expounded, "It's a game humans play".

"You mean like tag?" Chirped in Little. "Me and my friends play that all the time."

"Not exactly", continued Daniel. "The game is played by professionals."

Little scratched his head. "You mean you watch a game, but do not play? That doesn't make any sense."

"We pay them to play," Daniel went on.

"What is pay?" asked Little.

"It's like a reward, so they can earn a living," said Daniel.

"Wait a minute," Little asked exasprated. "You give them rewards to play, but do not play yourselves?"

"That's the way it works," Daniel went on explaining to Little.

"And Bart they are not rocks. They are called balls and the limbs are called bats. There are numerous rules about how to play and these humans are the best at doing it, is why we pay them."

"Wait a minute," Little questioned. "You pay them to play a game cause you don't want to play?"

"No," Daniel went on patiently. "We all would like to play but they are the best at it."

"Well. Well. Well."Exclaimed a frustrated Little. "We are back to the list of dumb human activities."

"My friends and I get rewards for playing tag," Little went on.

"Really" asked Daniel "And what is the reward you get?"

"It is called fun, dummy."

"Okay Little. You are missing the point. We pay them because they train to play and we would like to but don't have the time to train."

"You don't have the time to have fun?" asked a confused Little.

"We just enjoy watching them do it." An exasperated Daniel went on.

"Okay, so you enjoy watching them play. You don't play yourself and the players are what you call professionals."

"Now you got it Little".

"Well actually I don't get it, but if it makes you happy. Then TAG you're it."

The Most Important Thing

Daniel went out for his morning communion with Mother Nature and there awaiting him was his three friends. Bartholomew the stately elm, Patricia the young lovely Pine and Little One, the bushy tailed squirrel.

"Good Morning you guys," he greeted them.

Hello came back the chorus of replies.

"Why all the serious long leaves and twitching tail?" he asked.

"We were just discussing the most important thing in life, each of us feels," projected Bart.

"I tried to tell them," complained Little "But they have their own ideas and surprise, surprise. No one listens to me."

"And what did you tell them?" questioned Daniel.

"Just that almonds were the most important thing in life," quipped the squirrel.

"Little," said an irritated Patricia. "You are really such a pain in the bark. To me it is the rain. It cleanses the air, it gives water, coolness in the summer and nourishment all year long."

"How about you Bart?" Daniel asked.

"To me it's the changing of the seasons. The fall discarding of the old leaves, the winter a time of rest, spring the birth of new growth, and summer the warmth of a full growing season."

"And you Daniel," projected Bart in a serious tone. "We all want to hear what a human thinks of as the most important thing in life."

"Well" Daniel started. "First thing you must understand is that every human probably thinks something different. For me honor and integrity are a must for a human. Without them, power and wealth, are a meaningless waste of time. But if pressed. I would have to say the most important thing in life is true love."

"Yeah", responded Little. "A bushy tail will fire me up in a heartbeat. I bet it even gets old Bart's sap flowing."

"I don't think that is what he means Little," intoned Bart.

"Right you are Bart." Said Daniel seriously. "True love is not about passion my little friend. It is a pure emotion and one that gives comfort and security."

"What could give more comfort and security than a bunch of almonds," Little asked.

"No he's right Little," said Patricia in a somber tone. "Don't get me wrong. I love when the pollen turns my needles yellow, but true love gives it all meaning."

"Very insightful Pat," Daniel replied. "Unfortunately many creatures can't see the subtle difference and separate the two."

"Thank you for sharing that Daniel." Complimented Bart. "I think that maybe creatures of this world are not so different after all."

A Day of Rest

Daniel went outside early Saturday morning to speak to his friends. The sun had just broken the horizon.

"Good Morning Bartholomew. Good Morning Patricia." He greeted them. "Where's Little?"

"And a good morning to you Daniel." responded Bart. "Little's just off scurrying around. He'll be back soon. What have you got planned for this glorious day?"

"Well remember how I explained how humans kept track of time with labels. Today is Saturday. My wife does not have to work on Saturdays or Sundays so we can be together all day and relax."

"Patricia and I have often talked about you and your mate. Few humans are so connected to each other." Bart went on.

"Yes we were fortunate to meet each other and we blended well together. It was just luck and we don't even have to work at it. Us being together just comes naturally." Daniel explained with a far away look in his eye.

"Yes I agree," injected Patricia. "You both are very lucky."

"Did I hear lucky?" came the small squirrel voice. "Must be time for breakfast almonds."

"Hello Little," replied Daniel "And a good morning, and yes I brought your almonds."

"So as you were saying, before we were interrupted by the starving Little?" questioned Patricia.

"Remember when I explained baseball?" Daniel asked.

"Yes we do."

"Well today is the first day of the World Series." He went on.

"What?" screeched Little. "You mean there is more than one world. And you keep track in a series of them?"

"No Little," Daniel continued, "It's just a name. When the two best teams at the end of the year play each other."

"Okay, But why is it so special," asked a confused Little.

"Because it will be on television and we can watch it. Even though the teams are far far away." said an excited Daniel.

"Is that when you stretch out on the sofa to watch the game?" Little inquired.

"Yes it is."

"Now that is when I first thought of you as special," Little quipped. "You keep track of what's happening on the television without even watching it."

"What are you talking about?" Daniel asked.

"I have watched you. You close your eyes. To be able to see through you eyelids is a special trick. Almost magical." Little said reverently.

"No Little, my eyes closed meant I was asleep. Remember me telling you about sleep?" a frustrated Daniel responded.

"Then how do you know what's going on?" Little asked.

"I ask my wife." interjected an irritated Daniel.

"Now that seems dumb."

"Shut up Little" Patricia almost yelled "You don't understand. So Daniel who's playing to get you so excited?"

"Well the Houston Astros are playing for the first time in the series. Houston is where my wife's father and mother live. And by the way we are going to visit them in about two weeks." Answered Daniel.

"That's a long way to go," Bart stated.

"I know," Daniel said miserably. "We are going to fly."

"I have talked to many of my bird friends and they are impressed by your airplanes," Bart stated.

"Well they say it's the safest way to travel, but I don't know." continued Daniel.

"What can you think of that's fastest or safer?" Little quipped.

"Well a safer way to travel would be walking," responded Daniel.

"Okay, you may be right but that's a long walk and I would probably starve by the time you got back." Lamented Little.

"So who are your wife's mother and father," said Bart adroitly changing the subject.

"Her parents are Tom and Leslie, they live in Houston. They have a big Arizona Ash, that I plan on talking to, in their back yard surrounded by a wooden deck." Daniel went on.

"Do they have a small dog named Foxie?"Questioned Patricia.

"Yes" Daniel answered, "In fact they do."

"Yikes they have a pet fox?" Little moaned.

"No Little. It's a dog and her nickname is Foxie." Daniel explained.

"Well a nickname is descripitive,"Little went on. "Just like I call you no tail."

"And Sam called you fuzzy butt." Daniel rejoindered.

"Not funny Dan." Little paled. "I can't help it."

"Okay you two." Bart growled. "Just stop it. Daniel I know this place. And the tree's name is George."

"And I must say he's a hunk." Patricia quivered.

"How could you know him?" asked a puzzled Daniel.

"When will you understand?" Went on a patient Bartholomew. "Every flower, every tree, every animal is part of this planet. We are all part of Mother Nature. Only humans, can't seem to tap into the collective consciousness.

We don't have to work at it, we just know each other and sometimes we talk. Be sure and tell George hello for me."

"And tell him I said Hello too,"Patricia pleaded. Her pine needles actually quivering.

"I certainly will Bart. And I'll give him your best Patricia." Daniel promised.

"Now I must go inside, eat my breakfast and get ready for the game." Daniel pronounced.

"Eat some almonds for me," chipped in Little. "And best of luck to those Astros."

Hurricanes

"Hey Daniel," announced Patricia. "Why the angry look on your face this morning?"

"Sorry Patricia," explained Daniel. "I was just watching the news on television."

"And what did you see to upset you so?" She continued.

"Hurricanes in Florida." Came the reply.

"Why would that make you angry," inquired a puzzled Bartholomew.

"It's just the way humans deal with the problem," answered Daniel barely able to control his temper.

"But hurricanes are a natural event," Bartholomew went on.

"Well if you listen to the news broadcast, it's like the end of the world." Daniel continued. " They act like they have never seen one before and there is nothing they can do."

"Would you mind expounding on that statement," Patricia inquired.

"Sure Patricia," Daniel stated. "Back in the 1930s the people in charge required houses be built to a higher standard. Built to withstand such forces. Now they just tell the people to evacuate until it's over. Never giving a thought to how much it cost in panic and pain not to mention money."

"Wow!" exclaimed Little. "Another dumb human idea."

"They tell the people it is mandatory and to survive they must leave their homes. Then they allow the meteorologist from the weather channel to come in to cover the hurricane event."

"Why?" Little could barely contain himself.

"It's to boost their ratings. Twenty four hours a day coverage." Daniel explained. "To make more money for them."

"Are we back to the list of dumb human activities?" asked Little.

"Weather is not that exciting." Chimed in Bart.

"It is if there is a possibility of losing their homes."

"Then why don't they raise the standards for building a house?" came Bart's logical question.

"Because that would cost too much and make the leaders unpopular and therefore they would not be elected again," Daniel said.

"But the cost after a hurricane's destruction of a badly built home would be more." Protested Bart.

"Well that would take looking at the long run," Daniel explained. "Not something they are used to doing."

"I have a solution," quipped Little.

"And what is that Little?"

"Plant more almonds," came the reply.

"Oh No," moaned Daniel.

"I have many friends in Florida," Bart said. "They accept hurricanes as a part of life and something that must be dealt with."

"I guess my objection comes from the way they try and scare people." Daniel went on. "They try and make them feel stupid and unable to think for themselves. If someone doesn't evacuate and something bad happens, the coverage is merciless. The people who don't evacuate and survive just fine don't make the news."

"Well Daniel," Bart philosophized, "It's almost four thousand miles away and there is nothing you can do about it.

"Plus there is a more serious issue here," intoned a serious Little.

"And what pray tell is that." Questioned Daniel.

"Breakfast almonds," responded Little. "I'm starving."

World Series

"Good Morning Daniel," greeted Patricia. "Why the long face this morning?"

"Houston lost the world series." Daniel replied.

"How sad for you and your wife's parents." Bartholomew joined in. "Any reason why?"

"Simple," retorted Little. "They didn't eat enough almonds."

"No," Daniel responded. "They just didn't get any breaks and played somewhat poorly."

"I'm telling you it was lack of almonds." Countered Little.

"Okay, Okay," An exasperated Daniel exclaimed.

"So who won?" a sympathetic Patricia asked.

"The Chicago White Sox." Came the answer. "They haven't won a world series in 88 years, so I guess it was good news for them." He explained further.

"Well just come on out here and sit awhile with us," Bart intoned, "We will try and cheer you up and if we can't we can just dance. That always seems to help."

"Thanks Bart, I feel the need for some cheering up."

"I think it's a dumb human game anyway." Little chirped in. "No one gets to be it and the only rewards are money."

"Not really, Little." Daniel responded. "The rewards are a feeling of accomplishment of doing a good job for an entire year."

"Pardon me if I'm wrong." Came Bart's serious tone. "But didn't they come in second, and beat all the other teams that played during the year, just to make the series?"

"Yes Bart." Daniel went on. "But for humans, second place is a let down from the expectations of winning."

"See?" quipped Little. "Another of those dumb human ideas."

"Little." A serious Daniel agreed. "It may be dumb but it is the reason humans have ever accomplished anything. They simply will not tolerate second place when they had a chance to win."

"Well maybe you could just tell them to dance with the trees. That should help." Patricia suggested.

"I can't." Daniel replied. "They would think I was crazy."

"Just because they can't talk to us doesn't mean they can't enjoy Mother Nature's music and dance awhile to feel better." Patricia reasoned.

"Well, I'll suggest it to them, but I'm not sure of their response." Came his reply.

"Then tell them to just eat some almonds." Little suggested. "That will help any creature to be in a good mood and they can't help but feel better."

"Irrefutable logic again, Little." An exasperated Daniel said. "Is everything so simple for you."

"Of course it is." The little squirrel replied. "It's only when the world uses dumb human reasoning, that the world is in trouble."

Houston

"George," called Daniel, as he walked out onto the deck of his wife's parent's house.

"Hello Dan." Boomed the large Arizona Ash. "I've been expecting you. Bartholomew contacted me and told me to expect a surprise. I didn't know he meant communicating with a human."

"I've only just recently learned projection and to communicate," Daniel explained. "Bartholomew and Patricia live next to me and they were the first and only ones I've been in contact with. We dance together a lot."

"Well, dancing is a great way to start and Bartholomew is a good dancer. Patricia is better, but that is only my opinion" George went on. "What do the old elm and young pine talk about?"

"They ask questions about humans. I explain as much as I can of how humans think." Daniel expounded. "And to be honest, most of the time they are puzzled with the explanations but are patient and we get along just fine."

"I am glad for them and somewhat envy them." George said sounding happy." Do you know their friend the squirrel?"

"Yes." Answered Daniel. "I call him Little One. Or just Little for short. I hear you have a friend too. She's called Foxie."

"The squirrel has cousins here and I do know Foxie." Retorted the big Ash. "Which raises a human concept I don't grasp. As long as you're here maybe you can help me understand."

"Be happy to help if I can and it will keep me in practice." Came Daniel's reply.

"Why do humans say they have a pet? That is the term, I believe, and they sound as if they own them." Asked a puzzled George.

"Humans feel the need to be in control of everything, and that they provide for their pets for the things the pet cannot otherwise acquire." Came the explanation.

"That's just dumb. Foxie takes care of Tom and Leslie and gives them comfort and happiness which is more important than food and shelter." George went on.

"True enough," said Daniel. "But, doesn't Foxie play along to give them the joy of feeling needed?"

"Yes that's true." Intoned a serious George. "And it explains Foxie's actions.

"You would love Little, he calls most ideas of humans dumb." Daniel expounded.

"They may be dumb but of all the creatures of this world their hearts are in the right place."Reasoned a thoughtful George.

"So that's about all there is to it George." Daniel finished.

"Well thank you for clearing that up for Me." said George. "Bartholomew and Patricia are very lucky to have you."

"Glad to be of help and by the way Patricia said to give you her best." Daniel said smiling.

"I'm too old for her best, but it's a nice thought. Take care going home and do give my best to them." George went on. "And if I remember Little correctly, give him some almonds. He really loves them."

Coming Home

"Hello everybody," called Daniel. "I'm back."

"Welcome home Daniel." Greeted Bartholomew. "How was Houston?"

"It was a great trip and we had fun." Daniel answered. "It was great to see my wife's parents. It has been too long a time gone by."

"How was George?" inquired Patricia.

"He was doing well. We had some interesting talks and by the way he said to give his best to you."

Patricia needles quivered and Daniel didn't think it was just the wind.

"He told me Bartholomew and he were old friends and he would probably be contacting you in the future to talk." Daniel informed Bartholomew.

"You're late." complained Little. "I'm starving."

"But I left out a supply of almonds for four days." Daniel defended himself. "You didn't eat them all the first day, did you?"

"Yes he did." Bart said.

"Hey," Little began his defense. "I didn't want some possum to get them."

"Yes, I understand." Daniel asked. "What else is new?"

"Fall is progressing nicely," Bartholomew intoned. "Shedding the old leaves for my winter's rest."

"Myself," added Patricia "I'm just moving my sap to the roots in case we have some hard freezes."

"I'm putting on extra fur." chimed in Little. "And putting on some extra fat. Just to help keep me warm, you understand."

"Well I missed you all and it's good to be home." Daniel said sincerely.

"We missed you too." Bartholomew said. "Nothing big happened while you were away."

"Except I almost starved," Little chirped.

"Little you look as fat as when I left, if not fatter." Daniel rejoinered.

"There was one small problem." Bartholomew went on.

"And what was that?" Daniel questioned.

"We couldn't resolve the feeling of loneliness we all felt not having you to talk to."

"Yeah. Great. Another dumb human emotion." Little lamented.

"When you get used to something, it becomes a routine, and you never miss it till it's gone." Daniel explained.

"Maybe that was all it was." Patricia went on. "But it was uncomfortable."

"Have you ever had anyone go away before?" questioned Daniel.

"No." answered Patricia. "We tried to contact you but were unsuccessful. It caused us to worry that something had happened to you."

"Well with the stress of the airplane ride and visiting with my wife's parents, I just didn't have the time or the alpha state of mind I needed. I am still new at this and not as proficient as all of you." Daniel apologized.

"Not to worry, Daniel." Bartholomew answered in a serious tone. "You are back now and we can resume our daily talks."

"Yeah," Little chimed in. "And I won't have to worry about starving."

Halloween

"Top of the morning to you Daniel." Greeted Bartholomew, the stately elm, as Daniel made his way out onto his back patio.

"And a fine morning it is." answered Daniel.

"Hi Dan," said Patricia, the voluptuous young pine.

"Hello Pat, you are looking especially lovely this morning."

"Hello, Hi, Good morning." came Little's projection. "Did you bring my almonds?"

"Yes I did my little friend." Daniel offered.

"Daniel we have another question we need to ask and have you explain about humans." Bartholomew inquired.

"Sure," Daniel quipped. "Ask away. I'd love to help."

"We really appreciate your patience my friend," the elm went on seriously. "We have noticed that around this time of the year humans put large orange gourds out in front of their caves, with holes cut in them to mimic distorted human faces."

"It's called Halloween. It's a holiday held on the last day of October every year."

"Well what does that entail?" prompted a curious Patricia.

"On the last day of October, children go around their neighborhoods dressed in scary costumes knocking on peoples doors. The gourds, or pumpkins as we call them, indicate to the children who is participating in the festivities. When the people answer the door the children yell "Trick or Treat."

"And to what purpose is this done?" inquired a puzzled Bartholomew.

"If you don't give the children free candy they will play a trick on you," Daniel explained.

"What is candy?" Patricia asked.

"It usually consists of something that tastes sweet."

"Like almonds." Little chimed in.

"No Little. The sweets are usually made from sugar. They taste good, but are usually not very healthy for the children," Daniel went on.

"Do these children have parents?" Little inquired.

"Yes. It's a holiday so certain concerns are ignored for the day," expounded the patient human.

"Okay," Little went on. "Let me see if I've got this straight. Human children dress up in scary costumes, so no one will recognize them. Then they go from cave to cave scaring the humans living there and and threatening them with "Trick or Treat" to extort free candy from them. Which from what you say is not healthy yet their parents approve this activity. Is that about it?"

"You got it." Daniel agreed.

"Okay I understand." Little responded.

"Me too," Patricia joined in. "It sounds like fun."

"How about you Bart, you understand?" Daniel asked.

"Yes,"Bartholmew answered. "Now I understand.Thank you."

"Two more questions, if I may Daniel." Came Little's concerned voice.

"Any thing to explain and make you happy my friend."

"First question. Is there any end to the list of dumb human ideas?" Little asked.

"Second. Are you familiar with jokes?"

"Of course." Daniel expounded.

"We have heard human children communicating a type of joke called a Knock Knock joke. Are you familiar with that type of joke?" Little continued.

"Yes," came the exasperated reply. "It's usually a dumb joke done by children."

"Well.Knock Knock." Asked little.

"Who's there?" came back Daniel's question.

"Trick or Treat." squeaked the small squirrel.

Daylight Saving Time

"You're late," scowled Little as he greeted Daniel coming out onto his back patio.

"Well, today we changed over from daylight savings time so I got an extra hour of sleep." Daniel explained.

"Is this one of those human time things?" asked Bartholomew.

"Yes it is Bart," Daniel answered.

"We don't understand humans perception of time and how you track it." Bartholomew went on puzzled.

"There are sixty seconds in a minute, sixty minutes in an hour and twenty-four hours in a day." Daniel expounded.

"Is that what you call time?" Patricia chimed in.

"Yes, Pat, we humans have clocks to keep time to let us know precisely what time it is each day. We have clocks on the wall of our homes and watches on our wrist so we can know the exact time of the day it is." came the explanation.

"Seems a bit overdone." Bartholomew observed.

"It lets us know when to get up, when to eat and when to go to work." Daniel said patiently.

"Then what is this daylight savings time." Little quipped.

"We move our clock ahead each spring and back each fall, so we can have an extra hour each day." Daniel went on. "It gives us an extra hour of sun during the summer."

"What is the purpose of that?" inquired Bartholomew.

"We plan everything we do. Daylight saving time allowed farmers to have an extra hour to get their products to market before the people buying those products arrive." Daniel explained.

"Sorry Daniel." Little chirped in. "You are not a farmer. You seem to have trouble growing hair."

"Every human goes by the same clock so all our activities are coordinated." Daniel extended his explanation.

"Still seems a bit overdone.' Bartholomew went on. "A day is a day no matter how you keep tract of it."

"Never the less." Daniel countered. "We get to plan our days with the knowledge that everyone is on the same schedule."

"But you don't really have an extra hour. It's all just an illusion." Patricia inquired.

"True Patricia. But it makes us feel we are in control of something." Said Daniel philosophically.

"Okay. I guess that explains it. Seems a bit too precise for me, my day is a day and not counted by some abstract measurement." Bartholomew offered.

"Think of it, as Little says, as another dumb human idea." Daniel proposed.

"All I know is one thing." Little said.

"And what is that, pray tell." Daniel questioned.

"You're late." Little scowled again. "I'm starving out here."

Smoking

"Morning no tail." The small squirrel's projection greeted Daniel as he walked out onto his back patio.

"Good Morning Little." Daniel returned.

"And a good morning to you, Daniel," acknowledged the big elm.

"It is in fact a glorious morning," piped in Patricia, the young voluptuous pine.

"Anything on your consciousness this morning?" Question the retired civil servant.

"Well now that you asked." Bart answered, "We do have something we would like explained," he went on.

"Yeah,"Patricia continued for him. "Why, when you come out here first thing in the morning, do you put a weed in your mouth and light it on fire? Bart and I don't object you understand? But fire makes us both kind of nervous."

"It's called smoking," Daniel explained. "Humans do it to ingest nicotine into their systems. It is a drug that relaxes us."

"I understand the drug but not the smoke." Bartholomew went on philosophically. "That can't be a healthy activity for a human."

"I didn't say it was healthy Bart. I said it relaxes us." Daniel expounded.

"Then why do it?" Patricia inquired puzzled.

"It's called an addiction. That is an activity that is very hard to stop, no matter the consequences."

"And the list of dumb human ideas goes on and on." Mumbled Little.

"If it is so unhealthy." Reasoned Bartholomew. "Why don't the leaders of the humans make it unavailable to the help stop the addiction? You do have things called laws to prohibit some activities, don't you?"

"Well, Bartholomew," Daniel went on. "The leaders make a lot of money off selling the cigarettes, that's what we call them, and they don't want to give that up. It pays for a lot of services for the humans."

"Don't they care about the individual humans?" Questioned an incredulous Patricia.

"No," Daniel extended his explanation. " If they can get a few humans to pay for the services of all by the addiction then they are satisfied. They know a certain number of humans will never stop smoking and they can charge whatever price they want. Look at the automobile. It pollutes the air for all, but they allow it. It is much worst for humans than cigarettes."

"Personally I think they stink. I like the smell of almonds," Little quipped. "If almonds are an addiction then I understand your problem."

Thanksgiving

"Good Morning Daniel." Greeted Bartholomew. "Did you have a restful night?"

"In fact I did." Daniel rejoinered. "But I did have some troubling thoughts, and thought you and Patricia might be able to help me."

"That would please us greatly." Intoned the old elm. "What would you like to know?"

"Well the humans have a holiday coming up. Its called Thanksgiving. It's the day when the Europeans came to America and celebrated a meal with the Native Americans." Daniel expounded.

"He means the Day of Mourning." Patricia said.

"Yes, my dear young one, I believe you are right." Bart mournfully replied.

"What do you mean? Day of Mourning." Daniel asked puzzled.

"It is the day we mark, as the day they became infected." Bartholomew went on.

"In what way do you mean?"

"I'm not sure which term to use." Bart said uncertainly. "Infected or addicted. Anyway it was when they began to stress individuality. Up to that day they had made some progress into becoming part of the overall consciousness of the planet."

"But all humans are individuals," protested Daniel.

"Not true," Patricia answered, "Look at you and your wife. You are married and suppressed your individuality for the union of a better existence. It took a long time but you finally realized that the union was better for joy and comfort in the long run."

"All creatures of the existence understand that?" Questioned Daniel.

"Yes." Bart replied. "Even Little shares his almonds." "How?"

"Do you ever see me burying the almonds?" Little quipped.

"Me and most humans assume you do so to have something to eat later," came Daniels explanation. "Then just forgot where you buried them."

"That's insulting." Little responded annoyed. " I bury them so the bacteria brothers can break them down for food for the trees and replenish their food source."

"So let me get this straight," Daniel went on. "Every thing is done for the overall consciousness."

"Yes Daniel," Bartholomew explained. "Part of the learning curve the Fire Lords set up was for all creatures to understand everything is related. Do you think the trees could not protest being cut down and overwhelm your consciousness and destroy you?" Bartholomew questioned sarcastically.

"Hadn't really thought of it that way Bart." Daniel answered.

"The Fire Lords set this up as a way for all creatures to benefit from their existence and to enable them to come into the light at the time when they are finished with their carbon based life form." Bart answered patiently.

"So death is not the end." Daniel asked questioning.

"Humans think it is." Patricia explained. "They even hunt other creatures and kill their carbon based life forms prematurely. I don't know why but they call it sport. I don't understand the term."

"So what happened to me?"Queried the retired civil servant.

"Not really sure," answered Bartholomew smiling. "But we rejoiced when you made contact. It means there may be hope for humans after all."

"If we can realize the consciousness of everything we may have a place in the light," Daniel asked hopefully.

"Hey," quipped Little. "Even I have enough sense to share my almonds."

Smart and Dumb

"Good morning everybody," greeted a smiling Daniel.

"And a good morning to you Daniel." Bartholomew responded. "Fall is here in full swing and I notice you seem to be rising later and later each day with the rising sun."

"And, if I might add," quipped Little. "Making me wait longer and longer for my breakfast almonds."

"Sorry about that Little," Daniel said. "But I feel great this morning."

"Why is that?' Patricia inquired.

"I went to a new doctor this week and she is doing wonders to improve my health." Came Daniel's reply.

"She is so smart."

"Smart and dumb, are but human ideas." Bart retorted.

"No." Daniel replied. "That is a fact. Some people are smart and some people are dumb."

"Well," responded Little. "At last we agree on something. Human ideas are dumb."

"Stop it Little," an annoyed Patricia responded. "Bartholomew explain it to him."

"Daniel smart and dumb are but misinterpreted human concepts," Bartholomew expounded." All humans with the few abnormal exceptions have the same brain. It's what you put into it that gives you the illusion of smart and dumb."

"What are you talking about?" Quailed Daniel.

"All human brains pretty much have the same capacity for thought." Bart explained patiently. "Only the chemicals you use to make them work differs. The foods you eat have different chemicals in them and affect your ability to think."

"Example please." Queried Daniel.

"You have a drug called alcohol, right?" Bart continued. "Have you ever ingested to much of it?"

Daniel smiled. "Yes it's being called drunk."

"And did it make you dumb?" Questioned the old elm.

"Yes." came Daniels reply.

"Permanently?" Bart asked.

"No. Just while it was in my system." Daniel conceded.

"Well some drugs you ingest make you smart, as you think of it, and some drugs make you dumb. Some impair your brains so much that people have committed suicide because of it. They are not to blame they just didn't understand. Some humans have more knowledge than others. That does not make them smarter or dumber." Bart went on.

"Wait." Daniel stopped him. "I remember a study in Canada, done about 50 years ago about heroin addicts. Some were recovered and some still addicted. Their IQ was on the average about 40 points higher after the drug."

"That was because the drug opened doorways or paths to different thought processes. It didn't make them smarter." Bartholomew continued patiently. "They still had the same brain. As did you when you were no longer drunk."

"So why do humans think in terms of smart or dumb?" came the question.

"Humans just misinterpret the store of fact or knowledge as intelligence or as you put it being smart. It's really very simple." Bartholomew went on.

"So, you're telling me, most all humans have the same brain capacity." Daniel reasoned. "It's just what chemicals we employ to use that capacity."

"You got it." Answered a relieved Bartholomew.

"What about you and Patricia." Daniel asked.

"We passed that misconception years ago and moved on." Came Bart's reply.

"And what about Little?"

"He just believes almonds make his thought capacity greater than for any of us." Patricia rejoinered.

"Hey," quipped Little. "That is just a fact, plus they taste good."

Retired

"Good morning," greeted Daniel as he walked out onto his back patio. "Everyone awake?"

Bartholomew replied, "Patricia and I are always awake Daniel. We don't do what you refer to as sleep until winter. Then we transfer our sap to our roots for safekeeping and rest until spring. As for Little I don't know. I haven't seen him around this morning."

"I'm down here by the pond, no tail." quipped the little squirrel. "Washing my face and paws, waiting for you to bring out my breakfast almonds, and trying not to starve till you made it out."

"Hey little fuzzy butt. As Sam called you, I'm retired so I sleep later than my mate. I have no need to wake up early." Answered the retired human.

"Speaking of that Daniel, what does the phrase being retired mean?" questioned Patricia.

"Well, when a human works all of their life, they save up enough money so they no longer have to work to make money to buy things." Daniel explained.

"What things do you buy?" asked a puzzled Bartholomew.

"Mostly food, shelter and labor saving devices." He went on explaining to the old elm.

"Labor saving devices?" Questioned Little. "Like what?"

"Dishwashing machines, vacuum cleaners, microwave ovens to save time cooking our food." Daniel expounded.

"You work, to make money to buy food?" Inquired Little.

"Yes." said Daniel.

"And to save time you work to buy labor saving devices to save time?"

"Yes," Daniel explained patiently.

"I give up!" said Little exasperated.

"It doesn't make a lot of sense." Patricia said. "Mother Earth gives food to humans. It grows everywhere and you don't have to work for it except to gather it."

"We have others gather it for us, prepare it for storage and then pay them to provide it to us when we need it." Daniel went on. "It makes for a convenient system for humans and we don't have to worry about having food when we need it."

"Like me having to wait for breakfast." Little put in.

"Exactly." Daniel answered proudly. "You got it."

"So you no longer have to work to make money?" Questioned Little. "And you buy labor saving devices to save time. Okay, then why is my breakfast late?"

Writing

"Good morning Bartholomew," said Daniel. "Good morning Patricia."

"Hello Daniel," Patricia answered.

"And a fine morning to you," Bartholomew joined in. "You are a constant mystery to me and Patricia with your puzzling human activities."

"Okay," Daniel replied. "What did I do now?"

"We observed you in the middle of the night and were puzzled." Bartholomew explained. "You were watching the small television and moving your hands rapidly. We know you were not asleep, as you call it, because your eyelids were open."

"That was the computer not the television." Daniel responded. "I was typing."

"For what purpose?"Quiered the elm.

"When I can't sleep at night, I sometimes get up and write. I've told you before about human writing." Daniel rejoindered.

"And what do you write?" asked a curious Patricia.

"Poetry mainly. I've published a poetry book called Eclectics and am working on another." came the reply.

"What is poetry?" questioned Patricia.

"It's human thoughts and emotions put into words that rhyme and flow, kind of like the songs we dance to." He explained further.

"Well if your poetry is like your dancing. It must be wonderful." Patricia exclaimed.

"It's just human thoughts and emotions put down in words. Hopefully they will help some humans or at least give them joy." Daniel said reflect fully.

"Well, what do you write about?" inquired Bartholomew.

Daniel answered, "Life, love, joy, sorrow, even dancing with you two."

"So if people like this book, you get the reward of making them feel better?" came the next question.

"Yes, plus if they buy the book I may even get some money." Daniel went on.

"Wait a minute." Squeaked Little's voice. "You may get some extra money besides the retirement money?"

"Exactly," came Daniel's hopeful response.

Little exclaimed, "Then buy more almonds."

The Day After Thanksgiving

"Good Morning Daniel," greeted Bartholomew in the early morning light. "You seem up earlier than usual this morning."

"Hi Bart." Daniel explained. "It's the day after Thanksgiving and the noise of the traffic woke me up."

"It does seem heavier than usual," echoed Patricia. "What's happening?"

"Well" Daniel expounded. "The first day after Thanksgivings signals to humans the beginning of the Christmas season, and they all go shopping to buy gifts for the season."

"Shopping we understand because you have explained it to us. But what is Christmas?" Patricia questioned.

"It's a religious holiday," Daniel went on. "To celebrate the birth of what many humans think of as our creators son."

"Uh, Oh,"chirped in Little, the small squirrel. "I feel another dumb human idea coming on."

"We understand the concept of holidays." Bart intoned. "But what are the human traditions of this one."

"Well we usually celebrate by getting a Christmas tree, decorating it with tinsel and lights, then on December 25 giving gifts to our loved ones." Came the human's explanation.

"Why do you use a tree to help celebrate?" queried Patricia the young pine.

"Patricia," Bartholomew jumped in. "Humans use trees for many of their religious beliefs."

"Like what," she asked.

"Like when a human dies." he went on. "They prefer to be buried in the earth in a pine box. Probably so they can be surrounded by a tree and feel protected."

"So that's where that story comes from." She exclaimed.

"What story?" Daniel asked inquisitively.

"The story told down through history goes like this." She then quoted, "When the Holy family was pursued by Herod's soldiers, many plants offered them shelter. One such plant was the Pine Tree. When Mary was too weary to travel longer the family stopped at the edge of a forest to rest. A gnarled old pine which had grown hollow with its years invited them to rest within its trunk--then it closed its branches down and kept them safe until the soldiers had passed. Upon leaving, the Christ Child blessed the pine and the imprint of his little hand was left forever in the tree's fruit--the pine cone. If a cone is cut lengthwise the hand may still be seen."

"But why decorate it?" Little asked.

Daniel replied, "The decorated Christmas tree can be traced back to the ancient Romans who during their winter festival decorated trees with small pieces of metal during Saturnalia, a winter festival in honor of Saturnus, the god of agriculture. And another legend goes like this" Daniel went on. "Saint Boniface, an English missionary, known as the "Apostle of Germany", in 722 came upon some men about to cut a huge oak tree as a stake (Oak of Thor) for a human sacrifice to their pagan god. With one mighty blow, Saint Boniface felled the massive oak and as the tree split, a beautiful young fir tree sprang from its center. Saint Boniface told the people that this lovely evergreen, with its branches pointing to heaven, was indeed a holy tree, the tree of the Christ Child, a symbol of His promise of eternal life. He instructed them henceforth to carry the evergreen from the wilderness into their homes and to surround it with gifts, symbols of love and kindness."

"Well that's all fine and good," Little chimed in. "But I only know three things. One. Growing Christmas trees provides a habitat for wildlife. Two. Christmas trees remove dust and pollen from the air. And three. 2-3 seedlings are planted for every harvested Christmas tree. Human dumb ideas make no sense but sometimes it comes to a good end."

"Well," Bartholomew said seriously. "The use of evergreen trees to celebrate the winter season occurred before the birth of this Christ. So your explanations are sound and good but the human traditions may have a variety of reasons for why they do things."

"So if you go shopping," Little said pleadingly. "Pick up a gift for greyboy my cousin in Houston and if you are thinking of a gift for me. I may make a suggestion. Almonds."

Winter Solstice

"Good Morning everybody," greeted Daniel early on the morning of December 21st. "Happy Winter Solstice."

"Good Morning Daniel." Answered Patricia the young voluptuous pine.

"Good Morning," Bartholomew, the old stately elm, joined in. "What is Winter solstice?"

"It means he brought extra almonds." Little quipped hopefully.

"No Little." Daniel explained. "It is celebrated as the shortest day of the year by humans."

"Daniel?" Bartholomew questioned. "You explained to us before that humans measured time as sixty seconds in a minute, sixty minutes in an hour and twenty-four hours in a day. Did something change?"

"No Bart." Daniel went on. "It's just the tilt of the earth nearer or farther from the sun. So the amount of light the earth receives varies. The Winter solstice is the day when we receive the least amount of sunlight. The Summer solstice is the day when we receive the most amount of sunlight, the autumn and spring equinoxes are when the amount of sunlight is the equal to the amount of darkness we receive in the night time."

"Okay, stop," moaned Little. "You have a longest day, a shortest day, and two days that are equal, but they all are still twenty-four hours long."

"Exactly." Daniel replied happily.

"I'm getting a headache." The little squirrel complained.

"Daniel, the earth gets the same amount of sunlight each day, requardless of its tilt." Bartholomew reasoned.

"That is true Bart." Daniel explained further. "These days are for the northern half of the earth. They are reversed for the southern half. It's how we mark the changing of the seasons. Winter solstice is the official start of winter. It prepares us for the coming season."

"That's not a very accurate way of preparing." Patricia exclaimed.

"No, it's not." Daniel agreed. "But it's the best we've got."

"Okay." Bartholomew answered stocially. "I understand the humans reasoning."

"Me too," Patricia joined in.

"I need an almond!" Little chirped.

Depression

"Good morning guys," mumbled Daniel as he walked out onto his back patio.

"Good morning," answered Bartholomew.

"Daniel! You look terrible!" exclaimed a worried Patricia.

"Sorry Pat. I had a bad night. Didn't get much sleep." he replied.

"What was the problem?" Bartholomew questioned. "Anything we can do to help?"

"No. I had a bad case of depression last night and had to fight it off. It left me worn out, but hey at least I didn't commit suicide." Daniel rejoinered.

"What is depression and what is suicide?" Little asked as he joined in the conversation.

"Depression is a bad state of human emotions that sometimes results in suicide. Suicide is where a human ends their life." Daniel explained.

"Well, of all dumb human ideas, that has to be the dumbest." Little went on.

"Little! If you don't shut up, I swear I'll drop a pine cone on your head." Patricia practically shouted.

"It's Okay Patricia." Daniel said. "Most humans don't understand depression either, and therefore are not too sympathetic to it, or its repercussions."

"Didn't you tell us," queried Bartholomew. "You had found a new doctor and she was helping you?"

"Yes." Daniel responded." But sometimes it's just too much and I fall back into a bout of depression. It's happening less and less these days, so maybe I'm getting better."

"What do you do to help?" asked Patricia.

"Well most people tell me to look at the good things in life. Look at bright colors. Listen to music, and concentrate on the bright side of life." He answered mournfully.

"Does that help?" questioned Bartholomew.

"Sure." Daniel explained. "But if I could do all that, I wouldn't be depressed to start with. It's merely a chemical imbalance in my brain and I am taking medicine to correct it."

"That I can understand." Stated Patricia. "I had a cousin who had a nitrogen deficiency and couldn't get his colors to turn green enough to get sufficient sunlight. The less sun he got, the more nitrogen deficient he became. It was a self replicating situation."

"Well that's kind of my case." Daniel replied. "But the medicine is helping and I am getting better."

"Well Daniel. You have been a joy to know and talk to." Little said seriously. "Almonds always helped me, and if it could help you, I'll be more than happy to share my almonds."

Disagreements

Daniel rose late in the brisk morning's light. He put on his coat and went outside to his back patio.

"Good morning Bartholomew. Good morning Patricia." He greeted his friends. "Where's Little."

"Good morning Daniel," came the chorus of replies. "We are not sure where he is this morning."

"Down here by the pond, no tail. You're late! A squirrel could starve to death here waiting for you." Chided Little's thought.

"Sorry my friend," Daniel explained. "I had a bad couple of days and slept in late."

"Anything we can help with," inquired a thoughtful Patricia.

"I just don't understand people," came Daniel's mournful answer. "Why when people disagree with me, do they feel threatened? They act like I'm insulting them and calling them stupid if they disagree."

"Well Daniel," intoned Bartholomew. "Every issue has two sides. One is correct and one incorrect."

"They explain the disagreement as it is their opinion that differs and is not incorrect."Daniel went on.

"Sorry friend, but no. Opinions are not an explanation. One side is correct and one side is incorrect. The incorrect side is just ignorant of all the facts and it is not an insult. Failure to discuss an issue to find the source of the disagreement is the only thing that is truly not intelligent. Failure to not explore all explanations by definition would be considered stupid." Bartholomew went on. "Patricia and I do not feel stupid or insulted when we ask for human explanations, just ignorant of human reasoning. Such explanations are the only way to knowledge and understanding. Opinions have no place."

"I understand but everyone else seems to feel insulted. Even Little felt insulted by Sam calling him fuzzy butt." Daniel rejoinered.

"It was an insult," Little argued.

"No Little. It was a description. Whether you like it or not, you have a fuzzy butt." Came Bartholomew's rebuttal.

"Hadn't thought of it that way." Little agreed. "Plus a fuzzy butt is a good thing on a morning like this."

"See what I mean." Daniel replied." Even Little is not immune to perceived insults."

"Well." Little responded, "At least I have a reason for feeling that way."

"And what is your irrefutable reasoning this time, my friend?" Daniel questioned.

"Simple." said Little. "Lack of almonds that morning."

Winter Rest

"Hello Daniel." greeted Bartholomew in the early morning.

"Bartholomew. Patricia. Good morning." answered Daniel.

"We have a question this morning," asked the old stately elm.

"And what might that be?" Queried the retired civil servant.

"Patricia and I were wondering why," continued Bartholomew. "Lately when you come out here you seem to have put on more and more coverings on your body."

"Well," Daniel explained. "Winter is approaching and the air is getting colder so I must cover up to keep warm. Humans don't tolerate the cold well."

"Ah yes, I understand." Bart answered. "Which brings me to another point. Patricia and I will soon send our sap to our roots and begin our winter's rest. Kind of like the sleep, as you explained before, that humans do."

"Humans sleep every day and cannot sleep an entire winter." Daniel went on. "Some animals do, it's called hibernation, but not humans."

"Well," Bartholomew said sadly. "Patricia and I will soon go to our winter rest and be out of communication with you. We have enjoyed the summer and all the talks we have had."

"And the dancing,"Patricia joined in. "You dance very well."

"Human's have a lot of dumb ideas but at least they can dance." Came the small squirrels voice.

"Hello Little," greeted Daniel. "Looks like it is just going to be me and you for awhile."

"We will miss our daily talks," reflected Bartholomew. "But we must retire to rest for the winter."

"And we will miss dancing with you." Patricia said sadly.

"We hope you will still be here in the spring when we return." Bart said hopefully.

"I will be here and so will Little, we can talk and dance all spring, summer and fall." Daniel said happily.

"Yeah." Little joined in. "I'll be here unless I starve because no tail here forgets my breakfast almonds."

"Enjoy your rest and I look forward to talking and dancing with you both in the spring." Daniel rejoinered.

"Then, until the spring," said Bartholomew solemnly. "Until the spring."

Conversations in the Spring

Introduction to Conversations in the Spring

The continuing conversations between the four friends first recorded in Conversations, Daniel the retired civil servant. Bartholomew the tall stately Elm. Patricia, the young voluptuous pine, and Little, the sarcastic almond loving squirrel.

Index to Conversations in the Spring

1 Awakening
2 Poetry
3 The Song of Earth - Poem
4 Stopping Smoking
5 Dancing
6 Rain
7 My Sister Diane - Poem
8 Birthday
9 What is Life?
10 Unique
11 Memorial Day
12 Jokes and Puns
13 Big Fish
14 My Dad Has Passed -Poem
15 Guilt
16 Gratitude
17 Characteristics
18 Harriet and Jonathan
19 Ghosts
20 Speeding
21 Funny Poetry
22 The Void
23 Frequencies
24 Summer Soltice
25 Fourth of July

Awakening

"Good morning you guys," Daniel projected as he went out onto his back patio. He had sent the same greetings each morning for three weeks, but had not had a reply yet.

"Good morning Daniel," boomed Bartholomew, with a yawn. "We're awake now."

"Hi Daniel," chirped Patricia the young voluptuous pine, sounding as perky as always. "We had a really good rest and can't wait for a new growing season to start."

"Anything happen to the world while we were resting?" inquired Bartholomew.

"Nothing worth mentioning, just the Christmas season in which my wife celebrated by sending gifts on the twelve days before Christmas to all the relatives, " came the answer.

"What are the twelve days of Christmas," asked a confused Patricia.

"Probably the most misunderstood part of the church year among Christians who are not part of liturgical church traditions. Contrary to much popular belief, these are not the twelve days *before* Christmas, but in the Western Church are the twelve days from Christmas until the beginning of Epiphany (January 6th; the 12 days count from December 25th until January 5th).

"And what is the Epiphany," Patricia inquired further.

"Epiphany is traditionally celebrated as the time the three Wise Men or Magi arrived to present gifts to the young Jesus," Daniel explained. "Well that, and just cold dreary days, that were boring and long."

"Thanks a lot", piped Little, the sarcastic, almond loving squirrel. "Nice to know that my company was so boring."

"Sorry Little, I didn't mean it that way. It was a long winter and I missed talking to Bartholomew and Patricia." Daniel replied. "I just wonder what it would be like to sleep that long?"

"Humans do not sleep that long," Bartholomew went on. "But you seem to resent sleeping at all. What is that all about and where do you get such feelings?"

"Remember when I talked about human feelings of what we considered right and wrong."

"Yes, we remember," answered Bartholomew. "If I remember correctly, humans considered such things you labeled wrong as a sin."

"That is the term we use." Daniel expounded. "And a great philosopher named Carl Jung one said, "Unconsciousness is the greatest sin of all." So I guess that's where I get my feelings from."

"What else did he believe?" questioned a confused Patricia.

"Jung's most famous concept was the collective unconscious. Much like the universal awareness Bartholomew often talks about. It is there but most humans can't tap into it or even believe it's there." Daniel responded. "He had a deep influence not only on psychology but also on philosophy for humans."

"He sounds like an interesting human," Bartholomew intoned. "Anyone else with his influence."

"He was from Switzerland and his counter part was a human known as Sigmund Freud, but they had differences. Jung believed in dreams and led him to explore religions of every type known to humanity. I believe he just felt that humans need to believe in something, no matter what. The collective unconsciousness filled his needs fine."

"What about this Freud fellow." Inquired Patricia.

"He just believed every human question and answer had a basis in sex."Daniel answered solemnly.

"Dreamy," said Patricia.

"Another in the list of dumb human idea." Little joined in." You just need to eat more almonds."

"Not everything is that simple." Chided Patricia.

"Well just cross pollinate with an almond tree, Pat." Little countered.

"Watch your mouth fuzzy butt." Patricia replied angrily.

"Sorry" said Little chastised.

"Anyway," Daniel jumped in. "Those were two of the most famous philosophers of the modern age and humans would rather take their word for things and not have to think for themselves."

"Well, thank goodness for you, my friend." Bartholomew went on. "Or we would never have answers to human thoughts and feelings."

"Plus more importantly," said a solemn Little. "No free Almonds."

Poetry

"Good morning." Daniel greeted walking out onto his back patio.

"And a good morning to you." Came the replies.

"We have another question." Bartholomew stated. "We have noticed you at your computer late at night when most humans have gone to sleep, what are you doing?"

"Writing." Came the retired civil servant's answer.

"And what are you writing?" Asked the curious old elm.

"Poetry."

"What is poetry?" inquired a curious Patricia.

"It's just putting down on paper human feelings and thoughts. It employs a rhyme scheme to make it flow kind of like a song." Daniel explained further.

"Will you read some of them to us." Asked Patricia excitedly.

"Sure thing Pat." Daniel went on. "If we talk about a subject that I have written about, I will read the poem to you."

"Do you have one now." She inquired.

"Yes." Daniel answered. "It talks about the song of earth. The one we dance to."

The Song of Earth

Do not let this day pass,
        Without looking to the sky.
To hear the song of the Earth,
        To see the clouds float by.

Enjoy the heat of summer,
        Relish in the cleansing rain.
The touch of winter's briskness,
        Will help to keep you sane.

Just see the colors of the Earth,
        Such joy in the array.
The birds, the ants, and the animals,
        Ignore them not, a single day.

For you have to make a living,
        But no requirement to make it grave.
Be careful viewing money,
        Be it's master, not it's slave.

For in every city that we build,
        All concrete walls and steel.
The dandelion breaks the pavement,
        To show us what is real.

Mother Earth she sings a song,
        To teach us joy and trust.
A way to live our lives,
        Our buildings, she turns to rust.

So try to meet your deadlines,
        To make your schedules tight.
The Earth scorns your depression,
        And makes her flowers bright.

I tell you fellow mortals,
        Be yea enemy or friend.
Relish in the song of Earth, because,
        You shall not pass this way again

Stopping Smoking

"Good morning Daniel," chorused his friends as he stepped out onto his back patio in the early mornings light.

"Morning," grumbled Dan.

"Well you sure look and sound to be in an uncomfortable way this morning," Bartholomew commented.

"What's the matter Daniel?" inquired a concerned Patricia.

"Remember when I talked to you about human addictions?" Daniel asked.

"Yes," Bartholomew answered. "We remember that particular conversation very well."

"Well I'm trying to quit my smoking addiction." Grumbled a mournful Daniel.

"Most of my anger is against my fellow humans and their condescending attitudes about how it feels to quit and how I should be handling it."

"Well for what it's worth my friend." Bartholomew intoned." You have our sympathy."

"Thanks for that. At least you're not preaching at me about how it feels." Daniel replied.

"We said you have our sympathy, not empathy."Bartholomew continued. "To try and give you empathy would be a great gift, but it is simply impossible for any intelligent creature to express empathy on a subject that they have no knowledge of."

"That doesn't stop most humans." Daniel explained. "The other day I was talking to a woman in a store and she told me she was still trying to get over her child dying last year. I told her she had my sympathy but I could not offer her more. I could not conceive what she was going through. She said most other people told here "I know how you feel." How could they know unless they had lost a child themselves? She was as angry as I am now. How dumb is that kind of a statement?"

"I can understand now how frustrated you must be."Sympathized Bartholomew." But didn't you tell us you were seeing a new doctor. A doctor of naturopathy? And you also told us she found your lack of certain chemicals in you body that led to your depression."

"Yes." Daniel agreed.

"And that all humans handle chemicals differently?" Bartholomew continued.

"Yes." Daniel agreed again.

"Then wouldn't it be safe to assume that because of your body makeup that you simply cannot quit smoking. And that it has nothing to do with your willpower, as you call it?" Bartholomew went on.

"Well that makes sense Bart." Daniel conceded.

"And for what it's worth, Daniel." Patricia said quietly. "We're here for you every day. Whether you stop smoking or restart. We care for you either way."

"Hey, Daniel." Came Little's voice. "No one understands what you're going through except me. I sympathize and empathize with you friend. I once tried to give up almonds."

Dancing

"Good morning everyone," greeted Daniel as he walked out onto his back patio. "And what a glorious morning it is."

"Oh Daniel it certainly is." Patricia answered happily. "The breeze this morning is a gentle one and harmonically beautiful. Come and dance with us."

"I would love to Patricia," Daniel responded. "But sometimes watching you and Bartholomew dance so gracefully, I just feel clumsy, but I do love it so."

"You don't do so bad for a human." Patricia said respectfully. She then asked. "Are you sure you don't have some roots down there?"

"Yes I'm sure Pat, I don't have any roots." Daniel answered.

"We noticed some music coming from your computer earilier,"Bartholomew joined in. "It sounded nice and while it was not as rhythmically pure as Mother's songs, it was nice. We have heard some music other humans make and it was not as pleasant. It seemed too complex and almost demanding."

"That's because most humans who make music feel that it must have a complex rhythm and be difficult to play on their instruments." Daniel explained.

"How absurd!" Bartholomew retorted. "Rhythmic simplicity is the true beauty of music."

"I agree Bart," Daniel conceded. "But if it is too simple, humans feel it has no worth."

"Are they deaf to Mother Nature's songs?" inquired a curious Patricia.

"I'm afraid so my dear." Daniel expounded " But let us just enjoy this morning breeze and gentle song."

"Hey, you three." Came a small squirrel voice. "You gonna dance all morning or feed me. I'm starving out here."

"Good morning Little." Daniel replied. "Come dance with us."

"Squirrels don't dance!" Little countered haughtily. "They scamper."

"Well I've seen you scamper, my friend, and I must say you do it very well." Daniel rejoinered.

"It takes a lot of energy and a lot of skill." Little went on. "And if I say so myself, of all my cousins, I'm one of the best at it."

"I brought you your breakfast almonds, but I just wanted to dance a little while." Came Daniel's reply.

Little quipped. "That's fine Mr. No Tail, as long as you realize. That scampering takes a lot of energy and I'm starving."

Rain

"Good morning everyone," greeted Daniel as he stepped out onto his back patio glancing at the cloud and rain filled morning sky.

"Good morning Daniel," Patricia said enthusiastically. "And what a wonderful rainy morning it is. A perfect start for a spring day."

"Hi Dan," Bartholomew replied. "Looks like I get enough to drink today."

"Why don't you three stop being so happy?" Exclaimed the grumpy little squirrels thoughts.

"What's the matter Little?" Questioned Daniel.

"I'm wet, cold, and my almonds are soaked." Little continued complaining.

"Well I'm sorry my friend." Daniel went on. "I can't help how I feel. Rain just reminds me of the happy times of my youth."

"What are some of those memories, my fine and favorite human?" Patricia asked her enthusiasm overflowing.

'I remember." Said Daniel reflecting. "Taking long walks at night in the rain with my older sister Diane. It was a pleasant time and we were so comfortable with each other we wouldn't feel the need to speak in human talk. We would both just enjoy Mother Nature's rain song. We both seemed to hear it and didn't want to show disrespect to her by interrupting her song."

"That is a wonderful memory my friend," Bartholomew stated. "Where is she now."

"She's on the other side of the country. I haven't seen her in a while." Daniel replied mournfully. "It's about 2,755 miles away."

"Why don't you visit her?" Patricia inquired. "You went to see your wife's parents in Houston and you visit your mother in Eugene often."

"There are actually three reasons." Daniel answered. "One, my health. Two, I don't like to fly. Three it really costs a lot of money."

"Those are really poor and sorry reasons." Quipped a contemptuous Little.

"Little if I spend too much money. I won't have enough to buy you your breakfast almonds." Daniel intoned.

"How silly of me," exclaimed a shocked Little. "Did I say poor and sorry? I meant proper and swell. The words start with the same human symbols and I must have gotten them confused."

"Right." Answered a skeptical Daniel.

"We haven't heard about her before." Bartholomew jumped in. "Does she have trees and squirrels like your wife's parents and your mother."

"Yes," came Daniel's reply. "In Houston the tree out their back door is named George and their little friend is named Greyboy. My mother's back patio tree is a large oak named Horace and her little friendly squirrel is named Rusty. I don't know about my sister's tree or Little's cousins there. She does have a tree in the front yard but her patio is in the back. The tree is a pin oak but she hasn't seen any squirrels."

"Can you tell us anything else? Does she have any children?" Bartholomew continued questioning.

"Yes she has four but only one who visits her regularly. Her name is Sherri and she has children of her own." Daniel answered.

"Okay. I think we have her now." Bartholomew replied after a few minutes of silence. " The pin oak's name is Scott and he says she has not made contact. He has seen her swaying when the wind blows and believes she is hearing Mother Natures song on an unconscious level and feels the dance."

"If she wants to dance she couldn't have a better partner." Patricia chimed in. "Scott's bark is smooth, he is a real beauty, plus in the fall he turns a bright crimson."

"Well Diane always was a very good dancer." Daniel explained. "She naturally feels rhythm."

"None of my cousins go there." Said Little joining in. "Maybe if she put out some almonds they would come in."

"Well I'll suggest it to her, but maybe it just rains too much up there for them. If they have your opinion about rain they may not come out." Said Daniel accusingly. "Is there anything good about a rainy day that you can think of to say Little."

"Sure." Said Little defensively. "Using your format three things. One it cleans the air. Two it gives water to all living creatures. And three it softens my almonds so they are easier to chew."

Danny L Shanks

My Sister Diane

I had a sister growing up,
    Diane was her name.
However being a great sister,
    Does not seem to qualify for riches or fame.

By the time I got to high school,
    Had no car and that was a pain.
Yet she had finished high school,
    Got a job and bought a new Ford Mustang.

On the weekends,
    She would come up to me.
Say "Have Fun"then give me the keys,
    These were always given where no one else could see.

After high school,
    I was sent to Viet Nam.
She never once forgot me,
    My other siblings didn't seem to give a damn.

She wrote me constantly,
    Sent cookies always wishing me well.
It helped to ease my pain,
    Making tolerable my season in hell.

She moved away from the family,
    But I never told her how much she eased my pain.
That regret I carry with me,
    Forever burned in my brain.

So if by some chance she sees this,
    By whatever means, being published or some other.
I would like to tell the world and her,
    "Thanks for everything", from your young stupid kid brother.

Birthday

"Top of the morning everybody. And a fine morning it is if I must say." Daniel effused as he walked out onto his back patio.

"Well good morning to you also Daniel." Greeted Bartholomew the stately elm. "What has got you so chipper this morning?"

"Today is my birthday." Daniel explained. "It's a holiday."

"You mean like Halloween, Thanksgiving and Christmas?" Patricia the young voluptuous pine asked.

"Yes Patricia." Daniel went on. "Except it's on an individual basis. All humans have a holiday and celebrate the day on which they were born. They have parties and are given gifts. They use the birthdays to keep tract of their age."

"And how old are you today?" inquired Bartholomew.

"Today is my 56th birthday." Came the answer.

"Well congratulations my friend." Patricia said happily. "We will really have to dance some today."

"I can't think of a better way to celebrate. However I do feel that I'm getting old. That's the only downside to the day." Daniel said reflectfully.

"But Daniel." Reasoned Bartholomew. "Just look at the life you've had so far. The life you have left and that you are closer to the light."

"I understand all that Bart." Daniel went on explaining. "But going into the light is somewhat scary from a human standpoint."

"Daniel being transformed into the light and becoming part of the universal understanding. Should be a joyous thing." Bartholomew expounded.

"I agree." Daniel conceded. "But the transformation seems scary and comes at the cost of some pain."

"That's just because you're male Dan." Patricia joined in. "Ask any human woman and they can explain. They have pain when giving birth to a child, but when it's over it's forgotten and the pain was a small and short price to pay for what they got in return."

"Plus that is a long way off." Bartholomew argued.

"You're both right." Daniel said happily. "So for today we can just dance and celebrate."

"Daniel." Inquired Little. "Did you say you got gifts?"

"Yes." He answered.

"You mean like almonds?"

"Yes." He answered again.

"Well now that I think on it. Guess what?" Little asked. "Today is my birthday too."

What is Life?

"Good morning Daniel.' Greeted the retired civil servant as he walked out onto his back patio in the early morning light.

"Hello Bartholomew. Hello Patricia." Said Daniel as he returned their greetings. "Anything on your minds this morning?"

"Just the usual questions we have about human feelings and thinking my friend." Came the answer.

"Well I have some questions myself this morning." Daniel rejoinered.

"And what are those?" inquired a curious Patricia.

"Bart, on my birthday you mentioned my death and going into the light. The transformation from the Fire Lords would explain everything and I would see the universe in a different way. Well, my friend what is life?" Daniel asked.

"That's a big one for this early in the morning." Bartholomew replied. "Maybe we should ask Sam the old oak."

"Hey you guys. Easy on calling up Sam. I haven't eaten breakfast yet." Wailed Little.

"Oh be quiet Little," Chided Patricia. "You won't starve."

"Okay," conceded Little. "But don't say I didn't warn you."

"Hey Sam." Called Bartholomew.

"What now? " came the grumpy answer. "Didn't I just talk to you guys less than a year ago."

"Right Sam," Bartholomew said respectfully. "But we need you to explain something to the human again."

"No problem Bart." Sam replied. "Is little fuzzy butt still there also?"

"Hey you old relic." Came Little's heated response. "Kiss my furry tail."

"Well at least nothing has changed." Sam said and asked. "What is your question?"

"Hi Sam," Daniel jumped in. "It's just me again and I wanted to know the definition of life."

"Hi Daniel." Sam answered. "Do you remember my explanation of energy and the universal awareness of all living beings. And that when you transformed to the Fire Lord state you would become energy and understand how every living being was included."

"Yes," Daniel went on. "But I wondered about bacteria and viruses."

"Yes Dan they are included as living beings." Sam explained further.

"Viruses and bacteria can cause human deaths. They are looked on as bad." Daniel expounded.

"They are no different than you. They are just trying to survive also. Do you not kill other beings to survive?" Questioned the old oak.

"Sure." Daniel answered. "But those are humans and have a higher intelligence level."

"An expected response from a human but, so what. Viruses and Bacteria have a right to life also, my friend." Sam went on patiently. "And when you are transformed, all those silly differences will not exist. Human concepts of what is good and bad will just no longer be there."

"Plus," said Patricia joining in. "Didn't you tell us Daniel, that sometimes human kill not for survival, but for sport, which is suppose to be fun for the humans."

"Point taken." Conceded a chastised Daniel.

"So my friend." Sam questioned. "Do you see now that life consists of any living being? Whether you designate them as good or bad.

He then asked, "As for the meaning of life. What meaning? You are alive and that's it, enjoy and stop looking for some deeper explanation."

"Thanks Sam." Daniel thankfully said. "I really appreciate your explanation and knowledge."

"Great!" Little chimed in. "Can we eat now."

Unique

"O Yeah." Shouted Little. Daniel heard shockingly, as he walked out his back patio into a full-blown argument.

"These two hard barked thinking trees are just wrong." Little told Daniel with a softer thought as he came outside.

"Our bark is hard. Not our ability to think." Patricia countered irritably.

"We were just having an intelligent discussion on the one characteristic humans have that makes them so unique." Answered Bartholomew, the tall stately elm. "For me, I thought it was your ability to solve problems."

"And I say it's the ability to love." Patricia chimed in.

"And I told you two, it's the ability to harvest almonds." Little responded almost shouting.

"Please resolve this discussion Daniel. Or at least tell us what you think." Pleaded a distraught Patricia.

"Well to start with." Daniel began his explanation. "The ability to solve problems is great. It took us out of the caves and let us create the civilization that we now enjoy. Love is also an admirable trait, but it is not unique to humans. Many creatures mate for life and demonstrate affection or love for their mate or offspring. Many creatures also harvest the fruits of Mother Nature. But if put on the spot and had to answer. I would have to say the most unique characteristic of humans is their imagination.

"What is this imagination you speak of?" Inquired a curious Patricia.

"It's the thought process that allows us to deal with the reality of the world." Came the thoughtful answer. "When we can't figure anything out our imagination gives us answers that we can reconcile the world's inconsistencies with."

"That is unique." Bartholomew conceded. "Can you give us an example?"

"Sure." Daniel went on. "Did you ever hear of stories about witches."

"What the dead bark is a witch." Little asked.

"The stories to which I refer involved thirteen of them going into the woods and knocking on wood. Usually a tree. The purpose was to wake up the nymphs who lived there.'

"No one in here but me." Said Patricia laughingly.

"What I believe they sensed was the universal awareness, and to resolve those feelings they created the image of a wood nymph who lived there." Daniel expounded.

"That's kind of an insult to us." Patricia said poutingly.

"Sure it is my dear." Daniel consoled her. "But they couldn't go into an alpha state and talk to you so they created the alternate explanation of a magical fairy nymph that gave them an answer."

"Just sounds like more dumb human ideas." Said Little contemptuously.

"It may be dumb." Countered Daniel "But you have to admit it's unique."

"Well I'll give you that." Little stated concedingly.

"Now I understand." Bartholomew stated consoling the little squirrel. "That is truly a unique quality."

"Okay." Little conceded. "How about some of those harvested MotherNature fruits for breakfast. I'm starving."

Memorial Day

"Good morning Daniel," greeted Bartholomew and Patricia, as he exited onto his back patio in the morning's sunlight.

"And a good morning to you all also." Came the retired civil servant's reply.

"About time." Responded Little mumbling grumpily. "I'm starving out here."

"Daniel, we were wondering where your mate is? She sometimes sits out here with you. She has not been able to make contact with us yet but we can feel her presence and it is a joy." said Bartholomew inquiringly.

"It's true she hasn't made contact yet, but her love of living things and her love of life radiates from her like the rays of the sun. It is a pleasure just to have her here when you come outside your cave." Patricia commented.

"Hey," Little joined in. "I like her a lot. Plus she gives me more almonds than Mr. No Tail here."

"That's not fair Little," said Daniel defensively. "I'm just trying to keep you from getting fat."

"I didn't say a thing about being fair." Countered Little. "I just said I liked her a lot."

"Anyway," Patricia asked. " Are there any holidays coming up. She seems to be here when you have one of your human holidays."

"In fact we do have a holiday coming up when she will be off work and can come out to see you all." Daniel answered. "It's the Memorial Day holiday."

"And what is this holiday for." Patricia questioned.

"It is a day set aside to honor and remember all the soldiers, men or women, who died in a war fighting for this country." Daniel went on explaining further.

"We really don't understand this concept you refer to as war." Queried Bartholomew.

"Well the human governments claim it's about the way other countries live and believe, but to be honest it's usually fought over control of a piece of land." Daniel expounded sorrowfully.

"But no one owns land," Bartholomew protested. "If there is an owner it's Mother Nature and she shares it with all living creatures."

"Yes," Daniel agreed. "But I was a soldier in such a war. Every year with this holiday I remember my friends who died. I do not feel honor for their deaths but regret and sorrow. I miss them."

"Why do the governments have such a holiday? It seems insensitive to the ones who survived and remember, with pain, the ones lost." Asked a puzzled Patricia.

"Governments believe they can inspire other young men to fight if they know they will be remembered and honored" Daniel went on explaining. "But basically they want to own and control some particular piece of land and will take it by force or buy it if they can't."

"Okay," Wailed Bartholomew mournfully. "Much as it pains me to say so. Little may be right. That is a dumb human idea."

"About time you realized how smart I am." Quipped the small squirrel.

"So what do you mean you honor them?" questioned a perplexed Patricia. "If you honored their lives you would never have asked them to fight in the first place, much less asked them to die in doing so."

" I didn't say I agreed with it Patricia." Daniel answered. "I was just giving you an explanation."

"Well that is not as joyous a holiday as are the rest." Bartholomew intoned seriously. "But the only bright side is that your mate will be off work and can share a day with us."

"Plus," chimed in Little happily. "I get more almonds."

Jokes and Puns

"Good morning everyone." Daniel greeted his three friends as he walked out onto his back patio.

"Morning Daniel." Came back the chorus of replies.

"We have another question." Asked Bartholomew the stately elm. "We would like some help. It has us puzzled somewhat."

"Sure Bart." Daniel rejoinered. "Just let me give Little his breakfast almonds first."

"No problem my friend." Bartholomew replied. "But for the record. I don't think our small friend will starve. He's getting kind of fat."

"Hey you old hard barked piece of sap." Little cried feeling hurt. "Your getting as bad as Sam."

"That is not an insult Little." Bartholomew intoned. Then continued his question. "Daniel, what is this human trait of laughter, and the exchange called jokes. We have been meaning to ask you since last Halloween when you and Little exchanged one."

"Well a joke is kind of a short story with an unexpected ending that conjures up an image humans find funny. Most humans do not make up jokes but retell ones they have heard or read somewhere else. The only original jokes people make up are called puns." Daniel explained further. "These are not stories but a play on human speech, which can give a double meaning from the expected one. It usually gives a ridiculous answer and although funny most humans groan. The protocol seems to be laugh at a joke, but groan at a pun."

"Can you give us an example of each?" Patricia asked inquiringly. "Be happy to my dear." Daniel stated. "A man takes his Rottweiler to the vet and says, "My dog's cross-eyed, is there anything you can do for him?"

"Well," says the vet, "let's have a look at him." So he picks the dog up and examines his eyes, then checks his teeth. Finally, he says, "I'm going to have to put him down."

"What? Because he's cross-eyed?"

"No, because he's really heavy."

"I get it." Patricia practically squealed. "The Veterinary wasn't talking about putting the dogs life out, but just mean the dog was getting heavy from holding him and he had to literally put him down."

"Right Pat." Daniel said. "And now a pun. A dyslexic man walks into a bra."

"I don't get it." Patricia lamented. "What's a dyslexic?"

"It's a human who sees the letter of words in the wrong order." Daniel went on. " Instead of bra, which means a woman's garment, the word should have been bar, which is the same letters rearranged plus that is the way many jokes start and therefore kind of a dumb misplay of words."

"Well that certainly explains the groan for a pun." Patricia expounded morosely.

"Does that answer your questions?" Asked Daniel.

"Are humans the only creatures to laugh?" inquired a curious Bartholomew.

"Actually no." Came Daniels reply. "It has been proven recently. That dogs also laugh, but I don't know what about?"

"I do." Little chimed in.

"And what are they laughing at?" Daniel questioned.

"Just look at your fellow humans." Came the sarcastic reply.

"Enough said Little." Daniel complained. "Just shut up and eat your breakfast."

Big Fish

"Good morning all," Daniel mumbled as he walked out onto his back patio.

"Morning Daniel," Greeted Patricia the young voluptuous pine.

"Hi Dan," Bartholomew said. "You sound kind of pensive this morning. What's on your mind?"

"It was just a movie I watched last night," came the thoughtful reply. "It was called Big Fish and reminded me of my father. It reminded me of all the stories my father had told me over the years. Fascinating stories. It also reminded me that I had never told those stories to my daughter." He continued regretfully.

"Well if you never told anyone, why not tell us about them. We would love to hear them." Asked Patricia inquiringly.

"I would love to hear them also." Little chirped in. "I'll even wait for my breakfast almonds."

"Thanks guys," Daniel replied. "First things first. My Grandmother left my Grandfather and ran off with another man. My Grandfather got sick and my dad sat in his room at age thirteen and watched him die. My Grandmother didn't want him so he was sent to live with his Grandparents. Being a wild child, he ran away from their house and rode the boxcars of a train for a while. When it became too much he went back only to be sent to a Catholic orphanage in Arkansas. He told me stories about the priest and nuns there and his religious training. Being an orphan he wanted children. So he got married and had six. I was the youngest."

"I remember one story he told about alcohol." Daniel went on. "He gave up all alcohol while his children were small. He never took a drop from the first day his first child was born. On the day I turned eighteen he came home with two beers. He told me what he had done and now that I was eighteen and a man his job was done and he felt like a beer after over 30 years."

"Didn't you tell us alcohol was an addiction" Queried Little.

"Yes it can be." Daniel answered.

"That must have been hard." Little said sympathetically.

"True," Daniel said. "But he was committed to his children and the life that he had been denied because his father drank."

"Anyway," Daniel continued. "He never finished high school and soon got a job pulling splinters out of men's hands at the local wood mill. From there he worked his way up to being an assistant plant manager. He supplemented his income with various jobs. He once told me about catching an eight-foot gar from the Mississippi River. About him and Ferd Gazee fishing illegally with nets on the lake and catching a three foot wide logger head turtle in their nets. They thought it was dead but it woke up and they gave it the boat. Also stories about fishing on a Cyprus Swamp called Old Town Lake and being attacked by water moccasin snakes."

"Then about being in the Navy in World War II and meeting Gene Kelley the famous movie star. About firing Conway Twitty the famous singer because as my dad said, "He could sing Okay but he was worthless as far as manual labor."

"I loved my dad and his stories." Daniel said with a tear in his eye.

"He told me of stories about the men he had worked in his life and that when told he would have to move to Chicago Illinois after twenty two years he quit. "I will never raise my children in that town," he declared." Daniel explained further.

"He told me about Shorty," Daniel told his friends. "About how the owner of the mill put him in a doll's house to live and worked him so hard. He was furious with the state congressman owner and never recovered when one night Shorty lay down on the railroad tracks and never got up. The train engineer said he saw Shorty raise his head and lay back down. Shorty would stack the cut wood coming off the saws and my dad was amazed he would stack each piece precisely while he was asleep."

"Did the mill owner ever apologize to Shorty's family?" Asked an angry Patricia.

"No," Daniel responded. "Shorty had no family."

"Well does the former state congressman still own the plant?" Questioned Bartholomew.

"I don't know," Daniel answered. "But the injustice of it still makes me mad at all the people who use others for their financial gains."

"I never saw my Dad cry, except once when I told him that I had joined the army and was being sent to Viet Nam. I sent money home to help out. I just sent it. I would never humiliate my Dad, by making him ask for it, as did some of my brothers and sisters. My parents were always in debt and I remember bill collectors knocking on our door in the middle of the night. I swore my daughter would never want for anything or be burdened with the guilt that the Catholic upbrings had caused. My father died on April Fool's Day in 1973,"Daniel went on. "I wasn't there. But I miss him so much."

"Well thank you for sharing that with us, my friend." Bartholomew intoned seriously.

"I can't imagine your sorrow. But if you need anything we are here." Lamented Patricia.

"And my no tailed friend." Said Little jumping in. "Tell your daughter, the stories."

My Dad Has Passed

It's been 30 years,
    April 1st was the day.
They called to tell me,
    That my father had passed away.

I remember the agony,
    When they said that he was dead.
All I could think of was,
    The many things I had left unsaid.

Why was I so hardheaded?
    Are all children that way?
Do they believe any parent ever woke up thinking?
    "How can I screw up my child's life today?"

Is every child so blind?
    That to such a future fate.
That when they all decide to say those things,
    That it all comes a little late.

I didn't get to tell my Dad,
    How much I appreciated what he did.
The sacrifices he made for me,
    I felt like such an ungrateful kid.

But he comes to visit me,
    Slipping into my dreams in the middle of the night.
Reminding me of how to look at the world,
    And not to be blinded by the sight.

Only then can I tell him,
    In that somewhat mystical way.
But he always gives me his smile,
    As if to say its O.K.

So if you've not told your parent,
    Do not be subjected to my fate.
Tell them now how much you appreciate,
    Their sacrifices, and their life, before you are too late.

Guilt

"Good morning all," Daniel greeted his friends walking out onto his back patio much later in the morning than usual.

"You are much later today than ordinary,"Bartholomew replied. "We were concerned that something had happened to you. Little went to the big glass door and looked in and didn't see you at your computer."

"Hey Mr. No Tail human," squealed Little. "Glad you could finally make it. I'm starving out here."

"Sorry about that my friend." Daniel rejoinered. "I brought you some extra almonds to make up for being late today."

"Extra almonds?" Little queried excitedly. "Be late any day. I can wait."

"Daniel?" came Patricia's response. "Why did you bring extra almonds? Were you late by choice or did something happen?"

"I didn't sleep well last night and slept in a little long this morning." Daniel answered guiltily. "I brought the extra almonds to make up for Little's breakfast being late. I felt kind of guilty."

"What is this emotion called guilty," Inquired a puzzled Patricia.

"It's when a human doesn't do something they should have for no good reason." They call it guilt and try to make amends by bringing gifts. Hence the extra almonds." Daniel explained.

"But you said you were up late and needed sleep." Bartholomew protested. "No need to feel bad about that."

"Well Bart." Daniel explained further. "I feel that humans have three courses of action in their lives. One is what they should do. Two is what they want to do. And three is what they do. Sometimes all three can be different. Guilt and the resulting guilty feelings come from not doing what someone feels they should have done but didn't."

"Daniel." Little jumped in. "This is one dumb human idea that I can handle."

"Thought you may feel that way my friend." Daniel replied happily as he brought out the almonds.

Gratitude

"Good morning Daniel," greeted the retired civil servant as he walked out onto his back patio.

"Morning Bartholomew. Morning Patricia." Daniel replied. "What's on your minds today?"

"Just one thing my friend" answered the stately elm. "Thanks."

"Okay thanks." Inquired Daniel somewhat puzzled. "Thanks for what?"

"For taking the time and having the patience to explain human feelings and thoughts to Patricia and I." answered a somber Bartholomew. "You seem to understand it so well."

"I have spent my lifetime," Daniel explained. "Studying and trying to understand human thinking and the whys of human actions."

"Well we just haven't expressed our appreciation to you before and wish you to know how much it means to us." Patricia intoned solemnly. "You make it all so simple and easy to understand. Did you train at one of the human schools to learn this?"

"No Patricia I didn't" Daniel went on explaining. "There are humans who do and the study is called philosophy, the pursuit of truth and knowledge, and the humans who do it are called philosophers. They train for years and study great books of knowledge, teach at the schools and even write books to achieve such status."

"And are they rewarded for such efforts?" Bartholomew asked.

"Yes," Daniel answered further. "They get financial compensation and fame among other humans as seekers of knowledge."

"You should get some rewards for helping us." Complained Bartholomew.

"Oh but I do my friend. I do." Daniel expounded.

"And what rewards do you receive that amount to human riches." Asked a concerned Bartholomew.

"I get the joy of friendship, peace of mind when we talk, and I get to dance with Patricia." Daniel effused.

"Watch it human." Patricia said quivering. "Flattery will get you everywhere."

"So Daniel." Bartholomew continued. "You and your mate have a child, as you told us. Do you talk to her and her mate?"

"No." Said Daniel regretfully. "If I talk too long to them they get bored and irritable."

"They don't appreciate your knowledge?" inquired a shocked Bartholomew.

"No Bart. They are just young, full of life and in a hurry." Daniel went on.

"I know about that." Quipped Patricia. "Many of my young cousins have the same problem. We call it too much pollen."

"Well I thank you my friend," Bartholomew said seriously. And if anyone wants my opinion. I think you should be called a philosopher."

"In my dreams Bartholomew. In my dreams."

Characteristics

"Good morning Bartholomew and Patricia." Daniel greeted his friends. "You are both looking very nice this morning and seem to be taking full advantage of the growing season."

"Thank you Daniel." Came the reply. "We relish the spring and the summer for our fulfillment. By the way we noticed you on the computer late last night. What on earth were you doing?"

"I was just doing some research." Came Daniels casual reply.

"And what were you researching?" Inquired a curious Patricia.

"Well to be honest, I wanted to know more about you two." Daniel answered sheepishly.

"And what did you find out?" Bartholomew questioned.

Daniel began his explanation of what he had found. "That elms grow up to one hundred and fifteen feet tall and can live for over three hundred years, and just like the human cardio-vascular system of arteries and veins, you have a vascular system of long thin vertical tubes. This vascular system takes the water and nutrients from the roots and distributes them throughout you. You have cells that produce the vascular tubes and are found just beneath your bark in a layer called the cambium. After each growing season, the inner part of the cambium dies. A new cambium is formed the next spring. You have tree rings and each ring is a cambium layer. You soak up carbon dioxide from the air, producing life-giving oxygen in return. In you, breathing takes place in the leaf. Chlorophyll (the substance causing the green color) absorbs the carbon dioxide and uses it along with water to dissolve minerals taken up through your roots. After the chemical reaction is completed, your leaves release oxygen and water vapor through it's pores. There are two ways that you can take in water: through the leaves and through the roots."

"Very impressive Daniel." Bartholomew replied. "But why didn't you just ask me?"

"Well I didn't want to take up our time talking about something you probably find boring." Came Daniels apologetic response.

"And what did you find out about me?" Queried Patricia.

"Well I didn't have time to research much about you Pat. The only thing I found was a human myth or story that goes like this," Daniel continued. "When the Holy family was pursued by Herod's soldiers, many plants offered them shelter. One such plant was the Pine Tree. When Mary was too weary to travel longer the family stopped at the edge of a forest to rest. A gnarled old pine which had grown hollow with its' years invited them to rest within its trunk--then it closed its branches down and kept them safe until the soldiers had passed. Upon leaving, the Christ Child blessed the pine and the imprint of his little hand was left forever in the tree's fruit--the pine cone. If a cone is cut lengthwise the hand may still be seen."

"It is nice that you thought about us enough to do research to try and understand us better." Bartholomew intoned seriously. "That is similar to what we do when we ask about human thoughts and feelings."

"Hey Daniel." Called Little's squirrel voice. "What did you find out about me?"

"Nothing I didn't already know without researching." Came Daniel's sarcastic reply. "You like almonds."

Harriet and Jonathan

"Good morning everyone." Daniel said morosely while walking out onto his back patio.

"Morning Daniel." Came the greetings from Patricia and Bartholomew.

"You sound upset this morning." Bartholomew continued. "Anything we can do to help?"

"Yes you can. Can you explain something that happened to me this morning?" Daniel asked.

"What happened?" Inquired a concerned Patricia.

"Well I came outside really early this morning. I noticed two ducks down in the pond. A mallard and his mate. So I went up to them and asked their names and how they were. I even tossed them a few of Little's breakfast almonds that I had extra." Daniel explained further. "But they never answered me. Was I projecting wrong?" he questioned.

"No." Patricia answered. "Your thought projections are fine. In fact they get better each day."

"Then what did I do wrong?" Daniel asked.

"Well." Bartholomew mumbled embarrassedly. "That was Harriet and Jonathan."

"So what did I do wrong?" Daniel questioned further.

"Tell him Bartholomew." Patricia said.

"He won't." Came Little's reply as he jumped into the conversation. "So I guess I will have to do it. I don't know why all the hard and unpleasant jobs always fall to me, Daniel." Little began his explanation. "Harriet and John will never answer you no matter what you say."

"Why not." Queried a perplexed Daniel.

"You're human." Little answered. "They feel superior to humans and will not communicate with them."

"And why would they feel superior?" Came the retired civil servants inquiry.

"Because they can swim." Little retorted.

"But humans can swim also." Daniel reasoned.

"Yeah, but you don't have feathers." Little explained irritably.

"But Bartholomew explained to me that all creatures are part of the universal awareness and will exist in the light as equals." Daniel answered pe·plexed. "Did I misunderstand him?"

"No." Little went on explaining patiently.

"Bartholomew is just a dreamer." Little expounded. "He thinks all living creatures should act as if they had gone into the light. Only problem is that they haven't gone yet and Harriet and John are just stuck up and arrogant. Don't sweat it. You didn't do anything wrong."

"Okay. I understand now." Said a relieved Daniel.

"Oh, and Daniel." Little said irritably. "Don't give them any more of my damn almonds!"

Ghosts

"Good morning everyone," Daniel greeted as he went out onto his back patio. "Morning Daniel." came the chorus of replies.

"We have a question." Bartholomew said stoically.

"Well go ahead and I will do my best to answer it." Daniel effused.

"Last Halloween holiday, we noticed a number of children going out to Trick or Treat covered with a cloth of complete white." Bartholomew inquired. "What was that all about?"

"They were disguised as ghosts." Daniel explained.

"And what are ghosts?" Patricia questioned puzzled.

"Oh boy," Daniel answered. "I'd better get some more almonds for Little to snack on, this could take a long time."

"And what human explanation doesn't?" Quipped Little.

"Little just shut up and eat your almonds." Patricia replied exasperatedly. "Daniel go on."

"To start with we need to explain swamp gas." Daniel started his explanation. "The pond, as we call it but it's really just a swamp, has bacteria that breaks down certain elements and converts them into a gas. If the electricity in the air is high enough it will react with that gas exciting it and it will glow and give off light."

"Is that such a hard concept for humans?" Bartholomew questioned.

"No Bart," Daniel went on. "In fact humans use that concept in many of their homes. It's called florescent lighting. When the gas used gives off a colored light, it's called neon and used in many human advertising signs."

"Where do the ghosts come in?" Mumbled Little with his mouth full.

"Little." Exclaimed an angry Patricia. "I won't tell you again. Shut up and just eat."

"That part of the explanation is just to demonstrate human thinking. They create myths about the lights to explain their fears of the unknown." Daniel expounded. "The ghosts come from that same human imagination. Silicon is the most abundant element on the planet. Silicon dioxide is just plain sand to most humans but the silicon is the element used in their computers. I have seen a demonstration of someone using a computer by nothing but brain waves. So low electrical charges are all that is needed to operate the silicon chips in a computer. With that in mind remember that silicon is the most common element on the planet and is everywhere. So if you apply a big enough electrical charge, as someone's brain gives off when they die or has a traumatic event, the silicon will crystallize like the chips in a computer. That is how they make the chips in the first place. Then to operate these natural occurring chips just takes an electrical charge. Now recently humans have learned how to make a hologram. That is an image you can see but has no substance. It is purely an optical illusion created by the silicon chips in a computer or as I say by Mother Nature when everything falls into place."

"That makes a lot of sense my friend, but still does not explain the ghosts." Bartholomew complained.

"Okay," Daniel went on. "If the naturally occurring chips were made by the strong brain waves from someone who died unexpectedly, then the crystallization would take the form of the person in question. Therefore most people who claim to have seen a ghost identify them as someone who died. They also relate myths about seeing them accompanied by cold. This familiar person and cold are interpreted by most humans as a visit from a dead person and scares them."

"I'm beginning to understand what you have explained, but where does the cold come in. I assume that many humans have reported it for it to become part of the legend." Patricia inquired.

"Right Pat." Daniel went on patiently. "Have you ever experienced a storm coming in?'

"Yes I have." Patricia answered.

"Well humans have a term for when it comes. It's called first chill. That is when the barometric pressure drops quickly and creates the cold. Plus when a storm comes in there is usually a lot of electrical energy in the air, which is what sets off the naturally occurring silicon chips and hence the hologram."

"That is so simple Daniel. Then what is the mystery?" Questioned a perplexed Bartholomew.

"Well it requires much thought and most humans won't do it so they create myths and legends to explain it all." Daniel answered. "I guess that is what Little would call a dumb human idea."

"No Daniel," Little jumped in. "That is a dumb, a neurotic, and a totally paranoid idea."

"Well I hope I have explained it well enough." Said Daniel expectantly.

"Yes my friend." Came Bartholomew's reply. "Thank you for another explanation of human ideas and thoughts."

"Well if it helped, then that is good. But it has made me tired and so if you guys don't mind, I'll just stay out here to be close to you and take a nap." Daniel replied as he settled comfortably into his chair and closed his eyes.

Speeding

"Morning Daniel." Greeted the retired civil servant as he went out onto his back patio.

"Morning." Came his grumbled reply.

"Daniel?" Inquired a concerned Patricia. "Is something wrong? You seem angry this morning."

"Sorry Pat. Didn't mean to take it out on you. It's not your fault, but yes I am upset this morning." Daniel answered.

"Anything we can help with?" Questioned Bartholomew the stately old elm.

"No Bart." Daniel went on. "It's just that I get tired of coming out here each morning and watching the traffic out in the road speeding."

"Are they doing something wrong?" Bartholomew questioned. "I am not familiar with the term speeding."

"They just constantly break the speed limit. That's what speeding is." Daniel explained.

"What is a speed limit?" Patricia asked.

"Humans have rules about almost everything." Daniel explained. "They put a limit on how fast you can go and the traffic out here seems to break it on a constant basis."

"Didn't you tell us that humans make things called laws to enforce the desired actions?" Queried Patricia.

"Correct again." Daniel intoned seriously. "But the people who enforce such laws are few and can't be everywhere all the time, so people push the law hoping not to be caught."

"They don't have laws concerning almonds do they?" asked a concerned Little.

"No Little." Daniel answered smiling. "Nothing about almonds."

"Whew." Effused a relieved Little.

"Why do the humans break the laws?" asked a perplexed Patricia.

"They seem to fail to understand, that a society has laws to keep everything in order. Such order benefits everyone." Daniel expounded.

"Yet they put personal goals above the society's welfare." Bartholomew inquired shocked.

"It's a philosophical concept called tragedy of the commons." Daniel went on expounding on the explanation. "It states the tragedy is that each man is locked into a system that compels him to limit his goals and in a world that is so limited he needs to sacrifice his goals for the benefit of the whole. Ruin is the destination toward which all men rush, each pursuing his own interest in a society that believes in the freedom to pursue their own goals regardless of the cost to society."

"That's just dumb." Quipped Little.

"Can you give us another example?" asked Patricia.

"Sure." Daniel answered. "We have traffic lights that tell us when to stop and when to go. Red means stop and green means go. If a human comes to such a light and no one is around they will not go thru the red light for fear of being caught. Not for the realization that the society will benefit from their following the rules."

"Wow." Patricia exclaimed. "That seems awful small minded of them."

"No. Small minded would mean they had a mind." Daniel replied seriously. "I don't think they consider the larger picture at all."

"Well for what it's worth my friend." Bartholomew expounded philosophically. "I know of at least one human who seems to understand and adhere to the rules."

"Thanks Bart, and sorry Pat, I should know better by this point in my life and not let it upset me." Said Daniel thoughtfully.

"I can offer some advice my friend." Little chirped. "Eat more almonds."

Funny Poetry

"Hi guys," said Daniel walking out onto his patio. "Looks like it's going to be a hot day today."

"Yes Daniel." Replied Bartholomew the stately elm. "But hot is a relative term so it means different things to different beings as to whether it is hot to them or not."

"We have a request this morning." Patricia interrupted.

"And what could that be?" Daniel questioned.

"You told us that you write poetry." She went on.

"Yes." Daniel responded. "I've even had a book published. It was called Eclectics."

"Well," Patricia explained further. "The poems you have read us so far have been really good and flow like a song. Tell us one that is humorous."

"Okay Pat." Daniel effused. "Here is my favorite funny poem."

Roses are red,
Violets are blue.
Some poems rhyme,
And some don't.

Daniel was greeted with a stoned silence.

"I don't get it." Patricia said solemnly.

"Ugh." Little chimed in. "That's not funny, that's just dumb."

"The funny part is that it is a poem but doesn't do what a poem does and explains it as an excuse." Daniel explained.

"That didn't cause us to laugh." Little complained. "If it's a matter of perspective, my perspective is it was just dumb and it caused us to groan. Was that a pun?"

"No Little. It was just a whimsical bit of poetry." Daniel explained further.

"Was that in your book you had published?" Queried the small squirrel.

"No." Daniel went on. "That type of poetry would not sell."

"Is there a law against it?" Questioned Bartholomew.

"No Bart. No law against it but punishment just the same." Daniel expounded.

"If there is no law, and you have explained that only humans who break the law have to be punished. What punishment could you experience?" Bartholomew's questioning continued.

"No one would buy the book and that would be the price to pay for bad poetry." Daniel went on.

"So you would have to pay a price for such a bad poem?" Little inquired expectantly.

"Yes Little, it would be like paying a fine." Daniel replied seriously.

"Well then Mr. No Tail." Little said stoically. "For reciting that to us your fine is twelve almonds."

The Void

"Good morning Daniel." Greeted Patricia. "Isn't it a glorious morning?"

"Hi Patricia." Mumbled Daniel pensively.

"What's wrong handsome." Patricia inquired concerned.

"Ignore her Daniel." Little jumped in. "She effuses every conversation with her perky enthusiasm. It's as maddening as it is infectious. What's on your mind?"

"I had a bad morning my friend." Daniel responded. "I went to the void."

"You didn't go anywhere." Little said. "Bartholomew I need some help here."

"Daniel." Bartholomew questioned. "Do you know where the void is?"

"No Bart. I don't." Daniel replied. "Only that it is a dark place where demons live."

"The void is in your mind. Every living being has one and they visit them from time to time." explained the stately old elm. "Why did you go there?"

"I don't know. Maybe I went there just looking for answers." Came Daniel's solemn answer.

"No." Bartholomew retorted.

"Then why did I go?" questioned a confused Daniel.

"You went there, as all creatures do, looking for control." Extolled Bartholomew.

"And controlling my mind is a bad thing?" inquired an exasperated Daniel.

"What ever led you to think any living creature could control their mind?" Bartholomew questioned further.

"There has to be something in control." Exclaimed Daniel.

"Didn't you tell us once that you had ingested too much alcohol once and that you then lost control over your body's functions, both physical and mental." Asked Bartholomew continuing the analysis. "Then realize that the mind is controlled by the chemicals you ingest voluntarily or involuntarily. Not some mystical force."

"But you told me that when I died and went into the light the universal awareness would give me peace." Daniel demanded.

"The light gives peace, my friend, not control." Answered a patient Bartholomew.

"So you are saying that when I go into the light, I will no longer feel the need for control and that the desire will cease to exist?" Reasoned Daniel.

"Way to go Daniel. You got it." Little jumped in. "I can't wait to tell Sam that the human is not as dumb as I first thought."

"Daniel you are not the first creature to visit the void, be depressed, or consider suicide." Bartholomew went on.

"I thought only humans committed suicide." Daniel questioned further.

"Stop thinking like a human." Said Little. "You ever notice other mammals dead in the highway out there."

"Yeah." Daniel went on. "I just thought that they had just been too slow and been hit by a car."

"That's as insulting as you thinking I had forgotten where I buried my almonds. Most animals you see and think of as "Road Kill" were two or three times faster than any human and had twice the reflexes of your best athlete.

"Okay." Replied a thoughtful Daniel. "I hadn't really thought of it that way."

"That's because you still think like a human." Little responded. "Ever been to a zoo?"

"Yes."

"Look into the eyes of the animals there. Then go to a human mental institution and look into their eyes. It's the same look. They keep the humans inside, the same way they keep the animals in a zoo. It's to keep them from committing suicide and going into the light." Little continued angrily. "That is the worst thing that can be done to any living creature. I guess the humans doing it have an inferiority complex and it makes them feel that they have some control."

"So to prevent going to the void I just need to be more aware of what I put into my body." Daniel asked inquiringly.

"Right." Little went on. "It's as simple as that. The only way I would ever go into the void is if they had almond trees there."

Frequencies

"Morning friends," Daniel projected as he walked out onto his back patio, with the summer's morning sun just peeking over the mountains.

"Morning Daniel," intoned Bartholomew, the stately old elm.

"Hi Dan." Echoed Patricia the young perky but voluptuous pine.

"Did you bring my breakfast almonds?" Inquired Little the sarcastic almond loving squirrel. "And by the way good morning."

" I am a little embarrassed this morning." Daniel went on.

"Why would you ever be embarrassed with us?" Bartholomew asked.

"Well." Daniel began his explanation. "I was researching human brain frequencies on the computer last night and found that I had been mistaken on the state of consciousness that I had been experiencing."

"Would you mind explaining that to us." Bartholomew continued. "What exactly did you find?"

"That there are four states of human brain frequencies. Contrary to what we were taught in high school, the human body is mostly water and it runs on electrical energy which we generate from foods we eat.

First is the Delta state, which is pretty much asleep. Frequencies range from three and one half to five megahertz. Second is the Theta state or deep relaxation or hypnosis. Frequencies there ranges from four to seven megahertz. Third is the Alpha state, basically very relaxed but alert, with frequencies of eight to thirteen megahertz. The last is Beta, which is the most common human frequency and ranges from fourteen to thirty megahertz. That is when a human is awake. What I found was that astral projection usually occurs in the Theta state when the frequency is seven."

"Why would this upset you?" Bartholomew inquired further.

"Well Bart." Daniel answered. "I wasn't going into the alpha state all this time but had gone lower and reached the Theta state when I traveled with Sam and Little."

"Daniel those are just labels. Which one you were in, is irrelevant. You visited and traveled with us and that is all that is important." Bartholomew reasoned.

"I know." Daniel went on sheepishly. "But it just makes me feel so dumb."

"Awareness of dumb." Little jumped in. "That is the first step to becoming not so dumb."

"Daniel." Consoled Patricia. "We do not think you are dumb. You are the first human to make contact with us and that counts for a lot."

"I guess you're right." Daniel answered consoling himself. "The contact is the most important thing."

"Second most important thing." Little corrected him. "First thing is almonds."

Summer Solstice

"Good morning my friends." Daniel exclaimed excitedly as he went onto his back patio. "Happy Summer Solstice."

"Happy what?" inquired a curious Little.

"Summer Solstice." Daniel continued. "Remember when I told you about Winter Solstice? Well today is June twenty first and it is the Summer Solstice or put simply the official beginning of summer."

"Well spring sure passed by quickly." Bartholomew stated.

"And it was a great spring." Patricia exclaimed happily.

"I couldn't agree more Patricia." Daniel said. "You looked radiant when you were covered with pollen turning you a lovely bright yellow, Bartholomew grew a new cambium layer, and even Little lost some of his winter fat."

"Hey watch it Mr. No Tail." Little countered. "I'm not the only one around here to put on some winter fat."

"True Little." Daniel conceded. "But I haven't been able to lose mine. Maybe you could teach me to scamper."

"Summer is always such a joyous time." Patricia jumped in her perky enthusiasm overflowing.

"Well I enjoyed the spring," Daniel countered. "But I will say I am looking forward to summer. Mother Nature's spring songs with the blustery winds seemed sometimes intense. Mother's summer rain songs and lazy heat filled days are an exercise in relaxation."

"How true my friend." Bartholomew went on. "So just relax and take a nap."

"Hey Daniel," Little cried out. "Before you snooze, how about some breakfast almonds?"

Fourth of July

"Good morning." Daniel called softly as he emerged onto his patio in the heat of a summer morning.

"And a good morning to you as well." Greeted Patricia the young voluptuous pine.

"Good morning Daniel." Greeted Bartholomew. "You seem to be moving a little slow this morning."

"I was out with the wife late last night." Daniel explained.

"Did you guys have anything to do with all that racket?" Questioned an irated Little.

"Yes and no. We didn't do anything to cause the racket ourselves, but we did attend the celebration." Daniel went on.

"That seems to happen about once a year." Bartholomew analyzed. "Is it another human holiday?"

"Yes." Answered the retired civil servant. "It's called the Fourth of July."

"You celebrate a certain day in a month above all the rest." Inquired a curious Patricia.

"We celebrate the date because of the significance of what happened on that date long ago." Daniel continued his explanation.

"Well tell us, while I eat." Little asked chewing on his breakfast almonds.

"Long ago." Daniel began his explanation. "This geographical part of the earth was occupied by a group of humans whose ruler was the King of England. They got tired of it and wanted to rule themselves. So they sent a message declaring their independence of him and of England. A war ensued and they won and became the United States of America. So on the Fourth of July every year they celebrate. Their feelings are called Patriotism, to honor their country and they set off fireworks to show how Patriotic they are."

"What are fireworks Daniel?" Asked Patricia.

"They are an extremely simple substance called gunpowder. Indeed, it is not even a compound, being merely a mixture of potassium nitrate, common charcoal, and sulphur. When ignited it explodes causing bright colored lights and a loud noise." Came the continuing explanation.

"Well that explains why I lose a lot of sleep once a year." Complained Little. "Where does that dumb human idea come from?"

"In one of the first battles of the war." Daniel went on. "A gentleman named Francis Scott Key, observed the battle and wrote a song about it. The flag of the new country was called the Star Spangled Banner due to the colors and stars it displayed. It became the song of the country and was held in high

Patriotic esteem to denote the pride the people held. It spoke of rockets red glare and bombs bursting in air. Hence the relationship to fireworks and the celebration of the song, date, and battle by shooting off fireworks."

"Couldn't they have come up with something a little quieter?" Little expounded.

"It celebrates the date this country gained independence and the society in which we live. Which by the way allows me to buy the almonds you have each morning." Daniel replied exasperated.

"Hey who am I to complain." Little exclaimed nervously. "Don't want to be a spoiled sport, or change anything. Let the fireworks begin."

Final Conversations

Introduction to Final Conversations

A modern version of Aesop's fables with a twist.

The third and final book of the conversations series between the four friends first put down and recorded in Conversations, Daniel the retired civil servant, Bartholomew the tall stately Elm, Patricia, the young voluptuous pine, and Little, the sarcastic almond loving squirrel.

This book is dedicated to my wife Dell. She who has meant so much to me and supported my work at every step of the journey from the beginning to the end. Never complaining about my time spent writing, or her time spent reviewing everything I wrote.

Index Final Conversations

1 Quotations
2 Casino
3 Hope - Poem
4 Insanity
5 The Universe
6 Grok
7 Hope Revisited
8 Automobiles
9 Reveling
10 Driftwood
11 Home
12 The Ballad of Danny and Dell-Poem
13 Children Screaming
14 Glasses
15 Human Nature
16 Suntanned
17 Shaving
18 Solitude
19 Little's Poem
20 Beverly Hillbillies
21 Brazil Nuts
22 True Meaning of Conversations
23 Final Conversation
24 To Katie on Your Wedding Day - Poem
25 Goodbye

Quotations

"Good morning everyone." Daniel greeted his friends walking out into the summer's morning on his back patio.

"Good morning to you." Replied Bartholomew the stately old elm.

"Hi handsome." Patricia effused her usual perky self. "You look good this morning, especially after last night."

"Almonds." Little chimed in.

"Little, I've told you before. Almonds is not a greeting. And Patricia" Daniel questioned, "what are you talking about when you said, especially after last night?"

"Sorry Daniel." Little quipped. "But I'm starving out here."

"What I meant." Patricia jumped in interrupting Little and avoiding any confrontations. "We observed you awake most of last night with the light by your bed on. What were you doing?"

"Remember me telling you about human books?" Daniel queried. "Well I was up late reading."

"Is this how you learned so much?" Bartholomew inquired.

"Sure." Daniel answered. "No one is born with knowledge, you have to work for it. Reading is one way humans have to share knowledge."

"How do you remember it all?" Asked a curious Patricia.

"I don't." Daniel responded regretfully. "But there are many ways humans have come up with over the years. One way is quotations. When someone writes or speaks of a thought that is profound, it can be written down and memorized as valid and worth remembering. Some are very thought provoking and some are just silly."

"Tell us a silly one." Patricia pleaded.

"Well." Daniel quoted. "Never put off for tomorrow, what you can do the day after tomorrow."

"I assume the silly part is that it is dumb and bad advice." Bartholomew intoned seriously.

"Correct Bart." Daniel went on. "But a serious one is that, there is a very thin line between genius and insanity."

"That is thought provoking." Bartholomew answered then questioned. "Why would you think of that this morning?"

"Well, it seems to apply to me." Daniel explained. "I have made the mistake of telling a few people of our conversations."

"I have noticed no one joining in." Bartholomew exclaimed.

"Right." Daniel explained further. "I don't know what they think but I suspect they think I'm going insane. I am usually greeted by one of three responses. One is stunned silence. Two an uncomfortable laugh. And three total denial."

"Could you explain that a little more?" Bartholomew asked inquiringly.

"They think that I make it all up in my head." Daniel went on explaining. "And that it indicates that I am losing my mind."

"They think that just because they cannot talk to us?" Questioned Patricia.

"Afraid so, my dear." Daniel went on. "Humans are very uncomfortable with the idea that something is going on and they are not part of it, or can understand it. So they create answers to explain it all away. In my case it's just that I am going insane."

"You humans have some very strange reasoning thoughts." Little jumped in. "But I think I know why."

"And what might that be." Daniel questioned the small squirrel.

"You guys just don't eat enough almonds."

Casino

"Good morning!" Daniel exclaimed happily as he walked out onto his back patio into the early morning's light.

"Good morning to you as well." Answered Bartholomew. "You sure seem in a chipper mood this morning."

"I am indeed." Daniel announced. "I came out ahead at the casino last night."

"What does that mean? Coming out ahead and what is a casino?" Queried Patricia curiously.

"Coming out ahead means that I left the casino with more money than I had going in." Daniel explained. "A casino is a business where humans bet on games of chance and can win money."

"If they pay out money, it seems from what you've told us, that would not be a good business investment and they would not be in business long." Decried Bartholomew.

"You don't always win. Most times you leave with less than you went in with." Daniel conceded. "The games have statistical odds assigned. The odds favor the business." Daniel went on.

"Then why go if the odds are against you?" Little asked confused.

"Because the odds are great against you but not impossible." Daniel explained further. "When you win you have beaten the odds. It feels great. Plus it is just enjoyable entertainment."

"Enjoyable entertainment." Scoffed Little. "What kind of entertainment is enjoyable with no rewards?"

"Okay." Daniel paused thinking. "How about sex. Even when humans don't want an offspring to come from the process they still engage in the process."

"Okay your point is taken." Little mumbled aggravatedly.

"What kinds of games do they play?" Patricia inquired.

"Hundreds of different kinds." Daniel effused. "Most are run by machines and are called slots. The buildings are lit with different colored lights, there is always music and the thrill of winning is ever present."

"Do a lot of humans go there?" Questioned Bartholomew.

"Oh yes." Daniel responded. "The casinos are always full."

"So you get interaction with other humans? That must be a good thing." Bartholomew reasoned.

"The truth is Bart. It is a good feeling and lifts ones spirits to see so many humans with hope in their eyes, even if they know the odds are against them."

"An interesting concept." Bartholomew mused. "This is a particularly good concept you humans have."

"I've got a good concept." Cried Little. "I'll bet you two almonds I can scamper faster than you."

"That's not a bet Little. The odds are too great and if I could scamper at all you would be much faster than I." Daniel said mournfully.

"You're no fun." Little bemoaned.

"Daniel." Patricia injected. "Surely you have written about this. Read us a poem."

Hope

What is this thing we call hope?
We revere the trait above all the rest.
And why must we continually,
Put it to a test.

Have you ever gone into a casino,
And the people just have to know.
The odds are all against them,
Yet their confidence does show.

See people skydiving,
It's really such a feat.
And their parachutes will always open,
It will be such a treat.

Bad things always happen,
To the other guy you know.
It never happens to you,
So to the wind, caution you do throw.

Do overs are in the movies,
Some things don't allow a second chance.
But people do things,
That seems stupid at a glance.

But hope is universal,
And so we all tempt fate.
Because while it may be dumb,
It's man's only enduring trait.

Insanity

"Morning." Daniel mumbled as he walked out onto his back patio into the early morning's light.

"My. My." Chided Patricia the young voluptuous pine. "Aren't you in a good mood this morning?"

"Sorry Pat." Daniel corrected himself. "Good morning."

"That's better. Now what's got you so upset this morning?" She queried.

"I'll bet it had something to do with Daniel being up most of the night." Said Bartholomew joining in the conversation.

"I noticed your light was on way past the time when most other humans, including your mate were asleep."

"Right you are Bartholomew." Daniel conceded.

"Were you writing?" Patricia asked. "I love your poetry. It flows like a song. Were you having a problem with it?"

"No Pat." Daniel explained. "My poetry is going fine. I have the book Eclectics published and Eclectics II is contracted with the publisher and waiting to be printed. Eclectics III is finished and waiting to be sent for review to the publisher."

"Are you having a problem with it being accepted?" Inquired Bartholomew.

"Not really Bart." Daniel went on. "Some humans like it. Some say I'm very talented. And others say I'm gifted. But what had me up most of the night was a statement my daughter said."

"You humans have more trouble with your offspring than any other mammals." Little exclaimed joining in.

"Little you don't even know his daughter." Complained Patricia.

"Well tell her to come down and I'll get to know her and even let her feed me some almonds while we talk." Little offered.

"What a sacrifice." Patricia scolded. "Tricking another human into feeding you almonds."

"Hey," Little said sheepishly. "Almonds are not a trick. They are serious."

"Anyway Daniel." Patricia went on. "What did she say?"

"It was just a human quote I've heard most of my life." Daniel answered quoting. "There is a thin line between genius and insanity."

"Sounds to me like she was trying to give you a compliment." Bartholomew intoned seriously.

"I'm sure she was," Daniel rejoinered. "But it led me to thinking about it."

"And what was your conclusion." Bartholomew asked concerned.

"Well," Daniel reasoned. "If it is true and there is a thin line between the two. Why the hell doesn't anybody tell me where it is?"

"Find that, my friend." Bartholomew answered consolingly. "And you will be famous among humans."

The Universe

"Good morning everyone." Greeted Daniel walking out onto his back patio. "I've had my coffee this morning and I feel wonderful."

"Great Daniel. You have all the coffee you want. Just don't forget my breakfast almonds." Little chided.

"Don't worry my friend. I didn't forget." Daniel answered carefully placing down the almonds. "And Bartholomew. Can I ask another question?"

"Sure." Came the old elm's reply. "You answer our questions without complaint. I would be happy if I could answer any question you may have."

"I talked with Sam about life and understand the universal awareness of all intelligent beings. But I wonder why it is so limited. I mean is Earth the only place it really exists?" Daniel questioned.

"O my goodness no." Bartholomew exclaimed. "The entire universe is just one big community. Life abounds everywhere."

"Even in the cold darkness of space?" Daniel questioned further.

"Daniel remember going to the Orion Nebula?" Asked Patricia joining in.

"Yes I do." Replied the retired civil servant.

"How do you think that much light, color and warmth could exist without life?" Patricia inquired.

"Even the stars?" Daniel asked.

"Certainly." Bartholomew injected. "The entire universe is full of life. Stars are born and they die. Some of the forms are not what you would recognize, but they all have one thing in common."

"I guess you're right. I limited my original conversation with Sam to creatures of the Earth only. What is the common factor?" Daniel inquired.

"All intelligent beings have a sense of humor." Bartholomew answered explaining.

"Really?" Came Daniel's incredulous response.

"Sure," Bartholomew went on. "Remember when Little told the joke about Andy losing a few protons and being negative. Sam responded by saying that it was the oldest joke in the cosmos."

"Then tell me a newer one. Something that is easily understood." Daniel pleaded.

"Okay," Bartholomew began. "Two asteroids were talking. One said,"I really don't like Mother Earth."

"Why." the second asked.

The first one answered, "She wraps that big oxygen layer around herself to make her look blue and acts like she's better than the rest of us."

"I know what you mean." Replied the second. "That oxygen thing really burns me up."

"That's the kind of jokes going around the universe?" Daniel asked unbelieving.

"Sure my friend." Bartholomew answered. "Humor is always silly. From what you have told us, humans think it has to be intellectual and serious. Sorry but humor is just silly and that's what makes it funny."

"Humans have things called practical jokes, but they are usually cruel, and at the expense of someone else's pain." Daniel went on.

"So, we're back to the dumb human ideas list." Declared and exasperated Little.

"Afraid so." Daniel said apologetically. "But it is a wonderful feeling to know that the universe is not empty but full of life everywhere, even if some of it we humans could not survive in."

"You will in time Daniel." Bartholomew explained refering to coming into the light. "You will in time."

Grok

"Question?" Came the greeting to Daniel as he walked out onto his back patio.

"Okay, sure." Daniel responded. "And good morning while I'm at it."

"Sorry my friend. Good morning." Bartholomew apologized. "But, I've been thinking all night and had to ask you a question."

"Fire away." Daniel replied.

"You read and study humans a lot. You read the books and even write them. Do you have a word in the language that might describe the universal awareness?" Bartholomew inquired.

"Yes." Came Daniel's answer and explanation. "The word is spelled G R O K. It was coined by science fiction writer Robert A. Heinlein in his novel "Stranger in a Strange Land". In Heinlein's invented Martian language, it is pronounced *grock.* Grok literally means to drink, and figuratively means to understand, to love, or to be one with."

"So he knew of the universal awareness?" Bartholomew asked further.

"That I don't know." Daniel replied. "The definition formally used is to understand so thoroughly that the observer becomes a part of the observed, and to merge, blend, intermarry, lose identity in group experience. It means almost everything that we mean by religion, philosophy, and science, and it means little to us, because we are humans and probably understand what it means as much as what color means to a blind man. So I don't know if he understood instinctively what it was, or he felt that something was there and he gave a name to it."

"How very interesting." Bartholomew intoned.

"Humans have instincts they sometimes don't understand and few will accept those feelings without a logical explanation." Daniel expounded further.

"They don't trust their feelings?" Patricia asked inquiringly.

"Not if those feelings don't have a simple explanation that they are familiar with." Daniel replied mournfully.

"Just another dumb human idea." Exclaimed Little joining in. "Even I Grok."

"No Little, you don't Grok. What you do is Groak." Daniel expounded.

"What's the difference?" asked Little with an offended tone.

"Well to Grok is to understand things by instinct. To Groak is what you did last night. It's watching someone eat, hoping to be invited to join in. Like a dog does when it sits staring at you when you eat hoping to get a bite. You stood outside the sliding glass door last night while I ate supper, and stared at me." Daniel explained.

"That sounds like Little." Patricia chided.

"Hey I don't understand human food." Little defended himself. "I Grok almonds

Hope Revisited

"Good morning everyone." Daniel exclaimed walking out onto his back patio.

"And a fine morning it is." Bartholomew replied. "Did you have a good night's rest?"

"Yes I did." Daniel responded happily. "Anything on your minds today."

"I have a question." Patricia injected. "Bart most of the time asks them but I have one this morning."

"Well ask away my dear. You know I would love to help." Daniel rejoinered.

"Daniel. First off you know I love your poems. They flow and rhyme so smoothly it makes me want to dance. But in the poem you read to us called Hope, you referred to it as man's only enduring trait. What is the term enduring and what does it mean?" Patricia inquired.

"Well Patricia. According to the human's dictionary, which defines words. It means simply long lasting or permanent, or to hold out against without yielding." Daniel explained.

"So it is a human characteristic that is good and should be prized." She queried.

"You would think so, but I have reservations about it." Daniel went on.

"That sounds ominous." Bartholomew stated, then questioned. "Care to explain that?'

"While it gives humans reasons to live, it makes them gullible to other humans whose intentions are less than honorable." Daniel replied sadly.

"In what way?" Inquired a puzzled Patricia.

"Like I told you about the casino. The odds are in favor of the business and they play on that gullibility and hope of winning to take money from them and don't have to work for themselves." Daniel responded explaining.

"That does seem less than honorable." Bartholomew mused. "Any other humans business's do that?"

"Unfortunately yes." Daniel went on. "We have humans who do not understand the light and prey on other humans fear of dying by promising them an afterlife that is full of joy and rewards for living a good, honest, and moral life."

"But that is what happens." Bartholomew argued. "What's wrong with that precept."

"Because the other humans teach that the only way they can attain such happiness is by listening to them and following their teaching. Also by giving them money. They call it tithing."

"What does tithing mean?" asked Patricia.

"It means giving one tenth of their income to those people so they don't have to work and will be supported while they do the teaching." Daniel expounded.

"Are you ever going to reach the end of the list of dumb human ideas?" Little injected into the conversation.

"No Little. It's not all bad. It gives people hope and joy and, if you remember Carl Jung's idea, something to believe in and a reason to live." Daniel countered.

"So hope may have some bad side effects but overall it is good." Patricia asked seriously.

"I believe in the end it is a good thing." Daniel answered solemnly.

"Then I can hope for you all to shut up, and feed me my breakfast almonds before I starve." Chimed in an exasperated Little.

Automobiles

"Good morning." Greeted Daniel walking out into the morning's light on his back patio.

"Greetings Daniel." Replied Bartholomew.

"Hi Dan." Patricia joined in Bartholomew's greeting. "We have a question this morning and surprise, surprise the source is Little."

"Well, that's a first." Answered Daniel seriously. "What's the question?"

"When Little was climbing around the other day he noticed that the big area across the road had hundreds of automobiles parked in it. We didn't know why." Patricia inquired.

"Is that where a lot of humans park their automobiles?" Asked Bartholomew.

"No." Daniel replied. "It is a car sales lot. That is where they store the cars they wish to sell."

"They must have a large demand for cars to store that many." Bartholomew responded questionably.

"No again Bartholomew." Daniel explained further. "They have so many because each one is different. Humans, as I have told you before thrive on individuality. Therefore, they need a lot of cars to cater to each human's desire to buy a car that is different from all the others."

"I understand my friend." Bartholomew replied. "That is quite an accomplishment, to have that many automobiles built so differently. The engineering for the motors must be almost unbelievable."

"Well no again for the third time my friend." Daniel explained further. "The mechanical engineering is pretty much the same on all of the automobiles. They haven't changed all that much in the last 50 years."

"Then why do you say they are different?" Asked a puzzled Patricia.

"The differences are in the outward appearance and accessories." Daniel responded.

"You may have to explain a bit more." Bartholomew questioned further.

"Using my former explanations I will list three." Daniel expounded. "One is the color. Two is the accessories such as radio, air conditioning, interior design materials, and automatic transmission. And three is body design of the automobile. The shape and curves that the engineers build it into."

"You mean the automobiles all function the same?" Argued Bartholomew shocked. "But the only differences are small changes to establish the illusion of uniqueness and individuality?"

"Afraid so Bart." Daniel conceded. "I have told you before how prized individuality is in humans."

"As much as it pains me." Patricia rejoinered. "Little may in fact have a point. That sounds like a pretty dumb human idea to make so many different versions of the automobile that all function the same."

"Yes." Daniel agreed chastised. "I agree it doesn't make a lot of sense, but that's just human behavior."

"Hey guys." Little exclaimed joining in the conversation. "Did Daniel explain all the automobiles in the area across the road?"

"Yes Little." Patricia explained. "He told us they all function the same but differ in style, such as body design, accessories, and color."

" Wow." Stated Little. "Then if I can choose make mine the color of Almonds."

Reveling

"Good morning all." Daniel exclaimed as he burst out onto his back patio in the early light of a July morning. "Isn't is a grand morning."

"Indeed it is my friend." Replied Bartholomew solemnly.

"Oh yes." Patricia said joining in. "You could call it glorious."

"I couldn't agree more. You voluptuous little pine." Daniel effused.

"Surely you must have written some poem to speak of a day like this." Patricia went on. "Read one to us."

"Well, the first thing I can think of is part of a poem I wrote long ago." Daniel responded. "Here it is."

Then one day I saw a dog,
    Lying in a field of clover.
Enjoying the sun and gentle breeze,
    Onto his back rolled over.
He did not strive to better his lot,
    No guilt to spoil his fun.
He took the day for what it was,
    And reveled in the sun.

"You know Daniel." Patricia said joyfully. "I love your poems. They rhyme so sweetly and flow so smoothly, they make me want to dance. But I don't know that human term, reveling. What does it mean?" She questioned further.

"It means to take great pleasure or delight in." Daniel replied explaining. "Just like we take great pleasure in this morning's light."

"It is a joy to be alive." Bartholomew injected. "And if I could use the term. I revel in our friendship."

"I revel in your poetry Daniel." Exclaimed Patricia. Her enthusiasm overflowing.

"Hey I revel." Came a small squirrel's voice from down by the pond.

"And dare I ask." Daniel questioned warily. "What do you revel in Little?"

"I revel in almonds."

Driftwood

"Good morning." Daniel greeted his friends as he stepped out onto his back patio.

"Good morning my friend." Replied Bartholomew the old stately elm.

"Hi handsome." Said Patricia coyly.

"Did you bring my breakfast almonds, Mr. No Tail?" Little asked anxiously.

"Yes I did Little. And there is no need to be insulting." Daniel rejoinered.

"Hey," said Little defensively. "As I remember it, that would be a description and not an insult."

"Fine. Do you guys have anything else to talk about except for Little's fixation on starving?" Daniel inquired.

"We do indeed." Bartholomew questioned. "Why do you have that big log on the edge of your patio?"

"That would be our big piece of driftwood. We have many smaller pieces in the home but that one just caught my wife's eye and she wanted to have it." Daniel explained.

"What's driftwood?" Asked an ever-curious Patricia.

"It's just parts of trees that have become dislodged from land and fell into the ocean. They drift around and eventually wash ashore. The pieces my wife collected are from the ocean shore in Washington State." Daniel went on. "The pieces that are really malformed are pieces she calls gnarly."

"But where did it come from?" Inquired Patricia further.

"That I don't know. The driftwood she has collected could have come from anywhere in the world. But eventually the tides and ocean currents finally deposited it here." Came the retired civil servants answer.

"So why does she feel the pull to collect it?" Bartholomew asked.

"Maybe she feels a subconscious attraction. The wood could have come from anywhere in the world and therefore she feels having it around connects her with the planet." Daniel replied thoughtfully.

"Maybe she senses the residual frequency emitted by the once living being." Bartholomew expounded.

"You may be right Bart." Daniel conceded. "Wood has always had a special place in human homes. They build all kinds of things with it. From tables, to chairs, and even to beds."

"They probably feel connected on a subconscious level." Patricia offered.

"Don't humans build things out of steel?" Questioned Bartholomew.

"Yes they do, but over the centuries wood has always held a premium place." Daniel explained. "And as far as a subconscious awareness, humans always refer to it as giving a warmth to a home."

"Your wife probably senses it and it gives her a connection to the universal awareness." Patricia reasoned.

"Could be my dear." Daniel agreed.

"I know why you have it." Quipped Little interrupting.

"And why is that my little friend." Daniel questioned.

"It gives me a place to eat."

Home

"Good morning." Daniel greeted as he walked out onto his back patio.

"Hi Dan." Patricia responded.

"Good morning." Bartholomew joined in. "We have a question or two this morning."

"Ask away, my friend." Daniel expounded. " I will, as always, do my best to answer."

"We are curious about you and your mate?" Bartholomew questioned. "Have you been mated a long time?"

"Well time is a relative term Bart. For humans we have been together a long time. Married for over thirty-five years." Daniel answered.

"And where were you living all this time?" Inquired the old elm.

"We have lived in many places." Daniel went on. "When we first got married, we decided that no job would determine where we lived. So occasionally we would move to a different part of the country and then find a job there."

"Where have you lived?" Asked a curious Patricia.

"We started off in Georgia, then to Wyoming, back to Georgia. Arkansas then Texas and finally here in Washington State." Daniel explained.

"Is that normal for humans?" Bartholomew questioned.

"Not really." Came Daniel's answer. "Some humans live and die no more than fifty miles from where they're born. Normal is probably somewhere in between."

"Wow." Little jumped into the conversation. "Daniel's not normal. What a shock. Can we eat now?"

"Little, shut up and be patient. You can eat later." Patricia scolded the little squirrel. "Daniel go on."

"Well we think we have found where we want to live permanently now." Daniel went on. "It's here in Washington State, especially out on the Olympic Peninsula. They have old growth forest out there and it has a temperate rain forest. There are only three places in the world where that happens. One is the country called Chili. Two is New Zealand. And the Third is here."

"Always back to the number three." Bartholomew mused. "I must confess I know of the old growth forest. Those guys make me feel like a sapling."

"It took us a long time to arrive here." Daniel replied. "But we got to see much of the country and had a lot of fun moving around."

"Have you written about your travels?" Inquired Patricia.

"Of course my dear. When will you realize I write about everything that is important to me?" Daniel responded.

"Can we eat first?" Little said pleading.

"Later Little." Patricia chided. "Daniel read us the poem."

Danny L Shanks

The Ballad of Danny and Dell

She was a Tarheel from North Carolina,
    He an Arkansas Razorback.
They hooked up down in Georgia,
    And they never have looked back.

Running from here to there,
    Never settling for long.
They seem to dance to another tune,
    A self composed sort of song.

Never playing by all the rules,
    Just enough to get by.
Never managed to win the game,
    But seemed to really try.

They would get so very close,
    Then off again, to run around.
Folks and family just shake their heads,
    Will those two ever, settle down?

They are just searching for paradise,
    A pipe dream if you may.
They flit from here to there,
    Hoping to find it, one fine day.

Well that isn't quite the whole story,
    Finding paradise, ain't what's cookin.
Cause after thirty years it ought to be obvious,
    The fun is in the lookin.

Children Screaming

Daniel rose in the early summer's light and went out onto his back patio. "Good morning Bartholomew and Patricia." He greeted.

"Thank goodness you are now awake." Came the old elm's reply.

"Yes." Patricia agreed. "You can help us."

"I assume you have a question about humans?" Daniel inquired.

"Most assuredly my friend." Bartholomew answered.

"And it has to do with Little." Patricia injected.

"What is the problem?" the retired civil servant asked.

"Well Daniel." Patricia began. "Around this time of the year we have sensed human children being tortured. Little says he can actually hear them."

"You bet I can." Said Little joining in the conversation. "It's about to drive me insane."

"You mind explaining that a little?" Daniel inquired further.

"Ever year and this one is no exception. I hear children being tortured every day. You can hear their screams all the day long." Little explained.

"Where does this screaming come from?" Daniel asked puzzled.

"The center of all these buildings." Little said continuing his explanation. "Where they keep the man made pond."

"Little." Daniel explained patiently. "They are not being tortured. They are having fun."

"They are screaming." Little argued.

"Yes they are." Daniel went on explaining. "For some reason, whenever human children play around water, they express themselves by screaming. They are having fun not being tortured."

"Well it is enough to drive you insane." Little complained.

"That is all it is my friend. Nothing more." Daniel intoned.

"Well at least we have that mystery finally explained." Expounded a relieved Bartholomew.

"And Little's paranoid reaction." Patricia chuckled.

"Hey, I didn't know." Little protested. "Just another dumb human thing, that made no sense to me."

"Well at least if it was going to drive you insane, it would be a short trip." Daniel said amused.

"What is that supposed to mean?" Little asked angrily.

"Well it would be a short drive for you to be considered crazy." Daniel went on laughing. "Humans have a saying, that you are what you eat. Little you're just nuts."

Glasses

"Good morning Daniel. You look different this morning." Greeted Bartholomew as Daniel walked out onto his back patio.

"Good morning Bart." Daniel answered. "I have new glasses."

"I think they're cute." Patricia chimed in.

"What in the world are glasses?" Questioned a confused Little.

"They are aids to help me see better." Daniel explained.

"Humans have aids to help their normal body functions?" Inquired a curious Bartholomew.

"Yes Bartholomew." Said Daniel and explained further. "When we get older some of our body parts cease to function as they did when we were young, so we make things to help us out. Glasses are something we wear to help us see as well as we did when we were young."

"How amazing." Bartholomew intoned.

"What else do humans have to help them?" Inquired a curious Patricia.

"We have knee replacements, stints to help the heart, hearing aids, and even false teeth to help us eat." Daniel went on explaining further.

"So when a part wears out you just replace it?" Asked an astonished Little.

"Many parts of the body we can replace." Daniel replied.

"And do these parts work as well as the originals." Queried Bartholomew.

"No." Daniel answered mournfully. "But they help keep us alive and able to function close to the original level we once enjoyed."

"Does that mean you can live forever?" Little questioned.

"No my friend." Daniel conceded "We all will eventually die, but the aids put it off for awhile and make the time we have more tolerable."

"That must be the most important thing in humans." Bartholomew expounded.

"I told you once my friend. True love is the most important thing for humans that I can think of." Daniel replied seriously.

"But it makes you live longer." Bartholomew argued.

"Bart." Daniel went on explaining. "One day of true love beats a hundred years of life without it."

"That makes sense to me." Patricia agreed.

"Myself." Little injected, serious for once. "My true love is almonds. I would not like to live a single day without them in my life. To heck with seeing better."

Human Nature

A chorus of good mornings greeted Daniel as he walked out onto his back patio.

"Good morning to you all." The retired civil servant replied pensively.

"What is the matter my friend?" Questioned Bartholomew the old stately elm.

"Well we have talked a lot about many human things." Daniel expounded sadly. "But we have never really talked about basic human nature."

"You have explained much." Bartholomew replied respectfully. "What would you like to talk about?"

"Just what makes us humans tick?" Came the reply.

"What would you like us to understand?" Inquired a curious Patricia.

"It is best explained by a statement once made by Sir Edmund Hilary." Daniel went on explaining. "When asked why he climbed Mount Everest, the tallest mountain in the world. He said, because it's there."

"What kind of a dumb human explanation is that?" Asked Little joining in.

"It demonstrates true human nature." Daniel intoned.

"What does the statement mean?" Queried Bartholomew.

"Just that humans feel the need to conquer." Daniel went on. "He needed to feel he conquered the mountain by climbing it."

"Do humans feel the need to conquer many things?" Bartholomew asked.

"Yes, " Daniel expounded. "We set goals we feel we need to conquer in our personal lives. We have sports in which we have the need to conquer another team. Remember when I told you about the Astros coming in second and everyone was sad. We are driven to be number one and conquer everything."

"So that hunting thing is just to conquer another animal?" Inquired a shocked Patricia.

"Yes Pat." Daniel explained further. "We have wars and contests and sports, all designed so that we can conquer any other being or thing that is sometimes weaker than us."

"That's disgusting and depressing." Little chimed in.

"I'm afraid I have to agree, but it seems to be the main driving force of human nature." Daniel conceded.

"So Daniel." Bartholomew questioned. "Is conquering anything good."

"Only one thing is worth conquering." Daniel replied.

"And what might that be my friend." Bartholomew inquired seriously.

"Just the human ego." Daniel replied. "Just the human ego."

Suntanned

"Good morning my friends." Daniel projected walking out onto his back patio.

"Good morning my favorite human." Patricia answered coyly.

"Hello Dan." Bartholomew greeted. "You look a little different this morning. You don't have the normal body coverings you usually have on."

"No Bart, I don't. It's just too hot to be all covered up, so I have on Bermuda shorts and a tee shirt." Daniel explained.

"Is that normal coverings for humans when it gets too hot?" Asked Patricia.

"Yes and no, Pat." Daniel went on. "I would never wear these coverings if I was going out in public among other humans."

"Why not." Inquired a confused Bartholomew. "It just makes sense to not be overheated by additional coverings."

"I would be too embarrassed." Came Daniel's reply.

"Why would you be embarrassed?" Questioned a concerned Patricia.

"I know." Chimed in Little joining in the conversation. "Because he doesn't have any fur."

"No Little, I don't. But the reason why is because I'm so white and don't have a suntan." Daniel admitted embarrassedly.

"Do all humans feel this way?" Bartholomew inquired further.

"No." Daniel answered. "Some humans have suntans, and are not embarrassed to wear less coverings."

"What is the significance of the suntan?" Asked Patricia puzzled.

"Well it denotes to other humans, that you have enough money to have leisure time to sit out in the sun and get a tan. Or that you are rich enough to take a vacation to where the sun is out. It rains a lot here in Seattle. Not a lot of sun." Daniel went on explaining. "It also demonstrates that the human goes outside a lot which usually means they exercise and are a healthier human."

"That seems a little judgmental to me." Bartholomew reasoned. "Are all humans this white."

"No." Little jumped in. "Just none of them have fur."

"Little shut up and let us ask Daniel for some explanations without interrupting." Patricia scolded the little squirrel.

"Just trying to help." Said Little chastised. "So, Daniel are all humans this white?"

"No Little they are not." Daniel continued. "Some humans have darker color skin and don't suntan."

"That must be a blessing." Patricia intoned.

"Not really." Daniel explained further. "Skin color denotes that they come from a different culture."

"And is that a problem?" Inquired a confused Bartholomew.

"It shouldn't be." Daniel conceded. "It just demonstrates and exemplifies their difference."

"Just the color of their skin?" Asked a shocked Bartholomew.

"More the difference of their culture." Daniel answered. "Many humans use this difference to define their individuality. Some are Hispanic, some African American, and some Asian."

"Wait a minute." Little questioned. "I thought you said they were all living here?"

"True." Daniel agreed. "But their parents may have come from a different place and hence their heritage or different cultured past."

"But aren't they living here now?" Little's inquiry came.

"Well, yes." Daniel explained. "But heritage is a big thing to humans. It sets them apart from the masses. Some people even speak a different language and teach their children a different language. They say they should not be forced to teach their children the common language."

"Doesn't that make it hard on the children?" Patricia asked.

"Yes Pat. When humans first came to America, from Europe, everyone had to learn English, which at the time was the common language. They were proud to do so, but in the last few years it seems, heritage is more important than being able to communicate." Daniel lamented.

"Okay." Little asked. "Let me see if I've got this straight. Humans came here from other places. They all agreed to live here and get along. Then some parents demanded their children learn to speak a different language that they spoke when their parents or even grand parents lived there, but no longer live there and now live here. Plus being able to get a suntan communicates a sign that you have money and leisure time."

"That's about it my friend." Daniel answered seriously.

"I'm getting a headache." Little complained. "Just one more question, if I may?"

"Anything for you Little." Daniel agreed compassionately.

"These humans come from everywhere, they agree to live in the same place to be part of a culture. Then they live expressing a culture they never lived in. How did they get together enough to harvest almonds?"

Shaving

"Good morning." Daniel said, walking out onto his back patio in the early morning light.

"Good morning Daniel." Bartholomew returned the greeting. "Mind if I ask you a question?"

"Go ahead." Daniel agreed.

"What is that red marking on your face and neck this morning?" He questioned curiously.

"That's just blood from shaving." Daniel explained.

"What is blood and moreover what is shaving." Patricia inquired puzzled.

"Well blood is the fluid that runs thru the body of mammals and gives us life. Little and I both have it. It's like the sap you and Bartholomew have." Daniel expounded. "Shaving is a human practice of cutting off our beards or fur as Little would call it."

"How is this accomplished?" Inquired Patricia further.

"We use a very sharp piece of steel to cut it off. Sometimes we cut ourselves in doing so, hence the blood." Daniel explained patiently.

"Yikes." Screeched Little. "You're going to cut your throat, bleed to death, and I'll starve."

"No Little." Daniel went on. "The steel is called a razor and they have safety features built in so that won't happen."

"Pardon me, my friend." Little lamented. "I have observed many humans and they are not the most coordinated and agile of Mother Earth's creatures."

"Little." Daniel intoned. "It won't happen. As I said the razor has a safety feature built in so that will not happen. I couldn't cut my throat even if I tried."

"Okay." Bartholomew jumped in. "Why do you do it? Is it like me dropping my leaves in the fall?"

"Kind of like that." Daniel explained further. "Human's beards, or fur, just grow back each day and we shave it off."

"Why would you do that?" Asked a confused Patricia.

"We just do it as a tradition." Daniel answered explaining. "Not all humans do it but many of us do."

"You have fur on top of your head also." Little argued. "Why not shave that off also?"

"Many humans do in fact shave their heads." Daniel went on.

"Talk about dumb ideas." Little said exasperated. "Patricia doesn't drop her needles and I don't shave my fur. You and Bartholomew are just dumb."

"Yes Daniel." Patricia reasoned. "I understand the tradition but why?"

"Well Pat." Daniel expounded patiently. "Some of us just feel it makes us look better. If Little shaved his tail, then Sam wouldn't call him fuzzy butt."

"If I shaved my tail, he may not call me fuzzy butt." Little argued. "But I wouldn't leak out my blood just to look pretty."

"Point taken my friend." Daniel conceded. "Point taken."

Solitude

Daniel walked out onto his back patio greeting his friends. "Good morning."

"And a good morning to you as well." Patricia replied. "Didn't expect to see you out here this early. Especially after last night."

"What happened last night?" Asked a curious Little.

"Daniel was up out here most of the night with us." Bartholomew explained.

"What did you guys talk about?" Little inquired further.

"We didn't talk." Patricia went on. "I wanted to but Bart said Daniel needed silence to be with his thoughts."

"I appreciated the silence. I did watch you and Bart dancing gently. I enjoyed your presence and consideration." Daniel said solemnly.

"When it gets dark, you are supposed to go to sleep." Little cried.

"Little be quiet." Bartholomew scolded gently. "Sometimes beings, and probably humans are no exception, need to be with their thoughts in quiet. Daniel do humans have a word for this."

"Yes they do Bart." Daniel replied. "It's called solitude."

"But you said you were aware of Daniel out here." Little protested.

"That is true my little friend." Bartholomew continued. "But we respected his need for quiet and silent companionship. We were just here."

"And my thanks to you and Patricia for it." Daniel exuded.

"I don't understand." Little went on. "After a full day of scampering around I need a full nights sleep."

"Little, in case you haven't noticed." Bartholomew went on patiently. "Daniel doesn't scamper."

"O yeah." Little exclaimed. "So what did you do in the middle of the night?"

"I just sat out here and listened to the city going to sleep. Listened to the silence build and watched Patricia and Bartholomew dance." Daniel explained quietly. "It was very relaxing."

"Well if that don't beat all." Little said puzzled.

"Sometimes silence with friends around is a beautiful thing." Daniel expounded.

"I guess so." Little conceded. "At least you woke up in time to bring me my breakfast almonds."

"That is something." Daniel answered solemnly. "I would never forget my friend. Something I would never forget."

Little's Poem

"Good morning." Daniel greeted to the early morning's light off his back patio. "Everyone awake?"

"Very funny Dan." Bartholomew countered, "Of course we are awake. The only ones around here who sleep every day are you and Little. Patricia and I slept last winter."

"Sorry Bart." Daniel apologized. "You would think by now I could get that into my head."

"Hey." Little protested loudly. "I need my sleep. Scrambling around all day is very tiring. What is the old elm squawking about this morning?"

"Nothing much." Daniel replied. "Just commenting on our sleep patterns."

"If he worked as hard as I do, he would be tired." Little expounded.

"True Little." Daniel went on. "Your single minded determination for almonds is truly inspirational."

"Hey." Came Little's response brightening. "You told us you write poetry when inspiration hits you. Well write a poem about almonds and me. What could be more inspirational than almonds?"

"Little just shut up and eat." Patricia chided.

"No Pat." Daniel went on. "He does have a point. Just give me a moment."

"Told ya." Little said smugly.

Daniel thought for a moment and then began reciting.

Let me tell you of a story,
 About Little the almond loving squirrel.
It will take away your breath,
 And leave your mind in awhirl.

Seeking out almonds,
 Was a task in which he did not fail.
Seeking them with every fiber of his being,
 From his paws to his bushy tail.

"I'm gonna be famous." Little gloated.

"O dear." Patricia lamented. "We won't be able to live with him now."

"It's okay Pat." Daniel consoled her. "He still can't dance."

Beverly Hillbillies

Daniel walked out onto his back patio and greeted his friends. "Good morning." He said pensively.

"Good morning." Bartholomew replied happily.

"Uh-oh." Patricia intoned.

"What is that suppose to mean?" Daniel asked defensively.

"Daniel." Patricia answered. "I've known you far too long not to recognize that look on your face. What's bothering you?"

"Guess I'm just an open book to you, my young voluptuous pine." Daniel responded sheepishly. "I was watching my television and saw an old television show I used to watch and enjoy. But with my new found awareness since I have begun to talk with you and Bartholomew, it took on a whole new meaning and was upsetting that I had missed it for so long."

"What was the show?" Patricia queried.

"The title was the "Beverly Hillbillies" and its premise was a story about an old country mountain man named Jeb who found oil on his land and became very rich. Then pressured by family and friends he moved to the modern city of Beverly Hills."

"That sounds like a happy story to me." Little quipped jumping in the conversation.

"On the surface." Daniel went on. "He was ignorant of the modern city ways and the show was built on that ignorance as funny. He had a banker who was supposed to be his friend but had become very rich keeping Jeb's money and using it to build his own wealth off Jeb's ignorance of modern city life."

"Was Jeb happy?" Patricia inquired further.

"It would seem so. But that's not what has me upset." Daniel answered.

"If he was happy then what was the problem?" Bartholomew asked confused.

"It's a very thin line of distinction Bart." Daniel explained further. "Jeb was happy but at the expense of his ignorance. The banker was happy because he was making a lot of money. People liked it because everyone was happy and they laughed at Jeb's ignorance. I've come to understand that to take advantage of someone's ignorance or weakness for financial gain is just wrong."

"If everyone was happy that is a very thin objection." Bartholomew reasoned.

"But it was wrong was it not?" Daniel asked pleadingly.

"Yes Daniel." Bartholomew agreed. "It was."

"I watched it for years and never saw the distinction." Daniel lamented. "It should not have been funny."

"Have you discussed this with other humans?" Little inquired perplexed.

"No Little." Daniel wailed. "They would jus think I was crazy."

"Guess what Dan." Little went on. "They think you're crazy already."

"I guess you may be right about that my friend." Daniel agreed mournfully. "So what does someone do when they see things so differently?"

"Just let it go." Came Patricia's reply. "Rejoice that you can see it, but let everyone else who doesn't be happy and come out here and dance with me."

Brazil Nuts

"Good morning." Daniel greeted his friends as he walked out onto his back patio in the early morning's light.

"Good morning to you as well." Bartholomew replied then asked concerned. "Another long night last night?"

"Afraid so Bart." Daniel explained. "I went to bed around ten last night and couldn't sleep. So around one I got up from my bed, came into the dining room and played on the computer for a while. I didn't get much sleep."

"Almonds." Came the small squirrel's voice. "You just need to eat more almonds."

"Little." Said an exasperated Daniel. "All of the world's problems are not solved by eating more almonds."

"What." Exclaimed a shocked Little. "Are you sure about that?"

"Yes I'm sure." Daniel went on. "Besides I eat nuts every day."

"Really." Little questioned. "What kind of nuts do you eat?"

"I eat four Brazil nuts each day." Daniel explained further. "That gives me my R D A of selenium."

"Daniel." Inquired Patricia confused. "What is R D A and furthermore what is selenium."

"Sorry Pat." Daniel apologized and then explained. "R D A is the Recommended Daily Allowance needed by humans for their health. Selenium is a mineral stored in the human brains that aid in their proper function and also the functioning of their thyroid gland."

"Yeah." Little rejoindered scornfully. "But I bet they don't taste as good as almonds."

"Well that is a personal choice." Daniel answered reasoning. "I like the Brazil nuts better. Have you ever tried one?"

"No." Cried Little defensively. "They would have a long way to go to be better than almonds."

"I will bring you one out now and you can try it." Daniel offered compromising.

Daniel went back into his kitchen and brought out a single Brazil nut for Little to try.

Little ate the nut while Daniel and Patricia looked on.

"Ha." Little shouted smugly. "The selenium is not working for your brain my friend you have lost your mind. The almonds taste better just like I told you."

"Well that is just your opinion Little. It is no more valid than mine." Daniel proclaimed.

"Bartholomew help me out here." Little pleaded to the old elm. "Tell Daniel he is wrong."

"Don't drag me into this argument." Bartholomew protested. "Daniel is right. Maybe not about the taste, but that each of you are entitled to your opinions, and each may be considered valid."

"Thanks for nothing Bart." Screeched Little. "I refuse to give up my almonds."

"You don't have to give up anything my friend." Daniel said consolingly. "I need the Brazil nuts. I didn't say you did. I have no intention of changing your eating habits. You will still get your breakfast almonds."

"Well that's a comfort." Little quailed relieved. "Don't scare me like that."

"That was not my intention my friend." Daniel went on. "We were just talking."

"That kind of talk is enough to take my appetite away." Little lamented.

"That would be hard to believe my little friend." Daniel replied. "That would be hard to believe"

True Meaning of Conversations

"Good morning all." Daniel greeted as he walked out onto his back patio.

"Good morning Daniel." Came the chorus of replies from his friends.

"I stand before you today humbled." Daniel replied meekly. " I feel the need to apologize to all of you."

"Whatever for my human friend?" Bartholomew inquired softly.

"I have spent the last year explaining things to you in great detail. I finally realized last night that my explanations were not for you but for me." Daniel explained further.

"That is all conversations are Daniel." Bartholomew expounded patiently. "Communication of ideas between beings. Many times the communication is in one's own self. Conversations are important so your thoughts can be brought to light and out in the open to others as well as yourself."

"I thought I understood it all." Daniel lamented.

"A common emotion." Bartholomew extolled. "Why do human parents talk so much to their children? It's to teach themselves as much as teach their children."

"How do you ever reach understanding?" Questioned a confused Daniel.

"Time." Came Bartholomew's serious answer. "True wisdom comes only from conversations with other beings. You don't know anything by pure instinct. Many things are pure instinct but wisdom. No. Only sharing ideas gives you perspective enough to understand anything."

"The more I understand things I find myself becoming more tolerant." Daniel went on talking feverishly. "That is a fact. I don't understand many of them at all. Some things that I was adamant about, I now find really weren't that important to begin with."

"Therein lies the beginning of wisdom." Bartholomew lectured patiently.

"There was a philosopher named Saint Augustine." Daniel told them. "He once said "All men seek happiness, but it amazed him that most went about it in ways that made it impossible to attain." I guess he was looking for understanding, and that would be his happiness."

"That is because most go after it by themselves." Bartholomew went on explaining. "Every being in universe has something to offer. True wisdom only comes from collecting as much of it as you can. Therefore the importance of conversations."

"Is this part of the learning curve before you die?" Queried Daniel.

"To a large extent. The answer is Yes." Bartholomew conceded.

"So my explanations have had no merit." Daniel asked humbly.

"Not at all my friend." Bartholomew went on. "We have found your explanations enlightening as well as entertaining."

"We thank you for them." Patricia acknowledged.

"And I must thank you as well." Daniel answered. "But what is the most important thing in this universe?"

"It differs for each being concerned." Came Bartholomew's thoughtful answer. "For me it's the sharing of ideas and conversations between intelligent beings, human or otherwise."

"For me it's just to dance." Patricia contributed her perky enthusiasm overflowing.

"Almonds." Came Little's serious declaration.

Final Conversation

"Good morning you guys." Daniel greeted his friends as he walked out onto his back patio. "How's it going this morning?"

"We are fine Daniel. The question is how are you?" Questioned a concerned Bartholomew.

"What do you mean?" Daniel asked. "I am fine this morning."

"Really." Inquired Patricia.

"Sure." Daniel countered. "What makes you think I'm not?"

"Just hearing your tone and observing you over the last year. I am concerned as are all of us." Patricia explained. "You seem to be better physically but we are concerned about your mind."

"I'm fine Pat." Daniel went on. "I am retired and have accomplished more than most humans dream of."

"Really." Patricia said again. "What have you accomplished?"

"I rose from poverty, worked my way through college. Then rebuilt motors, raced motorcycles, learned chemistry and physics. Studied philosophy and fought in a war." Daniel expounded. "Written books. Retired from working and now enjoy life."

"Really?" Questioned Patricia again. "What have you accomplished?"

"I don't understand the question?" Daniel argued. "What more could a human ask for?"

"Meaning to your life." Patricia countered.

"I have meaning to my life." Daniel argued further. "What could I look for that I haven't done already?"

"Daniel." Bartholomew broke in seriously. "You have accomplished much in a human's life. But what Patricia is asking is what is important to you. Do all the things you have done or accomplished give you peace and joy in the middle of the night?"

"I guess." Daniel answered.

"I'll take it from here Bart." Little jumped in.

"Dan what Bartholomew and Patricia are asking," Little went on explaining. "Is that, all that you have done or accomplished gained you stuff. Which I have observed from time to time is thrown out by you and your mate to clean up. Humans are social animals and they need family. In a social animal, offspring are the only thing that really matters."

"I did read once," Daniel went on. "That humans really cease to live once they lose the ability to recreate life."

"There is a reason that is true." Little explained patiently. "Humans only live for one thing. That is to procreate. All the other things you accomplish merely reinforce that need. Do all your accomplishments give you real joy and comfort or do they leave you cold?"

"Well now that I've done all that they say I should have, it does leave me kind of empty." Daniel lamented.

"Daniel you have had some bad instances with your child. Isn't that true?" Little questioned.

"So now to make up the need for social interaction you talk to trees and a squirrel?" Little inquired.

"I guess you may be right Little." Daniel conceded. "I seem to be looking for something, but I don't really know what."

"Offspring." Quipped Little.

"They may drive you crazy, and not do what you think they should, but at least you feel part of something."

Little continued. "The downsides of it are all overcome with the positive sides of it."

"I love almonds." Little went on. "But they do not compare with my little ones. They make me feel needed, a part of something important and complete. Do you feel that?"

"Not really." Daniel answered morosely.

"Call your daughter." Little told his friend. "Stop talking to us. But, don't forget my almonds."

"Surely you must have written her one of your poems. Read me one." Patricia asked softly

To Katie on Your Wedding Day

And so my treasured Princess,
Today you are to wed.
I do not know what I feel,
Unbounded joy or dread.

The emotions pull so strongly,
My chest feels as if it's torn.
For wasn't it only yesterday?
I remember you being born.

I held you in my arms,
Announced you Katherine Ellen Shanks.
Then offered up a silent prayer,
An offering of thanks.

My life was changed that day,
Though I could not see.
The road of ups and downs,
Awaiting there for me.

And so I watched you grow,
Learning to roller skate and ride your bike.
Which music you listened to,
Which foods you did or did not like.

I watched you learn to swim,
Tell jokes that all began "Knock Knock".
The thrill that was in your eyes,
When you skipped your very first rock

Walking through the forest,
Body surfing at the beach.
Watching your confidence grow,
Realizing nothing was beyond your reach.

And my pain of realization,
    That you needed me less and less.
But pride as you grew so strong,
    The conflicting emotions I confess.

So today I retire,
    Another has taken my place.
But that is the way life is,
    Or should be in any case.

I've never been at a loss for words,
    Yet today it's hard for me to say.
Out loud of how much you mean to my life,
    In every facet and every way.

You begin a new adventure today,
    But really you cannot go.
For in my heart you shall always be,
    With the memories of watching you grow.

And on some future day at work,
    Wading through file after countless file.
I'll remember you fishing at dawn on Lake Hartwell,
    And my face will start to smile.

The past is always with me,
    The future belongs to you.
I can only wish a life of happiness,
    And joy in all you do.

I wanted to tell you so much this day,
    Of memories, joy and pride.
But all I can say is "I Love You",
    And hang on for a helleva ride.

Papa
March 14,1997

Goodbye

"Thank you for the poem and for all the conversations my special human. I will miss you." Patricia said emotionally. "Goodbye."

Eclectics Revisited

Danny L. Shanks

This Book is dedicated to Katie and Chris Molina
with thanks to you both.
Without your help, total support and devotion it
would never have been published.

Contents

1. Birth of a Human..
2. Tailgating
3. The We ....
4. Does God Exist?
5. Zoos .....
6. Two Bits...
7. Rap Music....
8. Cancer from Smoking ..
9. A New Name ....
10. Power vs Right ...
11. Marriage Vows..
12. Crime Dilemma....
13. To Viet Nam Veterans .
14. Pets Revisited .
15. Hot Cocoa ..
16. Sick People...
17. Missed Breakfast
18. September 21st ....
19. Fool on the Hill
20. Christmas Truth
21. October Morning.
22. The Golden Rule .
23. Cows..
24. Take Us To Your Leader
25. God Doesn't Play Football
26. Columbus Day
27. A Night's Walk In October ...
28. The Triple Threat ..
29. Anger ..
30. October Country....
31. Olympic Rain Forrest.

32. Love, Love, Love
33. Autumn Storm .
34. Madness ...
35. Summers Gone...
36. Growing Up and Apart
37. Not a Likeable Guy ..

Foreword

I have written so much it sometimes seems a crime.
And with any crime I have the right to remain silent.
What I seem to lack is the ability.
Danny L Shanks
September 1, 2006

Birth of a Human

The miracle of birth,
 I've heard so much as to have had my fill.
Yet no one mentions that after the event,
 The roads of life, all seem uphill.

Yes, after the event,
 Written about in countless songs and verse.
With someone slapping your rear, no money nor clothes,
 And after that, things just get worse.

August 12, 2006

Tailgating

To study human nature,
    I have spent a lifetime telling jokes.
How people react to them,
    Tells me much of the feeling and beliefs of folks.

One I used to tell, was about tailgating,
    A practice to which many drivers are prone.
As the joke went on to explain,
    They just didn't want to feel alone.

Well when discussing it with my wife,
    As I am want to do.
I realized that the scary thing was,
    That is was not funny, but true.

That humans don't want to be by themselves,
    And history proves this out.
Inventions over the last hundred years show,
    Human relationships is what it's all about.

First came the telegraph,
    Communications in the blink of an eye.
Then came the radio,
    Someone in your home with no reason why.

Most songs are about,
    Human relationships, be they good or bad.
Instrumentals just conjure up memories,
    Making us happy or sad.

It made us feel the human presence,
    Just sitting in our home.
Followed shortly on its heels,
    The invention of the telephone.

Enabling us to contact someone,
    By picking up a phone.
Instant communications,
    So we no longer felt so alone.

Next was the television,
    Persons whom we came to see.
Every day the constant touch,
    Without commitments, allowing us to stay emotionally free.

The Internet is now the way,
    We talk and send email.
Praying strongly every day,
    That our computer does not fail.

Now the cell phone craze,
    To be in touch twenty-four hours a day.
Without really all that much,
    To talk about or say

For we humans are social animals,
    Who need the daily touch.
Of other humans, and I find,
    We need such contact very much.

And so you argue no,
    As a species we are not so insecure.
How can I be so cynical?
    How can I be so sure?

Just disconnect the Internet,
    Then turn off the cable.
That you are scared more than bored,
    Is the answer you can't give or be able?

To admit to such a supposed weakness,
    In human nature, for you won't go that far.
But it is just plainly and simply,
    Who we really are.

August 15, 2006

The We

My wife and I have been married,
    For over thirty-five years.
We have had our share.
    Of laughter, joys, and tears.

But I am concerned for the society,
    In America today.
For it seems that marriage,
    Has definitely lost its way.

People want to tell you,
    How your marriage should be.
That all chores should be shared equally,
    And no one gets a ride for free.

Who in the hell told them?
    That they have the rights.
To tell anyone how life is,
    To resolve their laughs and fights.

Just remember the beginning,
    You started out as friends.
And that my fellow humans,
    Is where true love begins.

Just two people,
    Trying to live this life.
Sharing it all by becoming,
    Simply husband and wife.

There is no I in it,
    And there is no she.
My wife and I call it,
    Simply "the we".

No fifty-fifty division,
    Of tasks that we must do.
We each do what we are able,
    To try and make it through.

We do what we can,
    No payback to expect.
For if you simply want that,
    Go get a job and a paycheck.

Cut the grass for a man,
    A woman's place is in the home.
Who in the hell made up those laws?
    And more importantly, are they now alone?

When my daughter was getting married,
    Many tried to offer her advice.
I told her then, as now,
    Take none, and let the friendship suffice

Just start each day when awaking,
    With no more than a simple kiss.
It reminds you of what you are,
    And the importance of this.

You are just two friends,
    Doing your best to get by.
Remain friends and the love will last,
    And you won't even have to try.

August 16, 2006

Does God Exist?

Does he Exist?
    A question that cuts me like a knife.
And I have searched for the answer,
    To that question, all of my life.

Well I finally found the answer,
    And here I use as my defense.
Logic and reason, because,
    None of it makes any sense.

Just look at the human body,
    Personality disorders, sex and hair.
Try to examine each,
    Don't be judgmental, just be fair.

To make it all up seems a bit too weird,
    So the discussions of God as a rumor.
Ends simply with,
    He exists but has a sense of humor.

August 18, 2006

Zoos

We have places in America,
Zoos they are simply called.
Yet, thinking about them the other day,
I was suddenly overwhelmingly appalled.

I had seen an elephant,
In a zoo, when I was a child growing.
But I have never been to Africa,
And I really don't plan on going.

So if I had never seen one,
Would the experience have been lost?
Not really, considering the elephant,
And the price it cost.

Yet people justify the cost,
They actually have the gall to dare.
To say they love the animals,
And that they really care.

The Native American Chief Joseph,
"Torture me", when captured said.
"At least in a week,
It will be over and I'll be dead."

But no creature should be denied freedom,
To be put in a cage.
For shortly they will lose their minds,
And feel nothing but rage.

But no my friends,
You say to them, for we have the strength and might.
Well, you may have that,
But who in the hell said you have the right.

But they may become extinct,
    Lost for all time, you say.
However you never asked them,
    If it's a price they will willingly pay.

Close the zoos,
    And then set them free.
At least they will have quality of life,
    Not just painful longevity.

August 19, 2006

Two Bits

Two bits, four bits,
    Six bits a peso.
I wish whoever created,
    That ditty would stand up and say so.

For then I would have the chance,
    To get my gun and shoot them dead.
And maybe, just maybe,
    I could get it out of my head.

For since I was a child,
    At any of the weirdest time,
It would pop up repeating,
    Over and over in my mind.

No rhyme, nor reason,
    To explain to me why.
And I can't get it out of my head,
    No matter what I try.

It makes no sense to me,
    But it will finally go away.
But as sure as the sun comes up,
    It will return on some distant day.

No warning of when it's coming,
    Nothing to prepare me for the coming of it.
It's just suddenly there, and won't go away,
    Leaving me in pretty much of a fit.

So ask Freud or any psychologist,
    If they would take the time.
To answer where such a ditty comes from,
    That it consumes so much of my mind.

August 24, 2006

Rap Music

I went outside yesterday,
    To enjoy the day, but instead I walked into a trap.
Next door were workers repairing the building,
    They were listening to some music they called rap.

Like a bad poem it rhymed,
    And the idea was not to sing but simply to talk.
Spoken rapidly for any delay, like pitching in baseball,
    Simply meant a balk.

So I investigated it some more,
    And the music was created by a machine.
As a background to the talking,
    And here I don't wish to be mean.

But if they used a machine and not instruments,
    And that was how it was slated.
Then how could you call it music?
    By any measure created.

But it did answer one question,
    For it was loud and far from gentle.
And there seems to be no,
    Rap Music Instrumental.

August 24, 2006

Cancer From Smoking

Smoking causes cancer,
    That's what all the opponents declare.
Yet, all the taxes collected,
    Go again. To where?

If it is so bad,
    Why don't the farmers of it be cursed from on high?
Because if smoking causes cancer,
    And they still subsidize them, then I ask why?

If cancer from smoking is a guarantee,
    Why do I see so many doing it when they are old?
Could it be that maybe,
    The whole truth is not being told?

When the FDA is worried,
    They seem to always have a plan.
Well if it is so bad, and cancer is a guarantee.
    Why not institute a ban.

But they are correct on one point,
    Cancer I do truly fear.
But it's the rectal and not the lung,
    From all the smoke they keep blowing up my rear.

August 30, 2006

A New Name

My doctor last week,
    Prescribed morphine, after we had a talk.
To ease my pain,
    And allowing me to walk.

I'm also now on Prozac,
    To help and cure my depression.
The two cures arrived at,
    After countless visits, and many a session.

Of course, I'd had been on a diet,
    And I had lost ten pounds of weight.
Yet after taking the morphine, I gained all of it back,
    After just a week, and I didn't have to wait.

Now I'm just dumb and fat, but happy,
    Truly the accomplishment of a hopeless feat.
Yet somehow after all of it,
    I still feel incomplete.

I feel I need a new name,
    Something poetic and musical.
Perhaps the "Flowering Danny", would do it,
    Naming me now, the new Washington State vegetable.

August 30, 2006

Power Vs Right

Reflecting on it lying in bed,
    Around 1 A.M. last night.
I could no longer attempt sleep,
    So I rose, and went to the kitchen to write.

I was thinking of how to explain,
    My lack of respect, for human life.
For when I was young,
    I believed in work, children, home and wife.

I had even had thoughts,
    Of becoming a catholic priest.
But marriage soon awaited me,
    Making that option one of my least.

But I still believed in human goodness,
    That overall everyone was decent.
Then they sent me to war,
    And the learning of my self deceit was recent.

An all American blend, good old boys from the mid west,
    And Southern boys with all their charm.
Who would always do good,
    Never inflict others with unnecessary harm.

So the Army tested,
    And with an IQ of 160 they could clearly see.
My potential in the military,
    So they classified me infantry.

My six-month in the service found me,
    In the 178th Battalion of the 23rd Infantry Division.
The central highlands,
    And what I saw there clouded my vision.

Ever heard of William Calley,
    Well the same battalion was his place.
While there is no atheist in a foxhole, but opposite for me,
    For I no longer felt part of the human race. .

I saw things done,
    By the good old boys over there.
For with no one watching,
    They could do whatever they considered fair.

So I came home,
    Finished a college degree.
Reading philosophy and great thinkers,
    I finally realized they could not see.

What I had seen in war,
    And the confusion that was in their head.
For they considered the power to do something,
    Gave them the right instead.

So wave a flag to them,
    Stand up proud and tall.
Support these fine young men,
    Remember those that fall.

Having the power over another,
    Does not guarantee.
That the one with the power,
    Can always be counted on to see.

Right from wrong,
    On whatever scale you use.
The misuse of power,
    But calling it right is just a ruse.

To justify their actions,
    Same as in everyday life.
For the truth sometimes cuts both ways,
    As does the proverbial knife.

Well I've bitched enough,
    To try and clear my head.
So goodnight to you all,
    As I return to my bed.

August 31, 2006

Marriage Vows

Words spoken so solemnly,
    Vows of commitment in our mind.
Years of good and bad,
    Pass swiftly before we find.

To honor and cherish, for richer or poorer,
    In sickness and in health, not just from the start.
Forsaking all others,
    Until death do you part.

Words spoken by many,
    Each day around the world.
Spoken by millions between,
    Some young boy and his girl.

But the years pass,
    The trials try and do their best.
To challenge each such marriage,
    As they put them to the test.

The vows that came so easily,
    Spoken in our youth.
Only as time passes,
    Do we learn the real truth.

Health eventually fails,
    And the money is all spent.
As each passes us by, we are left wondering,
    Where in the hell it went?

Yet two people stick together,
    Despite the challenge of it all.
Truly there lies true love,
    For they have heard the call.

Of what commitment means,
    To care for each other, and despite.
All adversities they encounter,
    And as a team of two, they face the fight.

September 4, 2006

Crime Dilemma

How do you stop crime?
    Book after book written, each explaining a theory.
And many a proposal suggested,
    To answer this specific query.

But overall the simplest answer,
    Always seems to be.
To issue such harsh punishment,
    And to never set criminals free.

But to issue such a punishment,
    An enlightened society would say.
That it makes you just as bad,
    And you would, have become, the they.

For it would have to be so harsh,
    To act as a deterrent.
It would have to scare the criminal,
    From having such intent.

It's for the good of society,
    Explaining it so they could see.
And never commit a crime in the first place,
    Nor risk the loss of being free.

I don't think that such a thought,
    Ever entered their head.
For they wish to have a better life,
    Or wish to be, simply dead.

For the rich always seem to get richer,
    The poor always seem to be poor.
Mankind does not seem concerned,
    To even out the score.

But how much is too much,
    To share it with a fellow being.
For then maybe crime would be lost,
    Never again to be seen.

September 4, 2006

To Viet Nam Veterans

The other day I watched a movie,
    In Viet Nam was it set.
Yet I could almost guarantee,
    And I doubt I would lose my bet.

That after forty years,
    To the vocabulary used they would find.
Being exposed to it again,
    That it was indelibly etched into their mind.

The highlands, the grasslands,
    The deltas, and the green.
Would never be understood by anyone,
    Those images that had never been seen.

A new vocabulary and soon,
    To speak it you must learn.
Only to have such language,
    Be in your mind forever burned.

A vocabulary of curses,
    From beginning to the end.
Of any conversation,
    Seemed to be the trend.

FUBAR we said,
    And you're frigging A.
To the max, and bet your ass,
    Seemed acceptable things to say.

A top, a cherry, a newbie,
    All used to help understand.
A greenie and fresh meat,
    All describing the category of a man.

A slick, a cobra, a pink team,
    And Puff the Magic Dragon that left no life.
After their sweep was made,
    Try explaining that, to father, mother or wife.

A three stepper,
    Was used to describe a snake.
That after it bit you,
    About three steps was all you would make.

And don't forget willie pete,
    To start an artillery mission.
We used the term road runner.
    To establish the starting position.

But we wanted so badly,
    For people to understan.
What it was that happened there,
    Where we became a man

Don't mean a thing,
    Seemed to be our cry.
For reason and logic had escaped us,
    And we couldn't understand why?

But if you made it back,
    To the real world and touched down,
The only thing awaiting you,
    Was a condescending attitude to be found.

Yeah, across the big pond,
    We returned to the real world.
But little tolerance was expressed,
    By the one left behind as our girl.

Forty years gone by,
    The memories fade at last.
Except for the nightmares,
    From experiences of the past.

And the desire ever so strong,
    That someone or anyone would know.
Left most of us confused and sad,
    So my advice is, to try and let it go.

September 5, 2006

Pets Revisited

I once wrote a poem,
Pets it was called.
Yet upon reflection,
Of what I said has left me appalled.

I was the youngest child of six,
Brothers and sisters all around.
Yet being the youngest,
No real companionship was to be found.

But I had a dog,
Sparkplug was his name.
Devoted and true,
With many a day passed in game.

I would tackle him,
He in return would tackle me.
Such fun it was,
To me a child of three.

Laughing in the fields,
Rolling over and over.
Such joy to have,
In the summer fields of clover.

But a mad dog came into our yard,
And Sparkplug never quailed.
Protecting me that day,
A task in which he would never have failed.

But the price he paid,
Left him tied to a tree.
Then a policeman came, declared him mad,
And shot him in front of me.

Told that was the world,
And deal with if I should try.
So I buried the memory of him,
And it was forty years later did I finally cry.

I was in the hospital,
And I was at death's door.
They pumped me full of drugs,
Then empirically kept their score.

Well I didn't die that day,
But it opened up my head.
Memories I had buried,
Of Sparkplug being dead.

And with the memories of him gone,
I found then that I could cry.
Forty years but I couldn't stop the tears,
And I didn't want to try.

In the years that had passed,
My wife and I had a girl.
And after seeing my wife in labor,
Decided that one would be our world.

So she grew and got married,
Moved out into her life.
Yet she had no children,
To call grandmother to my wife.

But growing she always had a dog,
For what else did she know?
Neither brothers nor sisters,
To help her mature and grow.

So she got a female dog,
Yoda was her name.
And as the years passed,
I watched the two, play their own game.

So I read the poem,
    And called such animals pets.
But it has left me,
    Full of bewildering regrets.

For I now see them for what they are,
    And I truly never meant to offend.
But such glorious creatures,
    Should instead be called friend.

September 8, 2006

Hot Cocoa

Summer is gone,
    Brisk describes the start of each new day.
Gone are the mornings of warmth,
    We found in June, July, and May.

And of all of mankind's discoveries,
    If you think, you will find it so.
That on such a morning,
    There is none greater than hot Cocoa.

The warmth it gives,
    As down your throat it does slide.
Starts each day you drink it,
    With a joy you cannot hide.

For we have been to the moon,
    Drive cars with cruise control.
Computers, television, and science,
    Each discovery making us feel bold.

Yet with all the things,
    That mankind has created.
Hot Cocoa seems to me,
    To be the one, that joy is best mated.

So start each morning,
    Savor a cup of the drink.
And it seems to give a greater joy,
    Than any others of which I can think.

So take the time to make it,
    Let nothing else start your day.
And drinking a cup will give you direction,
    As you go your way.

September 17, 2006

Sick People

When you remember your youth,
    Remembering it completely is the trick.
You did not want to be around,
    Anyone who was sick.

It did not mean you were heartless,
    That you were cold nor did not care.
But try and remember it honestly,
    And analyzing it, try to be fair.

For you never thought,
    That it would happen to you.
Yet it would come some day,
    That much you knew was true.

That fear was never spoken,
    Or acknowledged that it would someday come.
But surely it comes, as the changing of the seasons,
    Or the rising of the sun.

So you avoid all contact,
    Of anyone who was sick.
Subconsciously thinking,
    That this would be the trick.

To avoid illness,
    Anything you would try.
But it will eventually come,
    And someday you will die.

But denying it will not stop it,
    And you will simply fail.
And thoughts will intrude,
    Of a heaven or a hell.

Life will show you the way,
    Whether or not you care.
And realization that life, doesn't fit your description,
    Of what you think of, as fair.

September 17, 2006

Missed Breakfast

I was up reading a book,
    Late into the night.
I fell asleep finally,
    As the new day brought its light.

It was then that I discovered,
    My wife had already left.
Without a morning kiss, nor without my saying "I love you",
    She must have felt adrift.

But she let me sleep on,
    Late into the day.
And when I finally arose,
    I found the price I had to pay.

So I didn't get up with her,
    Nor kiss her goodbye.
Sleeping I didn't do all the morning rituals,
    And wasn't even awake enough to try.

But she knows I love her,
    And that is a love that will last.
But the price I pay for not getting up,
    Is simply to fix my own damn breakfast.

September 21, 2006

September 21st

The twenty-first of September,
    The autumn equinox has come.
The changing of the seasons,
    Sounding loudly as a drum.

Gone are the warm days of summer,
    Gone the soft breezes of June.
The fall has come,
    And Mother Nature sings a different tune.

The forest now explodes with color,
    Yellow and red dominate the scene.
As the fall comes full force,
    There is little left of the green.

The breeze will soon be brisk,
    And chill you to the bone.
You will soon crave hot chocolate,
    No more of summer's ice cream cone.

So relish the change of seasons,
    In any endeavor you choose to strive.
Relish the earth's variety,
    It helps you know you are alive.

September 25, 2006

Fool on The Hill

There was a song,
    That I loved in my youth.
It was called the "Fool on the Hill",
    And I believed it spoke of truth.

I also revered Man of La Mancha,
    For the ideals it proposed.
Truth, honor and nobility,
    A way of life I supposed.

That the world would agree,
    And believe as I believed.
Only now as I grow older,
    Does the world's reality leave me grieved.

For I thought if it was known,
    How a man should live his life.
That this above all,
    Would relieve most of his strife.

And the world would be better for this,
    That one man torn and covered with scar.
Still strove with his last ounce of courage,
    To reach that unreachable star.

That good would triumph over evil,
    That nobility would carry the day.
That a man's natural goodness
    Would give him a life, to strive for in every way.

Alas I now see the world,
    As it does truly exist.
No longer can I believe,
    Such reality I can no longer resist.

I tried to write it out,
    To tell the world the way it should be.
But it was just a waste of time,
    Expounded then read by no one but me.

It was just a dream,
    But as I grow older I wish for it still.
And the truth as it truly exists,
    Is that I am just a Fool on the Hill.

September 25, 2006

Christmas Truth

The Christmas season is coming,
    And I find I have a real regret.
It is because most of us,
    Grow older and seem to forget.

The true spirit of Christmas,
    We lose over the years.
We grow older and succumb,
    To all of our adult fears.

When you learned that your parents bought the presents,
    And that smug intelligence brought relief.
Yet you failed to see the cost,
    Of losing that belief.

For the magic of Christmas,
    In the joyous belief of a child.
While growing older made it impossible to see,
    The transformation after a while.

That the belief of Santa Claus,
    Was not a proven fact.
But in reality every parent became Santa,
    And that my friends is a fact.

And belief that the North Pole,
    Was where he kept his shop.
Well where else should it be.
    Than at this world's top.

That flying reindeer,
    Would pull his magic sled.
Allowing him to visit the world,
    While each child lay snugly in their bed.

So we grow older,
    Discount the stories with relief.
Yet the reality of our world,
    Does not make untrue all belief.

Do not give up on Christmas,
    Do not live in such a shell.
That you discount all beliefs,
    You once felt with the sound of a Christmas bell.

Relish the season of Christmas,
    Resist all logic given to you to train.
To disbelieve in the magic of Christmas,
    They try and force into your brain.

The season is truly magic,
    Joy and belief is what makes it true.
Do not let the doubters,
    Change the stories held in you.

To discount the stories as myth,
    Will not justify or relieve.
The true joy of the season exists,
    If you can only just believe.

September 27, 2006

October Morning

It's three o'clock in the morning and,
I find I cannot sleep.
I have grown weary of just lying there,
I tire of counting sheep.

So I dress warmly and retire outside,
To sit out back and watch the night go by.
The date is the first of October,
And my eyes turn to the sky.

A full moon is out there,
Floating in a cloud filled sea.
A light breeze is blowing,
The moon crosses the white waves for me.

I sit outside and relax,
No muscle spasms to twitch.
My sole concentration is all above,
For I am looking for a witch.

For it is the first of October,
A special time of year.
So I search the woods and sky,
For validations of my childhood fear.

Ghosts or goblins I seek,
Witches or black cats,
Anything crossing the moon filled sky,
Wearing a black and pointed hat.

But there is only the soft wailing,
Of the wind among the trees.
Who sway with leaves aquivering,
Among the gentle breeze.

No howling of wolves,
    No screeching of a bat.
Just the solitude of the night,
    And I must be content with that.

For the tales in my youth,
    Of October nights abound.
But growing older if find,
    None of those creatures could be found.

The terrors of my youth I've lost,
    Gone forever and a day.
But the loss just leaves me empty,
    And adulthood is the price I pay.

So many beliefs are gone,
    As older I have grown.
With the world changing so fast,
    Computers, television and the telephone.

So were the good old days that good,
    When everything was as real as Jack Frost.
I only know I miss them,
    And to me now, they are forever lost.

Yes gone are all the stories,
    That I feared, but cherished in my youth.
And all that remains now,
    Is the emptiness adults call truth.

October 1, 2006

The Golden Rule

"Do unto others,
As you would have them do unto you."
This was called the golden rule,
And was taught to me as a child as true.

So I spent all of my life,
Helping out others as much as I could.
Because if you had to choose,
Living that way you should.

But life is not always fair,
And as I grew older, I got sick.
So I expected others to return the help I had given,
And sadly I grew to realize life's trick.

For the golden rule,
Seemed like a good rule of thumb.
I now began to see,
That I was just gullible and dumb.

A belief taught to me as a child,
As a valid one of life's tools.
But the reality is simply,
He who has the gold makes the rules.

October 4, 2006

Cows

I was talking the other day,
To a devout vegetarian.
He professed to eat only foods,
Grown in the soil and therefore agrarian.

So I inquired what he had against cows,
And he launched into a tirade against the animal.
Flatulence from cows destroys the ozone,
And if the land were used correctly, the homeless would be minimal.

He inquired if I offered no hope,
To help save the environment.
And to stop eating such meat,
Was not such a stringent requirement?

They smell so bad,
And emit volumes of gas,
And if allowed to continue unchecked,
The planet will simply not last.

Somewhat chastised I said that I in fact did care,
So he asked me if I could demonstrate how.
I replied with logic and reason,
That I simply eat the cow.

October 4, 2006

Take us to Your Leader

Watching a science fiction movie,
    Earth had been invaded by an alien band.
"Take us to your leader" they cried,
    "The speaker for all of man."

Well we have so many cultures,
    Each determined to be free.
But how do we pick one human to speak,
    And just who might that be?

Some countries are proud,
    Some countries are meek.
Diversity prevents agreement,
    On even one language to speak.

Each culture and country self-righteous,
    Made mostly of mirrors and smoke.
But to suggest we had such a leader,
    Would have to be the ultimate joke.

October 5, 2006

God Doesn't Play Football

Watching a football game last weekend,
    I begin to remember things long past.
Lessons I had learned playing the sport,
    Lessons that I thought would always last.

But as I grow older I begin to wonder,
    What lessons do I really remember?
Only that I was in better shape,
    And by far much more limber.

I saw a receiver catch a pass and point up to God,
    As if to say thanks and it was God's will.
That he catch the ball,
    And it had nothing to do with his own skill.

So I began to think,
    Do we only give thanks with a win?
And if the player drops the ball,
    It's also God's wish and to catch it would be a sin.

Coaches always had a prayer for victory,
    Each coach had one, so whose took precedent.
Were they saying that the winner?
    Deserved the victory by being more decent.

How could you wish defeat?
    For your opponent in a game.
If the prayers asking for a win,
    Were in fact both the same?

So maybe I was misled,
    When the coaches prayed in the fall.
And in reality,
    God doesn't play football.

October 5, 2006

Danny L Shanks

Columbus Day

In the year 1492,
    Columbus sailed the ocean blue.
His claim that the world was round,
    He wanted to prove it true.

But before him came Nicholas Copernicus,
    Who had previously made that claim.
And the German mapmaker Martin Behaim,
    In 1492 made the first globe stating the same.

But we liked the rhyme so much,
    It is still taught in school.
And it seems facts are not as important,
    And pop culture seems to be the rule.

Leonardo Da Vinci wrote most of his notes,
    Backwards and it could only in a mirror be read.
Like the mirror was a new invention,
    And could only be used to reveal the secrets in his head.

But Archimedes was a mathematician and inventor,
    Who lived around 200 B.C.
And he developed the burning mirror
    That burned the ships of invading armies at sea.

And Jesus, who is listed as the Messiah,
    But it originally meant a divinely-appointed king.
And some argue that there is no "saviour" concept, as suggested in Christianity,
    The "anointed" one more closely means 'high priest' or a 'leader' thing.

Or why not a day for Nicolas Tesla?
    He discovered alternating current.
An electrical solution to modern life,
    For computers and how our Email is sent

We revere so many men,
    And others we simply do not.
Claiming all are equal,
    In the American melting pot.

But we celebrate some,
    Others we simply shirk.
But all I really care about,
    Is that my wife gets a day off work.

October 6, 2006

Danny L Shanks

A Night's Walk in October

An early October night,
    My wife asked if I wanted to go outside.
Happily I agreed and she got my wheelchair,
    Then took me for a ride.

It was a pleasant evening,
    With a full moon riding high.
Among the stars and clouds,
    Gracing the October sky.

The clouds did not seem to move,
    No wind stirred the trees.
Stillness and quiet prevailed,
    For there was simply no breeze.

And as we paused in our stroll,
    To stare at the moon up there.
Riding so high and lonesome,
    It washed away all my care.

For I felt a kindred spirit,
    With the moon's light up above.
And with the glow upon me,
    I felt the fullness of my wife's love.

For the moon sometimes seems lonely,
    But it has all of the stars.
And if that is not enough,
    It also has the planets Venus and Mars.

Well I have a companion also,
    And she is my lovely wife.
A pleasant night, a full moon's glow,
    What more could one ask of life.

October 7, 2006

The Triple Threat

I grow weary these days of my fellow humans,
And on the why would you place your bet?
The true nature of mankind exposed,
What I call the triple threat.

Being ignorant, arrogant and self righteous,
Three characteristics that give me pain.
I don't know how much more of it I can take,
Before I go insane.

They resent being called ignorant,
Yet all it means is that they lack knowledge.
And such wisdom comes from life,
Not some course learned in college.

The arrogance comes as a defense,
Offered to defend their point of view.
But if they actually researched the facts,
They would find some of theirs were not true.

The third is being self-righteous,
In this they find relief.
For the truth cannot compare,
To what they hold as belief.

So why do I try,
To show them what is true.
To expose their old beliefs,
With something that is different or new.

I am now so tired,
Weariness now fills my cup.
And I believe I will argue no more,
I will simply just shut up.

October 7, 2006

Anger

Two years ago I had to retire,
Rest and an end to stress to make me well.
Two years later and I now realize,
It has become a living hell.

I live in solitary confinement,
Just like in a prison.
Four walls drawing close,
With no life or human contact within.

The only relief I found.
For companionship in my world.
Was talking to the trees outside,
And to a small sarcastic squirrel.

Doctors said depression,
With arthritis's accompanying pain.
I began to fear,
That I was going insane.

They prescribed drugs,
And so those answers I bought.
And the result was.
For the first time I had suicidal thought.

Paranoid delusions continued daily,
For all I felt was rage.
The arthritis dominating me was usually experienced,
By someone fifteen years beyond my age.

So I took up writing,
Hoping that diversion was all it took.
Only to find further rage,
When no one cared to read or even buy my book.

My wife and daughter had always told me,
    My anger was something bad.
But how can it be described so,
    When it seemed to be all I had to keep from going mad.

So my wife took action,
    She did something most would call rash.
She took all the drugs they had prescribed,
    Then threw them in the trash.

Well it seemed to work,
    Yet did not relieve the physical pain.
But I have to live with that,
    For it seems the anger allowed me to keep my brain.

So now she accepts the anger,
    For it is the only way I might.
Keep my sanity,
    And allow me to see the light.

Accepting the pain, yet reclaiming my mind,
    Was something for which to strive.
For it reminds me daily,
    That I am still alive.

So before you condemn me,
    For the anger I still sometimes display.
Realize that it enables me,
    To face another day.

October 12, 2006

October Country

I slip outside this evening,
    To await the coming of the night.
Storm clouds race across the sky,
    With the fading of the light.

A full moon is out,
    Peeking through the breaks with it's glow.
Illuminating in full array,
    The autumn land below.

Thankful am I for the moon,
    For she allows me to fully see.
A land I simply call,
    The October Country.

Gone are the colors of summer,
    Yellows and reds now dominate the scene.
I love the display she offers,
    So much more vibrant than the green.

I suddenly notice movement,
    A cat has crossed my sight.
Cold black and moving sinuously,
    As if it controlled this night.

It's October I suddenly remember,
    Halloween is not far away.
A day when ghouls, ghosts and witches,
    Will demand to have their say.

The breeze is brisk tonight,
    The smell of fall is in the air.
Smoke from chimneys float across the land,
    A land stripped of leaves and left bare.

I relish this night,
Thoughts of youth cloud my mind.
Traditions and stories we seem to have lost,
And can no longer find.

But they are not truly lost,
For they still live in my memory.
And as long as I have those thoughts,
In October my youth will always remain free.

October 16, 2006

Danny L Shanks

Olympic Rain Forrest

The mist hovers over the mountain stream,
A battle with the morning's light.
The water babbles softly over the rocks,
Rushing in a hurried downhill flight.

A temperate rain forest,
One of only three on this earth.
The others are in Chile and New Zealand,
That fact alone determines its worth.

The evergreen firs stand large,
Majestically towering over all.
Reverence prevails in the forest,
And the silence dominates the call.

So here I sit in the quiet,
Yet I do not feel alone.
I do not miss the television,
Neither email, nor the telephone.

Dare I say I revel?
In the reverence and solitude.
Enraptured by the peace and joy,
Each demanding control of my mood.

For if I watch the news,
In a world gone totally mad.
In my peace of the forest,
I suddenly feel completely sad.

If I could only bottle it,
I'd give it to the entire world.
Like the whirlpool in the stream,
Going around each obstruction with a whirl.

If mankind could only solve their dilemmas,
By seeking an easier way.
Not butting everything head on,
Demanding to have their say.

But I cannot stop the wars,
Nor the conflicts, nor the fights.
By each group of humans,
Demanding to have their rights.

Yet here as sit in the forest,
I see so clearly the absurdity of man.
For I cannot change any of it,
And I just enjoy the forest while I can.

October 21, 2006

Love, Love, Love

Back in the sixties the Beatles sang a song,
That with all of life's push and shove.
To truly conquer it all,
All you need is love.

So many unaware starry-eyed youths,
Enthusiastically embarked on their life.
With this promise assured,
Became simply husband and wife.

Children came and bills piled high,
Putting the marriage to a test.
But they believed overall,
That love's answer would be the best.

So sweet a time it was,
But my friends let me tell you how I feel.
Love may indeed make the world go round,
But it's money that greases the wheel.

October 26, 2006

Autumn Storm

I'm suddenly awakened,
As I glance over to my sweetly sleeping mate.
The clock says five A.M,
But I do not wish to be late.

I feel a storm coming,
The wind beckons me outside.
For missing the first storm of autumn,
Is a regret I will not abide.

So I bundle up warmly,
Put on my coat and slip out back.
Sit in my easy chair,
And wait for the storm to track.

Feet propped up I wait,
For a wind more strongly than a breeze.
I relish its coming,
And the swaying of the trees.

The flag across the way is snapping,
The wind is brisk but not cold.
Music added to by the chain,
Beating gently against its pole.

The trees sway too and fro,
Leaves fall softy to the ground.
All of the storms coming,
Adding to the sound.

The wind calls to me,
Sleeping the town will miss it all.
But no one should deny themselves,
The first storm of the fall.

For I will forgo my bed,
    Willingly miss my sleep.
But the joy I feel being here.
    Is a cherished memory I shall keep.

October 29, 2006

Madness

It's one o'clock in the morning,
    I find myself writing once again.
For I feel the need to explain,
    The mind of a madman.

I was lying in bed an hour ago,
    When I noticed my first mind's twitch.
I knew it was coming,
    As if someone had thrown a switch.

The darkness settles over me,
    Settling softly like a silken veil.
Then it comes slamming home,
    Like the hammer on an anvil.

Where does it come from?
    Surely not from anything I had bought.
Yet gone is reasonable thinking,
    Gone all logical thought.

Conspiracy theories run rampant,
    Concerning the people that I love.
Each thought fitting perfectly,
    Like the wearing of a glove.

But I know these people love me,
    They do not plan my demise.
Yet trying to ignore this thinking,
    In my madness seems unwise.

Why do I not have the control?
    I once had in my youth.
When it was a simple chore,
    To reason out the truth.

For the thinking that overtakes me,
    Seems all so logical and real.
And it is simply hard to believe,
    That it is not how they feel.

So bear with the ravings of a madman,
    Writing in the middle of the night.
For these thoughts I know are not true,
    Yet in my mind I must alone face that fight.

November 1, 2006

Summers Gone

I went outside this afternoon,
    To watch the storm roll in.
Left the security of my home,
    Left my snug warm den.

To watch the coming of the storm,
    With it's stiff and brisk like breeze.
To be outside with my friends,
    My lovely dancing trees.

For I sense the dismal coming,
    Of the autumn rain.
Teardrops hang from their leaves,
    As if they are in pain.

I feel a strong empathy,
    That I wish to share.
Traffic passes and the world goes round,
    And no one seems to care.

They rise ever so tall,
    Each with its majesty.
And if by chance they look down,
    It's me I want them to see.

They are not alone,
    Waiting for the winter's blast.
For out here with them I sit.
    Telling them it will not last.

But they look so forlorn,
    All leafless now and bare.
I just want them to know,
    That at least one human does care.

That Mother Nature she has a plan,
And once again she will sing.
Seasons come and seasons go,
But it will soon again be spring.

November 03, 2006

Not A Likeable Guy

My wife was talking to me the other day,
And she told me she would explain why.
People did not want to talk to me,
Because I was just not a likeable guy.

The hurting of people's feelings,
Was not what I intended.
But hearing the truth spoken out loud,
Left most of them offended.

It was a trait my father taught to me,
That I would be often rejected.
If I spoke the truth out loud,
A truth to which they objected.

But that certain principles apply,
As to the honor and conduct of a man.
And rejecting their fantasies to explain it,
Would not gain me any fan.

So I've tried to accept things,
I knew were simply wrong.
But each sensed my true feeling,
And that it was just an act to get along.

For my father told me often,
A trait valued above all of the world's wealth.
Was to simply accept the truth,
And not to lie to one's self.

So even if I agreed out loud,
They saw my distain of their lies.
For I seemed to be unable,
To keep it from my eyes.

She said I made them feel stupid,
    But all I felt deep inside of me.
Was an explanation and a truth,
    I felt that they should see.

So I will write no more,
    No more revelations will I try.
And this will be the last poem,
    From a not very likeable guy.

November 7, 2006

Growing up and Apart

I had a daughter gifted to me,
    In the early days of my youth.
I vowed to teach her all I knew,
    Of justice, honor, and truth.

And so we both grew,
    Getting older every day.
Incorporating life's lessons,
    In every game we did play.

She got older and went to college,
    Got married and moved away.
But I can't help but think of her,
    Daily in every way.

She learned so much, my daughter,
    In a world ever changing and new.
Regretfully I began to realize,
    That outdated was my point of view.

I didn't understand the words of the music,
    But it had a really good beat.
That phrase my parents used on me,
    I found myself using as if sitting in their seat.

She seems to be doing good,
    I am proud of her in this.
And I still relish her whenever,
    She gives to me a kiss.

But I worry what she thinks of me,
    And of my well thought out plan.
But all I can hope for is, that she sees me,
    As nothing more than a man.

A Papa that tried to give to her,
    All that he felt he could.
And that goodness and honor,
    Were positions for which he stood.

But now I grow older,
    I realize the folly of my youth.
For her world is not what I grew up in,
    And that my friends is the truth.

November 5, 2006

The Poet's Curse

Danny L. Shanks

Contents

Foreword .

1. Poet's Curse . . . . .
2. December 11, 1971 Revisited .
3. Eulogy for Markie . .
4. Valentine Day 2006 . .
5. The Nature of Tragedy . .
6. Relax . . .
7. Medication .
8. Quantum Physics .
9. Breathing .
10. Mother's Day Poem
11. Speed of Light
12. Abortion VS Pro Life .
13. Fast Reading Revisited .
14. The Coming of the Night .
15. Back Patio
16. Particle VS Wave
17. The No Present Birthday .
18. The Sirens
19. Blue Lamp .
20. Dragons Storming The Castle .
21. Why Am I Still Sick?
22. Another Forgotten Man
23. Web Builder
24. Outrage of War
25. Parents
26. Narcissism
27. Goodbye
28. Margarine
29. I Lied .
30. July Night .
31. Advice Sayings

32. Goodbye—Revisited
33. Reality
34. Cook .
35. Brief Encounter
36. Wind
37. Poet's Curse Part II

Foreword

The front and back covers of this book are a quote from Miguel de Cervantes, author of *Don Quixote*. A voice from the past who has inspired me most of my adult life. I thank you Miguel for the impossible dream and the world will be better for this.

Danny L Shanks
July 11,2006

Poet's Curse

My name is Danny L Shanks,
 I am cursed as any soul can be.
My curse is simply writing,
 Well, writing poems is my vanity.

If you have seen my books,
 Eclectics one, two and three.
You will easily recognize the vanity's curse,
 That has afflicted me.

In the third book,
 The "Final Poem" it was called.
The last entry of the book,
 For I had recognized and was appalled.

How tightly vanity's curse had snared me,
 And held me in its grip.
But no more nightly visits to the computer,
 I would forestall making that trip.

Then I heard soft voices calling me,
 Like the Siren's lure.
To come and sit and write,
 Some poem, simple and pure.

Angrily I resolved,
 I would not move from my bed.
But the voices were so enticing,
 And would not stay out of my head.

So I tried some drugs,
 Counted sheep and even tried the Alpha state.
Anything to avoid,
 Being lured unto that fate.

For hours I fought the fight,
    But I lost the battle in my head.
Resigned I arose in the middle of the night,
    Went to the computer and left my bed.

As I wrote I found the peace,
    That had eluded me.
And realized that I was writing,
    For no one else but me.

It let me see a world,
    No reality could I see.
Just a world the way I wanted it,
    The way the world should be.

The wife noticed the computer on,
    Asking me what I had written.
I told her about the poems,
    And by vanity's bug I had been bitten.

She was happy for me and,
    Suggested I publish a new book.
With vanity's curse upon me,
    That suggestion was all it took.

So here I sit,
    It's 3 AM as I take the symbolic pen in hand.
Attempting to bring aware,
    The better side of man.

Be not so self righteous,
    Do not declare yourself a judge.
Keep an open heart and mind,
    Not so fixed, as not to budge.

Listen to others talk,
    Their ideas and belief.
Everyone has something to say,
    And some may offer relief.

Others may make mistakes,
    They may not have a good plan.
That does not eliminate them,
    From use of your helping hand.

So talk to others about everything,
    Do not become made of stone.
For you are on the third rock from the sun,
    And you are not alone.

Danny L. Shanks
December 1,2005

Danny L Shanks

December 11, 1971 Revisited

The dawn is breaking,
    I rise and go to the kitchen and take my seat.
A quick kiss good morning,
    Then concentration on my breakfast to eat.

Again you have fixed for me,
    Oatmeal with blueberries.
Thankful am I for the food,
    But more so the message that it carries.

The last few years have been tough,
    With illness and depression waiting in the dark.
Suicide waiting for me to come,
    My future looked at best described as stark.

But you never gave up on me,
    You stuck by me no matter the cost.
Gave me your strength,
    And never considered me lost.

I swore I would never write again,
    But what can I say.
To express my love for you, I write,
    On this our anniversary day.

You never lost faith in me,
    And though I still stumble and slip.
I would never have made it this far without you,
    And I thank you for the trip.

Words cannot express my love for you,
    And respect for your many ways and tries.
But just look closely at me,
    And you will see the love there in my eyes.

Never has a man had the support,
    To overcome the trials of his life.
Than to have you by his side,
    Such a lovely magnificent and reliable wife.

December 11,2005
Your thankful husband,
Danny

Eulogy for Markie

Today we got the news,
Markie had passed away.
It is a sadness that will forever,
Mark for us this day.

Eighty-Seven years,
And if the truth be told.
Years of sorrow and years of fun.
But the loss still leaves us cold.

My sympathies go to the children,
Bill Mack, Janie and Jim.
But she has gone to a better place,
And is now with her husband and her lifelong friend.

So goodbye to you Markie,
We will miss your laugh and wit.
Fond memories of you being cool,
And never throwing a fit.

For I remember your humor,
You shown like the sun.
A beacon to me the newcomer,
Allowing me to have some fun.

Yes I will miss you,
And all the family will too.
So give us a smile from above,
And remember us each, as one of your crew.

January 9, 2006
Danny

Valentine Day 2006

Valentine Day 2006,
    February 14th is the date.
But I didn't want to wait for it,
    Didn't want to be late.

We both know I think it's dumb to buy flowers
    But this morning I realized, that might be true.
Then realization that I was buying them,
    Not for me, but for you.

For they will get old,
    No matter what you try.
But hey guess what?
    So am I.

For you are the greatest joy,
    That I have in this world.
Undiminished for 35 years,
    Since you agreed to be my girl.

So Happy Valentine's Day,
    Again I wish you this year.
As long as we have each other,
    There is nothing in this world to fear.

Feb 14,2006

The Nature of Tragedy

There are riots in Paris,
    Nigeria has a civil war.
Well I don't know how to tell you folks,
    But this has happened before.

The centuries come and the centuries go,
    Conflicts abounding between man.
Each self-righteously fought over,
    Some insignificant piece of land.

We have the high moral ground, they say,
    We're righteous in our fight.
But in truth, the Nature of Tragedy,
    Is the conflict between right and right.

Feb 25,2006

Relax

I went to the doctor the other day,
He told me just to relax.
So I pulled out my dictionary,
Just to get the facts.

Well lax means to not be so strict,
Not to be so severe.
And re means to do again,
My understanding I began to fear.

Cause if I was not so strict,
Nor severe at the time.
How could I do it again?
Without losing my mind.

The word redundant,
Seems to jump out at me.
Cause if I were lax,
Doing it again I could not see.

March 9,2006

Medication

A prescription drug for pain,
    And one for depression too.
Both have kicked in and I'm now in love with the whole wide world,
    Best expressed by "Whoop Dee Do."

March 13,2006

Quantum Physics

I was watching a movie the other day,
    It was called "The Butterfly Effect."
I soon became lost in the story,
    No storyline could I reason or detect.

So I researched the term,
    And I was surprised to find.
Edward Lorenz coined the term,
    The year was 1960, to help him to define.

A theory called Chaos,
    For the new physics of the day.
To help explain the universe,
    In an original and innovative way.

He was a meteorologist,
    No degree in physics or math.
Twelve equations he created.
    To explain his thinking path.

Using the weather as examples,
    He soon reduced the number to three.
Regardless of the initial conditions,
    The universe was chaotic, and it was plain to see.

But when I was in school I was taught Newton's third law,
    "To every action there exists an equal and opposite reaction".
Taught as law and agreeable to nature,
    A balance for everything, each part and faction.

So the further I looked I found a new physics.
    M theory, String theory, and Chaos.
The variety was over whelming,
    And it left me at a loss.

For how could they teach both as true?
    And I don't mean to be intrusive.
But Newton's third law and Chaos theory,
    Are mutually exclusive.

They can't both be true,
    For each other they contradict.
Yet both are taught in the schools,
    Of what makes the universe tick.

So I decided to ask my daughter,
    She has degrees in physics and math.
She would know the answer I sought,
    Setting me on the correct path.

So I asked her to help her old man,
    "So give me the answer my love".
"Dad", she said with an enigmatic smile,
    "Quantum physics is just the dreams, stuff is made of".

April 24,2006

Breathing

And so you have high blood pressure,
    Well I certainly do not wish to deceive.
But to control such a condition,
    All you need is to learn how to breathe.

In through your nose,
    Then out through your mouth.
Slowly each breath,
    Will help your health from going south.

They sell machines to help you,
    Resperate is one to buy.
Or practice without a machine,
    All you have to do is try.

The machine is there to help you,
    A musical interlude.
To teach you how to breathe,
    With no intention of being rude.

Ten breaths a minute,
    Less if you train yourself.
Once learned you can retire the machine,
    And put it on the shelf.

Fifteen minutes a session,
    Three times a week.
You will see the lower blood pressure,
    That your doctors seek.

You say what a waste of time,
    You say your schedule is too tight.
You have to earn a living,
    You have to do what's right.

So you have to make a living,
    Don't have time to waste.
Well how much time do you spend living?
    How much of life do you taste?

So learn to breathe,
    Slowly if you can.
And you will find yourself,
    A healthier and happier man.

May 10,2006

Mother's Day Poem

Motherhood is the greatest gift for man,
    Of that there is no doubt.
For mothers are the one thing,
    The human race cannot do without.

They give their love so endlessly,
    Give devotion from their heart.
A hundred percent given all the time,
    Not just at the start.

The second Sunday in May,
    Is set aside to give.
Thanks to our wonderful Mothers,
    Who made it possible for us to live.

So on this day of thanks,
    We would like to say.
Thanks a million times over,
    Forever and a day.

May 14,2006

Speed of Light

I was taught in school,
The fastest thing was the speed of light.
As I get older, I wonder,
Could my teachers have been right?

Just think about an equilateral triangle,
Somewhere out in space.
With points A, B and C,
With a line between each traced.

You begin at B traveling to C,
In a clear spacecraft going the speed of light.
Then you turn on a beam,
You could see the beam, if I'm right.

Is it a particle, is it a wave,
Name it a photon called Jeffery.
But it exists regardless,
That you can plainly see.

So Jeffery is going the speed of light,
At least from where you stand.
That is the fastest thing in the universe,
According to the measurements of man.

But suppose I was at point A,
And I could see your craft and you.
We've established that Jeffery exists,
So could I not see him too?

But if I measure him for speed,
What measurement would I get?
Using the theory of relativity,
Would put my teachers in a fit.

For if you find just one exception,
    Then the law is not always true.
Then you begin to doubt,
    If there are not more than a few.

Professors teach the Poly Exclusion Principle,
    And the Heisenberg Uncertainty Principle both as fact.
But the fact is they contradict each other,
    Understanding their teaching, I lack.

We take so much we're taught for granted,
    Yet if you think it through.
It doesn't make much sense,
    To blindly accept it as true.

Abortion VS Pro Life

I was listening to an argument,
 It left me somewhat bemused.
Between an abortionist and a pro lifer,
 Their semantics left me confused.

Life begins at conception,
 The pro lifer did declare.
No, replied the abortionist,
 Only when the baby is born, would make it fair.

And so I thought of what I had learned,
 From biology class in school.
Trying to figure it all out,
 I needed every tool.

I remember reading,
 How much the sperm swims.
Hunting for the female egg,
 Not just a random movement of whims.

Once there the female egg must choose,
 Which one it uses to mate.
Millions of choices to make,
 Quickly so not as to be too late.

Well if the sperm chooses where to go,
 And the egg determines which one is best.
Don't those choices demonstrate?
 Proof of an intelligence test.

So if intelligence exists already,
 Is not that a proof of life?
The sperm and the egg make those choices,
 Not the husband or wife.

Yet the abortionist and pro lifer,
    Both are so self-righteous in their view.
Of what is the meaning of life?
    And what is precious and new.

If life already existed,
    Just waiting to began.
What kind of mass murderer was I?
    By my teenage human hand.

For a kernel of corn has life,
    But never into a stalk if you do not sow.
It into the earth and nourish it,
    And leave it alone to grow.

And so I listen to them rail,
    Argue their where and what for.
But all I could think of was that,
    Of all the mammals, only man, created war.

May 19,2006

Fast Reading Revisited

I once wrote a poem called Fast Reading,
In it, I explicitly warned.
Reading poetry too fast,
Was a practice that I scorned.

I now realize, as I get older,
That was not all that I should say.
That fast reading cost emotions and was not the only,
Price that you would pay.

Poetry should be read aloud,
Let your emotions rule your sound.
Be not embarrassed or fear ridicule,
Let your humanity abound.

Children are no longer taught to recite,
That is a lesson we should preach.
For if we do not teach it early enough,
They have to learn it in a college class called Speech.

So pull down a book of poetry,
Read it to your spouse or child.
Take whatever time is needed,
And turn off the television for a while.

For if you hide your emotions,
And do not read or speak aloud.
You will find you have trouble,
Talking to a crowd.

And if you put it off,
To do on a different day.
You will reach for the ability,
Only to find it has gone away.

May 19,2006

The Coming of the Night

I sit outside in the evening,
    I watch the fading of the light.
The darkness soon embraces me,
    Its touch is ever so slight.

The nighttime then enfolds me,
    Washing away all my care.
A challenge to my anxieties,
    If I'm bold enough to dare.

It cradles me so softly,
    Like a mother's new born child.
The breeze whispering endearments,
    Imploring me to stay awhile.

The silence that comes with it,
    A companion to make it quite.
Reminding me of how the world should be,
    When everything is right.

No stress to spoil the time,
    Or make me worry more.
Of what comes tomorrow,
    Or what it has in store.

So I sit in the stillness,
    Relishing the solitude.
With no worries of the world's problems,
    Night doesn't allow them to intrude.

Should I feel so very special?
    To enjoy my time in the night.
Everyone should have such time,
    For everyone has that right.

May 28,2006

Back Patio

It's 3 AM and I'm awake,
Mournfully again, I find.
So I get out of bed, go to my back patio,
Searching for peace of mind.

The nighttime there embraces me,
The silence greets me as a friend.
No expectations for me are asked,
No need to act smart nor even to pretend.

I sit in my chair and listen,
To the quiet in the night.
An owl flies by on feathered wings,
The sound ever so slight.

The sound of the field mice scurrying,
To get to the hole in the ground.
Once again to the safety of home,
Can't be out when Mr. Owl is around.

I hear a splash in the pond,
But neither do I rise nor am I drawn.
For it's probably just Mr. Raccoon,
Out fishing before the dawn.

In through the nose, and then out through the mouth,
I take slowly every breath.
It helps to make you live longer,
But cannot forestall eventual death.

And when the Grim Reaper calls,
I can only hope that it is so.
He finds me there and not in a hospital,
Out sitting on my back patio.

May 29,2006

Particle VS Wave

In physics, wave-particle duality holds that, light,
Exhibits properties of both of particles and waves.
Many men have studied this,
From their youth until their graves.

The photoelectric effect, was analyzed in 1905,
By Albert Einstein, and it won him the Nobel Prize.
But after looking at it with common sense,
Was he really all that wise?

Feynman asserted, that the photon is a particle,
Newton and Einstein thought it a particle and agreed.
But the Bohr model, when proposed in 1923,
Suggested that as a wave, it would fill every need.

Planck's constant validated Bohr,
For all know photons have no mass.
Broglie then published his hypothesis,
Proving that electrons really have waves that are fast.

So what *is* light?
Is the photon, a particle or a wave?
They use quantum physics,
Making mathematics act as their slave.

But light won't play their game,
Or fit in their equation.
For the light is life itself,
And simply evades their explanation.

June 1,2006

The No Present Birthday

Well it's birthday time again,
No present could I find.
That would express my love for you,
And I find myself really in a bind.

I guess I could take you out to eat,
See a movie, or go shopping at the mall.
For you would smile at me,
Say thanks, and that you had a ball.

But as I thought about it,
True realization I came to see.
Anything like that would not be for you,
But really just for me.

So what could I give you?
That would be special on your day of birth.
That would express how much you mean to me,
And what my love is worth.

Then it hit me, and I knew I had it right,
We would not get dressed or go out in any way.
We would stay at home,
And my gift to you, would simply be a no bra day.

June 9,2006
Love ya,
Danny

The Sirens

The Sirens are calling to me,
From across the River Styx.
Their proposal offered honestly,
Devoid of lies or tricks.

The promise that if I join them,
No more pain, lies or strife.
The cost is non-negotiable,
I must simply end my life.

The terror I felt in my youth,
Of their promises left me cold.
Those promises now hold no fear,
As I feel myself getting old.

Their offer is appealing,
An end to worry and pain.
Just a darkened respite,
To overtake my brain.

The lure from them is strong,
It puts me to a test.
For how can anyone resist,
The promise of everlasting peace and rest.

But I shall resist their calling,
For at least another night.
And stand the challenge of life,
Raising my sword of hope to face the fight.

June 12, 2006

Blue Lamp

I got a call from my daughter last night,
She wanted to help me but did not know.
This morning I was listening to a song,
Called Blue Lamp from the Heavy Metal picture show.

It seemed to be her singing,
With a big old house as my life.
For she had looked both inside and out,
But the only light left on was the Blue Lamp of my wife.

She let me know that she would find any guardian angel,
And give it to my wife without a doubt.
But if my wife were wiser in today's world,
She would just get out.

But in the upstairs they still laugh and cry and shine,
They were the stars of my dream.
As she listened through her and not to her, she realized,
My wife would never leave or break our team.

I was inspired and decided to fight,
Despite the struggles or strains.
Cause my daughter let me know,
That only the love remains.

June 27,2006

Dragons Storming The Castle

The dragons are storming the castle,
Arrows rise to arrest their flight.
And as the battle rages on,
No one stops to question, who's wrong or right.

Centuries have passed,
As we look for what is true.
But almost all the beliefs are old,
And nothing on this world is new.

The scale of justice is fragile,
To determine right or wrong.
Mostly the deciding factor,
Is simply weak from strong.

For perception is what we use,
To determine who has the high ground?
And if the strongest win then, it must be correct,
What other proof need be found.

But as an outside thought,
When determining wrong from right.
What if there were more than the two choices,
More than just black or white.

For a moment just open your mind,
And picture what could be seen,
If instead of just black or white,
There was another color of green.

Then a myriad of colors could be possible,
With the possibility of truth in each.
As many different answers as there are people,
All within our reach.

With a new way of seeing,
    Who is right or wrong?
Using reason and logic,
    Not just weak against strong.

Maybe if we just used our heart,
    Instead of our mind.
All things would be possible,
    And real truth could we find.

July 4,2006

Why Am I Still Sick?

I retired from the working world,
About a year and a half ago.
I could no longer take it,
And told others and my wife so.

Doctors shake their heads,
All the tests came back fine.
The only real answer left,
Seems to be, it was in my mind.

Depression and suicide thoughts,
Dominate my every day.
To beat them I use drugs,
But there has to be a better way.

And so I took up writing,
I declared it purged and cleansed my soul.
And I have said that line so many times,
Even hearing it, is starting to get old.

I now believe the writing,
Is the problem inside of me.
Why I never saw it before, I don't know,
For it was clear to see.

Was I just trying to validate my existence?
Declaring I still had something to say.
That I still had some worth,
To justify my getting up each day.

So I watched for people's reactions,
To the books I had written.
Seeking their approval,
Seeing if by my genius they are smitten.

That is the sickness in me,
    I don't know how to fight.
For it haunts me mostly,
    In the middle of the night.

I find myself asking my wife,
    What the others have said.
Did they like it? Were they moved?
    By the poems and stories that they read.

Seeking such fame and recognition,
    And dare I say the word glory.
Just because I wrote some poems,
    And some supposedly funny story.

And so on this day,
    I will try and change my life.
Not to consider writing,
    And just be a husband to my wife.

I will try not to worry,
    If any of my books have been sold.
For each inquiry returning a negative,
    Leaves me unbelievably cold.

For without writing,
    Or anything else to occupy my mind.
I feel empty and useless,
    Just waiting for the end of my time.

July 5,2006

Another Forgotten Man

I'm just another forgotten man,
They put a rifle in my hand.
They shouted "Hip Hooray," they sent me far away,
But look at me today.

Their analysis is endless,
Psychobabble till all I feel are screams.
As if they could see,
What was in my dreams.

Look on the bright side, they say,
Enjoy the sky and sun.
Don't dwell on negatives,
Get out and have some fun.

As if they could see my reality,
The memories and horrors in my mind.
So just take your self-righteous advice,
And stick it where the sun don't shine.

July 5,2006

Web Builder

She rises with the dawn,
    Mists still cling to the trees.
Her babies are coming and she must find a place,
    To build her web, and then she sees.

A human's trail creating an opening,
    This will be the perfect place.
For the flies of the wood will always congregate,
    To any open space.

Make the silk, attach and extend,
    Make more, but soon it will end.
For her babies must have food,
    Till they are old enough for themselves to fend.

Hours and hours pass,
    She could certainly use a rest.
But if Mother Nature has qualifications for motherhood,
    Then this will be the test.

Late afternoon arrives,
    Her labor has taken the entire day.
Now she can rest with the knowledge,
    Her babies will have a place to stay.

Concentric circles extending outward,
    Surely, this is a place that will stand.
Suddenly, along comes a self-pronounced nature loving human,
    And the web disappears with the casual swing of a hand.

The human continues down the trail,
    Unawares of the drama unfolding behind him.
That he has created such sorrow,
    By exercising such a casual whim.

Her sorrow and loss will go unnoticed.
    For tomorrow is another day.
She will try and postpone the babies,
    Till she can build another place for them to stay.

As the sun slowly sets,
    And the earth goes round and round.
Most creatures live unaware of other life,
    And how precious it is to be found.

July 06,2006

Outrage of War

If a rabid dog came into your yard,
Then tried to kill your pet.
Would you not defend it?
Meeting any of the mad dog's threat.

Would you not kill the madness?
In defense, you understand.
But why kill the mad dog?
As if it was something that it planned.

It was just the rabies,
That had changed the way it felt.
Does that mean you have to kill it,
As the only way with it to be dealt.

Well any child raised by its parents,
Believe everything they are told.
Never doubting the truth,
About the beliefs that they are sold.

So when told they must help to kill,
Any infidels in their land.
They gladly go with full knowledge,
Of the overall existing plan.

So the destruction of the children,
Hurts us and makes no sense.
But to prevent such an outrage,
We should kill such unworthy parents.

July 9,2006

Parents

So you decided to have a child,
To bring another life into this world.
A healthy baby you want,
If it be boy or girl.

Soon they start to grow,
And you prepare them for this life.
Truth they will be told,
Of politics, wars and strife.

There is no Santa Claus you say,
No tooth fairy or Easter bunny.
They should abandon such fantasies,
They are not real nor funny.

They should learn responsibility,
To deal with the problems of life.
Sorry my friends but no,
The responsibilities, lie with husband and wife.

Who in the hell told you?
A child should have no fantasy.
But see the world as it is.
Should be their only destiny.

You would destroy their hopes?
And dreams for this test?
Well look around and see,
The world is in a mess.

Let the children play,
Have their dreams and hope.
For soon enough they will have to deal,
With life's reality and its slippery slope.

Youth passes soon enough,
    Without your vanity imposed.
On any child or youngster,
    Without your fears exposed.

July 11,2006

Narcissism

Seven books I have published,
    An author's status I now hold.
Yet, I finally realize the cost to me,
    And it has left me cold.

For I no longer can make a claim,
    And that failure just makes me sick.
For I have lost the right,
    To claim I am not narcissistic.

July 11,2006

Goodbye

I went outside last night,
Just to my back patio to see.
If I could talk to my three friends,
Little, Bartholomew and Patricia the young pine tree.

For I had not spoken to them for a very long time,
Since, my doctor had demanded I make choices.
For the depression and what was in my head,
To deal with reality and stop the voices.

He put me on drugs,
Prozac to help me heal.
So I took it and it helped me,
I took it for my wife and against my will.

I spent the entire night outside,
Calling over and over to the friends I had lost.
But only silence greeted me,
And then I knew the cost.

I could no longer reach the alpha state,
The drug took the ability from my life.
A sacrifice I made willingly,
For above everything else, I love my wife.

Yet, I had to give them up,
I felt alone and empty, but I don't want to preach.
Never again to become one with the universal awareness,
I had once touched, but now was beyond my reach.

So goodbye Little my friendly squirrel,
Bartholomew and Patricia my favorite trees.
I will miss you all so very much,
As I embark alone on uncharted human reality seas.

July12, 2006

Margarine

To fatten up turkeys,
    Margarine was first created.
But it killed the turkeys,
    So another use must be slated.

The people who had put all the money,
    Into the research wanted a payback.
So they put their heads together,
    To figure out a different tact.

It was a white substance,
    With absolutely no food appeal.
So they added the yellow coloring,
    Then flavoring to try and clinch a deal.

To sell in place of butter,
    Surely the public they could fool.
But it is so close to plastic,
    Differing by only one molecule.

Purchase a tub of margarine,
    Then leave it somewhere in your back yard.
Within a couple of days you will notice,
    Several things and it won't be hard.

Even flies will not eat it,
    And it doesn't rot or have a different smell.
Because it has no nutritional value,
    And in America, that should sell very well.

July 12, 2006

I Lied

The other day I was talking,
    To my wife and she corrected me.
So thinking quickly I said I had lied,
    And if she were thinking clearly, she would see.

Surprisingly I found the story worked,
    Coming from my lips sweetly like a song.
And it was easier to say I had lied,
    Than to admit to her I was wrong.

July 13,2006

July Night

A summer's night, it's mid July,
    I retired to my bed for the night.
Yet lying there I find I can't sleep,
    With a window full of summer's moonlight.

The wife left the window open,
    And I hear the night calling to me.
Come join all of us outside,
    Seems to be the plea.

So I rise and make my way,
    Onto my back patio.
It's as if the night planned my coming,
    My way lit by a full moon's glow.

And so I ease myself down,
    To the chair I keep out there.
Relaxed I am enjoying the night.
    Without a single care.

The honeysuckle smell is in the air,
    The fireflies light the sky.
In the distance I hear the lonely whistle,
    Of a freight train passing by.

Maybe I could sleep out here,
    The thought pleasing to me.
So I relax and began counting sheep,
    But only make it to three.

The sheep change into unicorns,
    Flying over an enchanted land.
A land with maidens fair,
    And knights are in demand.

All the wizards are nice,
Evil is always defeated by good.
Minstrels sing and poets quote,
Simple songs and poems easily understood.

No wars to threaten the people.
Mothers and fathers love their young.
Children are polite and show respect,
To all creatures under the sun.

This is not real I realize,
I must have fallen asleep.
But would this not be a place,
That in my heart I should keep.

Maybe it's not reality,
But it is a better place to be.
The summer's night with its gentle breeze,
Decided to show it to me.

So I look up to the sky,
I watch the clouds float by,
It could be reality,
If only people would care to try.

July 13,2006

Advice Sayings

Listening to a conversation,
I heard some advice that was just a stupid thing to say.
Then thinking about it I started remembering,
How many dumb things are spoken every day.

The only thing I have,
To use in my defense.
Is that none of these sayings,
Makes any kind of sense.

A few examples follow,
"A penny saved is a penny earned."
Well folks to get the penny to save,
You have to earn it first is all I ever learned.

"A Stitch in time saves nine."
So I pulled out my copy of the book.
The Time Machine by Mr. Wells does talk about time,
But never mentioned sewing wherever I chose to look.

"Don't count your chickens before they hatch."
And why would you, if you had my luck.
Because soon as you did,
One of the eggs would be a duck.

And financial advice is no better,
"Neither a borrower nor lender be."
Great advice if your calendar,
Happens to read BC.

"Never look a gift horse in the mouth."
Well I've never seen a gift horse, in any of my lifetime trips.
But if the horse was Mister ED,
Then I guess you could read his lips.

"A watched pot never boils."
    Fearing it was true not watching it I might.
So I timed a pot not watched, then timed one I watched,
    Discovered they were not right.

Everyone knows these sayings,
    Advice taught and preached over the years.
For not having anything to teach,
    Seems to be one of our biggest fears.

July 14,2006

Goodbye—Revisited

To my three friends in the alpha state,
I wrote a poem last week called Goodbye.
For I could no longer reach them,
Regardless of how hard my try.

Then laying in bed last night,
I had a realization in my head.
The failure to reach the alpha state,
Was not the drugs, but me instead.

Controlled breathing exercises,
Incorporated with meditation as one.
But suddenly I realized,
It simply cannot be done.

The breathing had blocked me,
From reaching the alpha state.
Not some conspiracy of drugs,
From the doctor and my mate.

So I stopped worrying about breathing,
Just did the meditation required.
It came to me easily,
Even though I was tired.

I felt the identifiable pulse,
In the upper side of my brain.
It was a reassuring throb,
And took absolutely no strain.

So I went outside this morning,
I sat in my back patio chair.
Sure enough I went to sleep and the alpha state,
Only to be awakened by a squirrel's icy stare.

"Hello Mr. No Tail," he said,
    "Glad you decided to come back."
"For I have missed your conversations,
    And I have felt the lack."

I felt so good and warm,
    My three friends I did miss.
And the feeling of being part,
    Of the Universal Awareness.

It was my own stupidity,
    No other failure for me to atone.
It was just comforting and reassuring,
    That I was no longer alone.

July 18,2006

Reality

I was talking to someone the other day,
    And they asked me if I would mind a bit.
To tell them what reality was,
    And what was the center of it.

I pulled down all my books on philosophy,
    Then went to the Internet.
To find the best and simplest,
    Answer I could get.

For if I failed to answer them,
    It would surely be my demise.
For if I failed to find an answer,
    How could I consider my self wise?

After hours spent searching high and low,
    The answer rang in my head like a bell.
It's just a bloody seven-letter word,
    And at its center is the letter L.

July 20,2006

Cook

And so you decided to have a child,
Another life brought into this world.
All you wanted was a healthy child,
Be it a boy or a girl.

The child is now grown,
A full adult they be.
But the child turned adult,
Is not the person you did foresee.

So you look for answers,
Of what made them so.
Surely you cannot be blamed,
It must be someone else you know.

Sorry folks, it's not a conundrum,
With which you are faced.
For a cook cannot prepare a meal,
Then complain about the taste.

July 25,2006

Brief Encounter

Late July, my back patio,
    Sitting in my chair watching traffic pass by.
Out of the corner of my eye a blur,
    Then I see the landing lightly of a fly.

He walked up and down my hand,
    Then began to circle around.
Looking intently for a snack,
    But nothing could be found.

He cocked up his head,
    Stared at me face to face.
As if to say, "My, but you are large,"
    "But without a snack. Why are you in my space?"

Then he lifted quickly,
    And gracefully flew away.
For without a snack to be had,
    It was not a place to stay.

Just a brief encounter,
    Our understanding sharp as a knife.
On this planet, we both shared,
    Between two simple forms of life.

It took only a minute,
    The encounter that we shared.
But I could not help but wish him the best,
    And hope that well he fared.

July 26,2006

Wind

I sat out back today,
    Watching the wind blowing through the trees.
Watching the swaying of their trunks,
    Watching the quivering of their leaves.

For I know the definition of wind,
    And the scientific explanation.
But watching it this morning,
    I began to question its creation.

Its everywhere on this globe,
    It seems to be in every place.
Be it summer breeze or winter blast,
    Each blowing in your face.

Comfortably warm or bitterly cold,
    It can change how we react.
But it is the same wind that blows,
    And that my friends is a fact.

But this morning it was enjoyable,
    Gentle and warm for a summer's morn.
Perhaps the changes are like life,
    Being flexible is why we were born.

July 28, 2006

Poet's Curse Part II

Vanity I once wrote in a poem,
    Is truly the poet's curse.
Well, that is true, but there is a part II,
    And it is viewed by many as worse.

Talking to a friend the other day,
    They asked me why all my poems were dark.
Pessimism, cynicism, and depression,
    Painting the world as stark.

To explain my writings,
    I must first declare, I am part of the human race.
Although my writing will not change the world,
    I can at least feel I have left a trace.

To point out evil and injustice,
    And a way to help others cope.
For in the midst of all the misery,
    Stands a small light called hope.

I cannot change the world,
    I can only say the way it should be.
Hopefully I can point my fellow humans,
    To a way they all could see.

I see the world as it should be,
    Never blurred is my sight.
Yet regardless of seeing it as it is,
    Does not diminish hope's everlasting light.

July 26,2006

Questions Matthew 7.1

Danny L. Shanks

This book is dedicated to Johnny Robert Shanks. My father. A very religious man,
who had so many many questions. However they were simple questions. Too simple.
As a result he died without an answer.
I do miss him so.

Contents

1. What is God? .
2. Belief . . .
3. Why .
4. What do We Think of God. . . .
5. Rain Worries . . .
6. Why Did Jesus Have to Die .
7. What Value Has Man? . . .
8. Knowledge . . . . . .
9. Absence . . . .
10. Commandment Misunderstanding . .
11. Simplicity . .
12. Older and Wiser .
13. Saved
14. Blasphemy . . .
15. Changes
16. Judgment . .
17. Religious Dogma
18. Faith .
19. A Godless Child .
20. Evolution
21. The Sign of the Cross
22. Trinity . .
23. Conversation with Myself
24. First Fridays .
25. Alicia.

What is God?

We are carbon-based life forms. We generate electricity in our bodies thru chemistry, and as a result energy. The energy created gives us intelligence. Do any other beings in the universe generate energy? How about the stars? They create energy and therefore must be intelligent according to our definition of life. Or does life have to be carbon based? If so, what about plants? The experts say we live thru instinct. What is instinct? Geese fly in a V formation. Each one is behind and slightly higher than the one in front of it. They make flight easier by drafting. Did they learn the laws of aerodynamics thru instinct or were they taught. A mother has instinct to protect a child. But experiments with monkeys', show that a chimp taken away from the mother, will, when grown up, not know anything about mother hood and will ignore their own offspring and even abuse them. Some mothers have killed their children because they became inconvenient. So much for instinct. Minnows will flee from a larger predator. Even to the point of going into shallow water and thrusting themselves on land. When whales do it. We assume some magnetic field flux because we cannot imagine a predator bigger than a whale that would chase it. We have not discovered one yet. But there are miles and miles of the ocean undiscovered. Salmon will go up stream to breed and die. Do they know they are going to die? I don't think so. They are under an illusion that they will survive the trip. Only the pacific salmon die. They may even go to a different stream, and not their natal one. And so we are all under illusions. We gamble and play the lottery armed with the foreknowledge that we will probably lose. We label this emotion, as hope instead of calling it what it is, stupidity. Our lack of accepting things as they are gives us illusions. God as we think of it is a wise and caring being. All God really is, is a possible flow of energy in the universe that we all occasionally tap into and learn, even unaware that we are doing so. The massive flow of energy in the universe seems to come from everywhere. So we must contribute to it and by definition. We are God.

March 17, 2007

Belief

So you prepare your argument,
Research the point in every way.
Fully prepared you are,
For the discussions you have today.

How can they not see?
How can they even pretend?
To not see the reason,
You use to defend.

Your point of view,
But here is the real trick.
Never ever argue,
With someone who's a fanatic.

Doesn't matter the topic,
Argue it all day long.
Physics, religion, or politics,
Or even the value of a song.

But argue you will,
And here I offer some relief.
Because you cannot prove or disprove,
What is simply called a belief.

March 27, 2007

Why

Sitting out back the other night,
    With questions running rampart through my brain.
A disturbing one arose,
    And to ask it, I could not refrain.

If God is omnipotent as we believe,
    And can do anything he chooses to try.
On the sixth day in the bible, he creates man,
    Then I have to ask why?

Was he lonely?
    Did he need praise from a lesser creature?
Those come from human frailties,
    And not from a superior teacher.

And so answers I got none,
    Left to stew in my confusion.
Because reconciling God and a superior being,
    I could not transcribe fusion.

July 7, 2007

What do We Think of God

Sitting out back today,
    Rational, clear minded and lucid.
A question arose in me,
    What if God was just plain stupid?

He is supposed to know it all,
    The future, the present, and the past.
Then why did he create the Garden of Eden?
    If he knew it wouldn't last.

And why create a sexual desire,
    And why make it so strong.
In men at 18 and women around 40,
    Was it planned, or did he get it wrong?

We were created in his image,
    A plan that would pay the bill.
But when you think about it,
    Isn't that a plan that is less than original?

And does that plan call for,
    A little bit more tack.
Or it is it just a joke for us to have,
    Arthritis or a cataract.

And then to have a child,
    He decided to come into the world.
Could he not find or create,
    A better more desirable girl.

The child he named Jesus,
    Had to die to correct our sin.
Could he not have forgiven it?
    At the beginning of the trend.

So much of it makes no sense,
    And it leaves me very confused.
Or was it a shot in the dark,
    A way he could stay amused.

Was intelligent design his plan?
    When he created us.
Well let me remind you my friend,
    He also supposedly created the platypus.

July 22, 2007

Rain Worries

I went outside this afternoon,
    To watch the falling of the rain today.
Mother Nature was there to teach me a lesson,
    A lesson I will share metaphorically, if I may.

The rain was like the worries in my life,
    The tree leaves like my soul.
How to deal with them each,
    Was the lesson that I was being told.

For the leaves did not reject the rain,
    But welcomed it as a part of life.
Did not fight it or get depressed by it,
    Or consider it as another thing of strife.

And so I realized that I too,
    Should let the worries go.
Not to spend time on them,
    Not to worry so.

For the leaves were not crying,
    With the drops falling off each.
Just happy to be there,
    With joy within their reach.

And I realized that Mother Nature was giving a lesson,
    In how to deal with pain.
Just let worries roll off you,
    And you will have so much to gain.

July 23, 2007

Why Did Jesus Have to Die

Why did Jesus have to die?
    Crucified on a cross.
And at such an early age,
    It truly seems a loss.

He died for our sins,
    That is what I am told.
What sins are those?
    If I may be so bold.

The ones we have not committed yet,
    Or the one from the Garden of Eden long ago.
For a God that preaches forgiveness,
    That seems a long way to go.

And why should he have to pay,
    For the sins of man.
He supposedly wasn't even there,
    When they all began.

And to subject him to such pain,
    Really seems too much of a cost.
When God could just forgive them all,
    It leaves me at a loss.

So I began to question,
    If he was a God or a man.
Because either way you look at it,
    It doesn't seem a good plan.

If he was a Man then,
    A God it could not be.
And so I ask for answers because,
    The contradiction escapes me.

July 24, 2007

What Value Has Man?

The elephant is larger, stronger and swifter is the horse,
The butterfly more beautiful and the mosquito more prolific.
Even the sponge is more durable,
If you want to be specific.

He has no claws,
No cover of simple fur of any kind.
No teeth to bite any prey with,
And nighttime leaves him blind.

So what value has man?
He has the ability to think.
To ask questions that have no answers,
And from uncertainty does not shrink.

This ability sets him apart,
From all creatures of this world.
To question his existence,
In the face of either boy or girl.

He's just looking for some answers,
As to why he is here.
He faces the truth whatever it is,
Even if it holds his greatest fear.

July 24, 2007

Knowledge

Sitting out back today,
Listening to a song.
I tried to remember who sang it,
Only to find the knowledge gone.

I must be getting old,
Dementia affecting my recall of fact.
Knowledge I once had,
Now expressed vividly by its lack.

Suddenly I had an insight,
Knowledge must be shared.
Daily with other people,
Whether or not they cared.

Older people's memory doesn't fade,
And vanish overnight.
They just don't have anyone, with whom they can share,
Or define as wrong or right.

And now I sit at home daily,
No outside company to relate.
Like older people who are alone,
And are cursed to endure such a fate.

Getting older is not the problem,
Of someone's memory loss.
It's the lack of other's company,
And it comes at a hell of a cost.

So if you feel,
You are losing your mind.
Just remember, it's merely companionship,
And with them spending time.

July 25, 2007

Absence

Absence makes the heart grow fonder,
Is a phrase I often heard said.
I must take exception to it and wonder,
If the people saying it aren't brain dead.

Absence just allows you,
To remake someone you have met.
To create a personality in your head,
And as for reality, to forget.

It doesn't make you miss them more,
You either miss them or you don't.
Absence is just a way to forget,
Whatever annoyances you want.

But don't tell me you miss them more,
Just create whatever feelings work for you.
And their mere absence,
Is what makes it true.

July 26, 2007

Commandment Misunderstanding

I don't understand many things,
    But yes, I understand God wanting to have a son.
But why would he choose to have it,
    With an already married woman.

It raises many questions,
    And the top one that puzzles me.
Is what in the wide world of sports?
    Constitutes adultery.

He didn't have sex with her,
    Is argued as a defense.
But they also argue, that sex is only to produce children,
    Talk about straddling the fence.

But if God is the father,
    And is not married to the mother.
Then Jesus is a bastard,
    By definition of any other.

July 28, 2007

Simplicity

When religion was first created,
    To save the priest from being part of the working class.
They created a number of gods,
    To save their sorry ass.

Some male and some female,
    Each designed with a specific trait.
And each with the promise,
    Of delivering a man from certain fate.

A creation fable they then generated,
    Of how they all began.
And of how the world was created,
    All for the benefit of man.

How could a person believe this, you question?
    People are not that dumb.
Well a person is not, but people are,
    As a general rule of thumb.

As the generations went on,
    A new religion was generated for all to see.
One devised for the people,
    Devoted to the idea of simplicity.

Just have one god,
    Not the many to cause frustration.
And put it all down in one book,
    Begin it with Genesis, which means simply generation.

And to scare the people into believing,
    Create the concept of sin.
And tell them that this,
    Is where it all begin.

When they die,
    Which no one can disprove or tell.
Create the stories and fables,
    Of a heaven and a hell.

Don't tell them as the ancients did,
    About the river Styx.
Correct that error and misconception,
    And put in a better fix.

There are so many religions,
    Spread all around this place,
With supposed truths to validate them,
    Just to save the priest's face.

The female gods had to go,
    Only a male god could stay.
Testosterone driven ego,
    Being the order of the day.

So why did these religions rise,
    When all the others did fail.
Christian, Jewish and Moslems,
    Each with simplicity and a threat of hell.

And so we war with each other,
    Each preaching the moral high ground.
Until we kill each other off,
    And only the animals will be around.

July 30, 2007

Older and Wiser

I keep growing older and wiser,
Day after countless day.
The wiser I can handle,
The other comes at a price I'm reluctant to pay.

Yet older and wiser,
I must report with great regret.
Can't have one without the other,
They come as a perfectly matched set.

August 2, 2007

Saved

A woman asked me the other day,
If I had been saved yet.
Well pardon my misunderstanding,
But to be saved, it has to be from a threat.

It apparently was not a physical one,
But more of the mental kind.
And the threat could only be seen,
In the recesses of my mind.

It was not something I did,
Apparently it was something given when I was born.
So I'm expected to pay for something, like a shirt,
Without it being worn?

She asked if I had found Jesus,
If I had accepted him in my heart.
Well I didn't know I was looking for him,
And I didn't understand that part.

There seems to be many things,
The religious people profess.
What they mean and what they're for,
I can't even begin to guess

August 6, 2007

Blasphemy

The existence of god you question,
Or in the bible to have any doubt.
This is the worst of sins,
To question what it's all about.

Yet it puzzles me at times,
If we were given the ability to use our mind.
Why would we not question the things?
Whose answers we could not find.

Why would it be a sin, to question the Bible?
If some of the stories make no sense.
For if we were made in his image,
Wouldn't that be a plausible defense?

But I hear it said,
Over and over to me.
Don't question the word of God,
For that in itself, is blasphemy.

Just to voice a concern,
Is now considered a sin.
When the hell did that change,
And when did it begin.

August 7, 2007

Changes

Small are the changes,
    Yet left to their many ways.
They spell a danger to us all,
    In varying and destructive ways.

Changes in our attitudes,
    Of what we accept as being okay.
Priest abusing children,
    Now is acceptable this day.

Drinking is another vice,
    We accept as being all right.
As long as no one becomes abusive,
    During the middle of the night.

Music moved to the black soul,
    As Motown set the trend.
It has evolved in to a verbal travesty,
    Cursing from beginning to its end.

Drug use is now a joke,
    Every one tells the tale.
Well it used to be a drug abuser,
    Had a special place in hell.

That one we can see,
    Of where it all began.
Pharmaceutical company's greed taking over,
    Getting everything they can.

You used to not go out,
    Could not leave the house looking a mess.
Well that has gone to hell,
    Just as all the rest.

We lied to the Indians.
    And then the president lied about an affair.
A bit naïve, I must say,
    When we look at the pair.

When the wife and I were dating,
    And we were left alone.
I would never go in her house,
    If her parents were not at home.

Morals change and are now gone,
    And we are left to lament.
Gone are family values.
    And where in the hell they went.

But to cling to the old ways,
    Means you're just out of step with the times.
Not current with modern thinking,
    Or accepting of new rhymes.

You say that I no longer am relevant,
    That I am just getting old.
Just because I won't accept,
    All the bullshit I'm being sold.

Society is changing,
    Out with the old and in with the new.
Well that sadly is the way it's going,
    And this much is true.

For to object to the changes,
    You are accused of being a Jesus freak.
But what is really means is you are willing.
    To stand up, and not be weak.

So what is the answer?
    To societies woe.
Just that we are going to hell,
    And I tire of going with the flow.

August 13, 2007

Judgment

The world will come to an end,
No matter what we try.
We will all then be judged,
But then I must ask you, why?

If you believe in God,
And everything that he created.
Then where do the standards come from,
Enforcing the rules to which we are fated.

If the rules were made by him,
How can he judge us in the end?
When it was he that set up the commandments.
Before it all began.

He didn't just pick them up,
At the local morals shop.
They had to come from him,
Had to come from the top.

It seems a little bit twisted,
And somewhat out of sync.
If you question it at all,
If you use your mind to think.

August 18, 2007

Religious Dogma

We are born, and live for a while,
Then we simply die.
Death is forever.
But then why do we try.

Life is fleeting, yet transitory,
Fixed and finite.
So nothing taught to us could ever compare,
To the promise of an afterlife.

Teach it to them young,
While their beliefs you can easily mould.
And they will become inflexible, and fixed for life,
Even when they get old.

Freethinking is only for the young,
Teach them young, or at least give it a try.
Or they will eventually stop trying,
And it will wither and die.

The dogma religions teach,
Be it stupid or absurd.
Teach it to them young, or when aged,
They will sit and listen to every word.

August 21, 2007

Faith

Life as we know it,
    Is meaningless and cold.
Sacrifice is the only way they say,
    To save your immortal soul.

Yet life is meaningful,
    Why should you sacrifice enjoyment?
For some unknowable reward,
    Offered at the end of it.

For no one has returned from the dead,
    To give us any fact.
This evidence is punctuated,
    By its simple lack.

For those of us that don't believe,
    Believers develop and intense hate.
For the greatest sin of all,
    Is simply the lack of faith?

The stories we are asked to believe in,
    Are self-evident, as they are told.
Yet the facts of those stories are simply,
    That they are getting old.

They live for death,
    What more can be said.
Because it comes only then,
    Reward after they're dead.

Jump off a building,
    To test your faith you can fly.
But don't you dare flap your arms,
    It would demonstrate a flaw in your faith if you try.

But what does all this sacrifice,
    In the end really show?
Do we know the creators wishes?
    What do we really know?

August 21, 2007

A Godless Child

I raised a Godless child,
    And for that I apologize.
For looking back on it now,
    I'm not sure it was all that wise.

For thinking about it now,
    I did not want such thoughts to intrude.
No prejudices to interfere,
    No judgments to delude.

To give her mind a free hand,
    To make choices denied to me.
No teaching to make her think,
    And therefore allow her to be free.

So I taught her science,
    And taught her how to think.
I did not see the cost to her,
    I never feared such costs, and never did I shrink.

So she never was taught the fear,
    I was raised with as a child.
Taught her the truth of the universe,
    To question everything and to be a little bit wild.

Proud of her I was,
    To be free and be a little bit bold.
But I now felt it left her,
    Feeling a little bit cold.

To be left without a place to stand,
    A rock given on which to put her trust.
To base her life on,
    Believing so, I felt I must.

But in doing so I left her,
    No place in which to hide.
To retreat to in times of woe,
    Done so to appease my pride.

She now has no faith per se,
    Except in herself as such.
And does not feel the need,
    To believe in god, as a place of trust.

Too late to change that now,
    To give her a place to hide in times of woe.
To forestall her fears and to give her an answer.
    A place where she can go.

I felt the words I used,
    I raised her best I could.
Allowing her to think,
    As I felt she always should.

She doesn't think as others think,
    She doesn't feel the need.
To eat like others eat,
    To dine upon their feed.

I am so proud of her,
    Vanity makes it so.
But what you reap in this world,
    Often do you sow.

Yes I raised a godless child,
    Free to think and free to feel.
But the feeling she now has.
    Have left me a little bit ill.

For she thinks like a free spirit,
    Nothing to cloud her brain.
Able to think and not be prejudice,
    Was a goal I wished to obtain.

To give to her freedom,
    I did what I thought was right.
So I hope she will forgive me,
    When the world brings to her a fight.

March 17, 2007

Evolution

Thirty-one days,
After an egg has been fertilized.
Before it has even began,
To get arms, legs or eyes.

Predecessor cells take over,
Developing the cerebral cortex.
Really unique to the human race,
Making our thinking very complex.

One per cent is the genetic difference,
Between gorillas and the human race.
Yet our cerebral cortex is four times larger,
Than theirs at any pace.

Interesting is the fact that predecessor cells,
In other animals have never been found.
The cells are really unique to humans,
As long as we have been around.

Neurotransmitters are the key,
Chemistry is what makes us feel.
The rush of happiness or the pain of loss,
The chemical process is what makes it real.

August 23, 2007

The Sign of the Cross

Something taught to me from an early age,
Was a gesture called the sign of the cross.
But over the years, it's meaning and importance,
Has left me at a loss.

A term applied to various manual acts,
Which have this at least in kind.
That by the gesture of tracing two lines intersecting angles,
They bring symbolically, Christ's cross, to mind.

Regarding the sequence of which shoulder is touched first,
Different practices in the order have come to light.
All Christians originally, signed themselves, in right to left,
Then the Christians in the West moved from left to right,

Venetian merchants would cross themselves in the Western fashion,
And in the Eastern fashion when meeting with East.
This duplicity supposedly led to the coining of the phrase double crosser,
To mean someone who professes alignment with one party, but is aligned with another, none the least..

The sign of the Cross is extremely powerful,
Making the sign of the Cross over a human body by choice.
Even once, dispels the demon's bewitching,
And those who making the sign of the cross make those in heaven rejoice.

The Christian custom of gesturing the sign of the cross,
Was originally with the right hand thumb and across the forehead.
The custom originated during the second century,
As a supersticion to protect even the dead.

Kind of a ward,
Against the evil eye,
It takes nothing but faith,
And all you have to do is try.

Yet why is the act so powerful?
    Are we really that naïve?
Do we believe that alone such an act?
    Would save us if we believe.

September 5, 2007

Trinity

Three persons listed,
    The Father, the Holy Ghost, and the Son.
Three persons rolled into God,
    And labeled simply as one.

Ican understand one person,
    Having the personality of three.
But three acting as one,
    I just cannot see.

The shamrock they say,
    Is three parts acting as one.
Well that's just a plant,
    Not the individual who created the sun.

A split personality would,
    Explain the three.
One person having multiple sides,
    But three acting as one, I just cannot see.

So pardon my ignorance,
    Of finding the idea hard to conceive.
But you ask me to accept it all,
    You ask me to just believe.

You ask me just to accept it,
    And not from the idea to shrink.
Well I would if I could find the ability,
    To exist and not to think.

September 20, 2007

Conversation with Myself

It's 11:30 pm on a Thursday night and I feel the need to have a talk with myself. I've been sitting outside on the back patio this evening waiting for the coming of the fall equinox, and thoughts have been running through my mind. I recall Carl Jung's reprimand that a man must believe in something. Well I don't believe in God or in heaven nor hell. History bears me out on this and none of it makes any sense. Yet I also recall something my daughter said. Quantum physics is just the dreams stuff is made of. Well as I think on it I recall quantum physics is about possibilities. If you put a cat in a box with a poison button and close the lid. The cat is both dead and alive. Both are possible. Only when you look inside the box does reality take place. The same with light. Shine it through two slits in a page and you will get five shadows on the far wall. These are the possible paths of the light. Physicists say this proves that light is a wave. But if you put a photon detector on the other end the display will show only one possibility. That's because it is reality. Reality solidifies the dreams. Observation is what solidifies quantum possibilities. Yet the dreams are real when they exist. Just like the cat. Is it alive or dead? It's both. Nothing I've read leads me to believe in a heaven or a God, but like the song goes, I can swear there is no heaven but I pray there is no hell. The Jews understood this. The symbol for the male was a triangle The female symbol was an inverted triangle But you combine the ying and yang of the two, and guess what? You get the Star of David. Both are the symbols of life. Combined in a possibility. Maybe this is what life's about. Maybe we live in a quantum universe and it's all about the possibilities of dreams. Tonight I watched Man of La Mancha and something he said struck home. "Maddest of all, is to see life as it is, and not as it should be." Maybe this is what it's all about, not reality but possibilities. Carl Jung may have been trying to tell us something. You have to believe in something or why even try.

September 21, 2007

First Fridays

When I was a child,
    My dad was a very religious man.
Catholic dogma was a way to live,
    A place for him to believe in, and stand.

One of the beliefs, First Fridays it was called,
    And taught that if you made communion on nine of them in a row.
A priest would be at your side,
    When it came time for you to go.

I went with him to them all,
    Took communion and went through the mass.
Because the payoff was peace of mind,
    When it came time for us to pass.

Well, he died in the kitchen,
    Lying on the linoleum floor.
No priest within ten miles,
    So how much faith could I put in store.

Of my first Fridays meaning,
    A safe passing for me.
Sure didn't work for my dad,
    That much was clear enough to see.

So they lied to me about the dogma,
    I put faith in what they said.
I guess no one comes back to argue the point,
    Once that they are dead.

So how much else is wrong,
    How far did the lie extend.
Stretching the truth for peace of mind,
    And at what point did it begin.

You wonder why I have no faith,
    Why I don't believe in God.
Shame on me for believing it once,
    Shame on you for the façade.

September 22, 2007

Alicia

Alicia moved silently through the neighborhood. It was actually called an apartment complex these days, but all she knew or cared about, was that it housed a great number of humans. She was coal black and moved with purpose as she continued her rounds reaching out to touch and read humans minds and feelings. She loved to read the human thoughts. They were so confident and misguided. The only thing bigger than their stupidity was their ego. They thought they had a good bead on things. She paused probing the human thoughts. The human nearby was watching a movie called "The Mummy." She chuckled when the movie actor referred to cats as guardians of the underworld. First off, the underworld as they so politely put it, didn't exist. And secondly, she was not a guardian, but a level 8 controller. How dumb humans were. She was in charge of moving the dead human's energy to Ismer, the energy flow that ran throughout the universe. The human conception of another life after the one they were living was just a misconception fostered by the religions of the world. The fact was that being part of the energy flow was about as close as they would come to living again. She moved on pausing in her walk to note an energy flux where she had stepped. She lifted her foot and harmonically adjusted the flux. Again she chuckled to think of the humans. They related her purr to an emotional state. Not an adjustment to the magnetic flux she had just encountered and corrected.It was well past midnight and silent, when she noticed a figure sitting on the back patio of his apartment. Quietly she moved on past only to be halted when a voice called out to her. "Who goes there?" came the deep throaty voice. "Who wants to know?" Alicia replied offended that a mere human would address her. "It's just a lonely midnight companion." Came the response. "Okay." She replied. "I'm Alicia. How did you hear me?" "Didn't hear you at all." Replied the voice. "I sensed you." "Sensed me!" Alicia said clearly baffled. "No one can sense me." "You're a controller." The voice went on. "Your scent is unmistakable." "Oh. Yeah." Alicia replied now intrigued. "Well just who in the hell gave you the power of scent?" "Sorry. It comes from long years of training." The dim image said as if explaining something. "I have sensed much that the rest of the humans don't know exist." "That's an understatement if I ever heard one." Alicia replied haughtily. "Yes. Well I have been close to death a number to times, and I guess the controller's presence became familiar." He lamented sorry fully. "You're not afraid." Asked the shocked Alicia. "Why be afraid? There isn't a lot I can do about it, is there?" Came his inquisition. "No. Actually there isn't." Alicia replied, somewhat feeling pity for the lonely human. I've just never met a human who was not scared to death, pardon the pun, of dying." "Apparently you are not here for me tonight." He continued. "So make your rounds as quietly as you can and don't take to many of us with you tonight." "I'll be quiet as I can and will look forward to seeing you again in the future." Alicia replied and moved off quietly as the silence of the night returned.

August 9,2007

Short Stories

Cats

It had been four months ago. Samantha and her sister Angel had arrived on the back patio of the closest apartment from which they had been born. Scared and hungry they had tried to get the attention of the humans but were ignored. The days went by and finally the male of the species acknowledged them and gave them something to eat. They rewarded him by sitting on his lap and cuddling close. Angel had told her that if they could win the attention of the male, half their battle was won. The female would be an easier mark. Sure enough it seemed to work. The female of the species took them in and not only got them a house but some good food. The only problem was their names. She insisted on calling them by the names of Smokey and Snowflake. But the food was good and the house comfortable and warm so they adapted and fell into a comfortable existence. .

Time passed and they soon could come inside the house. The male became affectionate and the female proved to be a soft touch. They grew comfortable and life seemed to be without care. The only problem was getting into the house when the male was opposed to it, but as fast as they acted they soon were permanent members of the household. The male was affectionate and would spend hours scratching them wherever it felt good. Under the chin for Angel, and around the stomach for Samantha. When it wasn't that cold he would sit outside with them and allow them to jump up onto his lap spending hours enjoying the comfort of being held, warm and loved.

It never occurred to either of them that the affection he showed was beneficial to him as much as it was to them.

They soon became aware of other animals. Birds ate from a bird feeder and there was also a squirrel that came around. They would chase the squirrel whenever the male would open the sliding glass door oblivious to the fact they had no intention of catching it. They would spend hours staring at it as well as staring at the birds in the feeder. The human male seemed fascinated by their attention. He seemed to enjoy having them and all the other wild life around. If only he could speak. They had much to tell him and yearned to speak.

Maybe one day soon he would be able to understand them and realize the purring was talk and had a purpose.

Contact

Daniel was sitting on his back patio enjoying the night air with Smokie and Snowflake sitting on his lap. It was around 2 AM on July 23 and he was thoroughly enmeshed in the night air when he felt himself drifting off to the alpha state. Recognizing the feeling he embraced it and allowed it to envelope him when he overheard a conversation-taking place between the two cats.

"Smokie? Snowflake?" he inquired.

"Yikes?" Yelled Snowflake and jumped about three feet in the air.

"He can talk." Piped in Smokie clearly astounded.

"Yes I can." Replied an equally astounded Daniel.

"When did this happen?" Snowflake asked.

"A few years ago. I've been talking to the creatures of the world for many years." Replied the human.

"And you decided not to tell us till now." Smokie said sarcastically.

"Well I was just sitting here when I noticed your conversation and thought I'd join in." Daniel answered solemnly.

"That's great" Snowflake replied genuinely. "Welcome aboard. Who did you used to talk to and what about?"

"Mostly about how humans thought and explained it to two trees named Bartholomew, Patricia and a squirrel named Little" He answered.

"Well I can tell you how humans think." Smokie said sarcastically.

"How's that?" Daniel questioned.

"Simple." Smokie went on. "They like to be quiet and then scare the hell out of two simple cats enjoying the night air."

"Sorry about that." Daniel repeated. "I didn't know you could understand my talk."

"O Yes". Snowflake said. "We can understand anyone talking in the alpha state. We just didn't know you were capable of it, and by the way my name is Samantha and my sister is called Angel."

"Sorry about that." Daniel replied again with remorse.

"It's OK." She said. "Your names work for us just as well."

"Then why don't you respond when we call you?" He questioned her.

"Because we're ignoring you." She answered then explained. "If we're busy you don't exist for us"

"Well I'm here." He said and went on. "Anytime you want to talk."

"So what shall we talk about first?" Samantha asked.

"Well I talked to a cat called Alicia" Daniel said. "She was a level 8 controller and her purring was an adjustment to the magnetic flow abnormalities."

"Well she was much older than us and we are still young and can't do many things." She explained. "What else do you want to talk about?"

"Well first I'd like to know about intelligence." Daniel inquired. "What makes the humans so unique."

Samantha answered him. "Thought and thinking are mental forms and processes, respectively ("thought" is both.) Thinking allows beings to model the world and to deal with it effectively according to their objectives, plans, ends and desires. Words referring to similar concepts and processes include cognition, sentience, consciousness." She went on. "It is simply put, it is the flow of energy."

"But the stars have energy." He questioned.

"And there are about 40 billion of them." Smokie replied. "So what was the question about being unique."

"But we reason thing out." Daniel protested. "Like cats can't see colors."

"Says who?" Quesioned Smokie.

"Although they certainly do not have anything remotely close to the color perception of humans, many owners can testify that they certainly have some means of distinguishing some colors. It is thought that cats can distinguish between red, blue, and white, but green, yellow and white all appear gray. In a cat's use of its sight, it may be that movement is the dominant factor and color is not all that important. And even though cat's eyes, or irises rather, come in a wide variety of colors, for example, red, blue, green, and gold, it bears no particular relevance to the cat's ability to see." Daniel replied.

"Says who?" Smokie demanded.

"The experts." Daniel answered.

"Are these the same experts who say bumble bees can't fly?" Inquired a curious Smokie. "Ever ask a cat?"

"Yes." Answered an abashed Daniel. "Okay, what about the stars."

"They have untold amounts of energy." Samantha replied. "So why wouldn't they be intelligent?"

"Yeah." Smokie joined in. "They should come together and join in the fellowship every creature has on this planet."

"Most stars are in fact in groups." Daniel answered. "Betelgeuse appears as a star in the constellation Orion. But it is in fact a group of 5 stars. So I guess you are right,"

"What about nebula." Samantha asked.

"Good point." Daniel answered. "It seems most stars are in a group."

"Then why do you find it so hard to accept?" She asked.

"Because our sun is alone." Came the answer.

"So if it is alone, maybe it created us for company." She questioned.

"You mean that much intelligence would just need company." He asked.

"Sure." She replied. "Look at your history. People who contacted races who were not so advanced as us, thought of us as Gods. Face it. That much energy has to have a bigger intelligence. Just by definition. And higher intelligence doesn't preclude it for getting lonely."

"The Egyptians used to call the sun, RA. They believed it was god." Daniel said begrudgingly.

"Okay enough talking for one night." Samantha said. "Nap time."

Daniel turned off the light and went to bed. Feeling secure that he had found someone to talk to and snuggle with in his bed.

Albert

Albert woke to the secure safe feeling of being useful. Surrounded by the earth he helped invigorate every day. He sighed and decided to lay there a little while longer before beginning his day of manipulating the soil into a useful product the plants could use. His was a simple existence and a happy one. He had his work and a mate at home, whom he loved that was all any-one could ask for. His mate Sonya was fat with children and about to birth the lot of them. He then thought about his friend Bill which produced a frown on his face. Bill had an accident the other day, which was worrisome. Bill had his tail cut off by a giant. It was an inconvenience but he would re grow it and be fine. However the accident made Albert think of the giants. Huge creatures who lived above the ground and had appendages growing out from their bodies. The horror stories he had heard made him shiver. Stories of his people being hunted, and put into a container made of tree bark. The tree bark was processed till it was smooth, white and in the shape of a square. They would group together in a ball for security, but the giants pulled them apart one by one. The giants would then torture them by piercing their bod-ies with sharp curved metal rods before throwing them into the water. The ones that survived told stories of great beasts in the water that would come by and take a bite out of them. He shivered to think about these things and hoped his children would never have to experience such a horror.

Well he had dawdled long enough. He shook himself and started working through the soil. He had his section of soil to reprocess and Sonya waiting fo: him at the end of the day. He would think no more of giants. Apparently they did not know of the work he did and how important it was. Contented he went back to work and burrowed through the soil.

Alicia

Alicia rose in a smooth flight of the warm spring air. She was in mid life for a firefly. She had emerged from her larva stage and developed into a full grown adult, no longer eating slugs or snails but pollen and nectar

from the plants all around her. She was a soft brown color with two antennas and six legs. And she felt good today. She had an inner glow that she was proud of. She had glowed as an egg, as had all her brood, but now as an adult she could call upon her inner chemistry and glow.

Not like males, who could only glow every five seconds, but every two seconds if the mood struck her. She had been alive for four weeks and had another four to go in this life. She would mate with as many males as she saw fit and hopefully one would impregnate her and she would be able to lay eggs before she went to the next world. She had heard about the next world, where all fireflies went when they died and there, was her hope. Not to be stuck in some awful place, but in a world of beauty and light where she would be light as a feather, and her inner glow would shine. She wasn't sure about it, but it sure sounded better than anything else she could imagine. She flew about in a place she did not know, but it was called Tennessee, as we know it. She had been flying there for about four weeks and had mated repeatedly and as often as she could. The night would find her flying free as could be, and flashing her inner glow as often as possible. She was proud of her glow.

It came from her. Her friends had told her stories that it came from chemistry and was not attributable to her attitude, but she did not believe them. She was young, free and beautiful. She would fly on the winds of this world, mate, and glow whenever she felt the desire. She felt a part of the world and with the thought of her eggs now growing in her she felt she would contribute to the beauty of this place she called home. As she flew into a group their lights could be seen a mile away. She felt good and a part of the natural order of things.

AMANDA, ABIGAIL AND ABNER

Chapter 1

Daniel walked out onto his back patio to a greeting of hellos from his three friends.

"What a glorious day." He declared.

"Yes it is." Agreed Patricia.

"The sky is blue with so many clouds it is truly inspirational." Daniel went on.

"Right." Agreed Little. "Did you bring my almonds?"

"Yes I did." Daniel told the little squirrel.

"Going to sit outside a while?" Questioned Bartholomew.

"I thought I would Bart." Daniel told the stately old elm.

"Trying to think of something to write?" Patricia asked.

"Well it is such a glorious day I hate to let it go without writing something.

But I don't have anything new to write about." Daniel said morosely.

"Have you tried the clouds?" Patricia went on.

"What?" Asked the puzzled human.

"Why not." Queried Little. "You have found other creatures by trying."

"By talking to the clouds?" Daniel asked.

"Sure." Patricia answered. "What have you got to lose?"

"Point taken Pat." Replied Daniel "What do I say?"

"Try something like Hello." Little said sarcastically

Chapter 2

"Okay." Daniel replied and then concentrating on the cloud above projected.

"Hello."

Slowly the clouds began to form three distinct forms and then appeared solid off his back patio about three feet in the air. Open mouthed he stared at the three horses and then asked. "Who are you?"

"Good Lord." Said the first horse. "A talking human."

"Hi there yourself. Who are you?" Answered the second tall white horse with its wings spread wide.

"My name is Daniel." He answered.

"Okay you two." The third horse piped in. "I'm Amanda. This is Abigail and Abner. Pleased to make your acquaintance."

"Wow." Said the startled retired civil servant. "What are you?"

"Well we are white and can fly. What in the world do you think we are?" Asked Amanda.

"I don't know." Daniel answered. "Versions of Pegasus the winged horse."

"Right." Said Abner sarcastically. "The human can talk but he sure is dumb."

"Quiet down Abner." Amanda chided. "Can you not see he's confused?"

"Yeah I'll quiet down." Abner replied. "Look at our heads stupid."

As Daniel stared he noticed each had a long horn extending from its head.

"You're unicorns?" He said amazed.

"Correct." Amanda said softly. "I'm assuming from your reaction that you have never seen one before."

"No, I've only read about them in stories." Daniel explained.

"Dare I ask what you have read?" Abner inquired.

Chapter 3

The unicorn (from Latin *unus* 'one' and *cornus* 'horn') is a mythical beast usually depicted with the body of a horse and one usually three foot long spiral horn on its forehead." Daniel explained. "The unicorn's clear blood and horn are said to have mystical healing properties."

"What else?" Amanda asked.

"Well." Daniel continued. "Medieval knowledge of the fabulous beast stemmed from biblical and ancient sources, and the creature was variously represented as a kind of wild ass, goat, or horse. The unicorn, tamable only by a virgin woman was well established in medieval lore. Unicorn horns could neutralize poisons, the true horn sweats in the presence of poison, and the true horn, when thrown into water, sends up little bubbles."

"That's all about the horns." Chided Abner.

"Place the horn in a vessel and with it three or four live and large scorpions, keeping the vessel covered. Four hours later the scorpions will be dead, or almost lifeless," He went on. "Enclose a spider in a circle drawn on the floor with an unicorn. If the horn is true the spider will not be able to cross outside of the circle and will starve to death inside it."

"Well that's not all we do." Said Amanda quietly.

"What else do you do?" Asked a curious Daniel.

"We fight dragons and bad wizards." Amanda answered.

"We don't really have dragons, wizards or even castles here." Daniel said.

"What?" Abner sneered. "Your condos don't have dragons. I'll bet you don't even have moats."

"Enough Abner," Said Amanda scornfully. "Those are things of the past. But now that you mention it we must be going."

Chapter 4

"We must be getting back to Europe where they have all those things and we are still needed," Abigail piped in.

"Thanks for stopping by." Daniel said thankfully. "It was a break in my day and a real pleasure meeting you."

"No problem Daniel." Amanda said. "And if you ever need anything call us."

"Yeah watch out for those dragons and bad wizards." Abner said scornfully.

"Never know when they can pop up."

"All right Abner." Amanda complained then said in a compassionate voice. "Goodbye Daniel. It's been a real treat for us too."

BLACK HOLE TROUBLE

Chapter 1

Daniel woke to the early morning light coming through the window into his bedroom. He slowly got out of bed and went to wash his face. He then proceeded to the sliding glass door and went out onto his back patio.

"Good Morning Daniel" projected his friend Bartholomew.

"Hello Bart," replied Daniel. As he observed the tall elm tree he had come to know as Bartholomew.

"And top of the morning to you Patricia".

"Hey good looking," replied Patricia. The pine tree he thought of as a female because of her curved trunk.

Daniel had only recently begun to understand he could communicate with the trees by allowing his mind to go into the alpha state. His mother in law had given him a book on how to do it so he had been practicing it one morning when he got the shock of an unexpected reply from the trees.

Since then he talked to them each day and really enjoyed their company.

"Hey no tail, you gonna feed me or stand there all day talking." He looked down to see he other new friend the small squirrel who he had taken to calling Little One.

"Sorry Little, I didn't know you were starving to death out here."

"You bet your bushy tail I am." Replied Little, "Well that is if you had one", came the sarcastic reply.

He really loved the little squirrel even if he could be a trial at times.

"We seem to have a bit of a crisis this morning" Bart intoned. "That is other than Little's starvation obsession."

"Hey kiss my fuzzy butt" came back Little's rapid rejoinder.

"This is serious," Patricia went on. "Andy has stopped collecting light."

"Are you kidding me?" Suddenly Little lost his humorous attitude.

"What?" asked a puzzled Daniel.

Andy is the black hole at the center of the galaxy Andromeda answered Bart.

"Well what does that mean?" asked Daniel.

"I will try to explain it to the human", answered Little. "And I will use small thoughts so maybe he can understand."

"Just stop being a smart ass and explain it to him", Patricia replied barely able to contain her irritation.

"Okay," said Little. "I'll try".

Chapter 2

"Daniel" he started. "You do realize that light is energy? And all life comes from energy." Little explained.

"Yeah so what?"

"Well in about 7 million years the Milky Way galaxy and the Andromeda galaxy will collide and the black holes of each will merge and give off light. That means the continued existence of the cosmos and all of us including my great grandchildren as you think of them. If Andy stops collecting light there will be no continuation of life, as we know it.

"Ok" Daniel replied, "How will that affect us?"

"Stop thinking like a human for a second and think of the overall picture," and exasperated Little explained.

"There is more at stake here than your existence."

"You need to have a talk with Andy" Bart explained.

"How do we do that", Daniel asked.

"O great" said Little, "I suppose all of this will all fall to me".

"Now think closely Daniel and I'll try to explain, plus I'll use small concepts so you can understand."

"Life is energy. It is created by the interaction of the cosmos. It is stored in black holes, till it is needed to start a new universe. Then the black holes come together and evaporate releasing the stored light and creating a new universe. It is really very simple."

"Well how do we talk to this Andy?" asked Daniel.

"We have to go see him," was Little's reply.

"If he's 7 million light years away that sounds impossible".

"Ever hear of astral projection?" asked Little.

"Yes but how does that relate to us?"

"How do you think we are communicating now?" an exasperated Little asked.

"But the time difference is massive," Daniel went on.

"Only because you think small. Wasn't it only recently that human's thought there were only 4 dimensions instead of thc 11 that exist. Well, we will go to him by astral projection."

"I don't mean to rain on your parade Little, but that will be a little late by the time we get there. I mean 7 million light years takes a long time.

Little's exasperation was becoming obvious. "You still think the fastest thing in the universe is the speed of light."

"Well isn't it?" asked a confused Daniel.

"Look Dan. Thought makes the speed of light in your understanding, a turtle. We can go talk to him and be back by suppertime."

"Okay." Chirped in Patricia, "Before we let you two take off. We need to talk to Sam."

"Who's Sam?" asked Daniel.

Chapter 3

"Sam is the old oak out here." replied Bart. "He was old when I was just a sapling, and if anyone knows what to do it's him."

"Great," said Little.

"I don't know him," commented Daniel.

"That's because, he's a pain in the tail and never responds to conversations."

"Never the less," Patricia continued. "He has forgotten more than most of us will ever learn."

"Good point Pat," replied Bart. "Let me call him."

"Hey Sam."

"What!" came a loud cranky voice.

"Hi. This is Bart and we need your help."

"Did you forget how to drop your leaves in the fall? Is that Patricia with you? She doesn't need to drop anything she's an evergreen."

"No Sam. We need help to explain something to a human."

"Explain something to a human, that is the dumbest thing I've ever heard."

"Yeah, well maybe you just can't explain anything to anybody, human or otherwise," chirped in Little.

"Is that Little I hear". Boomed Sam "I can't communicate with him because I don't speak stupid."

"O Yeah," cried Little. "Then just get someone else to bury your nuts next year."

"Okay. Everybody calm down. Sam the problem is with Andy. He's stopped collecting light and the human has agreed to try and talk to him and Little is going to help any way he can."

"Well shut little bushy butt up and I will try. I assume he can hear me in the alpha state.

So here's the situation. This has happened before. Last time was with Virgo. It was just a bad case of depression. Jim and I talked him out of it but it took about 50 years. I was much younger then but Jim was older with a lot of experience and wisdom. Experience and wisdom results in a higher level of intelligence. Something fuzzy butt wouldn't know about."

"O yeah!" yelled Little. "Well just kiss my bushy tail you old relic."

"That's enough Little," chided Bart.

"Same goes for you Sam. Both of you are being immature and we need to focus on the problem at hand."

"Sorry," said Sam.

"Me too," Little chirped in. "But nobody can get me going like he can."

"I apologize Little. It's sometimes too hard to pass up at my age. Maybe I'm just jealous of your youth."

"Apology accepted", Little said chastised. "Guess I can be a little irritating at times. It's just my inferiority complex from being so small, compared to you.

Well" said Sam, "Let's get started. Daniel, is it. Sit down in your chair.

Little jump up into his lap and I will transport us all to Andy. Time will fold space, so it may seem like a long trip, but you will be back here in what passes for about an hour's time in this dimension, but longer when traveling. We will need to stop by the Orion Nebula to talk with the fire lords, so keep a stiff upper lip as you humans say and Little don't start complaining about the smell. The problem is simple to understand but harder to resolve. Andy probably feels unappreciated. He works for centuries and centuries, and most creatures that owe their existence to him don't even know he exists. How do you think that would make you feel?"

"Okay, I'm ready", Little declared.

"Me too" Daniel said unsure of what to expect but felt compelled to ask. "Sam, can you explain some of this to me".

Chapter 4

"Sure" replied Sam, "Humans usually only think in 3 dimensions, but think if 3 blind men grab a lion. One grabs the tail and declares string theory explains it all. One grabs the lion's ear and says no, it is all flatland and two dimensions will answer any questions. The third grabs the lion's leg and says you are both wrong. The universe has 3 dimensions. Well they all are right, and wrong. Their observations are correct for what they experience, but they miss the total picture of the lion. Humans have recently come up with an M Theory to explain it. In my opinion the M stands for Magic. They try to explain everything in terms of the physical but ignore the essence of life. Ask a physicist what is light and they will argue for an hour about whether it is a particle or a wave. The only thing they agree on is that it is energy. Therein lies the complete answer. Life is what it's all about, and light is the source of life's energy. Understand?"

"I understand", said Little," but where do almonds fit in?"

"Look," stated an exasperated Sam. "The only one who even came close was Einstein. E=mc2, is the correct equation but most physicists miss the main point. Time is a perception. And once it is noticed, it slows down. and at that point, the energy becomes mass. Hence the universe is created."

The discussion of dimensions is irrelevant. Just as is our travel across the galaxy, so here we go."

Daniel felt a slight disorientation and was soon looking at the Orion Nebula.

"Nebulas are the greatest source of light in the universe," explained Sam, "and therefore life. For this part of the galaxy the Orion Nebula, is where the fire lords live and our first stop."

Daniel marveled at the colors in the Nebula and was dumbstruck when it spoke to them. "Hello Sam. Long time no see. Who are your friends?"

"Just a couple of dreamers on a fools mission." Replied Sam.

"Anything we need to worry about?" questioned the fire lord.

"No just Andy's stop collecting light and the known universe will end".

"Okay" came the slow reply "Let us know if we can help."

"Well we would like some advice on how to change his mind.," replied

Sam. "After all you did create him for the purpose of continuing the existence of life.

"Sure no sweat. Just offer him something to show he's appreciated."

"Great", said Little, "A neurotic black hole with an inferiority complex."

"Be quiet Little and listen," scolded Daniel.

"Okay," said Sam. "Thanks for the tip we will think of something."

"You call that a tip?" Screeched Little. "I could have gotten that from a fortune nut."

"Hey, it's a starting point," offered Daniel.

"Well I think that it was a total waste of time," Little complained.

Daniel grinned and replied," As Donald Sutherland said in the movie Kelly's Heroes. Just stop with the negative waves."

"That's the answer!" shouted Little. "He's just lost a couple of protons and is feeling a little negative."

Sam groaned. "That has got to be the oldest joke in the cosmos.

Chapter 5

Suddenly they were facing the Black Hole but did not feel the gravity pulling them in.

"Hello" Sam called. "Andy you home."

"Who wants to know?" came the sullen reply.

"It's just Sam with a couple of earth creatures," he explained.

"Go away," mumbled Andy.

"Come on Andy. We've come a long way to talk to you."

"Yeah, and I skipped breakfast," complained Little

"Well forbid I caused any such creature, so small and fat, to miss a meal. What do you want?"

"We heard the you had stopped collecting light." Daniel explained.

"And we wanted to know why?"

"No one cares anymore so why bother."

"I care and so do my friends. We need you." Daniel pleaded.

"Why," Andy's question boomed.

"Without you life and the universe would cease to exist."

"And why should I care?" came the sullen question.

"Because it is the reason you exist, for one thing" Daniel reasoned.

Andy asked "Why should you care if I exist or not,"

"Because that is what life is about for us. And only you can make that happen. No one else can do it."

"And why should I believe you. Mr. Carbon Based Biped."

"Because I will forgo waiting. To kick start your gravity fields again, and to save this universe I will come into the light right now," Declared Daniel.

"You're joking." Said Andy incredulously.

"I will forgo the fire lords learning curve, and go right now." Daniel stated.

"That is some sacrifice you are proposing," said Andy, his respect growing.

"Not really," explained Daniel. "If it will start you up again I will just go now. I won't have that chance later if you stop forever."

"Good logic my friend. Hadn't really thought of it that way," reasoned Andy.

"Okay," I'll restart. But only because of your willingness to make such a sacrifice, and start now instead of several million years later if at all.

"Glad we got that settled." Daniel replied relieved.

Chapter 6

Soon he felt the gravity pull start up again as he, Sam and Little retreated.

He soon found himself back in his chair sitting in the sun with Little on his lap.

"Well that was refreshing" Daniel quipped.

"I'm glad you enjoyed saving the universe," Little stated. "Myself, I was scared to death. Plus I missed my breakfast."

"Don't worry," Daniel said seriously. "Long as I'm around you won't go hungry. And Sam, it was nice to meet you and I hope we can talk more sometime."

"Be more than happy to accomodate you human," replied the Oak.

"And Little, if you will get the hell off my lap I will get the almonds."

"It's about time," complained the little squirrel. "Saving the universe has left me starving."

CLANCY

Chapter 1

The sun was just breaking the horizon over Mount Rainier when Daniel walked out onto his back patio.

"Little." He called. "Come get your breakfast almonds. I don't have all day." "What the heck are you yelling about?" Came Little's mumbled response. "Do you know what time it is?"

"I know. I know." Daniel answered. "But I'm going out today to the Olympic Forest to hike and I need to get an early start."

"Okay." Little said. "Thanks for the breakfast. Where are you going?"

"Up to a state park called Staircase." Daniel explained further. "It's a place where the river comes downhill in a set of small falls like stairs.

Hence the park's name Staircase."

"Wow." Little grumbled. "You human's capacity for originality is under whelming. But I know this place and have a cousin there. His name is Reggie. Look him up but be careful."

"Be careful?" Daniel asked concerned.

"He won't do anything dangerous." Said Little reassuringly. "But the kid is a big practical joker."

"Okay." Daniel replied as he went back inside to get ready for his day in the forest.

Chapter 2

Upon arriving at the Staircase state park, Daniel began his leisurely hike through the forest. The quiet of the woods was reassuring and the babbling of the stream very calming.

After about a mile he decided the see if he could contact Little's cousin.

"Reggie." He called.

"Hello." Came the response. "Are you Daniel?"

"Yes I am." The retired civil servant answered. "Little said I should look you up and say hello."

"Little told me about you." Reggie said. "It seems you spoil him with almonds all the time."

"He does love them so." Daniel rejoinered. "Why don't you join me in a walk? I would love some company."

"Love to." Reggie agreed. "Maybe I can show you some interesting things out here. This is my territory and I keep track of everything that goes on."

"That would be appreciated." Daniel said. "I would like to see the forest through your eyes. My perspective of the world has changed much, since talking to Little and my friends Bartholomew and Patricia. I have learned that many of the things I took for granted are unique and special to others."

Chapter 3

After about a mile Daniel heard Reggie whisper. "Shush. Quietly now."

Daniel began walking silently using the heel, side of the foot and toe method his father had taught him when he was young.

"See that big brown bush ahead?" Reggie asked.

"Yeah." Daniel answered.

"Well go up and give it a poke." Reggie urged.

Daniel paused and then thought. This was Little's cousin and he would not do anything or ask Daniel to do anything dangerous so he crept up and poked the large brown mass.

"Arrgh!!!" Bellowed the bush and stood up spinning around to reveal a very large brown creature standing almost seven feet tall.

Daniel stepped back and was on the verge of panicking but then remembered Reggie would never have told him to do something dangerous and after having had so many revelations in the last year decided to try and communicate first. Then if that failed he could always run.

"Good morning." Daniel projected in the friendliest way he could summon.

"Blimey!" The creature responded. "A talking human."

Daniel calmed himself and said. "The correct response is Good Morning followed by your name. My name is Daniel."

"Cor!" The creature replied. "Sorry mate, you startled me. Good Morning.

My name be Clancy."

"I assume your not used to talking to humans?" Daniel questioned.

"Bloody right about that you are." Clancy expounded. "Most humans never get close enough before they run off in mindless panic. How come you didn't run?"

"Well back home I have a friend named Little, and he told me to look up his cousin Reggie. Reggie told me to give you a poke and I didn't think he would tell me to do anything dangerous so I thought I would try a greeting."

"Reggie." Clancy said scornfully. "He's quite the prankster that one is."

"Plus I've only been communicating with beings using the Universal awareness for a while and still find it amazing how much I don't know and am always open to new relationships."

"Well I hope I didn't scare you." Clancy said remorsefully. "Most humans appear scared to death and their first response is to run away.

Glad to make your acquaintance."

Chapter 4

"We humans have many legends about you." Daniel went on. "Some call you Sasquatch or Bigfoot or up north the Abominable Snowman. No one has made contact with you before. Why is that?" Daniel inquired.

"Well there are several reasons." Clancy explained. "There are not many of us plus if the truth be known we can't stand the smell. No offence."

"None taken my friend." Daniel assured him.

"There is one thing I would like to ask you." Clancy asked inquiringly.

"That is if you don't mind?"

"No problem." Daniel replied with a chuckle. "It seems all I do these days is answer questions about humans."

"The missus and I don't understand the human reproductive system."

Clancy went on. "It seems human women have litters of offspring but they age at different rates. We have observed a mate and his spouse with three or four or even five offspring and they seem to be aging at different rates.

We can't figure it out."

"Clancy they probably are no different than your offspring. They age at one rate. The reason you see families with a group of children is because they have had that number over a period of time."

"What?" asked a shocked Clancy.

"Its just a question of religious beliefs." Daniel explained.

"What is that?" Queried Clancy.

"Religion is a system of beliefs by humans of what is right and wrong and how to live their lives. It's all put down in books and the main book in America is the Bible."

"You have a book that tells you right from wrong and how to live?" Asked Clancy shocked.

"Yes." Daniel answered seriously.

"What about using common sense." Continued Clancy's query.

"There was a French philosopher named Voltaire who one said, "Sense wasn't common."

"Okay Daniel." Clancy continued, "How does this apply to offspring?"

"Well in this book there is a place that tells humans to go forth and multiply." Daniel offered.

"Does it say go forth and be stupid?" Clancy inquired sarcastically.

"No it doesn't." Daniel replied sheepishly.

"Do you humans have a thing we call math?" Clancy asked.

"Yes we do." Daniel answered.

"Well if you have one male and one female." Clancy patiently explained. "That makes two. If they have two offspring everything stays in balance. If they have more than two. The forest is going to get very crowded. In math multiplying is understood, but what you are talking about is an exponential factor."

"What can I say?" Daniel agreed sadly.

Chapter 5

"Well one thing I don't understand." Clancy went on. "How in the world did you sneak up on me? I know I was napping but no one has ever slipped up on me like that. I can smell most humans a mile off."

"Probably because I didn't take a shower this morning. I didn't put on deodorant and didn't shave so no after shave lotion." Daniel explained.

"That must have been it." Clancy reasoned. "You don't smell artificial like most humans."

"That's funny. Because most of the rumors I hear about you is that you smell bad." Daniel explained.

"I smell like Mother Nature made me." Clancy argued.

"I don't think you smell bad." Daniel said. "Most humans wear so much perfume and such that their sense of smell is pretty much useless."

"Well that's good for me I guess." Clancy said thoughtfully. "Keeps me out of trouble."

"That's what my mate says." Daniel replied. "Always look for the good side."

"Blimey." Clancy exclaimed. "Speaking of spouses I need to go do some fishing. I told mine I would bring back some salmon for supper and if I don't hurry, Marcus will get all the easy catches from the stream two mountains over. She will be put out with me."

"Who's Marcus?" Daniel asked.

"He's just our local bear and loves salmon." Clancy explained. "Well I gotta be going now. Enjoyed meeting you and talking. Come back and see me sometime."

Clancy waved a big arm goodbye, and went into the woods and quickly vanished from sight.

Chapter 6

As Daniel made his way back to his car, he noticed Reggie trailing along beside him.

"Hey Reggie. Quit hiding I see you over there." Daniel called.

Reggie looked out from behind a tree. "You mad at me." He asked sheepishly.

"Of course not." Daniel answered. "Clancy and I had a great talk and I enjoyed myself enormously."

"You mean you weren't scared?" asked the small squirrel.

"Not in the least." Daniel answered.

"You going home now?" Reggie inquired further.

"Yes I am." Daniel responded. "I'll tell Little hello for you."

"Thanks and tell him I said that you are no fun."

Easter 1971

It was Saturday, the day before Easter in Viet Nam, 1971. We just finished a two-week mission in the green. Back on the firebase we were enjoying a shower and looking forward to some sleep. Suddenly the sergeant comes up and tells us to grab some ammo and weapons. We were going to relieve C Company who had just got hit. So we got dressed grabbed some ammo and our weapons and went to board one of the eight choppers waiting for us in the landing field. We took off in the bright sunshine apprehensive to say the least. After about a fifteen-minute flight we changed direction. Word was D Company was worst off and needed immediate support. Nerves stretched we waited for the flight to arrive. Coming in we got a good look at the two choppers burning on the ground and we knew it was going to be bad. As we approached the Landing Zone or LZ as we called it. A Cobra Helicopter came past us in a blur. With mini guns firing and rocket pods blasting it was and awesome noise. But even with all the noise I could still hear the fifty-one caliber machine guns of the North Vietnamese firing away at us. We jumped out about ten feet above the ground. After seeing the two downed choppers, being on a chopper did not seem like a good idea. There were originally 20 men in D Company, but when we got on the ground there were only 4 left alive. Joe Schoolmester was my best friend and he was killed that day. Shot in the back he was propped up against a tree and bled to death. I still remember sitting in a bar about 2 months before and arguing with him about country music compared to rock and roll. Only after arguing for about three hours and many beers later did I ask him who his favorite country band was. He told me Credence Clearwater Revival. I explained that was rock and roll and we laughed about it. He died a virgin waiting until he was married. Now he was gone.

The LT came by to tell us to secure our positions and we would be out shortly. The air support was going to be with us till we could evacuate. I remember seeing a navy pilot fly into the valley then slid sideways to drop his load of napalm then hit the afterburners and climb vertically out of the mess. It was impressive but it didn't last. The air support disappeared but was replaced by artillery fire. This was supposed to last the entire night. It disappeared around 10 P.M. So we sat there all night. No food, no water, no mosquito repellant just our selves and the dead. The night was so black you couldn't see your hand in front of your face. There was a Vietnamese solider laying about 4 feet away. He had been killed earlier in the day and he lay there and stared at me all night. Around 3 A.M. I heard the sound of some one walking. Sound was the only thing we had left. It was the

North Vietnamese looking for us. I had my M-60 loaded with about 400 rounds and set to automatic. However if I fired they would know where I was and it would betray our position. There was an entire battalion of North Vietnamese looking for us, and only 16 of us. I literally began to shake but did not fire. The sound went away and was replaced by the sound of rain. Rain in the jungle makes a spooky sound. And we each were alone with the sound and the rain. So we got very wet. The mosquitoes would not let up and we spent the night awake, wet, and scared. Morning finally arrived and the relief choppers came to pick us up. I was the last to get on a chopper and leave. Waiting there with only the LT was as scary as the night had been before. But we made it out. So I now feel that everything back here in the real world is gravy. And it gives a new meaning to the phrase. "Don't mean a thing."

Elizabeth

Elizabeth was happy. Content with her life, as she knew it. She was warm and snug in her place, surrounded by earth with her food and water supplied by roots. But she noticed changes. She was getting larger. Every day she felt her limbs growing and extending out. Then one day, for the first time, felt hungry and thirsty, so she tried extending her roots and was relieved to feel them go out and supply her with water and food. She did not know where she had come from and didn't really care to ask. As long as everything was in control she was happy. Then one day the unexpected happened. The top of her head broke ground. The light was blinding and white, but it was warm and really felt good. This is neat she thought, and extended her limbs to catch more of the sun's rays. She noticed other plants rising from the ground and she was shocked to find she was not alone. There were literally hundreds of other plants around her rising to meet the sun. Then shock upon shock followed when she noticed the gods. They were smaller beings but were not a part of the Earth and could fly. Where did they come from she thought? She had no answer except they were just there and so she named them for what they were. Beings or bees. She also noticed that the gods were going from plant to plant. Landing on each plant's flower exchanging their pollen for another's pollen. This must be the answer to life she thought and began working to produce a flower of her own. Soon she had a bright yellow flower that the gods could visit and spread their food. She was saved. But as time passed she became discontent. She wanted to leave the earth and travel as the gods did. Her desire became overwhelming and she began to grow a stalk to assist her with mobility. While enjoying one day thinking over life and what it meant she felt a pressure.

"Who is that?" She questioned.

"It's just me." Replied the wind.

"Are you a god?" She continued her inquiry.

"Heavens no." The wind chuckled. "I'm just a pressure variance."

"What are you doing here?" Elizabeth asked.

"I just blow things around." Replied the wind. "You'll see soon enough."

So Elizabeth went back to basking in the sun and contemplating life.

She was feeling good and happy with her progress of a stalk when the unexpected happened again. The stalk began to get fuzzy. "What in the world is this?" She thought. Then asked the wind if he knew the answer.

"Sure Elizabeth." He answered in a casual tone. "Those are your seeds."

"My what!" She exclaimed scared out of her wits.

"Your seeds." The wind answered again. "Or simply what you are here for."

"What do I do?" She cried out worriedly.

"Just sit still and watch." Pronounced the wind as he created a mighty blast which spread the seeds to the wind.

"They're flying." Elizabeth shouted happily.

"Indeed they are." Said a contented Wind.

Then Elizabeth realized her purpose in life. The producing and spreading of her seeds. As she prepared for the night she looked out happily over the field of bright yellow flowers and for the first time felt at one with the world.

John

John woke to the bright sunshine of a spring day and leisurely began his flight up and down the rows of his garden. Cruising along comfortably he was startled as a black and yellow blur blew past him.

"Jake is that you?" he called out questioning.

"Hey old man," Jake replied. "Can't stop to talk I've got a quota to meet."

"Quota my rear," John growled. "The only quota you've got is in your head."

"No way," Jake replied. "I have a set number of flowers I must visit on my shift. Plus I have to dodge being smacked by the giants."

"You don't have any set number of flowers to pollinate, Jake," John replied warily. "As for the giants, just be careful."

"What is their problem?" Jake wailed. "Don't they have anything else to do but smack us?"

"The giants are truly a mystery," John explained. "They have been heard discussing the mysteries of the planet and unfortunately they are misguided."

"How so?" questioned a curious Jake.

"They seek to understand the how but not the why," John said solemnly. "According to their science we are even incapable of flight."

"What!" Jake exclaimed shocked.

"It's like the wind," John continued his explanation patiently. "They know the pressure variants and how they are created, but they do not know why."

"Then they are truly blind," Jake wailed sorrowfully.

"True," said John stoically. "It's kind a like us. According to their science we can't fly but we do. And why we do is what life is all about."

"Oh." was all Jake could think of to say and flew off to pollinate the flowers of his garden.

Music

It was a bright summer morning as Tim cruised across town at a slow 400 miles per hour, in his new Mercury Starfire. The wind was blowing his hair as he listened to the beat of the latest big hit song from Bogus belting out of his music box on the dash. He spotted the Starbucks where he was to meet his friend and instructed the car to stop. He went inside and ordered a triple espresso and smiled at the girl who waited on him. Damn he thought as he felt a stirring. He had forgotten to take his hormone-equalizing pill this morning and he was turning 16 very soon. Couldn't be forgetting that again. He spotted Horace his friend and sat down.

"How's it going my man?" Tim asked.

"Morning Tim." Horace replied. "SSDD."

"Same Shit Different Day." Tim interpreted.

"Yeah." Horace lamented. "Our professor gave us a lesson to solve last night."

"What was it?" Tim inquired.

"Just to solve the field unification problem from quantum mechanics." Horace said pissed off.

"What." Tim said sorrowfully. "That was done 600 years ago."

"I know. I know." Horace continued. "It was only busy work to keep us occupied. How about you?"

"Well I think I found a new problem I can solve for my PhD dissertation." Tim went on excitedly.

"Don't keep me in suspense." Horace cried. "Tell me."

"I was listening to the music box coming over." Tim explained. "You know that new song from Bogus. "Everybody eat my rust."

"O man yeah." Horace gushed. "That song is so kicking."

"Well it's been done before."

"You are kidding me. Bogus has been accused of stealing rifts before but never a whole song." Horace screeched.

"He didn't steal it." Tim said stoically. "It's an original song."

"Wait a minute?" Horace questioned. "If its been done before how could he not steal it?"

"That's what my dissertation is all about."

"Music." Horace said sympathetically." You know all the other guys studying math and science have been talking about you. Your almost 16 and don't have a degree yet."

"It's really simple once you think about it." Tim said and continued his explanation. "What you don't know, and nobody really knows, is why there are only 12 notes. Unless you count the pure ratio frequencies used in timbre as being an extra note. First, it's always a possibility that there may be no mathematical explanation why there are 12 notes. In the same way that science can't explain what it feels like to see the color red. It's mathematics. The chromatic scale was probably invented by Pythagoras. He noted that two strings of equal tension will sound very similar when one string is exactly half the length of the other, but the shorter string is higher in pitch, what we now call an *octave* higher. Next, Pythagoras began devising ratios of string length, and eventually came to a system of twelve tones, each one a mathematical ratio compared to a given length of string. For instance, the seventh tone has a proportion of 3:2, meaning the string must vibrate one and a half times as fast relative to the first tone. This became the mathematical foundation of the chromatic scale, as each note in the scale had a simple ratio such as 9:8. The reason, although Pythagoras may not have known this, is that the shorter string vibrates twice as fast. The pitch of a note is directly proportional to the length of the string. This is how stringed instruments like the guitar work the way they do. When a finger is pressed against the string, the vibrating portion is made shorter by pinning the string against the fingerboard, cutting off a portion of the string from the vibration."

"That's simple?" said Horace completely confused.

"What is means is there are only a fixed number of notes we can use." Tim explained patiently. "It's the year 2999. The new millennium is upon us. All the possible music has been written. Now they just repeat themselves. Although they may come up on it originally they can't create anything new. Mathematically all the possibilities have been exhausted."

"Nothing?" Questioned an inconsolable Horace.

"Well the words are different." Tim consoled him.

"The words?" Asked Horace.

"Yes." Said Tim. "The words are like Poetry. Always new with something to say.

NAN MADOL

Chapter 1

The sun was just rising when Daniel walked out onto his back patio.

"Good morning Daniel." Greeted Patricia the ever perky and optimistic young pine.

"Good morning Daniel." Greeted Bartholomew the ever stoic and serious old elm.

"Good morning." Came the retired civil servant's solemn reply.

"What's got you upset this morning?" Questioned Patricia.

"The ancient mystery of megalithic structures." Came the answer.

"The what?" Asked Bartholomew.

"The ancient practice of building very large stone structures. We don't know how they did it." Daniel replied morosely.

"Hmmm." Came Bartholomew's reply.

"Where were these built?" Queried Patricia.

"Mostly from the west." Daniel answered. "Nan Madol seemed to be where they started."

"Then why don't you go there and find out?" Bartholomew asked.

"Because the ruins are buried under 350 feet of water." Came the solemn reply.

"Well that is no problem." Bartholomew retorted. "Little come here."

"What's got you upset this morning?" Replied the small squirrel.

"Daniel wants to go to Nan Madol." Answered the stately old elm.

"What?" Little screeched. "That's ancient history. It doesn't exist anymore."

"I know." Bartholomew answered. "But why not take him. The outing would do you good."

"I don't know why I should have to do it." Quipped the small squirrel.

"Because you can." Bartholomew answered.

"All right." Said Little grumpily. "Haven't even had my breakfast almonds yet."

Chapter 2

Daniel felt the familiar tug of space-time continuance and opened his eyes to an underwater city.

"What in the world is going on?" Daniel asked Little.

"Be patient Daniel." Little said consoling his friend. "It will make sense soon enough.

Little began humming and juggling his almonds. He then recited an ancient Polynesian phrase. "Gromo Factos Homomous Raturia."

"Who dare disturb my sleep?" Came an outraged but clearly female voice.

"Sorry about that." Replied Little meekly. "But we need to see Nan Madol."

"Nan Madol." She huffed. "Nan Madol is a dead and long forgotten world."

"I know." Little replied, still astounded that the phrase worked. "But I have a human here and he needs to see the ancient world."

"Whatever for?" Came the imperious question.

"Hi." Daniel responded jumping in. "Sorry to disturb you, but I would like to find some answers."

"Concerning what?" Continued the questioning.

"The megalithic structures around the world." Came the solemn reply.

"Who are you?"

"I am the keeper of the timeline." Came the haughty response. "I was in the middle of a nap when your friend here woke me up."

"Sorry about that." Came Daniel's answer. "But I need to find out how they did it."

"Hmmph." Came the ever present but diminishing outrage. "You can call me, Bell."

She replied. "And now that I'm up, how can I help you."

"As I said." Daniel continued. "I'm looking for answers concerning how the megalithic structures were built."

"Well to see that we must go back in time." Bell said warming to the task.

"Uh oh." Little said.

Chapter 3

Daniel felt the time space continuum shift. When he opened his eyes the city was above ground and teeming with people.

Bell began her explanation. "About 12,000 years ago the sea was about 350 feet below what it is today. The earth's magnetic field was much stronger then. If you listen closely you will hear people humming. This was to offset the gravity. Gravity has a specific frequency, and if you hum at that frequency, it will set up a harmonic distortion offsetting the gravitational field. Therefore there was no mystery of how they moved the very heavy rocks and put them in place."

"But this whole structure is massive." Daniel replied awed.

"Yes it was." Replied Bell. "It was over 10 square miles."

"And the mystery of why it is in the ocean is that it was built when it was above ground." Daniel continued.

"True enough." Bell went on. "The people knew something was coming and built it to counteract the rising waters."

"Wow." Daniel answered overwhelmed.

"Not all the megalithic structures are here." She said.

"I know." Replied a humbled Daniel. "But here is where they are most prominent. So all the megalithic structures used the same technique?"

"Yes." Bell answered. "Does that answer you question."

"Indeed it does." Daniel answered relieved. "Now you can go back to sleep and we are sorry for the inconvenient trouble."

"Think nothing of it." Replied Bell. "I need to wake up and get ready for the next convergence."

"And when will that be?" Asked a curious Daniel.

"Soon enough. My friend. Soon enough."

Daniel felt himself being pulled back in time to the present. "That was far out." He said.

"Yeah, far out." Little said sarcastically.

Chapter 4

Daniel soon found himself back in his time with Little. They soon were flying back to his back patio where they were greeted by Bartholomew and Patricia.

"Find your answers?" Queried Bartholomew.

"Yes I did." Daniel answered.

"And did little fuzzy butt help." Patricia asked with a smirk.

"Yes he did." Daniel went on. "But how did he know the phrase to say."

"Universal awareness, Daniel." Came the response. "Universal awareness."

RALPH

Chapter 1

Daniel walked out onto his back patio in the blackness of full night. Settling into his chair he felt the tension ease from his shoulders. As he prepared for contemplative relaxation he suddenly heard a small voice.

"Hello?" The voice questioned.

"Uh hello." Daniel responded trying to pinpoint the source of the voice.

"So the rumors are true." Continued the voice. "You can speak."

"Yeah." Replied the retired civil servant. "But who am I addressing."

"Over here." Came the reply. And Daniel looked over his shoulder to spot a pair of small beady eyes staring at him.

"Bartholomew." Bellowed Daniel.

"Here Daniel." Came the old elm's response. "What do you want?"

"There is a creature talking to me and I can't see him." Daniel practically shouted.

"Oh it's Ralph." Bartholomew responded patiently.

"Who is Ralph?" Queried a confused Daniel.

"You can ask me." Came the voice's reasoning logic. "I am the local forest rat."

"The what?" Questioned Daniel.

"The local forest rat." Replied the voice inviting patience.

"Uh okay." Came Daniel's reply. "Bartholomew everything is fine.

Sorry to bother you. Ralph and I are just going to talk awhile."

Chapter 2

"So Ralph is it." Replied a confused Daniel.

"Like I said." Responded the rat. "I had heard rumors and I just wanted to see if they were true."

"Yes they are." Daniel agreed. "Come on out here in the open so I can see you."

"Sorry about that" Ralph said. "Old habits die hard."

The rat moved into the opening so he could be seen and assumed a relaxed pose.

"So what can I do for you?" Queried Daniel.

"I have also heard it said that you answer questions about human emotions."

Stated the rat.

"I try to do my best." Daniel said. "What is your question?"

"Why do human's hate rats so much?" Came the question.

"Well most of the hate is probably actual disgust and fear." Replied the retired civil servant.

"What is the disgust from?" Came the rat's question.

"The fact that rats live off garbage."

"Hello. Look around you. You are in a forest. See any garbage." Queried the rat.

"Actually no." Answered Daniel. "I don't."

"Exactly." Came the response.

"And what about the fear?" The rat questioned further.

"The fear comes from the plague." Daniel promptly responded.

"Great." Ralph answered. "More rat profiling."

Chapter 3

"Well rats do carry the plaque, and as such are considered vile creatures."

Came Daniel's response.

"Do rats have the plaque." Came the next question.

"Ummm. No." Daniel replied. "The fleas have the plaque and the rats carry the fleas. Hence the reasoning is that rats carry the plaque."

"Does that make any sense to you at all." Questioned the offended Ralph.

"Now that you mention it. No. But you are assuming that humans think rationally." Came Daniel's defensive argument.

"So the rats are considered vile just because they carry fleas?" Ralph responded shocked.

"Ummm. Yeah." Daniel responded defensively.

"And does that make any sense to you?" Continued the offended Ralph.

"No. Not really." Daniel ineffectively defended himself.

"So all this hoopla is just because a few lazy rats live off garbage and as most animals carry fleas."

"Well I guess you're right." Said Daniel. "Plus rats are nocturnal."

"So if any of this matters. Which is doesn't. The disgust and fear come from illogically reasoned thinking." Ralph defended himself.

"Yes. I guess you are right." Said a chastised Daniel.

Chapter 4

"Well I have to be going. Nice to meet you." Said Ralph. "Thanks for the time and explanation."

"No problem Ralph." Said Daniel. "Come on back and see me some time and we can discuss more."

"Only at night my friend. Only at night."

SERENDIPITY

Chapter 1

Daniel walked out onto his back patio with a frown on his face.

"Good morning." He greeted his three friends.

"Good morning Daniel." Came back the chorus of replies.

"What has you up this morning and in such a bad mood?" Patricia asked concerned.

"Sorry Pat." Came the answer. "I was up a lot last night and didn't get much sleep."

"Well what had you awake?" Questioned Bartholomew.

"I'm not really sure." Daniel answered. "Something was tugging at my mind and I don't really know what it was."

"Something on your mind?"

"Yeah." Daniel replied slowly. "I felt this need to write and I don't know about what or even where it came from."

"Uh oh." Patricia responded concerned.

"What?" Daniel asked perplexed.

"Sounds like Serendipity has been busy. What do you think Bart?"

Patricia continued her questioning.

"Sounds like something she would do." Bartholomew replied.

"What is a Serendipity?" Daniel questioned clearly puzzled.

"Hang on a second." Bartholomew answered then called aloud. "Serendipity are you here?"

Chapter 2

"Hi guys." Came the low sultry voice. "Just doing my job."

"What in the world?" Daniel asked now looking at the clearly visible young and beautiful woman standing in the dim light at the corner of his patio.

"Hi." She said in a deep throaty voice. "I'm Serendipity."

"Glad to make your acquaintance and if you don't mind my asking.

What are you?" Daniel asked.

"I'm an abstract." She replied solemnly.

"A what?" Daniel questioned further.

"I'm a muse stupid." She answered annoyed. "Not human or animal. I exist only in the mystical realm. What did you think I was?"

"You appear to be a young vibrant female," Daniel answered.

"Wrong," replied the muse. "A woman is defined by what is between her legs." She then lifted her silken gown to expose her smooth featureless flesh from her stomach to her knees. "See," she stated. "No definition."

"Wow!" replied a somewhat embarrassed Daniel. "I stand corrected."

"She's a muse, Daniel" Patricia explained. "She inspires people to write."

"Well what is she doing in my mind?" Asked a frustrated Daniel.

"She visits people often. No rhyme nor reason. She just comes." Patricia went on.

"You needed help." Serendipity replied. "You have not written in a long long time. So I thought I could offer aid."

Chapter 3

"So you just barge in." Daniel asked clearly upset.

"Sure." Serendipity responded. "You seem to need some inspiration and that's what I do."

"You inspire people to write?" Daniel asked. "About what?"

"Many things." Came the casual reply. "When people have writer's block I give them help, so they can write."

"Why don't you write it yourself?" Daniel asked perplexed.

"As I said I'm a muse. I inspire others to write. I don't do it myself plus who would read it?" Came the next question.

"Well if it was good any number of people would read it." Daniel replied.

"Not happening." Serendipity answered. "Who would I get to publish it and where?"

"I see your point." Daniel answered.

"I mean look at your books. They are good but even you have trouble getting people to read them." Came the haughty response.

"Okay." Daniel said. "What should I write about?"

"What have you not written about yet?" Asked a concerned Muse.

"I've written about everything I can think of." He responded.
"Everything?" Questioned the Muse.
"Well mostly everything." Came the answer.
"What are you forgetting?" Questioned the Muse further.
"Maybe Groundhog Day." Daniel replied.
"Then tell me about it." She asked.

Chapter 4

Daniel began his explanation. "It usually takes place on February 2 in Punxsutawney, PA.. It was originally a cross-quarter day, midway between the Winter Solstice and the Vernal Equinox. In traditional weather lore, if a groundhog emerges from its burrow on this day and fails to see its shadow because the weather is cloudy, winter will soon end. If the groundhog sees its shadow because the weather is bright and clear, it will be frightened and run back into its hole, and the winter will continue for six more weeks."

"There." Said the Muse contented. "You now have something to write about. Mission accomplished."

"Whoa." Complained the retired civil servant. "That's not something worth writing about. What if I write about you instead?"

"Feel free stupid." The Muse responded. "But no one will believe your story about an abstract."

"Okay." Daniel replied. "But you are far more interesting than a groundhog."

"Thanks for saying that." She replied. "And if you have trouble thinking of something to write about just look around you. Everyday life is full of things happening that people find interesting. I'm going now and if you feel a small twitch some night get up and write. You will think of something."

THE DRAGON'S GOLD

Chapter 1

Daniel sitting out on his back patio early in the mornings around four AM heard a soft wailing coming from the bushes.

"Woe is me." It wailed repeatedly. "Woe is me."

Upon looking closer he noticed a small man with an Irish costume about three inches high.

"Hello." Daniel greeted the little man. "Who are you?"

"O dear." The little man wailed. "Can anything else go wrong today?"

"What seems to be the problem my friend? Can I help?" Daniel asked concerned.

"Now I not only lost me gold, but I've allowed a human to see me."

The lament continued.

"Hi Dan." Little greeted. "Who are you talking to?"

"I don't know Little." Daniel explained. "There seems to be a wee tiny man in the bushes wailing."

"Oh. Hi Michael what are you doing." Little inquired. "Letting yourself be seen by a human."

"Hello Little, me fine lad." Michael answered. "I was so distraught about losing me gold that I didn't pay attention and let me guard slip."

"I need some help." Daniel cried. "Bartholomew. Are you awake?"

"Of course Daniel." Came the old elm's reply. "I only sleep in the winter, but I don't listen in to others conversations unless invited. What's up?"

Chapter 2

"I'm sitting here talking to a wee guy dressed up in Irish clothing and need some help." Daniel lamented.

"Little said his name is Michael and he's lost his gold."

"I know Michael." Bartholomew said.

"He is an elf and doesn't have any gold. Only dragons have gold and the only purpose in life for an elf is to keep and protect that gold. Who's gold is it Michael?" Bartholomew inquired.

"It be Angie's." Michael wailed even louder.

"Well then call her here and let's discuss it." He reasoned.

"Be sure and tell her to be small." Little quipped. "Daniel is a powerful magician and if he gets startled he could blast her out of existence."

"Little." Daniel whispered. "I'm not a magician."

"Quiet." Little replied, "What they don't know won't hurt em."

Michael closed his eyes and began to hum.

Chapter 3

Suddenly a small dragon appeared before Daniel. She was about six inches high and pink with gossamer wings.

"Who called me?" Thundered a deep voice.

"I did Angie." Michael answered meekly. "I seem to have a bit of a problem and this human said he would help."

"Indeed." Angie roared. "Could it have anything to do with my gold?"

"Aye lassie. It does." Michael lamented again. "It seems to have been stolen."

"I wasn't stolen." Angie said quieter. "I took it."

"What?" Michael screeched. "Why?"

"You hid it in that tree bole of the other side of the pond. During the wind storm last night the tree blew over and left the gold exposed for anyone to see of steal." Angie returned to thundering.

"Wait a minute." Daniel injected. "Bartholomew. Are Michael and Angie from the magical realm?"

"Yes Dan." Replied Bartholomew. "They don't exist in your world."

"And wouldn't you say that the gold is also from that realm?" Daniel asked further.

"Certainly my friend." Bartholomew conceded.

"Well there's your answer." Daniel expounded.

Chapter 4

"The only ones in this plane of existence who value gold is humans."

Daniel went on.

"What." Angie exploded as she started to grow larger and turned from pink to red.

"Wait Angie." Daniel explained further. "The only ones who would steal the gold are humans. The gold is from the magical realm. Therefore the humans can't see it. It would be safe just sitting there."

"Hadn't thought of that." Angie said softly returning to her small size and soft pink color.

"Neither did I, lassie." Michael said happily. "It was never in danger."

"You are not in danger either elf." She went on. "However, you human are smart. You also are cute, and would probably make a sweet snack."

"Angie." Daniel said. "It would be an honor to be eaten by any creature as beautiful as you."

"Silly human." She said blushing. "Don't you know that flattery will get you everywhere with a dragon. I would really like to stay and visit for a while but I must get back to where I belong."

At that she whirled and popped out of existence.

"Aye laddie and me too." Michael agreed. "You be having me thanks."

He danced a jig and disappeared same as Angie.

Chapter 5

"Well I'm glad that's over." Sighed Little.

"Interesting morning." Daniel agreed thoughtfully.

"Hey." Said Little perking up. "I know it's too early for breakfast almonds. But how about a early morning snack?"

THE LIGHT

Chapter 1

Daniel walked out onto his back patio with a frown on his face. "Good Morning." He greeted his three friends.

"Good morning." Came back the chorus of replies.

"Before you explain that frown on your face. Tell me you brought my breakfast almonds." Little announced.

"Indeed I did Little." Replied the retired civil servant then asked. "Bartholomew?

A question and a request."

"Sure thing." Answered the stately old elm.

"We are always talking about going into the light when you die."

Daniel questioned.

"Yes we are." Bartholomew answered.

"I want to go now for a visit." Daniel pronounced.

"What?" Bartholomew said clearly stunned.

"Why not." Patricia injected. "Daniel has talked to beings of the living realm, and to beings from the magical realm. Why not try the spiritual realm."

"I can see where this is going." Little lamented as he scampered up into Patricia's limbs.

"It has never been done before." Bartholomew practically wailed.

"So why not give it a try?" Daniel argued.

"Are you sure?" Bartholomew questioned further.

"Sure thing Bart." Daniel went on.

"Okay." Bartholomew sighed. "The smallest particle of light is a photon.

Correct?" Bartholomew asked.

"Yeah." Daniel agreed.

"Well picture one in your mind. Then go into it completely." Bartholomew explained.

Daniel pictured a photon and dove into it. He relaxed completely and as his breathing slowed he felt himself falling into the light. Suddenly he was in a world of nothing but color and light.

Chapter 2

"Incoming Michael" called a soft melodious voice.

"Got it Cupid." Answered a strong voice and added. "Take a break."

"After Valentines Day, I need one." Cupid answered.

"And what have we here?" Michael went on. "Bartholomew and Daniel. Wait a minute. They're not dead. We better call the Keeper."

"I'm here." Came the deep strong voice. "Bartholomew what are you doing?"

"Sorry your Grace." Bartholomew answered. "Daniel shows high awareness and strong ties to his father. I didn't know what else to try."

"No one is allowed into the light while they are still alive." Came the argument.

"I know." Wailed Bartholomew. "But he is more aware than any human I know, and he truly laments his father. I didn't know what else to do."

"Then I'll allow this one time." Came the Keeper's voice. "But one time only. Daniel what did you want to do? Talk to your father?"

Daniel fighting off shock answered. "Yes. If I may."

"Hold on." The Keeper replied and a shape formed out of the mist.

"Danny?" Questioned the apparition. "Is that you?"

"Hi Dad." Daniel replied. "You're looking good."

"I haven't heard that in a long time. Weren't you going up to visit your brother Ted this weekend."

"Dad that was thirty years ago." Daniel said sheepishly.

"My, my, but you sure lose track of time when you no longer keep it in human terms." His father replied.

"They allowed me to come see you this once." Daniel answered.

"No doubt to answer questions you have been asking." His father went on. "You always had such questions."

"Just looking for a few answers Dad." Daniel replied.

"Don't look any further my boy. Here all the answers are given. You no longer have the need." His father said consolingly. "We did have a few talks, though."

"I miss them." Daniel said morosely.

"Don't worry about it." His father went on. "Here all discussions are simplified."

"Can you tell me the meaning of life." Probed Daniel.

"No. You will understand it all once you get here for real, and not some dumb ass adventure." Said his father accusingly.

"Okay you two." The Keeper interrupted. "That's long enough. Daniel you go home and try not to think about it any more. Your father is in a better place and that's all you need to know."

"Thank you." Daniel sighed.

Chapter 3

Daniel woke up with a start to find himself on his back patio with tears streaming down his face.

"I assume all went well." Questioned a curious Patricia.

"Yes it did." Daniel answered then questioned Bartholomew. "Was that real?"

"The beings you saw were all in you mind, but yes it was real." Bartholomew explained. "Reality is a matter of the mind. What is reality for some is not for all. The three dimensions you recognize here are not the dimensions of reality."

"Wow." Said Little relieved. "Now how about some breakfast?"

THE WITCH WOLF

Chapter 1

Billy and Marjorie lay in the noonday sun. Sleepy after a full morning of scampering around the woods.

"Hey." Said Billy perking up. "I've got an idea."

"And whatever would that be my brother." Marjorie asked.

"Why don't we go dream walking?" Billy explained.

"On no." Squeaked his sister. "Uncle Little said that was too dangerous to do unsupervised."

"They're asleep so they will never know." Billy went on. "Come on.

Let's try it."

"What for?" She inquired further.

"Uncle Little is always telling us stories. About the witch wolf, traveling to the middle of the galaxy, and even talking to a human. If you can believe that." Billy explained patiently. "Let's see if any of that is true."

"How do you plan on doing that?" Marjorie queried.

"We could check out that mountain in the distance. I've always wanted to explore it. We could go to the astral plane and see if the cave Uncle Little talked about is even there." Billy expounded.

"I don't know." Said Marjorie thoughtfully.

"O come on." Billy chided. "Don't be such a sissy."

"Okay." Marjorie conceded.

She and Billy transferred to the astral plane and sped off toward Mount Rainer.

Chapter 2

Tap, tap, tap. Came the sound waking Daniel from his nap on the couch.

He went to the sliding glass door and out onto his back patio.

"Little." He inquired. "Was that you knocking at my door, and waking my up?"

"Yes Daniel it was." Replied the squirrel. "I have an emergency."

"I thought I fed you your breakfast almonds this morning." Daniel replied.

"You did." Little acknowledged. "This is more important."

"More important than almonds." Questioned an astounded Daniel.

"Yes." Little replied. "Billy and Marjorie, my nephew and niece are gone."

"What do you mean gone." Daniel asked.

"Their bodies are here, but their souls are gone. I'm afraid they've gone dream walking." Little explained frustrated.

"What is dream walking?" Daniel asked further.

"It's a cross between sleeping and astral projection. It can take them to places where there are some very unpleasant creatures." Little continued worriedly.

"Could this have anything to do with the stories you tell them?"

"Yes." Little replied meekly.

"What did you tell them?" Daniel asked seriously.

"Well about dream walking and one time I did it when I was very young and unsupervised. I met a witch wolf on Mount Rainier who tried to lure me into her cave with almonds. Bartholomew saved me by telling me to run like a hell cat was on my tail and not to look into her eyes."

"And what did you do?" Inquired Daniel.

"I ran like a hell cat was on my tail." Little answered. "They are both too young an inexperienced to run into her. I'm worried."

"There's Harriet and Jonathan. Let's ask them." Daniel reasoned.

"Good idea. Harriet." Little called. "Have you seen Billy and Marjorie today?"

"Why?" She answered. "Are the two little brats missing?"

"Yes." Little answered. "Do you know anything?"

"And why should I care. If they are gone good riddance." She replied huffily.

"Harriet." Said Little patiently. "They are family and I'm concerned"

"Well why should I help?" Came her haughty reply.

"See this big guy with me. He will make it very unpleasant for you if you don't." Little explained.

"How rude. I can't believe anyone would do such a thing." She rejoinered.

"Harriet." Said Daniel menacingly. "They are Little's family. Little is my friend. Believe it. I'm human."

"Well if it will help." Harriet replied chastened. "I saw two astral trails heading for Mount Rainier a little while ago. It could have been them."

"Thanks Harriet." Daniel expressed. "Now go back to eating and don't get your feathers ruffled."

He then took off after Little toward the mountain.

Chapter 3

As they sped toward the mountain Little called out to Bartholomew. "Bart have any of your friends seen Billy and Marjorie today?"

"Hang on and let me check." Came the stately old elms reply. After a short pause he said. "Henry the bald eagle said he saw two astral flows a short while ago heading for Mount Rainier. What's going on?"

"I'm afraid Billy and Marjorie went dream walking." Said Little explaining.

"Without supervision?" Bartholomew questioned.

"Afraid so my friend." Little responded.

"O dear." Said Bartholomew concerned. "Let me know if I can help."

"Sure thing Bart. And thanks." Little replied as he continued speeding toward the mountain.

Chapter 4

As Daniel and Little neared the mountain Daniel asked. "Where did they go?"

"I'm trying to remember." Little answered frustrated. "I think the cave is on the east side but I don't know. It's been a long time ago."

"Let's just start at the bottom and circle the whole thing till we get to the top." Daniel reasoned.

"Good idea." Little responded, "You take the west side and I'll take the east."

"Meet you on the other side." Daniel answered.

Chapter 5

Billy and Marjorie had long ago reached the mountain. They searched it from bottom to top before Billy saw the cave.

"Down there." He exclaimed and dove for the ground.

Marjorie was right behind him but pulled up quickly as she saw the old gray haired she wolf sitting outside the cave.

"Hey." Called Billy. "Are you the witch wolf of the mountain?"

"Don't know if I'm a witch but I certainly the wolf of this mountain." She replied.

"We're looking for the witch wolf." Billy said. "And it's been a long trip."

"You both look tired." The witch wolf replied. "Come inside and rest awhile. I even have some almonds for you to snack on."

"I don't know." Said Marjorie uneasily.

"It's okay. You can trust me." The witch wolf answered. "Just look into my eyes and you can see yourself."

Billy and Marjorie looked into her eyes of limpid blackness and felt their will drained.

Chapter 6

"Daniel." Cried Little. "I see the cave."

Daniel flew to join his friend and together they entered the darkness.

"Who are you?" Screeched the witch wolf.

"I am Little, this is my friend Daniel and those two are Billy and Marjorie my nephew and niece." Little pronounced pointing to the two comatose astral images.

"Oh I remember you." The witch replied. "But I don't know your friend."

"You had better not hurt them." Said Daniel angrily.

"Oh no." The witch replied. "You can trust me. Just look into my eyes and you will see the truth."

As Daniel looked into her eyes he heard Little scream.

"Nooooooooooo."

Daniel felt himself falling into the black of nothingness. He thought

"What's Happening? This can't be right." But try as he did he could not pull himself back. "This doesn't make any sense." He lamented. He tried to think of everything he had learned in his life to aid him. As his despair reached epic proportions he finally had a thought.

"Eight times five is forty. Eight times six is forty-eight. Eight times seven is fifty six." He said aloud.

"What are you doing?" The witch wolf screeched.

"Multiplication tables." Daniel replied. "Eight times eight is sixty four."

The witch wolf exploded in a million sparkles. Billy and Marjorie jumped and came out of their stupor.

Little quickly rounded them up and flew back to Daniel's back patio.

Chapter 7

"You want to explain what just happened?" queried Little confused.

"No problem." Daniel answered easily. "The witch wolf could not exist where reason and logic were applied. I recited the multiplication tables as an exercise in the science of mathematics and it created a paradox. She ceased to exist. The brain creates reality. Do the you see something with your eyes or with your brain? Many people have lost something such as keys and looked everywhere for them but they could not be found. Then they found them where they originally thought they had left them. Fact is when we thought they were lost, they did not exist. When we believed where they were, they reappeared. We create reality in our brains. When Christopher Columbus came to America the native Americans could not see him in the bay because nothing in their experience allowed it. Once the medicine man, who was more aware than most, pointed Chris out they could see him, before that, he simply did not exist in their world.

The Witch Wolf should not have had any control over me and once I realized that by using logic and reason she simply disappeared. Any story is reality. It exists. Only when told it's a lie does it become fantasy.

Pulsars

The sun had long ago set and there was a soft summer breeze in the air. Honeysuckle favor abounded it and wafted genteelly over Danny and his daughter as they lay in they lay on the grass under the stars.

"Dad" She asked inquisitively. "What is in the sky beyond what I can see?"

"Well." He replied lazily. "Novas, Quasars, black holes and pulsars to name a few. Many things we are just finding out about."

"What's the most interesting one in your opinion?" She questioned.

"That would have to be pulsars." He replied.

"Why?" Came the standard eight year olds question.

"Well because of what makes them up." Answering her question cautiously.

But she was an eight year old and he should have known that answer would not hold for long, so he tried to explain why. "Pulsars are neutron stars which pulse. They are massive stars, which have mass greater than 4 to 8 times that of our sun. Pulsars were first discovered in late 1967 by graduate student Jocelyn Bell Burnell as radio sources that blink on and off at a constant frequency. Now we observe the brightest ones at almost every wavelength of light. Pulsars are spinning neutron stars that have jets of particles moving almost at the speed of light streaming out above their magnetic poles. These jets produce very powerful beams of light. For a similar reason that "true north" and "magnetic north" are different on Earth, the magnetic and rotational axes of a pulsar are also misaligned. They called them they their discovery LGM-1, for "little green men."

"And why are these stars so special?" she continued.

"Well." He went on. "Neutron stars are formed when two black holes merge. The result is light."

"And the light is significant?" She inquired further.

"It could be a message from them sent to us. Many people believe that light is a source of intelligence. They talk about heart light and such."

"What are they saying?" Continued her questioning.

"Don't really know." Came his reply. "Haven't figured it out yet."

"Why don't we just ask them."

"Good point." He answered. "Problem is the closed one is about 280 light years away"

"So they may be trying to comminute with us?"

"Yes. But people can't communicate with each other much less an alien life form."

"Don't we have some way to communicate?" She asked the obvious question.

"Yes." He answered. "We have developed SETI."

"What's SETI?" She asked."

"The search for extra terrestrial life." Was the answer.

"Then why haven't those people answered the signal." She asked iniquitously.

"Because the closest signal is 280 light years away. We haven't been doing this very long." He chuckled.

"So the signal from an intelligent form of life could be coming."

"Or it could already be here but we haven't figured it out yet."

"Do these pulsars have life?" She asked skeptically.

"No. But they have Planets orbiting them which could sustain life." He replied using logic and common sense.

"You mean like Earth?"

"Maybe not like Earth but planets where life could have developed."

"So I should dedicate my life to finding the answer?" She asked.

"No. Just enjoy the summer night and the pretty stars."

Particle VS Wave

In physics, wave-particle duality holds that, light,
    Exhibits properties of both of particles and waves.
Many men have studied this,
    From their youth until their graves.

The photoelectric effect, was analyzed in 1905,
    By Albert Einstein, and it won him the Nobel Prize.
But after looking at it with common sense,
    Was he really all that wise?

Feynman asserted, that the photon is a particle,
    Newton and Einstein thought it a particle and agreed.
But the Bohr model, when proposed in 1923,
    Suggested that as a wave, it would fill every need.

Planck's constant validated Bohr,
    For all know photons have no mass.
Broglie then published his hypothesis,
    Proving that electrons really have waves that are fast.

So what *is* light?
    Is the photon, a particle or a wave?
They use quantum physics,
    Making mathematics act as their slave.

But light won't play their game,
    Or fit in their equation.
For the light is life itself,
    And simply evades their explanation.

June 1,2006

DANIEL AND GABRIEL

History of a writer

Danny was a just a young boy sitting by the banks of the Mississippi River in late June of 1955. He was five years old. His grandmother and two sisters were up the levee watching the river flow past when he noticed something in the water. It looked like a big tree boiling over and over in the turbulent water. It left a v shaped stream and when it finally rose to the top he found himself looking at the biggest fish he'd ever seen. It moved itself slowly upriver and seemed to be staring at him. He stared at it until it shocked him by speaking.

"Hello." It said in a conversational tone.

"What?" Danny replied agape.

"No. Hello." It said again.

Totally aghast Danny could only stare his voice gone.

"The correct response to a greeting is to return it." Said the big fish.

"Okay." Danny replied. "I may be stupid but fish don't talk."

"That may be true, but I'm not really a fish."

"What are you?" Danny still shocked asked.

"Well that's an interesting question, but seeing who asked it, I am not shocked." The Big Fish replied. " You can call me Gabriel and I'm what you would call an awareness."

"A what ness." He asked confused.

"Don't worry you'll understand later in your life." Was the answer.

"Some people call me an angel, some call me a wizard, some call me the light, and some call me a mere figment of an active imagination, but I'm none of those, just call me an awareness." Gabriel explained.

"I don't understand." Danny wailed.

"Don't worry about it." Gabriel answered solemnly "You will later in your life."

"What are you doing here?" Came the enviable question.

"I'm here to make sure you don't lose your innocence and perspective of this life." Came Gabriel's answer. "The World needs your talents and I'm here to make sure you don' lose them."

"Well my name is Danny, not Daniel." Danny protested.

"I like Daniel better." Gabriel replied.

"Okay. Now go, before someone else sees you."

"Won't happen." Gabriel assured him. "No one can see me except you."

With that Gabriel sank below the waters and Danny was left to question his sanity.

2

Danny didn't see or hear from Gabriel again for years and began to think it was just his imagination run wild.

He was 20 years old and was sent to Viet Nam when next he had an encounter.

Lying in a field next to the jungle he heard a voice.

"Hello Daniel."

"What?" Danny replied.

"Just me, Gabriel. "Checking up on you."

"I remember you." Danny said. "I thought you were just my imagination."

"No." Gabriel replied.

"So now you're a mouse." Danny noticed the little field mouse standing up on its hind legs and staring at him. "I told you my name is Danny not Daniel."

"I know. I know. But as an ethereal creature I can do pretty much what I like. Deal with it." Gabriel replied haughtily. " What's going on?"

"Well we're in this country against their will and we're meddling with their lives." Danny replied angrily

"Be careful about war. Keep your perspective. War is the ultimate insanity. Try to be more aware of everything going on." Came Gabriel's advice.

"How do I do that?" Came Danny's inquiry.

"Read." Gabriel answered. "Read everything you can find. Theology, Philosophy, and Science Fiction. That will help you accept me and keep your perspective in order."

'Okay but when can I expect to see you again?"

"Don't worry I'll be around." Came Gabriel's causal reply.

3

Danny finished his tour and returned home to have his father die a year later. He was close to his father and dealt with it by becoming an alcoholic. Gabriel returned this time in the form of his dog.

"Hello Daniel." His dog said one afternoon.

"Hello Gabriel." Danny replied, "And my name is Danny.

"Right. Just checking up on you." Gabriel said with a sneer. "Have you been reading?"

"Yes. And it changes my belief in many things."

"I know. But keep your perspective and innocence and stop your drinking." Gabriel said accusingly.

"Okay but why did my father have to die?" Danny wailed.

"May as well ask me why the sun comes up, I don't have an answer that you would understand." Gabriel said and asked. "How is the world doing these days?"

"Lousy and the president's nothing short of stupid." Came Danny's answer.

"Great." Gabriel replied. "Prepare yourself, you will be writing much much later, and you will have much to teach."

"Wonderful." Said Danny sarcastically. "Who will be reading it?"

"No one at first. But it must be said." He replied seriously. "The innocence must be shared with the world."

"But why me?" Danny asked.

"To be honest and I guess it's time you knew. You have the innocence and naiveté of a child. The World is in dire need of both." Gabriel said seriously.

4

The world went on and Danny soon graduated from college only to be told that he could not have a job he'd applied for because he was not a woman or a black.

This time Gabriel came to visit as a bird in his backyard.

"Hello." Danny greeted him. "Long time no see."

"What's going on?" Came the inquiry.

"Well the blacks are rioting and causing all kinds of hell." Danny responded.

"Is it justified?" Gabriel asked inquiringly.

"It appears so." Danny replied. "They fought and died for this country in Viet Nam and came home to be treated like second hand citizens."

"And does that appear fair?" He asked.

"No." Daniel answered. "I remember having a friend at church named Demeatrias when I was a child and we had lots of fun. There was no black or white we were just kids having fun. Now he's black and people discriminate against him. That's just not right."

"What are the blacks doing?" Came Gabriel's inquiry.

"There are riots and a lot of violence." Danny replied solemnly.

"Think you can change that?"

"I don't know. Some of them are just different."

"Only because of their upbringing." Gabriel answered seriously.

"I know." Danny said. "But they think differently also."

"How so." Came the inquiry.

"For example." Danny went on. At work I was talking to a black friend of mine and he was going on and on about how bad the schools were for him and all blacks and how it was just so unfair. So I asked him. "Did you finish high school and go on to college?" He replied yes. So I said why didn't he teach school and help out people of his race. He smiled and said he couldn't make enough money as a teacher and kept his job with IRS. As if that was explanation enough.

"Maybe I am just too naive." Danny lamented.

"Point made." Gabriel emphasized. "Keep your perspective."

5

Danny went on through his twenties and turned thirty before Gabriel returned. He had worked for the government for thirty years and was offered full retirement early so he took it. Now retired at fifty-five he had much time to sit and observe nature and relax, which he did. The only drawback was he had been diagnosed with depression and was given anti-depressants as a cure. Sitting on his back patio feeding a squirrel, which had taken, up residence there, he had a thought. "Gabriel?" he asked.

"Wondered how long it would take you to figure it out." Gabriel answered. "What's happening?"

"Well I'm retired now so I have much time to reflect on my life." Danny replied.

"Have you kept your perspective and innocence?" Gabriel asked.

"Yes." Danny replied. "And I took your advice about reading. To date I've read about 1,500 books."

"Good!" said Gabriel enthusiastically "Now you can begin your work."

"Work?" Danny asked puzzled "I just retired from working."

"You can write."

"I only write poetry and have done that for the last 30 years." He answered.

"So publish your work." Gabriel said.

"Publish what?" Came the question.

"Your Poetry." Came the answer.

"How can I put my perspective in poetry?" Danny asked.

"What else do you like?" Gabriel questioned.

"Fantasy." Danny answered quickly without pause.

"Then use that also to write about." It can be an outlet for your perspective.

"I know." Danny said after thinking a bit. "Carl Jung used imaginary characters in his work. I can do the same."

"Great." Gabriel effused. "Combine the two and call it "Poeantasy."

"I'll create a scenario using imaginary characters and explain things to them. I was at the casino the other day and someone asked the Dealer how to play Blackjack. The dealer tried to explain it but it was hard when the person does know the difference between a queen and a four." He went on. "I'll even use you as one of the characters."

"Okay get to work." Gabriel charged.

6

Danny went to work with a vengeance. He worked night and day for months all the while spending time with Gabriel every day talking and organizing his thoughts. Finally he was done.

"Okay Gabriel I'm done." He said.

"Done what?" Gabriel asked.

"I've finished my work." Danny replied. "I've published thirteen books. And I think that's enough."

"Why only thirteen or is that significant."

"Indeed it is." Danny answered then explained. "Thirteen is considered bad luck. Because the Pope sent out an order to capture and kill all of the Knights Tempter on Friday the thirteenth. Sorry but it's part of history that makes up the tons of useless junk in my head."

"So you have put all the poetry and trivia down in these thirteen books." Gabriel asked.

"Yes I have." Danny responded.

"Okay now you can rest and thanks." Said a grateful Gabriel.

Danny relaxed and sat back in his chair, soaked up the heat, and let the sun shine on him

Danny L Shanks
May 5, 2008

New Poems

36 Years

36 Years is today's anniversary,
    Wow, so much has passed.
Good times we cherished,
    Bad times we trashed.

It almost seems unreal,
    When you really think about it.
I mean so much of it has changed,
    Yet remains the same bit by bit.

We now fight more often,
    And that pains me even more.
It's like we're keeping accounts,
    And its like we're keeping score.

But I for one do not want to keep accounts,
    And I do not want to keep any score.
Because all I know is that I love you.
    Just loving you and letting it grow, more and more.

So when you leave this morning,
    Just give me a kiss for luck.
Taking on the world with everything considered,
    And it still doesn't suck.

For through it all,
    We've really only just begun.
White lace and promises,
    We started out walking, and learned to run.

And when the evening comes, we'll smile,
    So much of life ahead,
We find a place to grow,
    Before we wind up dead.

So stay around a while,
    I'll be here for you.
Just an old fat guy,
    And his sweet badoo.

With so much love, still after 36 years,
Danny

To Dell on your 56th Birthday

You've been on this earth,
For 56 long and glorious years.
And after all that time, I've watched you daily,
Conquer and defeat your fears.

Take on life's battles and troubles,
Responsibilities never did you shirk.
Raising a child, riding a motorcycle,
Or advancing thru jobs at work.

Never a more marvelous woman,
Did I, as a man ever see.
The only question I ask,
Is why you married me?

I'm not complaining you understand,
Thankful is what I feel.
For of all the crap in this world,
You alone are what makes it real.

From the kittens, to mother nature,
From the oceans, to the trees.
You and you alone,
Are a true child of the sixties.

Happy Birthday,
Danny

Autumn Memories

As the autumn winds gently blow
Through the trees of fiery red
My thoughts do travel back
To memories of a river bed

Walking by the riverside
Hand and hand you and I
Enjoying all that nature had to offer
Its water, its land and its sky

So when you ask my Papa
Were you a go father to me
With a exuberance in my heart
I answer most positively

Because some fathers may buy gifts
Of fine silver or shiny gold
But my gifts were from the heart
And thus their value is untold.

Love you Papa,
October 23, 2007

Believe

I watched a movie the other night,
The Polar Express it was called.
About a boy who could no longer feel Christmas,
Nor hear Santa's sleigh bells at all.

To relieve this condition,
He simply had to believe.
Not in some old fat guy with reindeers.
But in the spirit of Christmas to relieve.

To hear the sounds he longed for,
To have his spirit revive.
To believe in something good,
To let him know he was alive.

The message it spoke of,
And I finally got it, after all this time.
Was to believe in something good,
To ease the suffering of one's mind.

That the spirit of Christmas,
Was a feeling of goodness and joy.
That he had been lacking,
Since he had grown up, and stopped being a boy.

You don't have to believe, in the commercial side of Christmas,
Don't have to believe in the shopping trips to the mall.
But believe in the spirit it brings,
What it means to deck the hall.

What joy it brought to me,
To realize the truth in what it was about for the boy.
The joy and celebration,
Of seeing a child open the gift of a toy.

So don't listen to the salesman,
    Don't become an Ebenezer Scrooge.
Join in the holiday fun,
    Don't be such a stooge.

So have a Merry Christmas,
    Join in the celebration.
Don't let the spirit die,
    Because you got an education.

Danny L. Shanks
December 1, 2007

Chaos Theory

If you're looking for an answer,
To the Chaos Theory that's factual.
I'd suggest you look no further,
Than the simple fractal.

It's a geometric shape that repeats itself,
Over an over again.
And it does this repetition,
From the beginning to its end.

It was used in Tibet,
From days long long ago.
And is recorded in the Mandela's,
Check it out and you will find it's so.

To find you're inner self
As a path to self-awareness.
A way to deal with the world,
And a way to relieve your stress.

Many Theories abound,
About how fractals are made.
But they all use geometric shapes.
Repeating over and over down the page.

It cannot be defined by,
Quantum physics or math.
To find meaning to it all,
You must travel a different path.

It's grafting different functions,
And uses an imaginary number as a base.
It uses the recursion law,
So mathematicians can save face.

So look inside yourself,
    Look inside your soul.
And you will find a surprising answer,
    As to what makes you whole.

Danny L. Shanks
January 18, 2008

Counseling

I went to counseling the other day,
　　A trained psychologist to help me with my life.
The meeting was setup and appointment made,
　　By my lovely caring wife.

For I felt that no one loved me,
　　And that I had absolutely not a single friend.
And that such a depressing life,
　　Would result in a premature end.

Well the doctor seemed to care,
　　And he smiled a sympathetic smile.
He was caring and supportive,
　　That appeared to be his style.

But the simple truth of it was,
　　He cared until I walked out the door.
And I could have gotten that much,
　　From a late Saturday night whore.

He charged me just to talk,
　　To act like he was my friend.
But did he really care,
　　When the day was at an end.

They say prostitution is the oldest profession,
　　A job showing someone else cared about their life.
After all the crap going on,
　　In this somewhat boring life.

And why do people object.
　　To suicide, if I may be so bold.
It's just the scary fact,
　　That they have lost control.

So I'll keep my wife and life,
    She seemed to really care.
That will have to do for now,
    Because that is all that really seems fair.

Danny L. Shanks
October 19.2007

Disability

What the hell is going on?
    Emotionally I've lost my mind.
I try reason and logic,
    Both are elusive and instead I find.

I simply want to be pampered,
    Someone to cater to my every desire.
Not to make decisions,
    Something, which I find unbelievably, I could never tire.

Grow up I say,
    Life is simply not like that.
Its not a Dr. Seuss fairy tale,
    Like the preverbal Cat in a Hat.

Yet over and over I find,
    I want everyone to understand.
I am changed these days,
    I no longer am the man.

That cleaned the house and washed the windows,
    That drove the trips without sleep.
And acted like a good father,
    And took care of everyone in my keep.

So I'll try to be good,
    Understand that everyone must not cater to me.
Just deal with life as it comes,
    It's just a really tough thing to see.

Danny L Shanks
September 2, 2007

Danny L Shanks

Earth Abides

Sitting up last night, I caught a replay of Pink Floyd songs.
It was a moving theme, and it provoked much thought.
But looking back on it,
How much of it had I really bought?

And as I sat they're listening,
To song after endless song.
I began to wonder how much,
Of the good advice really belonged.

Kids today have lost their past,
They can't even count back change.
Respect for their elders,
Depressed and told they are insane.

They see a different world,
Than the one in which I grew.
How right was my thinking,
What in the world is new?

It's just different,
And they will get by.
Hear the music or see the light,
And all they have to do is try.

Every generation has a different life,
And aspires to a new set of rules.
Each determining what is best,
Each playing with a new set of tools.

The only constant in this mess,
That we so humbly strive to understand.
Is one rule that a is never changing,
To guide the development of man.

It was written down in a book,
    Where so many great thoughts hide.
Written by George Stewart,
    It was entitled, Earth Abides.

September 30, 2007

Euthanasia

Why is suicide such a topic to avoid?
    You can't even talk about it at home or at work.
Everyone takes offense,
    And your wife and child think you are a jerk.

But if you don't believe in God,
    Or in a heaven or hell.
Then why do you object so much?
    And why do you care, pray tell.

If you are content with the life you've led,
    And are happy how it went so far.
But you no longer find the joy,
    Or strength to measure up to the bar.

You can't do the things you used to do,
    Things that brought joy into your life.
The birth of a child,
    Or marriage to a wonderful wife.

So why can't you call it quits?
    Without everyone getting in a fit.
It's not like you don't care anymore,
    Or you're judgmental, or don't give a shit.

Maybe you're just tired,
    Of the daily grind.
And don't want to endure anymore,
    Of the bullshit of that kind.

But to end it all,
    Without the blood, or the use of a gun.
Just to lie down and end it all,
    To quietly turn off the sun.

Danny L Shanks
September 17, 2007

Memories

Photos in the albums,
Rock and roll songs on the radio.
Memories of days gone past,
Not so very long ago.

Why are they so potent?
These memories from the past.
Are we still just living there?
Trying to make them last.

It can't be just the music,
Notes that simply flow and rhyme.
It has to conjurer up thoughts,
Of a simpler and happier time.

The music is nice,
Words and thoughts sublime.
But the memories conjured with them,
Remind us of a happier time.

Would it be so strong?
This affection of the old songs.
And would the memories still be there,
And would they last so long.

Pictures taken of days gone past,
Stored forever in a book.
Only on days of nostalgia.
Do we pull them out to look.

Memories are a part of life,
They are ours to have and hold.
And they are there to remind us,
That we are just getting old.

Memories mark the passage of time,
    No other purpose is clear.
To remind us of happier times,
    And to relieve most of our fear.

Danny L Shanks
August 29, 2007

Mistakes

Mistakes made, or memories lost,
How much more of it can I really stand?
Before I lose all confidence,
Of my being a worthy man.

The kids jump on any mistake,
Of loss of memories they find.
As if that is an indication,
That I am losing my mind.

They seem to relish the thought,
That I have made a mistake.
And point it out repeatedly,
As if it is a valid point to make.

Even the wife joins in,
To point out when I am wrong.
Didn't we dance to a different tune?
When we sang a different song.

How much more of it can I take,
How much more of it can I stand.
Lost facts and knowledge,
And the memories of being a man.

Why did it happen?
This loss of knowledge and skill.
Was if nothing more,
Than to provide them with a thrill.

So the shotgun waits for me,
Just inside the bedroom door.
An end to all this rubbish,
A way to settle the score.

A simple pull of the trigger,
    Would put an end to all the pain.
Would I really lose that much,
    With so much to finally gain.

January 3, 2008

Suicide

What do you know?
    Why do people argue with you?
Why do you have to prove your point?
    Even when you know it's true.

Maybe you're just slow,
    Late to see what people see.
So you hang on a little bit to long,
    Waiting to be set free.

The reality of it is simple,
    And should be an easy role.
If you would just recognize,
    What you are being told.

It's really not hard to figure out,
    If you aren't a stupid shit.
Just think when you are talking suicide,
    Why no one tries to talk you out of it.

Danny L Shanks
August 18, 2007

The Past

The past is dead, and it's long since gone,
    They say it's just best to forgive, and forget.
Of words said and deeds done,
    Leaving you filled with regret.

No need for explanations,
    To try and set things right.
Of why things were as they were,
    And justification of a fight.

Time lost forever,
    But it's best to know.
My advice to you is simple,
    Just let it go.

Danny L Shanks
September 3, 2007

The Wild Duck

I had a child, once upon a time,
    And I raised her to be free.
Not to be restricted to beliefs,
    Or limited by rules such as me.

So when she was grown,
    To a full bodied woman as can be.
Was it a surprise that she was resented,
    For her lifestyle and beliefs, by the likes of me.

Henrick Ibsen's The Wild Duck,
    Applies to me no matter what I do.
I resent her, but am proud of her,
    That much is very very true.

Danny L Shanks
October 22, 2007

Valentine's Day Gift

It's really not normal,
    For a parent to give a valentine gift to a child.
But it is acceptable,
    And not all that wild.

Because it comes with love,
    From a mother's heart.
Something she made,
    Not bought in any part.

Its not all that hard,
    That is what she contends.
Just making hats,
    For Katie and two of her friends.

She made it over time,
    She chose the color ,yarn and all that.
And she hopes you like it,
    This charming pink hat.

Waiting at the Doctor's Office

Ever wonder why everyone at the doctor's office,
    Looks bored and extremely pissed.
That's because when most of us get screwed,
    We first like to be kissed.

When did it change? From days long past,
    When we were keeping score.
Ten minutes for an instructor, fifteen for a PhD,
    Before we were out the door.

Do they understand my time is as important as theirs?
    Swallowing that must be too bitter a pill.
They just better be thankful,
    That I can't send them a bill.

Why are they never early?
    But always seem to be late.
Can't they understand? An appointment means simply,
    A certain time on a certain date.

Danny L Shanks
August 30, 2007

What does it Matter?

Jesus lived and wrote great things,
Shakespeare and Plato did too.
Lincoln and Washington lived, and inspired great thoughts,
But what did they really do?

You live a good life,
Have a child and teach it to your best.
But at the end of it all,
What really is the test?

Of why we are here,
And what did we learn?
How much of it will pass beyond us,
We want it all, we want it so much, it burns.

The truth of it is really simple,
Nothing passes beyond the grave.
Nothing we learned, nothing we taught,
As a master, or as a slave.

A waste of time it is,
Yet we place so much importance to it all.
Nothing we lived, or nothing we taught,
Winter, spring, summer, or fall.

What is the point you ask?
Of living this thing we call life.
Dealing with the joys, dealing with the sorrows,
Dealing with all the strife.

It just is life,
We live it every day,
But there are no answers,
No price we're required to pay.

So we live out our lives,
    Longevity is the ultimate goal.
Enduing it all, until,
    It just leaves us cold.

Why are we so consumed?
    With living so very long,
Why is an answer we lack?
    Till we are simply gone.

Danny L. Shanks
October 9, 2007

Poeantasy II

Contents

1. Women are from Venus
2. Comfort
3. Grieved
4. Kids Today
5. Such Questions I Have
6. Valentine Day
7. We Were Soldiers
8. Frogs
9. Cults
10. Philosophy
11. Suggestions
12. The Answer to Life
13. Drug Commercials
14. The Bible .

Women are From Venus

Women are from Venus. Men are from Mars,
That my friends, is a fact of life.
For you may want to understand her,
But she is after all, just your wife.

And so you talk, And talk and talk.
But it would have been better,
For your health, that is, if you had just taken a walk.
Not that they don't listen,

They try to figure it out.
But really all they hear, is you beginning again to spout.
There is no communication,
They do not understand a single word.
To assume otherwise, is simply being absurd.

It doesn't mean there is no love,
They love us with all their heart.
But understanding us,
Is like trying in the wind to hear a fart.

Yes they love us,
And try to find a common ground.
But they get lost in the translation,
And similar understanding ideas are not found.

Love them you must,
For they are worthy of all we can give.
But you are alone after all,
And that is the way you must live.

Danny L Shanks
February 14, 2007

Comfort

I wrote a poem the other day,
And a lady told me she was offended.
That was not what I wished for,
Not what I intended.

But obviously she did not understand,
What I meant when I wrote that piece.
And what my feelings were,
Not even in the least.

But it is my duty,
Nay more of my role.
To comfort the afflicted,
And afflict the comfortable.

Danny L Shanks
February 18, 2007

Grieved

My wife was talking to a lady the other day,
She used a word that was hard to believe.
When she talked about her daughter going to college,
And she said it left her grieved.

It's not a term you hear much,
An older way to express.
It's an emotion that every parent feels,
Would have to be my guess.

You watch your child grow,
Every day from the start.
Yet nothing prepares you for,
The ache felt in your heart.

For you wish your child well,
But you can never see.
The cost that comes to you,
When you finally set them free.

You find yourself wanting,
To shelter them from the world.
To wrap them up and keep them safe,
This is after all, your baby girl.

But you have to let them go,
And you feel tremendous pride.
Yet the pain in losing them,
Is a pain you cannot hide.

For they will come to visit you,
Never staying for long.
And soon they will leave once more,
So you try and pretend you're strong.

And you realize that your world has changed,
    No matter what you try.
For it has become a world full,
    Of not hello, but of goodbye.

Danny L Shanks
January 21, 2007

Kids Today

I hear it said, "kids today",
Over and over it is repeated.
As if the people saying it,
Resented being treated.

As if they were ever, that young and stupid.
As the kids now appear to be.
And everyone says, they would all be better off,
If they would just listen to me.

But the kids will not listen,
As I didn't in my youth.
They think they are smarter than most,
And they alone hold the truth.

Vanity is what drives them,
They think they know what's right.
That life is simply not that hard,
And they can avoid the fight.

But as I grow older,
I now see the error of their way.
It is so clear to me,
As I live another day.

The "I told you so" speech,
Will not come for many years.
It's simply a waste of time.
And they will have to experience many tears.

It's not their fault,
In this I come to their defense.
For how can they know the truth?
If they are taught to straddle the fence.

Taught that they are wise,
    And the world is theirs today.
Old people just are not in tune,
    With the ways of the nowaday.

Yes, I now feel old,
    And in truth not that wise.
For what I know I cannot pass on,
    Without preaching in disguise.

So for now, I'll just keep quiet,
    Let them fumble and cavort about.
Life will eventually teach them,
    What it's all about.

And the pain that will come to me,
    As I watch in anguish the display.
That could have been avoided,
    If they had listened to what I say.

But it will not come,
    No matter what I try.
The wisdom of age,
    Is just a pipe dream in the sky.

But would they be better off,
    If they had listen to me.
And would their life have been that much easier,
    Is really hard to see.

So if you find yourself,
    Pining over your lost youth.
Take a moment and look at life,
    And realize the simple truth.

Wisdom comes with age,
    Can't get it any other place.
Kids today don't get it,
    So why should they change their pace.

What life you've led has taught you,
Can't be read in a book.
And that is irrefutable and disgusting,
As is the scorn of your look.

Danny L Shanks
February 10. 2007

Such Questions I Have

I have been married for 35 years,
    And I have come to realize.
My wife and life long friend,
    Does not think I'm all that wise.

We talk about sex,
    It is a trial at best.
She feels I am questioning her,
    On what actions are better than the rest.

It has been proven,
    That when we lose the ability to procreate.
We began at that point,
    To lose the life we so celebrate.

Depression sets in on us,
    We feel no need to continue.
Why does it affect us so?
    And what is the direction of that venue.

And why are fat people,
    So affected, more than the rest.
Do we just not feel sexy anymore?
    We do not feel our best.

And why are Black women never depressed.
    As much as most display.
It is because they still feel sexy?
    Regardless of the fat, they still are in play.

And smoking is harder to quit than heroin,
    It is what they say.
Then why is heroin illegal?
    And you can buy cigarettes any day.

How many people die,
    Of heroin addiction every year.
Cigarettes kill many of us,
    Do they tell us that to just instill fear.

And alcoholic's moment of clarity,
    Is not just a fable.
One can see everything at a glance,
    What is it that makes us able?

Throughout history it is shown,
    People rise up to fight oppression.
A lesson we forget,
    As we aid in fighting their suppression.

We must help them fight,
    To throw off the shackles of late.
The French and Russians,
    Had revolutions to determine their fate

Yet we send young men,
    To aid them in their fight.
To help them to establish,
    A government that we feel is right.

And to establish a new religion,
    May be the future in which we find.
Santa Claus is the leader,
    Doing what is best for all mankind.

The trend is there waiting,
    To begin a new way to relieve.
The stress of urban living,
    And all we need do is believe.

The Polar Express shows the way,
    To establish a worldwide trend.
A feel good movie,
    With a new and goodly friend.

Would it be far-fetched?
    It offers such an expression of relief.
If it offered to all concerned,
    And end to all stress with such a belief.

Such questions I have,
    So many discrepancies I find.
As I flounder around in my confusion,
    In the recesses of my mind.

Danny L. Shanks
January 22, 2007

Valentine Day

Valentine's Day, valentine's day,
    A day in which to rejoice.
To proclaim to the world,
    Demonstrating the wisdom of your choice.

A choice, which has given you,
    A better and kinder fate.
By the companion you have chosen,
    To be your lifelong mate.

A choice you have made,
    To get by in this life.
By choosing who would be,
    You husband or your wife.

Yet I can't help but feel lucky,
    For my judgment is a far superior voice.
I got her, but she got me,
    So who made the better choice?

Danny L Shanks
February 10, 2007

We Were Soldiers

We were young and soldiers,
    We were sent to war.
Why it took place and when,
    I still question, what for?

For they took my youth away,
    It was simply lost.
Later did I finally realize?
    What it really cost.

Try and find a solution,
    Some cure must be found.
But the only ones who have found it.
    Are six feet underground.

Posttraumatic stress disorder,
    Depression is what I've got.
While it states my illness,
    It does not say a lot.

The stress and disillusionment,
    Is not some illness that can be cured?
To be cured with a doctor's help,
    Is not something I am assured.

Drugs and counseling,
    Are what they say I need.
To rid me of dark thoughts,
    Which seem to always feed.

For the meaning of what we did,
    Though it causes much suffering and pain.
Was simply an exercise of bad judgment,
    And it was done in vain.

It cannot be changed,
    Cannot be reversed.
It is simply an affliction,
    One in which I'm cursed.

For the screams are always with you,
    No matter what you do.
Sad it is, but the fact remains,
    That much is always true.

So keep the banners flying,
    Sing the songs that must be sung.
For we were soldiers once,
    And we were just young.

Danny L. Shanks
January 19, 2007

Frogs

I went outside last night,
To hear the coming of the spring.
But all I heard was silence,
There were no frogs to sing.

So I said, "what's happening"?
To cause such a morbid change.
The singing nightly of frogs,
Was as soothing as the rain.

But they are no longer here,
No more will we hear that song.
And it is very simple,
All the frogs are gone.

No big uproar of them leaving,
Silently did they steal away.
A warning to all of us,
Who live in society today.

Frogs breathe through their skin,
And the toxins killed them off.
A warning to us all,
As chilling as the frost.

We did not notice there going,
Only now that they are gone.
And silence now greets us,
With the coming of the dawn.

Are we so blind?
That we no longer see.
Their fate will be our own,
If we fail to act responsibly.

Gone are the frogs,
    Unto a dismal fate.
So will be our own,
    If we wait too late.

Tree huggers you say,
    With a sneer upon your face.
But if we do not change the environment,
    What will be our place?

Yes the frogs are gone,
    So what must we do?
Clean up the environment.
    Act responsible and that is true.

For once they are gone,
    We cannot bring them back.
Gone are the nightly songs,
    And we feel the lack.

We cannot change the world,
    The fix is already in.
But we can stop the spreading,
    Of the more harmful toxins.

So raise your voice in anger,
    Put it the Internet blogs.
Try and change the world,
    Try and save the frogs.

Danny L. Shanks
February 24, 2007

Cults

Cults are everywhere,
    They are hard to resist.
For how can you fight them?
    When they claim that they do not exist.

But the signs are present,
    They are the same wherever you go.
They are designed to hide the truth,
    As their doctrines flow.

For they convince their converts,
    And denial is the hardest to fight.
For how can anyone argue?
    The fact that they are right.

First goes family,

They no longer feel the need.
    To belong to such a group,
As given by someone spreading their seed.
    Next is money,

Given to the cult in such an amount.
    So their doctrines they believe in,
And can forever flout.
    Then go friends,

Lost ,
    For time immemorial.
They belong to a group now,
    And in that group all friends are gone from that portal.

And so they capture their converts,
    Snare them in a trap.
They cannot escape from them,
    Without a reality map.

So try to understand,
    What drives the converts so?
Belief in what they are doing,
    Belief in what they know.

For they feed on the belief,
    They alone know the truth.
Everyone else is confused,
    And a little long in the tooth.

Families try to win them back,
    To show them the error of their way.
But it is just a waste of time,
    Trying to get them to stay.

Just let them go,
    And try to follow their heart.
They will eventually see the truth,
    And you will have done your part.

To release them to the cult,
    To try and free their mind.
They will come home once more,
    And then you will find.

They had not gone too far,
    And they could eventually turn back.
But the only way to do that,
    Is to travel that path, and take that tack.

The only thing lost is time,
    Gone forever and a day.
Time lost is time lost,
    No one there to pay.

For no one is lost forever,
    They all come home in the end.
And you can welcome them back,
    If you are there and have remained their friend.

Danny L. Shanks
February 23, 2007

Philosophy

I have spent my lifetime,
In pursuit of a philosophy.
An answer to life's questions,
As they apply to me.

One answer to it all,
To explain every thing I find.
All explanations to the function,
And working of the mind.

It was such a waste of time,
For I never found a clue.
That however did not preclude me,
From writing down everything as new.

But it did keep me busy,
And for that I am thankful.
And it kept me from,
Admitting it was bull.

For the really interesting questions,
Elude and leave me against a wall.
Questions I cannot answer,
Like why does rain fall?

Danny L. Shanks
February 24, 2007

Suggestions

Over and over the doctors say,
    When I visit, it's the same old thing.
I should lose weight, exercise,
    And most importantly, stop smoking.

If I do this religiously to be my best,
    Or at least I give it a try.
They one and all assure me better health,
    I'll be in when I die.

Danny L. Shanks
March 1, 2007

The Answer to Life

Many books have been written,
  Answers too toil and strife.
Ways to cope with everything,
  That is encountered in this life.

But why is so much written,
  Put down in text for us to read.
Maybe it is simple advice,
  Given for us to heed.

Written as true to the day,
  And here, I don't want to get sloppy.
But if anyone had it right, there would only be one book,
  And every one would have a copy.

Danny L. Shanks
March 1, 2007

Drug Commercials

Drug commercials on the television,
    They are starting to get old.
Advertising prescription drugs,
    And the brand name under which they're sold.

Drugs for diabetes, high blood pressure,
    And hypertension for sure.
But how many of these drugs,
    Correct symptoms and are not a cure.

Why do they advertise to the public?
    And not to the doctors for the drug.
Is it because they know the public,
    Will insist on having it, to cure a bug.

I didn't know there were so many illnesses,
    Affecting the human body, it was truly such a shock.
But the pharmacies companies had a remedy,
    And had a drug correction, as a lock.

Well folks I don't know how to say this,
    Or even, if I should try.
But each of us will eventually,
    Get sick and simply die.

The side effects of such drugs,
    Are as scary as the cure.
Our fear of dying is what it's all about,
    That much is sure.

But what are we so afraid of?
    An end to all our strife.
And what are we so concerned about?
    If we truly believe in an afterlife.

Danny L. Shanks
March 7, 2007

The Bible

The revered word of god,
    Perhaps demands a second look.
Written as a way to live,
    A good one, but still just a book.

The word of god as handed down,
    To every single man.
But why does all the advice given,
    Come to us second hand.

Perhaps Jesus could not write,
    And it's all in the past tense.
Yet anyway you read it,
    It doesn't make much sense.

So theologians study the words,
    And give us their interpretations,
But how many changes were made,
    With each of the translations.

But why does he feel the need,
    And this knowledge I do seek.
For an answer to the question,
    Why does god need to speak?

And why do we attach a gender,
    To a god up on high.
Are we just imposing our beliefs?
    That it must be a male up in the sky.

So many questions I still have,
    To this book in which we place such stock.
And why do we feel the need,
    To describe it thru the ages, as a rock.

Weren't the first words spoken,
    Was "Let there be light".
Before man was created,
    As if it were a slight.

For we can't define light,
    Even unto this day,
Is it a particle or is it wave,
    What do you say?

Maybe its just energy,
    And that is what god intended.
To make us flexible,
And to exist, without us being offended.

Poeantasy III

Contents

1. Web Builder
2. Hurry .
3. A Godless Child . .
4. Childhood . . . .
5. The Kids Don't Listen . . .
6. Surgery Today . . .
7. I Fear Death . . . .
8. The Importance of Being Important .
9. Looking Good . . .
10. The Kids Are Gone . .
11. Secrets . . . .
12. I've Gone Insane . .
13. Compromise . . . .
14. Doctor's Advice . . . . . .
15. Stupidity
16. Belief .
17. Offensive .
18. Summer Begins .
19. Diets .
20. Enunciation . .
21. Visiting My Daughter .
22. It's 3 AM .
23. Thirty-Five Years .
24. Pepie La Pew .
25. Life .
26. Knick Knacks .
27. Reason for Living .
28. America is Failing
29. Memorial Day . . . .
30. Flight of Fancy
31. Blue Moon . .
32. Memories of Youth

Web Builder

She rises with the dawn,
    Mists still cling to the trees.
Her babies are coming and she must find a place,
    To build her web, and then she sees.

A human's trail creating an opening,
    This will be the perfect place.
For the flies of the wood will always congregate,
    To any open space.

Make the silk, attach and extend,
    Make more, but soon it will end.
For her babies must have food,
    Till they are old enough for themselves to fend.

Hours and hours pass,
    She could certainly use a rest.
But if Mother Nature has qualifications for motherhood,
    Then this will be the test.

Late afternoon arrives,
    Her labor has taken the entire day.
Now she can rest with the knowledge,
    Her babies will have a place to stay.

Concentric circles extending outward,
    Surely, this is a place that will stand.
Suddenly, along comes a self-pronounced nature loving human,
    And the web disappears with the casual swing of a hand.

The human continues down the trail,
    Unawares of the drama unfolding behind him.
That he has created such sorrow,
    By exercising such a casual whim.

Her sorrow and loss will go unnoticed.
    For tomorrow is another day.
She will try and postpone the babies,
    Till she can build another place for them to stay.

As the sun slowly sets,
    And the earth goes round and round.
Most creatures live unaware of other life,
    And how precious it is to be found.

Hurry

No more strolls down the lane,
    No more rides in a horse drawn surrey.
It seems as if the world,
    Went and got itself, in one damn big hurry.

I remember a time in my youth,
    Spent from dawn to dusk was over.
Looking in a field of green,
    For a simple four leaf clover.

Cars go racing by,
    And planes speed overhead.
We race from everything,
    From our birth until we are dead.

No more letters to write,
    Phone calls seem the best.
To display the patience of waiting,
    Now seems to be a test.

To sit outside and watch,
    The rain falling in a pond.
Seems to be a waste of time,
    Displayed by the weak, and not the strong.

What's the hurry I say?
    As I pass through this life.
To attack each day so stringently,
    As if it were made of such strife.

Slow down I beg you.
    Do not be so bold.
For you will miss the days lost.
    Once you simply get old.

Danny L. Shanks
March 16, 2007

A Godless Child

I raised a Godless child,
    And for that I apologize.
For looking back on it now,
    I'm not sure it was all that wise.

For thinking about it now,
    I did not want such thoughts to intrude.
No prejudices to interfere,
    No judgments to delude.

To give her mind a free hand,
    To make choices denied to me.
No teaching to make her think,
    And therefore allow her to be free.

So I taught her science,
    And taught her how to think.
I did not see the cost to her,
    I never feared such costs, and never did I shrink.

So she never was taught the fear,
    I was raised with as a child.
Taught her the truth of the universe,
    To question everything and to be a little bit wild.

Proud of her I was,
    To be free and be a little bit bold.
But I now felt it left her,
    Feeling a little bit cold.

To be left without a place to stand,
    A rock given on which to put her trust.
To base her life on,
    Believing so, I felt I must.

But in doing so I left her,
    No place in which to hide.
To retreat to in times of woe,
    Done so to appease my pride.

She now has no faith per se,
  Except in herself as such.
And does not feel the need,
  To believe in god, as a place of trust.

Too late to change that now,
  To give her a place to hide in times of woe.
To forestall her fears and to give her an answer.
  A place where she can go.

I felt the words I used,
  I raised her best I could.
Allowing her to think,
  As I felt she always should.

She doesn't think as others think,
  She doesn't feel the need.
To eat like others eat,
  To dine upon their feed.

I am so proud of her,
  Vanity makes it so.
But what you reap in this world,
  Often do you sow.

Yes I raised a godless child,
  Free to think and free to feel.
But the feeling she now has.
  Have left me a little bit ill.

For she thinks like a free spirit,
  Nothing to cloud her brain.
Able to think and not be prejudice,
  Was a goal I wished to obtain.

To give to her freedom,
  I did what I thought was right.
So I hope she will forgive me,
  When the world brings to her a fight.

March 17, 2007

Childhood

The days they come, the days they go.
Passing swiftly in their flight.
Treasure each memory of lying outside, and watching the stars,
With your child on a warm summer night.

Such days go by so swiftly,
They grow up and are gone.
And you spend time now chasing them,
Trying to recover their childhood song.

Do not let a day go by,
And miss what is not understood.
The miracle of youth they have,
Labeled simply as childhood.

Don't grow up you warn,
It is vastly overrated.
Yet grow they will and soon leave,
It is what is fated.

Youth is wasted on the young,
For they simply cannot see.
The innocence held by them,
Of a world ruined by you and me.

Only do we see it,
When we are old and gray.
And then we miss the children,
Forever and a day.

Danny L Shanks
March 21, 2007

The Kids Don't Listen

The Kids don't listen,
    To anything that I've said.
It is simply because they are young,
    And do not have the fear of being dead.

But do not blame them,
    For not doing what they are told.
Do not criticize, nor blame them,
    For they are young and do not deserve such a scold.

In my youth I remember many things,
    Advice given by people who were older.
Advice given to me,
    But unheeded it went, and slid off my shoulder.

So why should the kids listen,
    And this should not come as a shock.
Advice given but unheeded,
    Advice in which they did not put much stock.

Youth thinks they know it all,
    And will not listen to you.
To any of your experiences,
    In anything you say or do.

But you are trying to keep them from pain,
    From making the same mistake.
And to give them a better life,
    That is what is at stake.

So do not despair,
    If your kids do not listen to you.
Realize that is the way of the world,
    And regrettably, that much is true.

Danny L Shanks
April 4, 2007

Surgery Today

Today I go to the hospital,
For surgery on my heart.
Everyone is well prepared,
And I have to do my part.

It is a simple procedure,
They have been doing it for forty years.
Everyone tells me this,
For comfort, and to relieve my fears.

Forty seems like a lot,
But you must remember this.
Mankind has been around for ten thousand,
Since Greece, Rome, and Atlantis.

Suddenly forty seems so small,
And not really a lot of time.
Actually less than one percent,
Of the recorded history of mankind.

So tell me something else,
To relieve my worry and fear.
Lie to me if you must,
Just whisper anything in my ear.

For it will be over,
Soon enough and that's true.
And if I come out the other side,
They say I'll be as good as new.

Danny L Shanks
April 6, 2007

I Fear Death

At eight years old, as a pallbearer I carried a friend.
To his grave from a simple baseball game,
Someone carelessly slung their bat,
And my world was never the same.

That same year while walking on the railroad trussle,
I stepped in a break, but came to no harm.
Saved from the sixty foot drop,
By my dad, holding on to my arm.

In Viet Nam while on patrol,
I stepped over a hidden land mine.
Placed there to kill me,
But I missed it at the time.

I came home to a car wreck,
Which destroyed the front of my car.
Memories reminded to me,
Each day when I look in the mirror at my scar.

Hemolytic anemia struck next,
As the doctor came and talked to me.
To get my affairs in order,
Because tomorrow I would not see.

Then came the heart attack,
That left me flat in a parking lot.
Flat out and prostrate,
And laying there I noticed, the pavement was really hot.

In two days once more I go for a procedure,
They shove a rod into my heart.
To clean out my arteries,
To give me a brand-new start.

Well after all this time of pretending,
    To be fearless of death is getting old.
For I am not as fearless as all that,
    And pretending is getting old.

To say I do not fear death,
    That I do not fear the grave.
Would make me appear much bolder,
    And I simply am not that brave.

The grim reaper has appeared to me so often,
    I should look upon him as a friend.
But fear him I do,
    And can no longer pretend.

I'm fifty-six years old,
    I tire of being so brave.
Tired of acting like,
    I do not fear the grave.

Death holds no joy for me,
    I tire of lying about it so much.
And I will miss my wife,
    And I will miss her touch.

Danny L Shanks
April 10, 2007

The Importance of Being Important

Wouldn't it be great?
At the end of the day.
To have someone seek you out,
To hear what you have to say,

It would be great,
And you would consider it nice.
If someone really cared to ask,
For your experience or advice.

But alas it does not happen,
And you question your value again.
Doubting your worth,
And your existence as a man.

Everyone needs assurances,
Of what they mean, or they begin to doubt.
The meaning of anything,
Of what it's all about?

Thoughts began to appear,
As you hold a shotgun in your hand.
But believe me people,
There has to be a better plan.

To explain why they are alive,
To give a reason why.
Of why they live each day,
Or a reason for which to try.

Meaning to why you live,
A daily existence in this life.
Meaning to more than a few,
Than family, child, or wife.

Benefits and goals set forth,
In which you do strive.
To validate your existence,
Of why you are alive.

To have someone care,
Is not a deadly vice.
To have people inquire, or,
Ask for your advice.

Cause if no one asks your opinion,
Or calls on your experience.
What answer do you have,
To validate your existence.

So people give up,
And they sometimes commit suicide.
Because they cannot exist,
With no place left to hide.

But I do not have an answer,
To that question in any way.
Of why you do the things you do.
Day after countless day.

To validate your existence,
May seem a bit out of hand.
But you are alive today,
Enjoy it all you can.

Danny L Shanks
April 18, 2007

Looking Good

I saw someone the other day,
    They said I was looking good.
I thought I had misheard them,
    Or simply misunderstood.

It was a compliment given to me,
    With no malicious intent.
But I began to doubt,
    What it really meant.

The implication is daunting,
    And the compliment may be swell.
But what it implies to me,
    Is before I simply looked like Hell.

Danny L Shanks
April 19, 2007

The Kids Are Gone

When they were young and dating,
    They hung out with us all the time.
A magical time it was,
    And everything was fine.

But they got married and moved away,
    As kids are wont to do.
And slowly everything changed,
    Going from old, to new.

Then one day they finally snapped,
    To the pressures building inside.
It came out as anger,
    An emotion they could not hide.

And as I hurt, I struck back,
    Saying and doing hurtful things.
Shutting myself off,
    From any more emotional stings.

They hung with us so long,
    And it really was so very cool.
But kids don't hang with their parents,
    Seems to be the rule.

I miss my daughter and son in law,
    The two are really a pair.
But things change in this life,
    And who's to say what's fair.

So now we call them infrequently,
    Don't see them all that much.
But I still miss them,
    And I miss their touch.

Danny L. Shanks
April 20, 2007

Secrets

We all have such secrets,
Buried down deep and dark.
As if anyone knew them,
Upon us it would leave a mark.

Things we've thought and things we've done,
Especially when we were young.
Dare not be admitted to now,
By a simple slip of the tongue

Embarrassing things we've thought and done,
In our youth and middle age.
But people everyone has read that book,
And they dog-eared that page.

Yeah secrets we keep,
Making us their slave.
And we keep those things buried,
Until way past our grave.

For we do not want anyone thinking,
We were just deprived.
Yet thoughts and deeds done,
Were just to know we were alive.

So do not fret the fear,
That I know you by what you shout.
For knowing and doing those things.
Is what being a human is all about.

Danny L Shanks
March 22, 20007

Danny L Shanks

I've Gone Insane

It's 3AM and I rise,
    Go outside to sit and listen to the rain.
And as I sit I realize,
    That I've simply gone insane.

For I feel the need,
    To shout and scream.
As if I am living through,
    Some horrible nightmare dream.

The wife is calmly sleeping,
    Unawares, warm and snug in her bed.
Of the thoughts tormenting me,
    On the inside of my head.

She loves me she declares,
    But alone I face the fight.
To ward off the madness,
    That faces me each and every night.

How can they fail?
    To recognize the torment inside of me.
For I have written about it,
    Countless times in my poetry.

And so here I sit,
    Quiet and silently alone.
For she simply does not realize,
    The thoughts to which I'm prone.

My daughter says think happy thoughts,
    Try and see the light.
As if that will help me,
    To try and win this fight.

So I try and fight them off,
    These thoughts inside my head.
But all I can think of,
    Is that I'd be better off if I were dead.

I don't feel good about myself,
    Self-esteem is at a low.
But I must continue to fight,
    This much I do know.

And so another night passes,
    Alone I still survive.
And as dawn breaks over the mountain,
    I find myself alive.

Compromise

My eyes are getting bad,
Just wear glasses they all say.
Everyone else does it,
So why should I not play.

It's like high blood pressure,
And I'm sure their hearts are pure.
But they keep treating the symptoms,
And they do not have a cure.

Just take a pill,
And relieve all of your strife.
And by the way, I might mention,
You'll be taking it, for the rest of your life.

Take a pill or wear glasses,
All signs of their profession.
But what I see and despair of,
Is another form of concession.

Danny L. Shanks
April 25, 2007

Doctor's Advice

Stop smoking and lose some weight.
    Is the advice all the doctors give.
And if you ignore them,
    You will simply no longer live.

So no morning donut, cup of coffee,
    Or even a cigarette.
All these things I love,
    Given up with great regret.

And if you do these things,
    Or even if you try.
You will be much healthier,
    When your time comes to die.

Danny L. Shanks
April 25, 2007

Stupidity

I grow weary these days,
    Of the stupid people I meet.
Cavorting at the beach, shopping at the mall,
    Or simply walking down the street.

Most are generally ignorant,
    Which means they lack certain knowledge.
It doesn't mean they are stupid,
    Nor didn't do well in college.

It comes from a way of thinking,
    And to really judge them I can't.
Stupidity simply comes from people,
    Who can't admit they're ignorant.

Danny L. Shanks
April 26, 2007

Belief

So you prepare your argument,
Research the point in every way.
Fully prepared you are,
For the discussions you have today.

How can they not see?
How can they even pretend?
To not see the reason,
You use to defend.

Your point of view,
But here is the real trick.
Never ever argue,
With someone who's a fanatic.

Doesn't matter the topic,
Argue it all day long.
Physics, religion, or politics,
Or even the value of a song.

But argue you will,
And here I offer some relief.
Because you cannot prove or disprove,
What is simply called a belief.

Danny L Shanks
March 27, 2007

Offensive

A friend gave me a C.D. the other day,
Warning me to not find it offensive.
So I began to wonder,
What was on it to make him so defensive?

As I listened I wondered,
What on earth was he thinking?
That I would object to songs?
All about sex and drinking.

And as I thought about it,
Society is what it's all about.
Not offending anyone,
Nor giving them reasons to shout.

But if you think about it,
Jokes are really so crude.
Given at the expense of others,
Without trying to be rude.

But jokes are offensive themselves,
Told at someone else's expense.
All jokes have a victim,
Or the joke doesn't make any sense.

As a child we had a dirty joke,
A white horse fell in a mud puddle.
Dirty it was, it's true,
And was not all that subtle.

We are so worried these days,
Trying hard as not to offend.
Society's way of coping,
Setting a politeness trend.

Well I simply was not offended.
    By anything that I heard.
By the sex or drinking,
    Or by any curse word.

So to find the answer.
    You need not be a detective.
It seems after all the talk,
    Being offended is in the perspective.

Danny L Shanks
April 27, 2007

Summer Begins

I went out to my back patio,
Early this afternoon.
A warm wind was present and promising me,
That summer would be here soon.

Warm was the wind,
A gentle but stoutly breeze.
Enhanced and punctuated,
By the gently swaying trees.

The leaves are already sprouting,
A beautiful and vibrant green.
It is the most wonderful thing,
That I have ever seen.

And as I sat, I chanced,
To look into the sky,
Unicorns and dragons were there,
Countlessly passing by.

I chanced to doze off,
Sleeping soundly if you may.
With security and peace abounding,
What a better way to spend the day.

The dragons and unicorns protect me,
Warding off depressing thoughts, which are bad.
Leaving me to enjoy the day,
With no feeling of being sad.

Summer's coming,
With no thoughts of being old.
Gone are the dark winter days,
That were punctuated by the cold.

So ignore me while I sit here.
    Relishing my new belief.
Summer's coming once again,
    And that thought brings relief.

Danny L Shanks
April 27, 2007

Diets

Cookbooks are the best selling books in America,
Diet books are solidly in second place.
It's as if we pay to learn how to cook the food,
Then pay to lose it to save face.

We have hundreds of diets in America,
Under different banners are they sold.
Wine and cheese or seafood,
Low carb will work we are told.

Well I had my fill of offers,
Telling me how not to be fat.
Pay a small price to them,
And I would soon be weighing just that.

So I decided to just not eat,
Starvation was not my desire.
But seemed an alternative,
To healthy eating to light my fire.

But you need to take supplements they said,
To give the body the results you seek.
I was told this tale,
Designed to intimidate the meek.

I didn't take the supplements,
And soon I was no longer fat.
So they can take all their advice,
And stick it in their hat.

For what I learned during this time,
And I'll translate it if I'm able.
You take off fat the way you put it on,
Simply at the dining room table.

Danny L Shanks
April 28, 2007

Enunciation

The way a word is said,
    Is considered its pronunciation.
The meaning of such a word,
    Changes with the Enunciation

Pretty is such a word,
    It defines the appearance one has.
The change of enunciation to purrity,
    Defines its pizzazz

Naked is another word,
    Kind of like purrity.
Naked means having on no clothes,
    Neck-ed means the same, but you're doing something dirty.

Danny L Shanks
April 29, 2007

Visiting My Daughter

My daughter called the other day,
She called up just to talk.
It lasted about as long,
As it does to take a walk.

She tells me that she loves me,
But I doubt her more and more each day.
Talk is cheap and is easier than visiting,
Seems to be her way.

I doubt if her love,
Is as much as I felt for my Dad.
Visiting him every day I could.
Grasping every second I had.

Then it hit me,
Like a bright but blinding light.
The answer to the riddle,
And I knew that I was right.

She loves me as much,
As I did my Dad in my youth.
However visiting me not as much,
And this sadly is the truth.

The truth hit me so squarely,
And strongly as a twelve gauge slug.
I am simply not as polite,
Nor as friendly as he was.

That is the real truth,
Of the difference between me and my Dad.
Not her fault, but mine,
And this makes me really sad.

Danny L. Shanks
May 2, 2007

It's 3 AM

It's 3 AM in the morning,
I go outside to sit in the rain.
I feel so all alone,
No one to share my pain.

As I listen to the rain,
Falling drop by drop.
Leaf to leaf, leaf to roof,
Never seeming to stop.

Everyone is asleep,
In the early morning mist.
No one to discuss the world,
Or point out what I've missed.

The night crawls by,
And I feel compelled to confess.
Should I question who am I?
And the world answers with a resounding, yes.

So here I sit again,
Listening to the rain.
As another night passes,
Wondering does anyone share my pain.

There is no wind tonight,
Not even a gentle breeze.
Nothing to disturb the silence,
To lure the dancing of the trees.

Night after night I sit here,
Watching the world go by.
Having no answers.
Or even the questions why.

Danny L Shanks
May 2, 2007

Danny L Shanks

Thirty-Five Years

Thirty-Five Years have gone from us,
It passed in the blink of an eye.
Yet looking back on it,
I really have to try.

To remember all the days passed,
And the things that happened to us.
Memories of days at the beach,
Of Halloween, Thanksgiving and Christmas.

The sun shinning down on us two,
Frolicking in the sun.
Plans of building a house,
And years of unbounded fun.

I got a job with FAA,
You stayed home to raise the kid.
But the plans fell away,
And we did what we did.

Then you got a degree to teach,
Kindergarten and it was cool.
I worked with IRS,
We employed each and every tool.

We moved to Washington state,
To continue on our quest.
To discover the life we wanted,
To discover what was best.

So now I'm getting old,
Not much more to live.
But what I have left,
I freely and truly give.

For I could say I Love You,
    And it would roll softly off my tongue.
Because I remember 35 years ago.
    When we had just begun.

So here I sit writing to you,
    In the middle of the night.
With no wind blowing the trees,
    And it is dark and quiet.

Where we go from here,
    I simply have no plan.
But with you I go,
    As a gentle and happier man.

Your Husband Danny
May 12, 2007

Pepie La Pew

I was remembering last night,
  Of the original casting crew.
Me, my Dad, and my dog,
  Named simply Pepie la Pew.

What at time it was back then,
  They're waiting for me on my college campus.
La Pew and my Dad in the car,
  And the reunion of the three of us.

My Dad watching us roll,
  Playing in the sun.
With a small smile on his face,
  As we frolicked in the warm Georgia sun.

The smile always there,
  As if he had secrets that he held.
That would come out expressed as laughter,
  Ringing like a bell.

For he could laugh at me,
  Like no one else ever dared.
Tolerating it I did,
  Because I knew he really cared.

Laughingly he taught me to be humble,
  Never condescending was he.
He taught me to laugh at myself,
  And allowed me to be free.

And soon I'd be laughing too,
  At the stupidity of the thought.
And marvel at the correction.
  And wisdom of what he taught.

But Pepe was hit by a car,
    We buried him in the wood.
And as my grief mounted,
    I knew nothing could hurt as this would.

But my Dad followed him about a year later,
    And as we put him in the ground.
Lost I became soon after,
    My center could not be found.

For I remember the talks we had,
    Hour after countless hour.
Walking in the woods,
    Picking the occasional bright May flower.

The way he could correct me,
    Showing me the error of my way.
Usually with just one sentence,
    Was all he had to say.

Well Pepie's gone,
    And so is my Dad.
Yet thankful am I for the pair,
    And the time that we had.

For I remember days spent,
    Reveling in the fun.
Memories cherished and memories lost,
    Both in the warm Georgia sun.

Danny L Shanks
May 12, 2007

Life

Life as we know it,
The passing of the days.
Seems to talk and tell us,
Of its many and wonderful ways.

The blue of the sky,
The ocean's crashing sound.
Birds singing it to us,
Each shouting out all around.

The squirrels and the flowers,
Even the dancing trees.
Are enough to bring a grown man,
Falling to his knees.

To dig his hands into the earth,
To feel the pulse of life.
To relieve all his worries,
To bring peace, instead of strife.

All given to us,
To relish in our day,
A gift from mother earth,
For our pleasure, if you may.

For I will truly miss it,
Once that I am dead.
Miss the clouds and sky,
And the stars shining overhead.

I will miss the flower's smell,
The trees, and my wife's touch.
And I will miss them all,
So very very much.

Danny L. Shanks
May 17, 2007

Knick Knacks

Knick-knacks are possessions,
    That you accumulate over time.
Slowly the amount you have,
    Grows till it is far from sublime.

Statues, paperweights, or stuffed animals,
    Even photos add to the collection.
Of things you can't live without,
    Yet their origins escape your detection.

Most have no practical use,
    Except to take up space.
Shelves are filled to overflowing,
    And everything has a place.

Memories they engender.
    Are enough to make you cry.
But your children will dispose of them all.
    The day after you die.

So how much time did you waste,
    Collecting all this stuff.
While throwing away nothing,
    For that would be too tuff.

I beg of you dear reader,
    Forestall yourself such a fate.
And I beg of you, do it now.
    Before you are too late.

For you still relish those memories,
    Silently hoping that they will last.
And not living life to its fullest,
    But simply living in the past.

Danny L. Shanks
May 18,2007

Reason for Living

What if there is no God,
    Nor Mother Nature to explain it all.
Would we still have four seasons?
    Spring, winter, summer and fall.

Meditation would be a waste of time,
    Seeking of a higher state.
What would be the reason for living?
    What would be our fate?

Yet we struggle for life,
    Trying to find a way to survive.
For it seems very important to us,
    That we are still alive.

For I have sought an answer,
    To explain the why and what for.
Of our existence on this world,
    And I have reached its core.

Animals are all we are,
    We are simply here.
No sight beyond tomorrow,
    Lacking an explanation our biggest fear.

So enjoy the day for what it is,
    Frolic in the sun.
Steer clear of an explanation,
    For it disappears with the setting sun.

Danny L. Shanks
May 21, 2007

America is Failing

Saying it out loud do you think,
    That I am just a fool?
That I never took a history or economics class,
    While I was in school.

Civilizations prosper for a little while,
    Then they simply fall.
And I speak of not one or two,
    But I encompass them all.

The Ming's lasted a 1000 years,
    The Romans 700 or more.
The Greeks lasted about 400,
    If anyone is keeping score.

After 200 years of life,
    We have begun our backwards slide,
It's not if, but when,
    And that we cannot hide.

For every civilization has fallen,
    After they prosper and began.
That seems to be the fate,
    And the history of man.

It begins with the loss,
    Of civil rights taken away.
Laws approved and then enacted,
    With every passing day.

And do you think we will last,
    Because we have technology?
The handwriting is on the wall,
    For everyone to see.

And so I hope and daily pray,
    That when we no longer survive.
I will not live to see it,
    And will no longer be alive.

Danny L Shanks
May 23, 2007

Memorial Day

Another federal holiday,
    Celebrating a day off work, to party down.
Go on a picnic, go to the beach,
    Or just get out of town.

So everyone join in the fun,
    Barbeque and have another beer.
Celebrate till the sun goes down,
    And keep your loved ones near.

So keep up the jokes,
    Laugh at depression instead.
After all it's just a holiday,
    Given to celebrate the dead.

Of those who gave up their lives,
    To keep America free.
To uphold the symbols we stand for,
    Truth, Justice and Liberty.

Danny L. Shanks
May 27,2007

Flight of Fancy

I went out back this afternoon,
    It was a bright and sunshiny day.
The 30th of the month it was,
    The last days of May.

Suddenly a blur caught my eye,
    Rising through the trees into the sky.
And my vision captured the flight,
    Of a beautiful butterfly.

So graceful was the transition,
    From the ground into the air.
I had the feeling to call it weightless,
    Would be considered fair.

For it rose so effortlessly,
    From the ground into the sky.
I felt tremendous joy in my heart,
    To witness the flight of a butterfly.

Danny L. Shanks
May 30, 2007

Blue Moon

Tonight we get a treat,
    We get to observe a Blue Moon.
It happens after midnight,
    On the first day of June.

Its comes when a second full moon,
    Of any given month you find.
But finding two full moons in one month,
    Could put you in a bind.

They are not generally blue,
    But red or brightly yellow in truth.
Caused by noctilucent clouds, from Krakatoa volcano.
    Look it up, if you need further proof.

Full moons are separated,
    By a total of 29.5 days,
So finding two in one month, is unlikely,
    Much less with an atmospheric haze

But poets write about it,
    Of the hopelessness of lost love, if you please.
And one author now quoted,
    Referred to it as being made of green cheese.

But it generally means not often,
    And they are really hard to find.
Because the next one to appear,
    Will be December 31, 2009.

Danny L. Shanks
May 31, 2007

Memories of Youth

So now you sit around remembering,
Your youth and days in the sun.
A thousand ways to entertain yourself,
A thousand ways to have fun.

Memories crowd your mind,
And you forget reality hoping it's just not true.
But old age has set in,
And the price is long past due.

But you keep the memories of what you did,
Hoping the memories will make it last.
Then you stumble and slip,
And fall ungracefully on your ass.

Alas the truth kicks in,
You are no longer young.
No more dancing, nor frolicking,
No more songs of youth to be sung.

So you sit by the hour,
Stretched back in your easy chair.
And you tell anyone who will listen,
That you just no longer care.

Danny L Shanks
June 1, 2007